He released her and stepped back, breathing harshly. "I told you this wasn't going to happen."

Ellie crossed her arms beneath her breasts, lifting them into mouthwatering prominence, though he was sure she didn't realize it. "You're not the boss of me, Conor. We aren't kids. And I don't have to take orders from you. I've been running my own life just fine."

"Quit flirting with me," he demanded, already undressing her in his head. Two things held him back. First, the memory of her dead husband. A year and a half wasn't long enough to work through that kind of grief. And second, the memory of how a younger Ellie had judged him and found him wanting.

And still, it was damned hard to resist her.

* * *

Second Chance with the Billionaire
is part of the Kavanaghs of Silver Glen series:
In the mountains of North Carolina, one family
discovers that wealth means nothing
without love

SECOND CHANCE WITH THE BILLIONAIRE

BY
JANICE MAYNARD

Published in Great Britain 2015
by Mills & Boon, an imprint of Harlequin (UK) Limited,
Eton House, 18-24 Paradise Road, Richmond, Surrey, TW9 1SR

© 2015 Janice Maynard

ISBN: 978-0-263-25272-9

51-0815

Harlequin (UK) Limited's policy is to use papers that are natural, renewable and recyclable products and made from wood grown in sustainable forests. The logging and manufacturing processes conform to the legal environmental regulations of the country of origin.

Printed and bound in Spain
by CPI, Barcelona

Janice Maynard is a *USA TODAY* bestselling author who lives in beautiful east Tennessee with her husband. She holds a BA from Emory and Henry College and an MA from East Tennessee State University. In 2002 Janice left a fifteen-year career as an elementary school teacher to pursue writing full-time. Now her first love is creating sexy, character-driven, contemporary romance stories.

Janice loves to travel and enjoys using those experiences as settings for books. Hearing from readers is one of the best perks of the job! Visit her website, www.janicemaynard.com, and follow her on Facebook and Twitter.

For all of you who remember the sweet rush of young love…sometimes it lasts forever.

One

Conor Kavanagh had been antsy ever since he heard Ellie Porter was back in town. In spite of the many celebrities and moguls who vacationed here, Silver Glen, North Carolina, wasn't all that big a place. Chances were he'd bump into her sooner or later.

The notion gave him goose bumps. But not the good kind. Ellie Porter was part of his past. A fantasy. A regret. A deep hurt he'd buried beneath layers of indifference. He didn't need the ghost of girlfriends past to tell him he'd messed up.

Hell, he'd made more mistakes in his almost-thirty years than a lot of people made in a lifetime. But he liked to think he'd learned from them. Besides, Ellie wasn't an old girlfriend. At least not in reality. He'd kissed her once, but that was it.

In the privacy of his imagination, however, he'd done a lot more. Ellie had featured in his adolescent fantasies on a nightly basis. He'd been head over heels, hormone driven, wildly in lust with her. Everything about her reduced him to shivering need.

The smell of her hair. The dimple in her cheek when she smiled. The way her breasts filled out a sweater. Even the tiny gap between her two front teeth had charmed him. He would have given his family's entire fortune for the chance to spend one night with her. To lose himself in her soft, beautiful body and show her how much he cared.

But Ellie Porter and her twin brother, Kirby, had been his two best friends in the whole wide world. So Conor had kept his daydreams to himself, and never once had he let on to Kirby that he thought of Ellie as far more than a pal, even after he'd finally kissed his buddy's sister.

She'd been popular in high school. A long list of guys had panted after her. Probably even entertained the same fantasies that kept Conor awake and hard at night. Each time she went out with a new date, Conor suffered. He wanted to be the one to hold doors for her and put an arm around her in the movie theater and walk her home on warm, scented summer nights.

But though he and Ellie had shared an undefinable *something* that went beyond mere friendship, Ellie had disapproved of Conor's risk-taking. Her rejection of an integral part of his personality had ended anything romantic almost before it began.

He'd often wondered what might have happened if the Porters had stayed in Silver Glen. Would Conor ever have persuaded Ellie to give him another chance? It was a question with no answer. And now they had both moved on. Ellie was married. Conor was still the guy who pitted himself against danger to prove he was alive.

Loud laughter at the table behind him startled him out of his reverie. The Silver Dollar Saloon was a rowdy place on the weekends. His brother Dylan owned the upscale honky-tonk. It wasn't unusual to see the second-born Kavanagh behind the bar dispensing drinks and advice and jokes along with the pretzels and booze.

Dylan was an extrovert and a people person. He'd settled down a lot since marrying Mia and adopting little Cora. You might even call him a family man. But he still loved the Silver Dollar.

Conor couldn't blame him. It was the kind of place where everybody knew your name. Locals and tourists alike were drawn to its atmosphere of camaraderie and fun. The music was good, the service above par and the burgers legendary.

Dylan made his way down to the end of the bar and stood in front of Conor, raising an eyebrow at the half-empty bottle of beer Conor had been nursing for the better part of an hour. "I'm losing money on you," he said. "You're not eating, you're not drinking. If I didn't know better, I'd think you were in love."

Conor finished off his beer and grimaced. "God forbid. Just because you're all gaga over marital bliss doesn't mean the rest of us have to follow suit. I'm perfectly happy as a single man. I like my freedom."

"You don't know what you're missing."

Dylan's smug assurance was designed to get a rise out of Conor, but it didn't work. Because deep down, Conor knew it was the truth. He'd seen his older brothers, one by one, succumb to Cupid's mischief, and the reality of the situation was, they were all happier than Conor had ever seen them.

Liam and Zoe, Dylan and Mia, Aidan and Emma. Even Gavin, who was a hermit and a curmudgeon at times, had been tripped up by the gorgeous and bubbly Cass.

So, yeah…it was hard to overlook the self-satisfied arrogance of his siblings, who were getting laid on a nightly basis. They practically oozed testosterone and caveman triumph.

But what really got to Conor was the look in their eyes when they were with their wives. When they thought no one was watching. Those moments when the alpha males softened and Conor could see the wealth of love that bonded each man with his spouse. That kind of connection was rare and wonderful and Conor would be lying if he said he wasn't the tiniest bit envious.

It wasn't in the cards for Conor, though. The one female who had ever inspired such a depth of feeling in him had dealt him a rejection that was very personal. Ellie had disapproved of his love for courting danger. In spite of his attempt to be honest with her and to explain why skiing was so important to him, he'd lost her, anyway.

Ellie had wanted Conor to change who he was. She'd begged him to be more careful. And in the end, she had stood by his hospital bed with sorrow in her eyes and told him they didn't have a future, because he loved the rush of adrenaline more than he cared about her.

Even then he had seen the truth in her words. As a child, he'd suffered from a respiratory ailment that kept him confined indoors. Once he finally outgrew the problem, he'd been determined to prove himself. He was driven to be the fastest and best at everything he did.

That blind determination to be number one had cost him.

Life was full of regrets. He should know. A man had to move forward or be forever cemented in the past. Personally and professionally, he'd had plenty of opportunities to learn that lesson the hard way.

Dylan handed him a menu. "Buy something. Flirt with someone. You're giving the place a bad vibe."

With a reluctant grin, Conor shook his head. "God forbid that you should let your brother hang out undisturbed. Bring me a Coke and a cheeseburger, damn it."

Dylan nodded, his attention drawn to the two men arguing heatedly at table six. "That's more like it."

When Dylan strode away to break up the potentially

violent situation, Conor watched the interaction with admiration. Somehow his brother managed to steer both men to the front door and outside without causing a fuss. The Silver Dollar didn't tolerate brawls.

While Conor waited for his food, he flipped through messages on his cell phone and frowned, not really seeing any of them. What would happen if he simply showed up at Ellie's front door and said hello? Would she look the same? Would he like her as much?

They hadn't seen each other in thirteen years, or was it fourteen by now? She wouldn't be sixteen anymore. So why did he still see her that way? It made no sense. All he was doing was torturing himself with one of those weird good-old-days memories that never held up under scrutiny.

Like the octogenarian who goes back to his childhood home only to find a strip mall where he used to play, Conor was keeping alive something that wasn't even real. Memories were not bad things. As long as you realized that the only truth was the moment you were living right now.

His accident years ago had cost him a skiing career. And had erased any possibility of having Ellie Porter in his life. Those two facts were irrefutable.

And what about Kirby? Conor and Kirby had been closer than brothers. They had studied together and played sports together and dreamed dreams together. Both of them had had big plans for the future. But their bond had been broken by something as mundane as Kirby's parents taking him to another hemisphere.

Could a friendship like that be resurrected? Only time would tell…but Conor hoped so.

He finished his meal and yawned despite the fact that it was not even ten o'clock yet. He'd been up at dawn. Had worked his ass off all day. He was the boss. He *owned* the Silver Mountain Ski Resort. But idle living had never suited him. Maeve Kavanagh had raised seven sons, mostly unassisted, and in spite of the Kavanagh fortune and the family's influence and reach in the town of Silver Glen, she had drilled into her boys the value of hard work.

According to Conor's mother, the size of a man's bank balance was no excuse for laziness. Her boys heeded the message. Liam ran the Silver Beeches Lodge with his mother. Dylan owned and managed the Silver Dollar Saloon. Aidan was some kind of banking genius up in New York. Gavin's baby was the Silver Eye, his cyber security operation.

On Conor's twenty-third birthday, he had officially taken over the ski resort. The move seemed obvious since he had spent a large portion of his childhood and adolescence gliding down those slopes. At one time he had dreamed of medals and podiums and national anthems being played in his honor.

But life had a way of smacking you in the face occasionally. His plans had changed.

Conor had a *good* life. And a great family. He was a lucky man.

So why did he still think about Ellie Porter?

The two blondes at table six were giving him the eye. They were both cute and looked athletic. No doubt, exactly his type. But tonight he couldn't summon up enough interest to play their game, even with a threesome in the realm of possibility. What in the hell was wrong with him?

"Conor?" He felt a hand on his shoulder.

Summoning a smile, he turned on his stool, prepared to make an excuse…to say he was leaving. But dark blue eyes stopped him in his tracks. "Ellie?"

She nodded, her expression guarded. "Yes. It's me. I need to talk to you."

Ellie found herself at a distinct disadvantage when Conor stood up. She had always been barely five foot five, and

Conor Kavanagh was a long, tall drink of water, several inches over six feet. The pale gold highlights in his dark blond hair were the result of many hours spent outdoors. Women paid a lot of money to get that look in a salon.

He wore his hair shorter than he had as a kid. But it was still far too gorgeous for a guy. Not fair at all. The only thing that saved his face from being classically handsome was the silvery scar that ran up the side of his chin and along his jawline. When he was twelve, he'd fallen off the ski lift and cut his face open on a rock.

She and Kirby had been in the seat behind him and had watched in horror as the snow below turned red with Conor's blood. But Conor had jumped up and waved at them, his typical devil-may-care attitude in full view. Even now, the memory made her queasy.

Conor had definitely grown into his looks.

His rangy frame was much the same as she remembered, though with more muscles, a few more pounds and a posture that said he was at ease in his own skin. The extra weight suited him. Back in high school he'd been on the thin side.

His passion for sports, skiing in particular, and his high-speed metabolism had made it difficult for him to take in enough calories. For Ellie, who had always battled her weight, his problem was one she would have gladly handled.

He stared at her without smiling, the expression in his gray eyes inscrutable. "I heard you and Kirby were back in town."

She nodded, feeling vaguely guilty. Should she have called Conor instead of simply showing up? "Grandpa isn't doing well. Kirby and I came home to look after him until my parents retire in nine months. They've opened their last clinic in Bolivia, so once it's up and running to their satisfaction, they'll move back to Silver Glen."

"I see."

Conor's reticence bothered her. At one time, she and Kirby and Conor had been thick as thieves, their friendship unbreakable. But then her parents had done the unthinkable. They'd become medical missionaries and had moved their family to the jungles of South America to dispense health care to the people there.

"We missed you," she said quietly. Even before the move, she and Conor had parted ways.

Conor shrugged. "Yeah. But it's a hell of a long way from Silver Glen to Bolivia. It's not surprising that we lost touch."

She nodded. For several months emails had winged back and forth between Kirby and Conor. The occasional snail-mail letter. But in the end, she and Kirby had been too far removed from their old life to maintain that thread. And Ellie had been too hurt by Conor's pigheadedness to write.

"We were furious, you know," she said. "In the beginning. We begged my parents to let us stay here with Grandpa and enjoy our senior year."

"I remember."

"But they insisted that the four of us were a family. And that we needed to stick together."

Conor shifted his weight, looking beyond her. "Let's grab a table," he said. "Have you had dinner?"

"Yes." She followed him and took the chair he held out for her.

"Then how about a piece of lemon pie? Dylan swears it's the best in the state."

"That sounds great." She rarely ate desserts, but tonight she needed something to occupy her hands and some activity to fill the awkward silences. In her head, she had imagined this meeting going far differently.

Conor's lack of enthusiasm for their reunion threw her. When they had placed their order, he leaned his chair back on two legs and eyed her unsmiling. "You've turned into a beautiful woman, Ellie. And that's saying something, because back in high school you were the prettiest thing I'd ever seen."

She gaped, totally taken off guard. Heat flooded her cheeks. "You're being kind."

"Not kind...merely truthful," he said, his expression guarded. "I was a guy, not a eunuch. Being your friend wasn't always easy."

Still that undercurrent of *something*.

"Are you angry with me?" she asked, not at all sure what was going on.

"No. Not now."

"But once upon a time?"

"Yeah. I guess I thought both you and Kirby could have argued harder to stay."

She bit her lip. "You don't know the half of it," she said softly, regret giving her an inward twinge. "We were typical sullen teenagers when we didn't get our own way. We yelled and pleaded and sulked. But Mom and Dad insisted we were a family and that we would be leaving the nest soon enough...that we needed to stick together. The thing is, they were right. Kirby and I had the most amazing experiences that year."

"What about your studies?"

"They homeschooled us. And we worked in the clinic. I wish you could have been there, Conor. The jungle is an incredible place. Dangerous, of course, but so beautiful."

"I'm glad things worked out." When he glanced at his watch, she sensed he was impatient.

Sadness filled her chest. At one time this man had known all her secrets. Had been at her side for most of the important moments of her life. "How about a dance?" she said impulsively. "For old times' sake."

His body language was one big negative, but he nodded. "If you want to."

The small dance floor was crowded with other couples. Conor held her close and moved them across the scarred hardwood with ease. Gone was the slightly gawky boy she had known. In his place was a powerful, confident man. Not that the young Conor had ever *lacked* confidence, but still…this Conor was different.

Her response to him took her by surprise. The sexual awareness might be a weak remnant of the past, but then again, she was a living, breathing woman, and Conor was masculinity personified. She'd come here tonight to plead her brother's case. Ending up in Conor's arms was both unsettling and frightening. She didn't have the right to revel in his embrace.

He smelled like an ad for expensive men's aftershave, but more on the faint and tantalizing end than the knock-you-down way some guys bathed in it. Conor was both achingly familiar and at the same time almost a stranger. The dichotomy was one she couldn't explain.

Her sundress left her shoulders bare. Conor had one hand at her waist and with the other, clasped her fingers in his. She wondered if he experienced the tingling that rocked her.

Over the years, she had thought of him, of course. Wondered how he was doing. But she didn't remember ever feeling this *aware* of his male appeal, even as a giddy teenage girl with a crush.

When the song ended, they returned to their table. Conor sighed. "It's great to see you, Ellie. But you said you needed to talk to me. And so far all we've done is exchange pleasantries. It's a beautiful night. Do you want to go for a drive so we can hear ourselves think?"

The noise level in the Silver Dollar had increased exponentially as the hour advanced. Conor's offer was appealing, but she didn't have the luxury of wasting time. "That sounds wonderful, but I can't be out much longer. I have a baby, Conor...a son. I put him to bed before I came, and Kirby is keeping an eye on the baby monitor, but sometimes he wakes up."

Though Conor seemed shocked by her confession, after several beats of silence, he gave her a genuine smile. "The baby or Kirby?"

"Very funny." She didn't know why she was so nervous about saying what she needed to say. Except that she still had a hard time accepting it. "I need you to spend some time with Kirby."

Her request came out sounding more like a demand, but Conor didn't flinch. "Of course," he said calmly. "It will be fun to catch up and rehash old times."

"That's not what I meant." She felt her throat tighten with emotion. Tears stung her eyes, foolish tears, because she'd had plenty of time to come to terms with what had happened. "Kirby needs you," she said. "He's had a huge blow, and I think it will help him to talk to you."

"Why me?" Conor's terse question echoed suspicion.

She couldn't blame him. He must wonder why no one else in her life had stepped forward to lend support. Conor been invited to her wedding by Kirby, but he'd sent his regrets along with an impersonal gift card. The fourteen years were an enormous void filled with only the slightest contacts from either side.

She rubbed her temples with forefingers. "You had a phenomenal future ahead of you as a competitive skier. Everyone knew it. You had made the American team as a not-quite sixteen-year-old. Everything you ever wanted was in reach."

"And then I blew out my knee." The words were flat.

"Yes. So you lost that dream and had to learn who you were without it."

"No offense, Ellie, but I'd just as soon not rehash that year."

"Sorry." She knew what it had cost him to give up his life's goal. The doctors had told him he could ski cautiously, but that if he tried to hit the slopes aggressively enough to win championships, he risked losing all mobility in his right leg. Despite the overwhelming disappointment, Conor had sucked it up and gotten on with his life.

"What's wrong with Kirby? What happened?"

She wiped the tears away, not embarrassed but feeling painfully vulnerable. "He lost a foot. Had it amputated just above the ankle."

Two

Conor's stomach clenched. "*Jesus*, Ellie." *Stunned* didn't come close to describing how he felt. The Kirby Conor had known could do anything. He'd played football, basketball and, though he wasn't a fanatic like Conor, he'd been a creditable skier. "Tell me…" He swallowed hard, not at all sure he really wanted to know.

Ellie was pale, her eyes haunted. "He finished medical school and his residency eighteen months ago. You would be so proud of him, Conor. He's brilliant. And as good a doctor as my parents are."

"That doesn't surprise me. He always ruined the curve for the rest of us."

Ellie nodded. "Exactly. I had to study, but Kirby could look at a textbook and remember almost everything he read."

"His brain isn't in question. What happened?"

"As a celebration, he wanted to climb Aconcagua. He went up with a group of other men, almost all of them experienced climbers. But they got caught in a freak storm. The ledge they were sheltering on broke and Kirby fell several hundred feet. His lower leg was caught between rocks. It took rescuers almost forty-eight hours to get to him."

Conor stared at her aghast, sick at the thought that Kirby survived two nights and days on the mountain only to lose part of a limb. "He's lucky to be alive."

Ellie nodded, tears glittering on her eyelashes. "He's had three surgeries and endless hours of therapy. He's walking on a prosthetic foot. But, Conor..."

He touched her hand on the table. "But what?"

"He thinks he can't be a good doctor anymore."

Conor saw how close she was to breaking down. Unbidden, old feelings rushed in. The need to protect Ellie, first and foremost. He'd always wanted to be her savior. Apparently, some things never changed. A crowded bar on a Friday night was not the place for this kind of conversation. "Come on," he said, pulling her to her feet. "I'll walk you to your car."

Outside, he took a deep breath. The night was humid... sticky. But he felt cold inside. Knowing what his friend had suffered made him angry and sad and guilty for all the times he'd grieved for his own lost career. His injury was nothing compared to what Kirby faced.

Ellie's profile in the illumination from the streetlight on the far side of the parking lot was achingly familiar. Golden-red hair slid across her shoulders. As a teenager he remembered that she always bemoaned her lack of curls. But the silky straight fall of pale auburn was perfect just as it was.

She was curvy, not thin. A very womanly female. He was assaulted with a barrage of emotions that didn't match up. Part of him wanted to explore the physical pull. But an even stronger part wanted to console her.

"I have to go," she whispered, the words barely audible.

"Come here, Ellie." He pulled her into his embrace and held her as she gave in to tears. The sobs were neither soft nor quiet. She cried as if her heart were breaking. And maybe it was. Twins experienced a special bond. Kirby's injury would have marked her, as well.

Conor stroked his hands down her back, petting her, murmuring words of comfort. Resting his chin on top of her head, he pondered the fact that after all this time, he still experienced something visceral and inescapable when it came to Ellie Porter. Holding her like this felt like coming home. And yet he was the one who had never left.

At last her burst of grief diminished. He released her immediately when she stepped back. Why wasn't her husband the one comforting her? Where was the guy?

"I'm sorry," she muttered. "I guess I've been holding all that inside, trying to put on a brave face for Kirby."

"Understandable."

"Thank you, Conor."

Was he a beast for noticing the soft curves of her cleavage above the bodice of her sundress? Or the way her waist nipped in, creating the perfect resting place for a man's hands?

"For what?"

"For listening."

He shook his head. "I'm glad you came to find me. And of course I'll spend time with Kirby. But I have more questions, and it's late. Why don't you bring the baby with you and come up to the ski lodge tomorrow? I'll even feed you."

"I don't want to intrude."

"All my guys have gone to Asheville for the weekend to catch an outdoor concert. You won't see anyone but me."

She nodded slowly. "I'd like that."

"Silver Glen has missed the Porters."

That coaxed a smile from her. "And Conor Kavanagh? What about him?"

He ran his hand down her arms, needing to touch her one last time. "Him, too," he said gruffly. "Him most of all."

Ellie drove the short distance home making sure all her attention was focused on the road. She was painfully glad Conor hadn't asked about Kevin. It would have been hard to talk about that on top of everything else. Her body trembled in the aftermath of strong emotions, and she felt so very tired. Emory was a good baby and slept well as a rule, but he was a handful. Between caring for him and looking after Kirby and her grandfather, she was running on empty.

Leaning on Conor, even briefly, had felt wonderful. He was the same strong, decent, teasing guy she had known so long ago, but even better. He carried himself with the masculine assurance of a grown man. He had been gentle with her, and kind. But something else had shimmered beneath the surface.

Surely she hadn't imagined the undercurrent of sexual awareness. On her part, it was entirely understandable. Conor was a gorgeous, appealing man in his prime. But maybe she had imagined the rest. She was exhausted and stretched to the limit and at least fifteen pounds overweight.

She couldn't even remember the last time she felt sexy and desirable. At least not until tonight. Something about the way Conor looked at her brought back memories of being a teenager and having a crush on her brother's best friend.

Many times she had envied the bond between Kirby and Conor. Though she and her brother were closer than most siblings, there was no denying the fact that an adolescent boy needed someone of his own sex to hang out with. The two guys had included Ellie in most of their adventures. It wasn't their fault if she sometimes felt like a third wheel.

And of course, she had never let Kirby see how she felt about Conor. Not even when Conor nearly killed himself and Ellie stood in a hospital room, scared but determined as she gave Conor an ultimatum. It was one of the few secrets she had ever kept from her brother.

That, and her current fear that Kirby was going to give up.

As she pulled into the driveway of her grandfather's tidy 1950s bungalow, she took a deep breath. She gave herself a minute to stare up at the stars before going inside. Loneliness gripped her, tightening her throat. For better or for worse, she was the glue that held this household together at the moment. The burden lay heavy at times.

Inside, she found Kirby sitting in the dark, kicked back in the recliner, watching a cable news program. She turned on a small table lamp and sat down across from him, yawning.

"Hey, sis," he said. "Feel better?"

She'd told him she was going for a drive to clear her head.

"Yes, thanks. I appreciate your holding down the fort while I was gone."

No need to tell him where she had been. Not yet.

Kirby shrugged, his expression guarded. "Even I can do that when our two babies are sleeping."

"How was Grandpa?"

"Not too bad tonight. He spent an hour telling me stories about Grandma and then took himself off to bed."

"Good." An awkward silence fell. No matter how hard she tried to pretend things were normal, they were anything but. She glanced at the clock on the wall. "Can I get you anything before you go to bed? Warm milk? A snack?"

Kirby's chest rose and fell in a sigh. "No. I'm good."

But he wasn't. He'd suffered wretched insomnia since the accident. Chances were, he'd avoid his bedroom again tonight and doze in the recliner until morning.

Feeling helpless and frustrated, she stood and crossed

the room. Pressing a kiss to the top of his head, she put a hand on his shoulder. "You'll call me if you need anything?"

He put his hand over hers. "Go to bed, Ellie. I'm fine."

After a quick shower, she climbed onto the old-fashioned feather mattress and lay beneath a cool cotton sheet, listening to the sounds of Emory breathing. The baby had been her salvation over the past terrible months. Her little boy was innocent and precious and totally dependent on her for care. She couldn't afford to have a breakdown or any other dramatic response to the soap opera that was her life.

She had shed her share of tears over Kirby but always in private. It was important to her that he not feel like an object of pity. Which meant she forced herself to walk a fine line between being helpful and smothering him.

Her own tragedy had been forced into the shadows, because caring for Kirby had taken precedence. Seeing Conor again made her dangerously vulnerable. Even though she had sought him out, she would have to be on guard when they were together. She didn't deserve his care and concern.

As drowsiness beckoned, she allowed herself to remember what it felt like to be close to Conor, first on the dance floor and later as he held her and comforted her. She shivered, though the room was warm. What would her life have been like if she and Conor had never argued so bitterly…if the Porters had never left Silver Glen?

It was a tantalizing question.

But the truth was, she now traversed a difficult road. Grief and fatigue could be dangerous. She should not mistake Conor's kindness for something more. Her life had not turned out according to plan. Even so, she would not wallow in self-pity. And she would not cling to a man to make it through this rough patch.

She was strong and resilient. She needed to keep her head up and her eyes on the future. The guilt she carried threatened to drag her under, and she would be mortified if Conor ever suspected the truth. His friendship would be a wonderful bonus, but only if the lines were clearly drawn. Perhaps, if he managed to coax Kirby out of the doldrums, the three of them could be the trio of friends they once were.

The following morning she fixed breakfast for the men in her life and then made sandwiches for lunch and put them in the fridge. She didn't like lying to her brother, so she had scheduled a well-baby checkup for Emory and said that she was going shopping afterward.

The doctor visit was real. Kirby wouldn't expect her back at any specific time. Fortunately, the pediatrician was on time, and the appointment went off without a hitch.

Emory was in a sunny mood. She wanted him to make a good impression on Conor, which was kind of silly, but as a relatively new mom, she was still so proud of her baby and wanted the whole world to see how special he was.

The trip to the ski resort didn't take long at all. When she pulled up in front of the large Alpine-style chalet that was command central for the winter ski crowd, Ellie was impressed. She'd spent a lot of time here in her youth, but clearly, major updates had been done over the years. The grounds and exterior were immaculate.

Conor waved her over to the door. Ellie slung a diaper bag and her purse over her shoulder and scooped up the baby. As they stepped through the double oak doors carved with fir trees and mountains, she paused to take in the lobby. Although large in scale, it had a cozy feel because of the quilted wall hangings, thick area rugs and half-a-dozen fireplaces scattered around the perimeter.

Enormous plate-glass windows afforded a view of the ski slopes below. In December it would be breathtaking. Even now, at the height of summer, it was impressive.

Conor urged her toward a mission-style sofa upholstered in crimson and navy stripes. "Have a seat. I'll round up some drinks and a snack." He paused to stare at Emory. "He's a cute kid."

"His name is Emory."

"Does he take after his dad?"

Her heart clenched. Was Conor deliberately fishing for information? If so, she wasn't ready to talk about that subject. Not yet. Maybe not ever. "I think he's beginning to look like me," she said lightly, nuzzling her nose in the baby's strawberry blond curls.

Conor stared at her and then looked back at Emory. "I suppose so."

Without knowing it, she had been holding her breath, because when Conor walked out of the room, she exhaled, all the oxygen in her lungs escaping in one *whoosh*.

Emory was unconcerned. He squirmed in her arms, wanting to get down. He was already close to walking and proved it yet again by cruising around the edges of the coffee table with confidence. When Conor returned, Emory gave him a big, slobbery grin.

As Conor set down a tray with lemonade and shortbread, Ellie lifted an eyebrow. "Somebody's domesticated," she said teasingly.

Conor shuddered theatrically. "Not me. I have a housekeeper who looks after my place and the chalet. She apparently thinks I'm in danger of starving to death, because every time she comes to clean, I find baked goods on the kitchen counter."

"She must like you very much."

Conor shook his head ruefully. "It's not like that. She's seventy-two years old. She likes the fat paycheck I give her because it supplements her income."

"If you say so." She had a hunch that the unnamed housekeeper had a soft spot for her generous boss.

Conor sat down beside Ellie on the sofa and chuckled when Emory let go of the edge of the coffee table and sat down hard on his bottom. The baby's look of indignation was comical. "He's going to lead you a merry chase as soon as he realizes he can go anywhere and everywhere."

"Don't I know it. I've already been baby proofing my grandfather's house."

"How is Mr. Porter doing?"

"He has his good days and bad. Sometimes he puts his reading glasses in the freezer and forgets to wear pants, but with Kirby and I around, he seems happy. I think he was afraid he would have to go into a rest home, so he's being extra sweet and cooperative."

"He's lucky to have you."

"That goes both ways."

Conor leaned forward, scooping up Emory and putting him back on his feet. "There you go, little man. The world is yours."

"Or at least this table." Ellie chuckled. She was torn between being excited about her son's prowess and worried that he would hurt himself. "He has no fear. Which scares me to death."

Conor nodded, his eyes on Emory's progress. "I don't know how my mom did it. Seven boys."

"That should qualify her for sainthood."

They both laughed and, for a moment, their eyes met. Ellie looked away first, her cheeks heating.

Conor leaned forward, his elbows on his knees, his gaze trained on the floor. "Are you going to tell me about Emory's dad?"

Ellie inhaled sharply, stunned that he would ask so bluntly. But then again, Conor had never shied away from difficult conversations. "No," she said. "I don't believe I am. I came here to talk about Kirby."

She saw Conor flinch. "You've developed a hard edge, Ellie."

"I'm not a child anymore, if that's what you mean."

He shot her a look over his shoulder, his warm, masculine gaze taking in her navy tank top and khaki skirt. "I'm well aware of that, believe me." Conor must have noticed that she didn't wear a wedding ring. Was that why he felt the freedom to say such things to her?

"I believe you offered me a snack," she said calmly, though her heart was beating overtime.

Conor sat back, his wry smile rueful. "I suppose that means I'm pouring."

She corralled Emory when he seemed ready to try his luck climbing onto the sofa. "No, sweetheart. No lemonade for you. I have your sippy cup of milk right here."

Conor shook his head. "Poor kid. I'll bet you won't let him have a cookie, either."

"Of course not."

Conor laughed as he handed her a glass. "I was only kidding. Even I know a little kid isn't supposed to have sugar. How old is he? I'm guessing his first birthday is not far off."

"Ten months. He's big for his age."

"I'll bet Uncle Kirby loves him."

"He does. The two of them are sweet together."

"So tell me about Kirby. Why do you think he needs to talk to me?"

Ellie took a long drink and set down her glass, still half-full. "The last year and a half has been really hard for him. Not only losing the foot, but being a patient instead of a physician. He's used to being the one in charge, the one caring for other people. So not only has he been dealing with the changes in his physical capabilities, he's gotten it in his head that he won't be a good doctor now. He has offers waiting from at least four prestigious medical centers across the country, but he refuses to deal with them."

"I'm not a counselor, Ellie."

"I know that," she said. "But you have some inkling of what it's like to have your whole life turned upside down. You've moved on. You've made new goals. You've accepted your limitations."

Three

But had he? Had he really? Conor didn't want to admit, even to himself, that he still grieved the loss of his adolescent dreams. He'd put on a brave face for his family... pretended that he was okay with no longer competing. But deep down, a tiny kernel of futile anger remained that he'd been robbed of doing the one thing that gave him such an incredible rush of exhilaration.

"I didn't get there overnight, Ellie. Acceptance takes time. And Kirby has lost far more than I ever did."

"That's not really true, if you think about it. You had to give up competing completely. But Kirby can still be a doctor."

Her words sent shock reverberating through Conor's gut. Had all his pretending been wrong? Would it have made life easier if he'd been up-front about his grief?

He cleared his throat, stunned that a woman he hadn't seen in a decade and a half could analyze the situation so succinctly. "I'll talk to him. If you think he wants to see me. But I can't promise miracles."

"I appreciate it, Conor."

Ellie's grateful smile made him uncomfortable. She glowed this morning, no other word for it. Motherhood suited her. If Conor started hanging out at the Porter household, he would see her regularly. That was probably not a good idea given his fascination with her.

Because there was still the mystery of Emory's father.

Even so, he was drawn to her warmth and caring. Or maybe it was simply the fact that he was sexually attracted to her. She had a body that was lush and ripe. He ached to touch her, much as he had as a teenager. Only now, he knew the kind of pleasure a man and a woman could share.

Imagining Ellie in his bed was definitely not smart. Tormenting himself was pointless. Conor hadn't changed. He still courted danger. He still relished the exhilaration of pitting himself against the elements. Which meant that Ellie would be as disapproving as ever when she found out the truth about him.

He picked up Emory and blew raspberries on his tummy, anything to distract himself from the image of Ellie's naked body. "When do you want me to see Kirby?" he asked, wincing as Emory grabbed handfuls of his hair.

"Whenever it's convenient for you. I know you have a business to run."

"In case you haven't noticed, it's the off-season. I'm not exactly tied to a desk. What if I order lunch from the deli and we pick it up on the way to your grandfather's house?"

"That would be perfect. I'd already made some sandwiches for Kirby and Grandpa and left them in the fridge, but they'll keep until tomorrow."

"You want to ride with me?"

"I can't. The car seat, you know."

"Ah. Yes. Does your grandfather still live in the same house?"

"Yes." She scooped up Emory.

"Well, in that case, I'll see you over there in half an hour."

He helped Ellie load up the car and watched as she drove away. Already he felt a connection that was stronger than it should have been given their long separation.

It occurred to him suddenly that he had asked questions about Kirby, but he still had no idea what Ellie did for a living. Though she downplayed her intelligence in comparison to her twin, he knew she had done well in school, also. The teachers had loved her.

Conor had *wanted* her. But her refusal to accept him as he was had kept his adolescent urges in check. Nothing had changed. He'd be smart to ignore this inconvenient attraction. Ellie wasn't the woman for him.

The deli was accustomed to him placing to-go orders, but they were surprised by the size of this one. The cute teenager behind the counter smiled teasingly. "Having a party, Mr. Kavanagh?" she asked.

Mr. Kavanagh? Hell, did he seem that old to this kid? "Lunch with some friends."

"We have fresh strawberry cake in the back. One that's not even sliced yet. You want a few pieces?"

"I'll buy the whole thing." Conor would take any help he could get in the way of a welcome offering. He wasn't at all sure his invitation from Ellie was going to get Kirby's stamp of approval. Men liked to hide out and lick their wounds. Kirby might not appreciate having Conor show up out of the blue.

At Mr. Porter's place, Conor parked on the street and unloaded the bags from the deli. With the cake box balanced in one arm, he made his way up the walk. The property was not in great shape. Not too surprising for an older person who didn't have the strength to handle fix-it jobs.

The paint on the house was peeling in places. He saw a section of rotting wood on a soffit. Several dead plants needed to be replaced. Even the driveway needed to be resurfaced.

Ellie and Kirby no doubt had plenty of financial resources to take care of things, but maybe Conor could offer to do a few odd jobs. It would give him an excuse to hang around, and maybe he could coax Kirby into holding the ladder or drinking a beer while he kept Conor company.

Ellie waited at the door, the baby on her hip. She looked anxious but incredibly beautiful. "I told him you're coming," she said. Her eyes were darker than usual. In their depths he saw worry.

"Point me toward the kitchen," he said. "And I'll dump all this stuff. What did he say when you told him?"

"Not much."

"Great," Conor muttered. "Does the term *busybody* mean anything to you?" He put the cold items away and leaned back against the counter. The kitchen was small and dated, but cozy and welcoming in a retro way. He and Kirby and Ellie had visited here on occasion as kids.

"That's not fair," she said, her gaze mulish as Emory yanked on a strand of her hair. "Kirby *needs* company. Even if he doesn't realize it."

"So I'm your token guinea pig?"

She shrugged. "I've done all I can do. If there's going to be a change in the status quo, I'm betting on you."

"No pressure." He was stalling, honestly scared that his longtime friend was going to kick him out after an obligatory five-minute visit. "Let's get this over with. But if he doesn't want me here, I'm leaving."

"We may have to ease him into it, but I know this will be a good thing."

"I wish I had your confidence." What did Conor possibly have to say to a man who had lost part of a limb? Yet even amid his doubts, Conor knew he would do anything to put a smile on Ellie's face.

Mr. Porter was napping, so Kirby was the only one in the living room when Ellie and Conor walked in. In a flash, Conor saw that Kirby had changed. More than Conor could have imagined. The teenage boy Conor remembered was a man with lines at the corners of his eyes and a tight jaw that spoke of pain suffered and battles fought.

Conor crossed the room, holding out his hand. "Hey, Kirby. It's great to have you back in town. Don't get up, man."

But Kirby had already risen awkwardly to his feet, his arms outstretched. "What took you so long?"

Conor hugged him hard, feeling a reciprocal level of emotion in his friend's embrace. "I had to pick up the food."

After a moment, they separated. Kirby settled back in his recliner. Conor took a seat close by. Kirby shook his head. "I've missed you, buddy. More than you know." The tone in his voice said a whole lot more than his prosaic words.

Conor had only a split second to ponder his next move. He tapped Kirby's knee. "So let me see this fake foot."

"Conor!" Ellie's shocked exclamation fell into a pit of silence.

Kirby blinked in shock. His jaw worked. And then he burst out laughing. A gut-deep, hearty, belly laugh that went on and on until Conor and Ellie joined in.

Kirby wiped his eyes, his grin a shadow of his former self but a grin, nevertheless. "God, it's good to see you." He lifted his pants and extended his leg. "Carbon. Latest issue. The best money can buy."

"Comfortable?"

"Hurts like hell most of the time, but I'm getting there."

Conor stood and gave Ellie his most reassuring look. "Why don't you give us some guy time? I'll keep little Emory if you don't mind. We have to train him up right."

"God forbid," Ellie said. But she handed over her son without protest. "I'll have lunch ready in half an hour."

Kirby nodded. "Thanks, sis."

When Ellie left the room, Conor juggled the baby. He'd assumed, and rightly so, that Emory's presence would fill any awkward silences. "So how are you *really* doing?"

Kirby grimaced. "Honest to God, I don't know, Conor. Most mornings when I wake up, it still seems like a dream, until I try to stand up and forget I don't have the damned prosthesis on. I can't tell you how many times I've nearly fallen on my face."

"Ellie worries about you."

"I know. She and my parents have been great through all of this. But sometimes I feel a little bit…"

"Smothered?"

Kirby glanced at the doorway and lowered his voice. "Yes. But she's been so good to me, Conor. I don't think I would have made it without her. So how can I tell her I need some space?"

"Maybe you won't have to. You and I have years to catch up on. If we're hanging out doing stuff, Ellie will be delighted, and it will give you a chance to venture out of the nest."

"So now I'm a baby bird?"

Kirby's disgruntled expression made Conor chuckle. "Bad analogy. But seriously…what do you think of the idea?"

"I'm on board. These walls have been closing in on me."

"Good." Conor paused, feeling vaguely guilty for what he was about to do. "Ellie told me a lot about you and her parents, but she's been reticent about herself. What does she do for a living? I assume she's on maternity leave?"

"Not exactly. She has degrees in political science and international affairs. Speaks several languages. A number of years ago she began working as a cultural attaché at one of the embassies in Buenos Aires. She's brilliant, Conor. But when I had my accident, she resigned to take care of me. And then, of course, the baby came along…"

"I see." Conor did see. Ellie was devoted to her twin. Generous and compassionate. But one more question loomed. He lowered his voice, not wanting Ellie to know he was snooping. "What about her husband? Are they divorced?"

"No."

The negative sent Conor's stomach into a free fall. "Oh." Disappointment knotted his chest.

Kirby shook his head, his gaze troubled. "She didn't tell you?"

Conor frowned. "Tell me what?"

"Ellie's husband Kevin was climbing with me when I had my accident. He fell also. Died of a broken neck. Didn't even know he was going to be a father."

Ellie set the large kitchen table for four and pulled the high chair to one end. She unwrapped all the food with a raised eyebrow. Conor had spared no expense. But the Kavanaghs were extremely wealthy, so it was no surprise. Their ancestors had discovered silver in these mountains several generations ago and thus solidified the family fortunes.

The town of Silver Glen was a popular destination for celebrities and public figures who wanted to get away from it all. The charming shops and wonderful restaurants, combined with year-round recreational opportunities, appealed to a well-heeled crowd.

The advisory council had taken careful measures to limit overbuilding and to keep the Alpine flavor of the community intact. Their care paid off. The Silver Beeches Lodge and the multitude of bed-and-breakfasts in town rarely had openings unless a patron booked months in advance.

Ellie checked her watch. She had given Kirby and Conor plenty of time. Taking a moment to summon her grandfather, she then returned to the living room. "Lunch is ready," she said, glancing from her brother to his best friend. The two men appeared to be enjoying themselves. Emory was curled against Conor's chest playing with a teething ring.

The meal turned out to be an awkward affair. Ellie's grandfather floated in and out, one minute coherent, the next saying bizarre things that made Ellie sad and discouraged. It was hard to see a loved one deteriorate.

At one point, Grandpa Porter sat straight up in his ladder-back chair and pointed an accusing finger at Conor. "I remember you," he said. "You used to have a soft spot for my little granddaughter, Ellie."

Though Ellie flushed with mortification, Conor took it all in stride. "Yes sir, I did. But that was a long time ago."

Kirby intervened. "Do you want some cake, Grandpa? It's homemade."

The ruse distracted the old man, fortunately. Ellie couldn't decide what was going on with Conor. He and Kirby laughed and joked together as if they had never been apart, but Conor scarcely looked at Ellie. Fortunately, Emory demanded much of her attention.

When everyone had finished eating, Conor stood. "If you all will excuse me, I have to get back to the ski lodge. This was great. Kirby, I'll call you tomorrow and we'll make a plan."

Again, Conor avoided eye contact with Ellie. "I'll walk you out to the car," she said, miffed that he was being standoffish.

"It's not necessary."

Was it only her, or did his smile seem forced? "I know that," she said. "But I want to."

Conor didn't even pause on the front porch. He strode down the path as if he had a plane to catch and not much time to make his connection. "Bye, Ellie." He tossed the words over his shoulder, barely slowing down.

"Wait," she said, grabbing his shirtsleeve. "Tell me how Kirby sounded to you. Do you think he's okay? This was the first time I've heard him laugh like that since the accident."

Conor pulled away but came to a halt, turning to face her. "He's going to be fine, Ellie. Losing the foot has knocked the wind out of him, but he hasn't given up, if that's what you're worried about."

"I *was* worried. Thank you for coming today," she said. "And thank you for the lunch."

Conor seemed uncomfortable with her gratitude. "No problem."

Well, shoot. "Did I do something to offend you?" she asked bluntly. "You're acting weird all of a sudden."

The tiny flicker of a muscle in his cheek told her that he understood what she was saying. He stood there staring at her, his expression impassive. But his hands clenched in fists at his sides.

The sky was cloudless, the sun beaming down unforgivingly. A trickle of sweat rolled down her back. Conor's posture was like stone. He was a completely different man from the one she'd spoken with at the saloon...or even at the ski lodge.

She saw his throat work.

"I owe you an apology," he said. The words seemed ripped from his chest.

"I don't understand."

"Kirby told me about your husband. About Kevin. I'm so damned sorry, Ellie."

His sympathy caught her completely off guard, though she should have guessed at some level that Kirby would spill the beans. "Thank you." What else was there to say? She couldn't tell him how she was feeling…how she had suffered. How she *still* suffered.

"To have dealt with that and also caring for Kirby… you're a strong woman." She could swear he was anguished on her behalf. But instead of feeling warmed by his empathy, it made her want to run.

She shrugged. "I don't feel strong. Most days I feel like a juggler with too many oranges and too few hands. But I don't see why this requires an apology."

"I flirted with you. I saw you weren't wearing a wedding ring and I assumed—"

"That I was divorced," she said quickly.

He nodded, his eyes bleak. "Lord, Ellie, I never even considered the fact that you were a widow."

"Does it matter?" She was shriveling inside, actively pained at the thought of discussing Kevin with Conor Kavanagh. Her guilt consumed her. What would Conor think if he ever found out the truth…the truth that not even Kirby knew?

"Yeah," he said, the word harsh. "I'm not usually such an idiot. I hope you'll accept my apology."

"You didn't do anything wrong. I *am* single, Conor, whether I want to be or not."

He ignored her words as if she had never spoken. "I'll do what I can for Kirby. And if I can help you in any way, all you need to do is ask. You're a mother and a daughter and a sister and a granddaughter. That's a lot for anyone to handle. I'd like to make things easier for you."

"Kirby needs your help, not me." She didn't want to be Conor Kavanagh's charity case. She was lonely and afraid and confused. The thought of resurrecting her friendship with Conor had kept her going lately. Now, even that was in jeopardy.

Conor stared at her, his gaze shuttered. "I'll be in touch with Kirby. Goodbye, Ellie."

Four

Conor spent a sleepless night, largely due to his dreams. Even knowing that Ellie was a grieving widow didn't keep his subconscious from going after what it wanted in erotic, carnal vignettes. The little devil on his shoulder pointed out the opportunity to take advantage of a vulnerable woman.

He wouldn't do that. Probably. Definitely.

When he heard Ellie had come home to Silver Glen, he had visions of reconnecting with the laughing, happy sixteen-year-old girl he had known. At some level, he resented the fact that she had an entire life he knew nothing about. He wanted her to be the girl in his fantasies. The childhood friend. The innocent first love.

Even to himself he had to admit the problem with that rationale. Though he had never married, he'd had two pretty serious relationships. Both of them had ended for different reasons, but he'd been emotionally invested each time. In between, he'd sown his share of wild oats.

He liked women. The way they smelled. The way they moved. The interesting ways their minds worked.

What he didn't like was the idea of competing with a dead man.

Did that make him petty? Or simply pragmatic?

Beyond that conundrum was the knowledge that he and Ellie were not suited for each other. He was still the kind of man she had once rejected. He hadn't changed. Not really. It would be better for both of them if he kept his distance.

He called Kirby early and made arrangements to pick him up at ten. "I'll wait in the car," he said. "And keep the A/C going. It's hot as hell today."

The stalled-out weather front was unrelenting. Humidity and a scorching summer sun alternately baked and broiled the town. But the real reasons he decided not to go into the house were twofold. He didn't want to see Ellie, and he *did* want to watch Kirby walk to the car.

He sent a text when he pulled up in front of the house. Moments later, as if he had been waiting by the door, Kirby appeared on the porch. As Conor watched, the other man made his way down the walk.

To a casual observer, Kirby's legs and gait would appear normal. But Conor looked beneath the surface. He saw the effort Kirby was making to walk naturally. Instead of looking toward the car, Kirby's eyes were trained on the ground as if something might jump up at any moment to trip him and send him flying.

Conor's heart contracted in sympathy, but he knew that kind of response would be the last thing Kirby wanted. Kirby didn't need Conor's platitudes. What he needed was to feel normal.

Leaning across the passenger seat, Conor unlocked the door and shoved it open. "Climb in, my friend. We've got a full day planned."

Kirby eased his big body into the car and shut the door.

His forehead was beaded with sweat and his lips pressed together in a white-rimmed line. "I'm looking forward to it," he said.

Conor drummed his hands on the steering wheel. Then he sighed. "Do you have a cane, Kirby? Do you need it?"

Kirby stared straight ahead, his tumultuous emotions etched in his body language. "Did I look that bad tottering out here?" he asked, the question clipped with frustration.

"You looked fine. Honestly. But I know you, man. You once played an entire quarter of football with a busted wrist. Today, though, we're not out to prove anything. So, tell me the truth."

"Yes and yes." Kirby's breathing was shallow, his skin clammy and pale. He dropped his head against the back of the seat and muttered an expletive under his breath.

"Do you have any objections if I go get the damned thing?"

Kirby shrugged, his eyes closed. "Knock yourself out."

Conor shouldn't have been surprised to find Ellie hovering just inside the door. She was wearing old faded jeans and a white tank top that showed off her honey-colored tan and more-than-a-C-cup breasts. "I'm here for his cane," he said. "Superman out there is trying to prove something, but I want to get him home in one piece."

Ellie nodded, relief on her face. "He's stubborn."

"I'd be the same way. In fact, I *was*," he said, thinking back to the long months after his skiing accident. "I was determined to show everybody that I was okay. That things were back to normal."

"And were they?"

Though he saw nothing but simple curiosity on her face, the question stung. "No," he said bluntly. "They weren't." He wanted to drag her into his arms and kiss her. But he couldn't. He shouldn't. Even though she smelled like vanilla and temptation.

He took the carved walnut cane and left without saying goodbye. He could barely look at Ellie now. All he could see was an image of her in another man's arms, another man's bed.

When he got back in the car and tossed the cane in the backseat, Kirby had recovered enough to give him a wry smile. "They tell me not to push it…that time is what I need. But I'm damned tired of feeling like a cripple."

"Is that how you would refer to one of your patients?" Conor started the engine.

Kirby's head shot around so fast it was amazing he didn't get whiplash. "Of course not."

"Then quit whining. Life sucks. Sometimes more than others. You've made it through the worst part. You might as well concentrate on having fun once in a while."

Kirby fell silent for the remainder of the trip to the ski resort. Had Conor offended him?

Once they arrived at the lodge, Conor was stymied at first. In ordinary circumstances, he would have asked Kirby to hike the perimeter of the property with him. As high school kids, fitness had been everything to them. That was a long time ago, though, and Kirby faced a new reality.

Kirby was a doctor, a pediatric specialist according to Ellie. All Conor had to do was persuade him that losing a foot didn't negate his training and his future.

Easier said than done. But Conor was determined to ease the grief in Ellie's eyes. She had come to Conor for help, and he would give it, even if it meant keeping his physical needs in check. He was no longer an adolescent boy with a crush on a girl. Still, his need to make Ellie happy had apparently survived the years of separation.

After a quick tour of the lodge, Conor made a snap decision. If they couldn't hike the property, they could at least see it from the air. "How about riding the chairlift with me?" he said. "We run it at least once a week to see if any problems crop up."

Kirby nodded, his mood hard to read. "Sure."

At the top of the lift, Conor elbowed his friend. "If that foot falls off, I'm not crawling all over this mountain to find it."

Apparently he hit just the right note, because Kirby chuckled. "Is nothing sacred to you?"

"If you were expecting me to baby you like Ellie does, you're in for a disappointment. You lost a foot. But you're still Kirby Porter. So get over yourself."

Truth be told, Conor was a bit anxious about how Kirby would hop up on the lift. But the other man managed the quick maneuver without incident. Once they were airborne, Conor relaxed.

Except for college, Conor had spent his entire life in Silver Glen. He loved the town, the valley and especially this mountain. He'd skied his first bunny slope the winter he was three years old. After that nothing had stopped him. Until the accident over a decade later.

When the doctors told him he could no longer compete, Conor had been wrapped in a black cloud of despair. He liked nothing better than pitting himself against an unforgiving mountain. Better yet, alongside other guys just like himself who had something to prove. Skiing was the way he released the fount of energy that kept him restless and active.

Ellie had visited him in the hospital and given him a choice. Either give up skiing, or give up her. They'd been on the verge of making their mutual attraction an official *dating* relationship.

In the end, though, Conor had lost almost everything. He'd had no choice but to adapt. No more black diamond descents. No more breakneck speeds. He'd had to find another outlet for his competitive nature.

Conor didn't think he was the only one who relaxed as they rode. But it was all the way down and back up and down again before Kirby spoke.

"Thank you, Conor," he said.

"For letting you ride the lift without a ticket?"

Kirby grinned, his face in profile. "For reminding me not to be a jackass."

"I don't mean to minimize what you've been through. I know it's been hell."

Kirby sobered. "I thought I understood the will to live. My parents are doctors. *I'm* a doctor. But it wasn't until I spent two entire days thinking I was going to die that I truly grasped what it means to fight for life." He paused. "I still have nightmares. It scares Ellie."

Conor inhaled sharply, imagining softhearted Ellie bearing witness to her twin's demons. "She's a strong woman."

"You have no idea. In those early days she never left my bedside. Sometimes she would throw up in a trash can because the morning sickness was so bad."

"And the funeral? Her husband?"

"His parents planned the whole thing. Ellie left the hospital…attended the service…and immediately came back to my room. It worries me that she hasn't had a chance to grieve. I'm afraid that one day she'll wake up and everything will come crashing down on her. Postpartum depression alone is dangerous. Ellie lost her husband on top of that."

"Does she talk about him?"

"Never. At first I thought she was angry because I invited Kevin to go on the climb with me. In fact, I even asked her if that was true."

"And what did she say?"

"She never answered me. It's like she's shoved his memory into a box she won't open."

"So she can concentrate on you."

"Exactly. We're close, Ellie and I, but you know that already. I've always been able to understand what she's thinking. Until now. Suddenly it's as if she's determined to forget the accident completely."

"Maybe that's the only way she can cope. Maybe it's too painful."

"I suppose so. But it's not good for her. She's given up her career. She's lost her marriage. And Lord knows, babies require the ultimate self-sacrifice. I've tried to get her to take some time for herself. To go away for a few days or get a massage. Anything. But she won't listen."

"Maybe I can think of something." Conor winced in astonishment as the impetuous words left his lips.

Kirby turned his head. "Like what?"

"Well…" His brain scrambled for answers. "In two weeks Mom and Liam are hosting a Christmas in August ball at the Silver Beeches Lodge. It's a fun thing they started doing three years ago. Brings in tons of extra visitors, plus, the townspeople are invited. Everyone dresses up. They'll have a 1940s band that plays Christmas songs. It's actually pretty fun. You could both come with me."

Kirby shook his head. "I want to do this for her—I'll stay at the house and look after Emory and Grandpa. That way Ellie will be more inclined to have a good time."

"Okay." Damn. Conor didn't want this to look like a date. Several times in his life he'd jockeyed with another guy to win a girl's affections. Sometimes he won, sometimes he lost.

But he was smart enough to know that going head-to-head with a ghost would be hell on a man's ego. He'd never met Kevin. And now he never would.

Kirby mentioned the guy as if he'd been a good husband. Conor was good at skiing. That was about it. Well, he was good in bed, too. But that wasn't likely to come into play.

He would take the grieving widow to a party and show her a fun time. That was where it ended.

Still, there was one more thing he had promised Ellie. And having her brother as a captive audience at the moment meant he could fulfill that pledge. "Ellie tells me you have some good job offers."

Kirby scowled. "All of which came in *before* I took a header off that mountainside."

"Is that a problem? You didn't get a concussion…right? You still remember all that stuff they taught you in med school, don't you?"

"There's more to being a doctor than what you read in books."

"Sure there is. Compassion. Empathy. You've lived through a traumatic experience. I'd say both of those qualities make you a better medical professional."

"It's not as simple as that, Conor."

The curt note in Kirby's voice told Conor he had pushed enough for the moment. The chairlift approached the lodge for the third time. "You ready for some lunch?" Conor asked, preparing to lend a hand if Kirby stumbled while getting off.

But his friend managed unassisted. "I could eat," Kirby said.

"I think I can scare up some leftovers and a couple of beers."

Over a meal consumed standing up in the kitchen, Conor was relieved to find out that he hadn't alienated his buddy. In fact, Kirby used the opportunity to turn the tables.

The other man crumpled an empty potato chip bag and tossed it in the garbage. "So tell me, Conor. Now that you can't go hell-for-leather down a mountainside anymore, how do you get your kicks?"

"You really want to know?"

"I asked, didn't I?"

Conor hesitated. Was his answer going to send his friend into an emotional tailspin? Conor was no shrink. But even he could see the irony. "I've taken up mountain climbing," he said.

Kirby's gaze sharpened. "Are you serious?"

Conor nodded. "Yeah…"

"Which ones?"

"I started with Whitney. Did Kilimanjaro two years ago and Everest last year."

"Damn. I wish I had known. We could have done some peaks together." He stopped suddenly, and Conor saw the exact moment his friend acknowledged that there would be no more hazardous mountains in his future.

It was a damned shame.

"I'm sorry, Kirby."

Kirby shrugged. "Adrenaline junkies have short life spans."

"Is that what you think we are?"

"It's who we used to be. I doubt either one of us has changed all that much." He paused. "So what's next?"

Conor leaned a hip against the industrial stainless steel counter. "I have plans to do Aconcagua this winter."

Kirby stared at him, jaw dropped. "Well, hell."

"Exactly."

"For God's sake, don't tell Ellie."

"I won't. But is this where you try to talk me out of going?"

Conor had been half expecting this moment ever since he heard Kirby's accident had happened on the very mountain in Argentina that Conor was slated to climb next.

Kirby shook his head slowly. "I wouldn't do that. Aconcagua is a phenomenal experience. I'm happy for you."

Conor felt a slither of unease. "You'd still call it phenomenal? After everything that happened?" In Kirby's position, how would Conor feel? The mountain had nearly killed Ellie's beloved twin. And it *had* killed his brother-in-law.

"It was a great trip," Kirby said, his jaw outthrust stubbornly.

"Right up until the part where Aconcagua kicked your ass."

"A freak accident. Could have happened to anyone."

"Mountain climbing is a dangerous venture. You knew the risks."

"And I did it, anyway."

"I get the feeling you're conflicted about that choice."

Kirby flexed his foot, the prosthetic one, his face grim and drawn. "I chose to go. It was my decision."

"And now you're paying. Is that it? You have to give up your career because you did this to yourself?"

"Damn it, Conor…"

Conor sighed, shaking his head. "You're wearing a hair shirt, Kirby. For no reason at all. The only thing that's changed is the way your shoe fits. Nothing's gonna hold you back but you."

After a taut, lengthy silence, Kirby sighed, shaking his head. "I can't decide if you're my therapist or my cheerleader, but it's creeping me out. Can we call a moratorium on talking about my situation?"

"Only if you promise to quit acting like a pathetic loser."

Kirby grinned, ending the verbal standoff. "Did I mention that I'm glad to see you again?"

Conor cuffed him on the shoulder, careful not to make him stumble. "Don't get all mushy on me."

"Moron."

"Half-wit."

"I can do this all day."

Conor chuckled. "Let's go find your sister. My work here is done."

Five

Ellie stood at the kitchen window, drying the same pot she'd been holding for the past ten minutes, and watched her brother and Conor play a restrained game of catch in the backyard. Conor had been back in their lives for a little over a week, and already she noticed a difference in Kirby's outlook. While she was delighted to see her sibling out of the house and showing interest in something other than television, she regarded Conor's intervention with mixed emotions.

With Kirby finally showing signs of moving forward, he would no longer need Ellie as much. At some level it hurt that she hadn't been able to coax him out of his funk. Kirby was her twin, the other half of her heart. She would do anything for him. Even if that meant taking a backseat while once again Kirby and Conor bonded as they had as kids and inadvertently left her out.

Kirby wasn't the only one whose future was a big, daunting blank. Ellie was equally adrift, though perhaps not so visibly. Once Kirby got settled in a hospital where he chose to do his work, and once Ellie's parents returned from the jungle to look after Grandpa, Ellie would no longer be needed.

Except by Emory.

She and her toddler would have to build a new life together. Without Kevin. Where would she start? She couldn't imagine going back to South America with all of her family now in the States, or soon to be. DC had the greatest possibilities for jobs. And she could certainly get good references. But did she want to raise her child inside the Beltway?

Her own childhood had been idyllic here in Silver Glen. A small town with an international flavor thanks to the high-end tourism trade. But the nearest embassy was far, far away. As far as employment went, her skill set was not exactly marketable in the mountains of North Carolina.

As she pondered the murky future, her sunny-natured son sat in his high chair, enthralled with a set of aluminum measuring spoons. She couldn't believe how quickly he was growing. Soon she would have to shop for eighteen-month-sized clothes. Though his birthday was still a ways off, he was big for his age...and tall.

A sudden knock at the back door startled her. Conor poked his head in. "Can you grab us a couple of water bottles, Ellie?"

"Of course." When she handed them over, her fingers brushed his. Conor smelled of hot cotton and male sweat and lime-based aftershave. It was a surprisingly alluring scent.

Conor didn't quite meet her eyes. "Thanks."

Before he could retreat, she put her hand on his arm. "How is he doing, Conor? Really. He tells me he's fine, but clearly he's not."

Conor moved casually, enough that her hand fell away.

"He's going to be okay. His head's still messed up. He blames himself for what happened. And he's still conflicted about the job thing. But give him time."

Though Conor was clearly impatient to leave, Ellie powered on, struck by the inescapable notion that she was about to miss something very important in her life if she didn't act.

"Conor…" She trailed off, at a loss for words, feeling the urgency of emotions tangled in her chest.

"Yes?" His body language was one huge rejection. But she was no longer a girl easily swayed.

"I'm glad you're here for Kirby, but *I've* missed you, too. I'm looking forward to the dance at the hotel next week."

He froze, his big frame taut, like an animal sensing danger. "My family will enjoy seeing you again."

"And what about you, Conor?" She put it on the line. No pride. No games. Just the need to *feel* something again other than worry and pain and distress.

He clenched one of the bottles so hard the plastic cracked. Water shot all over the kitchen. "Sorry," he muttered. He grabbed for a roll of paper towels, but she took it out of his hands.

"Leave it," she said. "I'll mop it up in a minute." Again she put a hand on his arm. "Can't we be friends again, too?" she whispered. The muscles in his forearm were hard and warm beneath her fingertips. He was a grown man, utterly masculine, breathtakingly sexy. She looked up at him, letting him see her confused searching, her yearning to feel like a woman again.

For long seconds, their gazes tangled, hers beseeching, his stormy.

At last, he spoke. "I *am* your friend, Ellie. But that's all it can be. I'm the same guy I was a decade ago. You told me way back then I had to choose, and you were right.

Now you're grieving and maybe lonely, but those are bad reasons to play with fire."

Before she could respond, he cupped her cheek with his free hand. His fingers were hot against her skin, lightly callused. Firm. Tender. She could swear the air in the small kitchen was charged with electricity. Though several window units cooled the house, her skin was damp.

"I assumed you were also the kind of man who lived for the moment. Has that changed?"

He shrugged, his thumb stroking her cheekbone, perhaps unconsciously. "No. Not really. But even I know better than to get involved with a woman who's lost so much and is still dealing with grief. I'll be here for you, Ellie. For talking and advice and even the occasional platonic outing. But nothing more. You'll thank me later."

"God, you're a patronizing ass," she said, feeling the burn of unshed tears in her throat and her eyes. "I'm a grown woman. I can make my own decisions."

He nodded. "I know that. But maybe I'm going to be the strong one this time. You've spent the last eighteen months taking care of everyone but yourself. You lost your husband. You nearly lost your twin. Your parents live a continent away. Your grandfather is fading before your eyes. You can count on me, Ellie."

"But only as a brother."

"Yeah…"

"I *have* a brother," she said, turning her lips against his palm and kissing him there. "I don't need another." The fact that his pompous speech held elements of truth was something she didn't want to admit.

His groan sounded like a man being tortured. "Don't do this, Ell. Please."

Though it took all she had, she pulled away. Conor represented an escape from the humdrum difficulties of her everyday life. He was alive and exciting and wonderfully familiar. She wanted to nuzzle into his embrace and never come up for air.

But there was too much history between them. And too much guilt on her part. "Fine," she said, the word as snippy as she could make it. "We're friends. I get it." She bent and began sopping up water.

Conor squatted beside her, forcing her to meet his gaze. "Please don't be mad, Ellie. I couldn't bear it. You and Kirby are very special to me. I'm damned glad you've come home."

He meant it. She could see it in his eyes. "I'm not mad," she said, concealing the depth of her disappointment. She stood and fished another water bottle out of the fridge. "Go play ball. I've got this."

Eight days later she stood in front of the bathroom mirror and second-guessed her wardrobe choice. She had lost most of her baby weight, but her breasts were definitely bigger. The red dress had seemed like a good idea for the holiday-themed soiree, but the just-above-the-knee frock exposed an awful lot of skin. Then again, it *was* August.

The silk fabric clung to her body like a second skin. Not slutty, but in the posh neighborhood next door. A plunging neckline and rhinestone spaghetti straps flattered her shoulders.

She had taken two thick strands of hair at her temples, braided them and twisted them around her crown. The rest of her hair fell straight to her shoulders. It had occurred to her to put all of it up in deference to the heat, but she remembered Conor teasing her about it when they were younger. Always touching her head or tugging a lock.

She wanted him to remember how close they had been. She craved a return to normalcy. Those years and days with Conor were some of the best of her life. A simpler time. An uncomplicated time.

As she walked into the living room, Kirby whistled long and low. "Wow, sis. You look hot."

She blushed. "Thank you. Are you positive you can—"

He interrupted her with an outstretched hand. "Stop right there. I'm a fully trained medical professional. Surely you trust me to take care of one old man and one little baby for one single evening."

"Of course I do, but you've been..."

"I've been dragging you down."

"Don't say that, Kirby. It's not true."

He came over and hugged her, resting his chin on her head. "I love you, Ellie. And I owe you more than I can ever say. I'm sorry it took me so long to get back on my feet."

"Oh, gosh, Kirby. That's a terrible pun."

He laughed along with her. "Sorry. It just came out that way." He held her at arm's length, his gaze locking on hers. "If you ever want to talk about Kevin, I want you to know I'll listen. God knows you've spent enough hours dealing with my tragedies. I'll never forgive myself for being so lost and unavailable when you needed me most."

"Stop," she said, almost in tears. "You nearly *died*, Kirby. Where else was I going to be than with you?"

"And have you let yourself deal with Kevin's death?"

His blunt question caught her off guard. She sucked in a sharp breath. "I don't want to talk about that."

"You never do, hon. That's the problem. A branch can only bend so far before it breaks. You've held everything in for far too long."

"And now that you're feeling better, you think you have the right to dig around inside my head?" She was angry with him for ruining her anticipation of the evening.

Kirby's warm, troubled gaze made her feel far too vulnerable. "If not me, then somebody. We can find a therapist here in Silver Glen. This is important, Ellie. I talked to Mom and Dad recently. They're worried about you, too.

I thought you'd shared things with them, and they thought you were talking to me. But turns out, you haven't said a damn thing to anyone."

"Back off, Kirby. I mean it. I'm a grown woman. I know how to take care of myself. If I need help, I'll ask for it."

He stared at her for long seconds, making her want to fidget in her high heels. But she held her ground. His shoulders rose and fell. "Okay. It's your call."

"Yes, it is." The subject demanded to be changed. "Do you have any questions about Emory's routine?"

"I live with you, Ellie. I think I'm pretty familiar with what goes on."

"And dinner?"

"I've already ordered delivery pizza for Grandpa and me. And I'll feed Emory exactly what you want him to have. Have fun, Ellie. Please. And if you don't come home until morning, it will be fine."

Her eyes widened. Hot color flooded from her throat to her hairline. "Why would you say such a thing?"

Kirby eyed her with a gaze that saw straight through to her jumbled emotions. "I'd have to be blind not to see the attraction between you two. I guess it was there way back in high school, but I was too stupid to see it."

"Conor and I are just friends."

"You could do worse when it comes to relationships. He's a good man, Ellie. The best."

She nearly blurted out that she had made her availability perfectly clear and Conor had shut her down. But she didn't want to do anything to cause discord between the two men. Kirby was very protective of his twin sister. If he thought Conor had hurt her, there would be hell to pay.

"Yes, he is," she said quietly. "But I'm only going to be here in Silver Glen until Mom and Dad return to the States. I'm glad Conor is back in our lives. That's as far as it goes."

The ring of the doorbell saved her from further uncomfortable conversation with her meddling brother. In all fairness, she had meddled in his life on a large scale. But that didn't mean she needed or wanted the tables to be turned.

When Kirby walked toward the door, she watched him, happy to see that he was more and more comfortable with his new foot. He had ongoing pain…that, she understood. But what she hoped was that he would get so accustomed to the prosthesis he would forget that his life had been compromised.

Conor entered the room and stopped dead when he saw Ellie. "Wow. You look amazing."

"Thank you," she said primly, wishing Kirby were anywhere else at the moment. "You don't look bad yourself."

That was the understatement of the year. Conor Kavanagh in a tuxedo made the angel choirs sing. His formal attire had clearly been tailored to fit his tall, lanky body. Broad shoulders, trim hips and long legs added up to one fine-looking specimen of manhood.

Thinking about his *manhood* was a really bad idea. For a woman who hadn't had sex in a year and a half, Conor was the equivalent of a steak dinner with all the trimmings. He was, quite simply, delicious.

She picked up her clutch purse and the cobwebby shawl that was supposed to protect her from any air-conditioned-induced chills. "I'm ready." She turned to her brother. "Promise you'll text me if anything goes wrong."

"It won't, but I will. Have fun, you two."

She kissed his cheek. "I love you, Kirby."

Conor took her elbow as they walked down the front walk toward his fancy European sports car. She knew less than nothing about automobiles, but the sleek, black roadster looked expensive.

When he held the door for her and she slipped into the passenger seat, she was greeted with the smell of warm leather. Oh, Lordy. She was trying *not* to think naughty thoughts, but this car was sex on four wheels.

She paused a moment to consider how many different women Conor might have slept with over the years, but she didn't really want to know. As far as she was concerned, her escort tonight was a grown-up version of the teenage boy she had once known and loved.

"Nice wheels," she quipped when he slid into the driver's seat.

"Thanks. Cars are my weakness. If I hadn't been a skier, I might have ended up being a race car driver."

"The need for speed."

"Something like that…"

She watched him out of the corner of her eye as they drove up the winding mountain road. His hands were confident on the steering wheel, his body relaxed, though he took the curves a little too enthusiastically for her taste.

Conor's assurance stood in direct contrast to her own mixed-up emotions. She was almost a hundred percent sure that tonight's outing had been Kirby's idea. Conor had made it very clear that he and Ellie were not supposed to be anything more than friends. But Kirby was worried about her, so he had probably badgered Conor into extending this invitation.

Even under those circumstances, she was glad to be here.

The trip was far too short for her taste. In no time at all, they arrived at their destination.

The Silver Beeches Lodge was a magnificent building set into the side of the mountain near the very top. It looked out over the valley below with a commanding presence.

When Conor pulled onto the large flagstone apron in front of the hotel, an employee appeared instantly to take the keys and park the car. Conor came around to open Ellie's door and helped her out, one hand on her elbow.

"I have fond memories of this place," she said softly, taking in every feature of the beautiful hotel. "Your mother used to let us do our homework in one of the empty guest rooms. We thought that was so cool."

"She'd be hard-pressed to do that now. There's rarely a vacancy anymore."

Sweeping steps led to imposing doors. Though the hotel was impressive on any given day, tonight it was even more so. Two huge Fraser firs, draped in twinkly lights and iridescent stars, stood like sentinels to greet guests as they arrived.

Conor and Ellie joined the snaking line of people and climbed the stairs. The festive air should have been incongruous given the blazing temperatures, but once inside, it was clear that everyone was prepared to get into the holiday spirit.

A uniformed employee stood in the lobby with a silver bucket, receiving donations for Maeve Kavanagh's favorite charity. Above and across the reception area, a large gold-and-cream banner proclaimed: Christmas in August...'Tis the Season for Giving.

Everywhere, clusters of mistletoe dangled from red velvet ropes, and plaid bows decorated the chandeliers.

Conor took her arm and steered her toward the spot where Maeve Kavanagh held court, welcoming guests and dispensing warmth and cheer. Conor kissed his mother's cheek. "You've got a great crowd," he said. "Congratulations." His mother looked beautiful and confident in a burgundy gown that took ten years off her age.

Maeve nodded. "Thank you, dear. I'm delighted my little event has been received so well."

Conor urged Ellie forward. "You remember Ellie Porter...right?"

Six

Conor watched his mother sum up his date in one all-encompassing glance. "Of course I do. And Kirby, also. I was so sorry to hear about your brother's accident, Ellie. I hope you'll give him my regards."

"I will, Mrs. Kavanagh. Thank you."

"How is he doing?"

"Better every day. Especially now that he and Conor have reconnected. The two of them are making up for lost time."

Conor could almost see the wheels turning in his mother's brain. She considered it a personal triumph that she had successfully married off four sons. Never mind that all of them were grown men with minds of their own. Maeve liked to think she had a hand in their romances.

Conor decided to nip any Cupid-like ideas in the bud. "Ellie and Kirby are only back in Silver Glen until the late spring. Her parents plan to retire and will be coming home at that time to take care of Mr. Porter. After which Ellie and Kirby will be moving on."

"I see…" Maeve's expression was one-part curiosity and two-parts Machiavellian intent.

"Mother…"

She lifted an eyebrow, trying to look innocent and failing. "What?"

Ellie seemed confused at the byplay. And guests were stacking up behind them waiting to speak to their hostess.

Conor took Ellie's arm. "Let's head on into the ballroom. We'll catch you later, Mom."

As they walked away, Ellie stared up at him with long-lashed eyes. "What was that about?"

"My mother feels the need to meddle in my love life."

"Didn't you tell her that you have no interest at all in me as a potential romantic liaison? That I'm a grieving widow who needs to be protected from her own dangerous impulses? That you're noble and stuffy and totally beyond temptation?"

Taking a detour at the last minute, Conor pulled his date into a narrow hallway and glared at her. "That's not funny."

"I'm not laughing." She took a step toward him, close enough now that he could see the tiny freckle on her right cheek. And the fact that her eyes sparkled with hints of green amidst the blue. She put a hand flat on his chest… right over his heart. "You're a gorgeous, sexy, wonderful man, Conor Kavanagh. The boy I remember has turned into a pretty special human being. I'm happy to be with you tonight."

Without warning, she went up on tiptoe and kissed him smack on the mouth. Somehow, his hands were around her waist and he was kissing her back. So many emotions. So many nuances.

He recognized the sexual need, a healthy man's response to having an attractive woman near. He also acknowledged the sweet sensation of holding his teenage fantasy in his arms. But what was more alarming was the sense of home-coming. Of rightness. As if every woman he'd ever known had simply been a placeholder…marking time until the real thing showed up.

The intense, unexpected feelings scared the crap out of him. He wasn't going to change for any woman. He released her and stepped back, breathing harshly. "I told you this wasn't going to happen."

Ellie crossed her arms beneath her breasts, lifting them into mouthwatering prominence, though he was sure she didn't realize it. "You're not the boss of me, Conor. We aren't kids. And I don't have to take orders from you. I've been running my own life just fine."

"Quit flirting with me," he demanded, already undress-ing her in his head. Two things held him back. First, the knowledge of her dead husband. A year and a half wasn't long enough to work through that kind of grief. And sec-ondly, the memory of how a younger Ellie had judged him and found him wanting.

"Fine," she said. "You're my other brother. I get the mes-sage. Can we go to the party now?"

She turned her back on him and headed for the ball-room, leaving him to trail in her wake. He was accustomed to being in control of his life. Of charting his own course. But Ellie challenged his preconceptions of her at every turn.

The view from the back didn't help his resolve. Her long tanned legs and narrow waist showcased a curvy bottom. That red dress had been created by some designer to drive a man insane.

So far, it was working.

He had assumed the ballroom would be neutral terri-tory. Too many people to make any rash decisions based on creamy shoulders and a feminine smile that made him ache.

Ellie's face lit up when she heard the band. "Oh, this is wonderful," she said. "I love this song."

It was a Bing Crosby classic about dreaming and Christmas and yearning for the past. Unfortunately for Conor, it was also a slow dance. He took Ellie in his arms with a sense of fatalism. She fit against him perfectly. Her light perfume teased his nose. But it was the slide of her hair against his hand that did him in. Silky. Thick. Like warm cider on a cold night.

It was a really bad idea to bring Ellie this evening. Too much romance in the air. Too many echoes of auld lang syne.

What did she want from him? If they had talked about Kevin before now, Conor might be more inclined to open up to her. But the fact that her dead husband was carefully sectioned off in a place labeled No Trespassing told him that Ellie had a long way to go before she would be ready to love again. Love didn't die in a mountain-climbing accident.

Maybe she was secretly furious with her husband for risking his life. And maybe that anger was manifesting itself in a flirtation with Conor.

He didn't like being used any more than the next man, but it was going to be difficult to say no, even if he really wanted to. Which he didn't.

Ellie Porter pushed all his buttons. She always had. Which meant that Conor was in a hell of a predicament.

The Bing song ended and another crooner took center stage, again singing a slow, haunting melody. Conor and Ellie hadn't exchanged a single word since he took her in his arms. If he were a whimsical man, he'd have said they were bound together by the magic of the past…by the years of playing together, studying together, growing up together.

They had so many shared experiences, so much in common when it came to their roots. But beyond that was an entire decade when they'd been on opposite sides of the equator...when life had taken them in each on radically different paths.

Ellie made a small noise, and he pulled back, incredulous. "Are you crying?" he asked, aghast.

"Of course not." She frowned at him, but her cheeks were damp.

Before Conor could deal with that information, the first of his brothers cut in. It was a half hour or more before he had a chance to dance with his date again. First came Liam and Dylan. They both remembered Ellie in passing. But they were older and not as familiar with her as Aidan and Gavin, who were closer in school.

Patrick, sixth in the lineup of Kavanagh brothers, also took a turn around the dance floor with Ellie. Only James, the youngest, was not in attendance tonight.

By the time Conor reclaimed Ellie, she professed herself tired and ready to hit the buffet. "I'm starving," she said. Her cheeks were flushed with color and her eyes sparkled. "That was so much fun. Your brothers are wonderful."

While Ellie was occupied with the Kavanagh men, Conor had passed the time by dancing with his sisters-in-law, each of whom was very dear to him. Zoe and Mia. Emma and Cassidy. The new additions to the Kavanagh clan were smart, sexy, beautiful women. His brothers were damn lucky.

It irked him that dancing with his siblings had made Ellie happy, while Conor's greatest achievement was to make her cry. But he kept his disgruntlement to himself.

Over hors d'oeuvres and wine, he studied Ellie when he thought she wasn't watching. Though she smiled and spoke to a number of people who remembered the Porter family, there was an aura of sadness around her. Conor wondered if he was the only person who noticed.

He sensed in her a fatigue that was more than physical. Perhaps he was seeing evidence of the mental toll she had endured. Some people in her shoes might have experienced a total breakdown. After months of worry and grief and unrelenting work, it was understandable if Ellie was fragile emotionally. And yet, she impressed him as one of the strongest women he had ever known.

He stole a large boiled shrimp from her plate and dipped it in cocktail sauce. "So tell me about life in the jungle," he said. "It must have been strange and exotic at the same time. Did you eat the local food? Speak the lingo?" Keeping the conversation light and impersonal was his way of coping with the evening.

Ellie nodded, licking a crumb from her lower lip. "Oh, yes. Aside from the fact that provisions were hard to come by, Mom and Dad wanted us to acclimate to the local culture. We became fluent in Spanish and Quechua. We learned how to build a hut out of banana leaves. We knew exactly which insects were harmless and which ones could kill us."

"I'm impressed. Maybe I should start calling you Jane of the Jungle."

"Does that mean you can picture me in a leopard-print bikini?" She swallowed a sip of wine and stared him down.

His temper fired along with his libido. "I'm trying damned hard to be a gentleman, Ellie. You're hurting. I get that. But having a fling with me is only going to make you feel worse."

She stared at him, spine erect, chin tilted upward the tiniest bit. "It must be lovely to be omniscient. Do you and God triage the world's problems every morning?"

"You're a piece of work, do you know that?"

She shrugged. "My husband is gone, Conor. I'm pretty clear about that. And *I'll* be gone from Silver Glen in no time at all. I have a baby who will never know his father and a brother who's struggling as much as I am. Is it so wrong for me to want you?"

Conor felt helpless and confused. The last time he'd felt this level of anxiety was in the aftermath of his horrific accident. Even now he could remember the moment he heard a dreadful pop in his knee and ended up facedown in the snow with one leg bent at an inhuman angle.

Surviving that moment in his life had been no small achievement. He'd hung on, because the alternative had been unthinkable. And he'd known he was right to let Ellie go, because he was not able to change the basic core of who he was. For years as a kid he'd watched his mother try to keep tabs on her gadabout husband.

The end of that struggle had meant heartbreak for everyone. Conor had learned a valuable lesson. He had to be who he was.

Now, here with Ellie, he felt a similar torture. Did he want her? Hell yes. But he couldn't get past the fact that she was acting out of desperation. He owed it to her to be the smart one this time. To make wise decisions.

He took one of her hands in his, not caring that they might have witnesses. "Will you tell me about Kevin?" he asked softly, trying in every way he knew how to communicate his compassion and his concern for her.

Ellie jerked free and wiped her hands on a snowy linen napkin. "No," she said. "I won't. This is a *Christmas* party, Conor. Your timing leaves a lot to be desired."

"It's August, not December. And you're putting a wall between us. I don't like it."

"Is that a requirement? You have to like everything I do?"

She was stubborn and angry and totally adorable. He chose his words carefully. "Maybe it's petty of me, but I'm not crazy about the idea of standing in for a dead man."

The shock on her face was almost instantly replaced by another expression. He saw in that moment she had never considered the possibility his mind might go in another direction.

She swallowed hard. Her hand trembled when she carefully pushed her plate aside. They were seated at a table in an out-of-the-way corner. It was doubtful they could be overheard. But she lowered her voice and leaned forward. "I'm embarrassed, Conor, that you would even think that. If we end up in bed together, I'll know exactly who I'm with. I'm lonely and sad and it's been so long since I've been touched sexually that I probably won't remember what to do, but I'll *know* you. It's you I want."

"Why?" he asked bluntly.

She shook her head, her eyes bleak. "I'm a single mom. I have no desire to go out and cruise bars. The chance of any man wanting to marry me knowing it's a package deal with Emory is slim. But I'm young and healthy and I have needs like any other woman. You're very special to me. I care about you. And I trust you. I think being with you in that way would be...well..."

She stumbled to a halt, the color in her cheeks rivaling her dress.

Conor bowed his head. When he finally looked up at her, he caught a flicker in her eyes that made his heart race. "Are you sure, Ellie? I don't want to hurt you. Things ended badly between us the last time."

This time it was *her* small hand that closed on his bigger one. Though her touch was light, he felt it all the way to his gut. His sex stirred even as his breath hitched in his chest.

"I'm sure, Conor. Very sure. But if you're not, we won't take this any further." She glanced around the room, restlessness in her body language. "Why don't we dance again?"

It seemed like a good idea. A socially acceptable way for him to be close to her while he sorted through the pitfalls he could see in front of them.

The room was crowded and loud. Despite what the calendar said, a holiday air permeated the assembly. The massive fireplaces at either end of the large salon were filled with pots of foil-wrapped poinsettias instead of roaring flames. Conor hadn't the slightest idea how his mother had managed to pull that off in the midst of summer.

Everyone seemed to be dancing—young and old... talented and awkward. Maeve Kavanagh had always possessed the gift of hospitality. Whether she threw a kid's birthday or a fancy affair, it was guaranteed to be a success.

The crush of partygoers made it necessary for Conor to hold Ellie close or risk having someone step on her. If he closed his eyes, this might have been many years ago. Kirby and Ellie had often attended special occasions at Silver Beeches. The first time Conor had ever danced with her, he had been fourteen years old. Having a girl in his arms, any girl, would have been plenty of stimulation for an adolescent boy. But since the girl was Ellie, well...he could be excused for fantasizing about that night for weeks to come.

And now here they were.

For a lot of men, this would be the perfect setup. Two adults indulging in a mutually satisfying sexual relationship. No expectations. No strings. No future. Conor had participated in a few such liaisons over the years. And never with repercussions.

But Ellie came with a whole laundry list of repercussions. Kirby's reaction, for one. For the first time in over a decade, Conor had his old friends back in his life. And it was pretty damn great. What would happen to their triangle if Conor took Ellie to his bed?

Then there was little Emory. Ellie needed to be on the lookout for a man who wanted an instant family...a man who would look forward to coaching Little League and shepherding Boy Scouts. Conor knew next to nothing about babies. He was learning from the additions to his brothers' families, but that didn't mean he was a fit parent.

In the end, though, his approach to life was what took him out of the running. Shouldn't Ellie wait for *the one*? Having sex with Conor would only postpone her chances to rebuild a life for her and her son.

Ellie rested her head on his shoulder, disarming him completely. All of his mental gyrations were nothing more than a smokescreen easily blown away. If Ellie wanted to be wild and irresponsible, was he really going to stop her?

She felt right in his arms, despite what his brain told him. He *needed* to have this time with her, even if he was still the same kind of man she hadn't wanted in the past.

Ellie curled a hand behind his shoulder and touched the place where his hair met his neck. His barber had done a good job. "I can almost hear you thinking," she said. "Chill out. Relax. It's Christmas." Her fingertips on his skin were like fire.

He laughed, but he wasn't really amused. It was easy to pretend for one night. Christmas was about dreams and special wishes and sharing love.

But tonight wasn't December 25, and he and Ellie weren't talking about love. That was something she had shared with her husband, marked by a wedding ring and vows. *'Til death do us part.* Never had that phrase seemed so starkly real.

What she wanted from Conor was far less cerebral. He had never been in love. The closest he had ever come was his adolescent crush on Ellie. But even he knew that such a juvenile emotion was only a pale imitation of what Ellie and Kevin must have shared.

The song ended, and part of the crowd began to drift toward the exits. Four hours had flown by though Conor had scarcely noticed. He glanced at his watch. "I should get you home," he said gruffly.

Ellie took his hand in hers, the simple gesture making his resolve crumble. "Yours first," she said.

He halted in the midst of the exodus, the throng of guests parting on either side of him to continue on their way. "What do you mean?"

"Take me home, Conor. To your house. I've never seen it. Wouldn't you like to give me a tour?"

Seven

Ellie had never thrown herself at a man so blatantly. If Conor didn't crack this time, she was going to back off. A girl had to have some pride, after all. "Come on," she said. "People are staring at us."

They said their goodbyes to Maeve, but the moment was brief, because Conor's mother was mobbed by well-wishers encouraging her to keep up the Christmas in August tradition every year. By the time Conor and Ellie made it outside, it was dark, the moonless night stuffy and warm.

Perhaps because Conor was the owner's son, a valet brought the car around to the side of the hotel so they wouldn't have to wait forever. There were definitely perks to being a Kavanagh. Even so, the line of traffic to exit the hotel driveway was slow moving.

Once they were in the car, Ellie felt totally alone. A silent Conor drummed his fingers on the steering wheel, his face in shadowy profile beneath the exterior lights of the hotel. He looked anything but happy.

"Take me home," she said abruptly. "It's late. I'm exhausted." And she was tired of battling Conor's scruples and misgivings.

Clearly he wasn't as interested in her as she thought. Or else he wouldn't be clinging so vehemently to his notion that the two of them shouldn't end up naked together.

"Make up your mind, Ellie." His grumpy response infuriated her.

Suddenly, she lost it. For months she had told herself life would get back to normal. She'd forced herself to believe it, even if the pleasant fiction was only a ruse to get from one day to the next. Seeing Conor again had been the first hint of happiness she had experienced since Kevin died.

But Conor didn't want her. Heartsick and humiliated, she threw open the door of the car, stepped out and slammed the fancy piece of metal. "I'll get a ride with someone else," she said, her tone as snarky as she could make it. She heard him yell at her, but she didn't stop.

She walked quickly into the dark night, circling around the hotel and disappearing into the gardens on the far side. Pausing only long enough to slip off her high heels, she moved forward blindly and quickly, trying to outrun the pain. Tiny pieces of gravel lacerated her feet.

She kept on. The neatly manicured gardens eventually gave way to a familiar rough path that led to a waterfall. The going was more difficult here. Roots and stones were silent adversaries in the inky gloom. Her lungs burned. Her chest heaved. Her throat was raw.

Sweat rolled down her back. Her beautiful dress was going to be ruined. She knew it and she didn't care. Nothing mattered. Nothing made sense. Behind her she thought she caught the sound of Conor's voice. Yelling. Demanding.

She ignored him. In some dim corner of her brain she remembered that the trail ended at the waterfall. What would she do then? Throw herself in? She had a son. That wasn't an option. Pain rose up inside her like a writhing beast.

Without warning, an unseen obstacle caught her toe and sent her crashing to the ground. All the wind left her lungs and the world went black as searing pain spread from her temple into nothingness…

Conor should have been able to catch Ellie easily. His long legs could far outstrip her stride. But he'd had to waste precious seconds easing the car out of the way so he wouldn't block the hotel drive.

By the time he bounded after her, she had disappeared.

He knew she wouldn't go inside the hotel…not in her condition. The only other viable option was the hotel garden. There he found her shoes. Tucking them in his jacket pockets, he loped after her, sure now that she was headed down the trail she and Conor and Kirby had traversed often as kids.

His heart jerked erratically in his chest as he ran. It was dark. The path was rough and dangerous in these conditions.

When he heard her cry out sharply, his blood congealed. Dear God. What had she done to herself?

He found her crumpled and still in the middle of the trail. In fact, he almost tripped over her. For several sick, stunned moments, he thought she was dead. But when he took her limp wrist in his hand, he found a steady pulse.

Should he move her? Had she broken anything? Breathing harshly, he grabbed his phone from his pocket and activated the flashlight app. Carefully easing her head to one side, he looked for damage. And found it. Blood oozed from a deep gash on her forehead.

Hell… His first-aid training kicked in and he began moving his hands over her limbs methodically. Everything seemed okay, but it was impossible to be sure.

He shook her gently. "Ellie. Ellie. Wake up, sweetheart. Talk to me."

The next minute and a half stretched into a lifetime, but finally she stirred. "Conor?" The word was slurred.

"Yes, love. I'm here." He pointed the beam of light away from her face so it wouldn't blind her.

She struggled to sit up. He helped her, though fear lingered that she might be badly hurt. "Where's Kirby?" she asked.

The odd question caught him off guard. "Um…at home."

"Oh." She put a hand to her head. "Why is my face wet?"

"You cut yourself when you fell. And you were crying."

Her chin wobbled. "I know. Because Kirby and I have to leave."

"You do?"

"We tried, Conor, I swear. But Mom and Dad won't budge. They're making us go with them to South America." She burst into tears.

Conor crouched beside her, stunned and more scared than he had been in a very long time. Something had happened. Something bad. And he had to get help. Fast.

Taking off his jacket, he wrapped it around Ellie. Her skin was ice-cold, she might be going into shock. Even though she had spoken to him, now she seemed to be drifting in and out of consciousness.

Taking a few steps away from her, he made two hurried phone calls…one to his brother Gavin and one to Kirby. Gavin and Cassidy agreed to head straight to the Porters' house to look after the baby and Mr. Porter. As soon as they arrived, Kirby would leave to meet Conor at the hospital.

Even though Conor was speaking in a low voice, Ellie should have been able to hear what he was saying. She should have demanded to know why he was calling her brother. Or why he was contacting Gavin. But she did neither.

With the plan set into motion, Conor knelt and scooped her into his arms. Her head lolled against his shoulder.

"Ellie," he said urgently as he stood and began rapidly retracing their steps. He wanted to run, but he couldn't risk dropping her or falling himself. She seemed so small suddenly…and fragile. God, what was wrong with her? A concussion?

The trail was not more than half a mile in length, but it seemed endless. He didn't waste time calling for an ambulance. He could get Ellie to the hospital more quickly, especially since the traffic from the party had now dissipated.

At his car, he set her gently in the passenger seat, reclined it and belted her in. "Ellie, honey. Can you open your eyes?"

She did as he asked, but though she smiled weakly, her gaze was unfocused and her eyelids fluttered shut again.

He knew in detail how to ski downhill at breakneck speeds, making the most of every curve and straight stretch. He'd been known to do the same in a car heading up and down this mountain. But now he was torn between speed and caution.

The trip became a blur. He drove automatically, his gaze flitting every five seconds to his passenger. Second-guessing himself again and again, he cursed beneath his breath. Maybe he should have waited for the ambulance.

Fortunately, Kirby had been cleared for driving since his right foot was intact. He sent half-a-dozen texts that Conor was not able to read until he hit a traffic light in town. Kirby was frantic. And he would be at least twenty minutes behind Conor.

The hospital emergency room was top-notch. The Kavanagh family had made numerous large gifts over the years. Plus, Conor and his brothers had kept them in business with various injuries. Broken arms. Sprained ankles. And, of course, Conor's torn-up knee.

When the admitting nurse passed them off to a physician, Conor spoke rapidly as the man assessed Ellie's condition. "I'd like to call in Dr. Milledge for a consult, if you don't mind. He's a family friend."

The ER doctor nodded. "No problem. I wouldn't mind a second opinion about this head injury. Tell me again what she said?"

"When I found her, she had tripped and fallen. There was a rock with blood on it, so that explains the cut. But when she opened her eyes and spoke to me, she didn't seem to be in the present."

"Got it." The doctor tucked a chart under his arm. "We'll call Dr. Milledge, but in the meantime, we'll see what we can find out. Are you her next of kin?"

"No. That would be her brother, Kirby Porter. But he'll be here shortly."

Conor watched helplessly as Ellie was rolled away down the hall on a gurney. Guilt choked him. He'd known she was in trouble…he'd known it in his gut. And yet still he had let her down.

The waiting room was like all hospital waiting rooms. Filled with fear and stale body odor and people with anxious faces. Only in this case, the furnishings and the reading material were upscale. Silver Glen catered not only to locals, but also to well-heeled visitors who often showed their appreciation of top-notch medical care by leaving large donations. Only last fall, an extremely famous pop sensation came down with the flu while spending a few weeks on hiatus. She was so happy with how she was treated that she had her accountant electronically transfer a six-figure gift to the hospital before she left town.

Conor was sitting, head bowed, elbows on his knees, when Kirby appeared at his side. The other man sat down and ran a hand over his face. "Give me an update."

"I've requested they call in Dr. Milledge. He's an expert on neurological stuff. I don't want them to miss anything."

"What in the hell happened?"

Conor swallowed. No matter how he told this story, he would cast himself in a bad light. But Kirby deserved the truth. "We argued," he said, his throat tight with regret.

Kirby's gaze sharpened. "About what?"

Conor stared at him, wondering how he could explain this delicately. "Well, I—"

"Oh, for God's sake, Conor. You're scaring the crap out of me. What the hell happened?"

Conor shrugged helplessly as the weight of his own fear and panic engulfed him. "Ellie wanted intimacy. Physical intimacy. I put her off, thinking she needed to deal with her husband's death before we acted on the attraction we both felt. Ellie got mad and ran away from me."

"Where?"

"The trail to the waterfall. It was dark. She tripped and fell and hit her head on a rock. But honest to God, Kirby, the cut doesn't look all that bad. She may need a few stitches."

"Who knows what else she might have damaged..." Kirby paused, his gaze locked on the far wall as if his physician's brain were assessing all the scenarios. "Tell me more about what she said."

"I roused her. Asked her to speak to me. She wanted to know why her face was wet. When I told her she had been crying, she nodded and said she was upset because your parents were making both of you go to South America."

Kirby paled. "Holy hell."

"Yeah." Conor was still hoping he had misunderstood her.

"As much as I don't want to say this, Ellie might have finally snapped. Not permanently. But maybe in a very bad way. Damn, Conor."

"I blame myself." The words felt like glass in his throat.

"She told me she needed to feel that physical connection again. To be held and touched as a woman. God, Kirby, she opened herself up to me and I told her it was a bad idea."

The hole in his chest grew larger by the minute. What had he done?

He dug the heels of his hands into his gritty eyes and waited for Kirby to lambast him. But when he finally looked at his friend, all he could see in Kirby's eyes was pain mixed with sympathy.

Kirby took a deep breath and let it out, absently massaging the leg that was missing a foot. "You were trying to do the right thing, Conor. Most men would have taken advantage of her vulnerability. But you care about her. Of all the people in her life, you're the first person she's reached out to...the first person she's been comfortable enough with to admit she's hurting."

"And I bobbled it." He jumped to his feet, feeling as if the walls were closing in on him. "I assume Gavin and Cassidy got to your house okay?"

"Yes. Grandpa and Emory are already asleep, so they shouldn't have any trouble."

"And Gavin and Cassidy's twins?"

"Mia and Dylan are keeping them at their house overnight.

Conor made a circuit of the small room, pausing to stare out into the darkness. A few hours ago he'd been dancing with Ellie, holding her close, feeling the pulsing current of need that made him hungry to taste her, to find release inside her beautiful body.

Ellie was everything he wanted in a woman. But he would forgo any chance of ever seeing her again if the Fates would let her be okay. Ellie didn't deserve anything that had happened to her. She had a big heart and a generous spirit. She was a steadfast sister, a dutiful daughter and granddaughter, a devoted mom.

He leaned his forehead against the glass…praying. After his accident in high school, he had prayed a lot. But those had been the selfish prayers of a teenage boy. He'd asked God to let him be whole again. To have the chance to be the best in the world at what he did.

How shallow he'd been in his tunnel vision. How little he had known of real life…of the things that mattered deeply. He had a lot to learn from Kirby and Ellie about dealing with tragedy.

Ellie had wanted Conor to help Kirby…to prove to him that there would be a good life after his amputation. But from where Conor was standing, the lessons were all coming *his* way. Ellie's selflessness. Kirby's bravery. The Porter twins had taught him a lot in a very short time.

At last, Dr. Milledge appeared and escorted Kirby and Conor to a nearby family room set up for private conversations.

Conor's heart was beating so fast he felt sick. One quick glance at Kirby's face told him his buddy felt the same.

Dr. Milledge took the lead, his expression composed as he addressed his comments to Kirby. "Your sister is going to be fine. But she's momentarily confused. Not uncommon under these circumstances. Can you fill me in on what might have triggered this?"

Kirby blinked, his jaw working as he fought to absorb the information. "She lost her husband eighteen months ago in the same accident that nearly killed me. Ellie and I are twins. At the time I was fighting for my life, she found out she was pregnant. She's spent every waking hour caring for me and worrying about me, even as her child was being born."

Dr. Milledge nodded. "Certainly enough trauma to trigger an episode, particularly if she has never processed the grief."

"She hasn't," Conor said. "We had an argument about

that very topic tonight. She became very angry with me. Ran away into the woods. And, well…you know the rest."

Kirby interrupted. "And the head wound?"

"She does have a significant concussion. Which likely was catalyst for this episode. We'll do X-rays and CT scans to make sure we aren't overlooking a skull fracture. But I don't think she's in any danger. We'd like to keep her overnight for observation."

"I'll take her to my house when the time comes," Conor said, his protective instincts in high gear.

Kirby frowned. "I'm a doctor. Why wouldn't she simply go home?"

Conor shook his head. "You'll have your hands full caring for your grandfather. Ellie knows me and trusts me. The ski resort is closed. There's no reason I can't give her my full attention."

Eight

The next afternoon, Conor and Kirby stood outside the hospital waiting for Ellie to be brought outside in a wheelchair.

"Standard operating procedure," Kirby muttered as a uniformed attendant came in sight with precious cargo.

Conor took a step forward, but Ellie never looked at him. Her eyes were glued on Emory, who wriggled in Kirby's arms.

Her face lit up, but her eyes brimmed with tears. "My sweetheart," she cried. "I'm so sorry. Mommy has missed you."

As Ellie stood, Kirby handed over the baby. Ellie cuddled Emory and smothered his head with kisses.

Ellie had responded well to rest and medication. She understood that she had sustained a head injury and that she had been concussed and temporarily confused.

Now was the tricky part. Kirby put his arm around her. "The doctors say you need to take it easy, sis. I have my hands full taking care of Grandpa, but Conor has arranged for you and Emory to spend a few weeks with him."

A hushed moment of silence fell. Kirby and Conor held their collective breaths. At last, Ellie acknowledged Conor with a small smile. "That would be nice. Thank you, Conor."

He'd been half-afraid he would see anger on her face... or stony dismissal. Hearing her agree to the plan eased part of the weight on his shoulders. "The car seat is in my car," Conor said. "Kirby will follow us up the mountain and help us get settled in."

Before Conor could make a move to put Ellie in the car, she took Emory, tucked him in his seat and slid in beside him, leaving Conor to play chauffeur. Over the roof of the vehicle, Conor looked at Kirby with a lift of his shoulders and a shake of his head. One step at a time.

Conor drove up the mountain with one eye on the rearview mirror and the backseat. It wasn't so much that Ellie ignored him but that she focused every scrap of her attention on the baby. Little Emory was blissfully happy to have his mother back.

Once they arrived at their destination, Conor decided to let Ellie move at her own pace. He grabbed the small bag Kirby had packed for her to have at the hospital. The three adults mounted the steps, Kirby following along behind. He was striding more naturally every day, and he seemed more at peace with his life. For Conor, it was a two-way street. He had missed his old friend, and having Kirby back in his life was a shot in the arm. Kirby would be leaving in the spring, so Conor was determined to enjoy the time they had.

And then there was Ellie. He watched her closely to see how she would react to his home. The house still smelled new. In fact, he had only completed the last bits six months ago. Building this structure had been a labor of love. He was much farther out of town than any of his siblings. But he relished the solitude.

Though his mother had gifted each of her sons with acreage on the mountain between the Silver Beeches Lodge and the ski resort, Conor had taken some of his own savings and bought property on the south end of the mountain. The terrain was rougher here, the sense of privacy more pronounced.

Ellie paused on the wide wraparound porch and smiled. "This is beautiful, Conor. I had no idea you had a house of your own."

"Well, I lived in an apartment in town for a while…and then a condo. But I suppose I finally grew up and decided I wanted to put down roots. I had lots of help with the architecture and the decorating. But I'm pretty happy with how it turned out."

All of Silver Glen conspired to maintain an Alpine theme in the picturesque town. The area was known for its atmosphere and its charm. Conor agreed wholeheartedly, but he'd always been drawn to Western design. He'd made several trips to Wyoming and Montana where he had procured large logs from abandoned buildings for the outer shell of his home.

His large porch and the floors inside were constructed of wide oak planking. But there was nothing rough or rustic about the place. He planned to live here for a very long time, so he had paid attention to comfort and luxury and, in some cases, outright decadence. He was deeply moved to know that Ellie and Emory would be his first guests.

In the living room, the three adults paused, no one quite at ease. Kirby spoke first. "I won't linger. I don't want to leave Grandpa for too long. Conor has given you and Emory a suite with a bedroom, bathroom and sitting room. Emory won't be right beside you every night like he was at Grandpa's house. You'll sleep better, I'm sure."

Conor nodded. "Make yourself at home. Take the tour."

"But what about all of our things? Mine and Emory's?"

Her brother grinned. "I packed it all up and brought it here yesterday. Turns out, I'm not quite as broken as I thought I was…and you aren't, either, Ellie. This is only a bump in the road. You took care of me night and day for months. I need the chance to return the favor and to show you I'm as good as new."

Conor was ready for Kirby to go. He wanted to be alone with Ellie. The knowledge that she would be sleeping beneath his roof made his pulse jump and his breathing ragged.

When the door closed behind Kirby, Conor hesitated. "How about some tea?" he asked with forced cheerfulness.

"I think Emory's ready for his nap. Will you show me where I can put him down?"

The baby was indeed yawning. "Of course. Right this way."

Conor stood to one side and watched as Ellie toured the quarters he'd given her. It had been important to him to add some finishing touches in the past twenty-four hours. Fresh flowers. A cashmere throw on the end of the king-size bed. A whimsical pair of bedroom slippers that resembled baby rabbits.

The rooms were done in shades of cream and pale green. With the large windows bringing the outdoors inside, this guest suite reminded him of a springtime forest.

Ellie tucked Emory in the brand-new crib Conor had bought and covered him with a light blanket. The house was air-conditioned comfortably, but the baby's arms and legs were bare.

Emory scarcely stirred as the two adults tiptoed out. To Conor's surprise, Ellie perched on the corner of her own bed and motioned him into a chair. "I'd like to say something," she said quietly.

He sat down and leaned back, trying to feign relaxation, but his gut was tight. "You have the floor," he teased, trying for a light tone.

But Ellie's expression was serious. "Dr. Milledge told me that you and I argued right before my accident."

"That's true."

"Conor..." She trailed off, her hands twisting restlessly in her lap. Today she was dressed simply in nice jeans and a white knit shirt with short sleeves. Her beautiful hair was caught up in a ponytail. The style drew attention to her high cheekbones and slightly pointed chin.

He waited, remembering the doctor's advice. *No pressure.* "Nothing to worry about, Ellie. You and I are fine."

"I'm sorry," she said, eyes downcast. "It was probably my fault. That's the thing that's bugging me. I can't remember."

She looked up at him, and he saw panic in her eyes.

Without overthinking it, he joined her on the bed. Hip to hip, but not touching. "It was nothing, Ellie. Really."

"I remember the party and the hospital, but in between is a blank."

He put his arm around her shoulders and drew her close against his side, unable to resist the need to comfort her. "According to the doctors, that's entirely normal for a head injury. Those brief hours may come back or they may not, but either way, it's no big deal."

She sighed, her expression hidden as she pressed her cheek to his chest. "It is to me," she said. "Please, Conor, tell me what we were fighting about."

Well, hell. What was he supposed to say? "It was more of a disagreement."

"I was running through the forest barefoot. It had to be something." One second passed. Then five.

Searching for a believable lie was not easy.

Ellie pulled free of his embrace and turned sideways so

she could look up at him, her blue eyes allowing him no quarter. "You can tell me. I'm not going to shatter into a million pieces. What did we argue about, Conor?"

He cleared his throat. "Well…"

"Was it about sex?"

He felt his neck heat. "Why would you say that?"

"I'm attracted to you. And I think you are to me. So it seems like the topic might have come up. But I don't know why it would be the kind of thing to make me so upset."

He cupped a hand behind her neck, steadying her… steadying himself…willing her to understand. "You wanted us to be intimate. I wanted that, too. But I was afraid it was too soon…that you hadn't dealt with Kevin's death."

She went white…so pale he thought for a moment she might faint. And he felt her tremble. "It must be nice to be right all the time."

While he struggled for the right words to say, Ellie stood up and went to the window, her back to him. "I'd like to take a nap now," she said. "If that's okay."

The dismissal was pretty clear. "Of course."

He didn't want to leave her, but he had no real reason to stay.

The house seemed to close in on him suddenly, and he wondered what in the heck he had done to himself. Ellie was already upset with him, and they hadn't even made it through the first day. Had he sentenced himself to an interminably long few weeks?

For half an hour Conor settled himself in front of the muted TV with a beer and his laptop to deal with a few things at Silver Slopes. But none of the business was really urgent. Not to mention the fact that he had an accountant and a host of other employees to handle anything that might come up.

Finally, he realized that he had to do something physical to diffuse the restless energy that thrummed through his veins. He wanted Ellie badly. And she was ensconced in his home. Close. Available. It was enough to drive him stark raving mad.

Surmising that Ellie and Emory would sleep at least an hour and a half, he went to his bedroom, stripped down to his boxers and donned a T-shirt and shorts. At the back of his new home he had added a state-of-the-art workout gym.

In minutes, he was sweating as he pummeled a punching bag. His knuckles would be sore and bruised tomorrow, but it was worth it. After that, he moved to the weight bench. Adding five pounds to his personal best, he lay down on his back, positioned his hands and concentrated fiercely as his arms strained to lift the almost immovable object.

Salty perspiration dripped into his eyes, making them sting and burn. His lungs ached for air, and his biceps quivered with fatigue.

The sudden sound of a woman's voice almost made him drop the weights. Gritting his teeth, he lowered the bar into its resting place. Taking a deep breath, he sat up and wiped his face with a towel. "I thought you were sleeping."

Ellie's curious stare made him restless. "I'm a good power napper." She crossed the room to stand beside him. "You're a very masculine man, Conor Kavanagh. I like looking at you." As sweat rolled down his shoulder, she ran her fingertip from the inside of his elbow up his arm and caught the droplet.

Her touch on his body burned him from the inside out. "I need a shower," he muttered, scarcely able to breathe. Arousal bloomed, hot and vicious. Surely Ellie wasn't this naive. "Will you excuse me?"

As he started to step around her, she placed a hand, palm flat, on his bare chest. He had stripped off his T-shirt before doing the weights. "No," she said. "I don't believe I will."

"Stop, Ellie." As a protest, it was weak at best. But the

last time he'd rejected her she had ended up with a concussion and memory loss.

"I've had professional medical care, Conor. You don't have to be afraid you're going to shatter my psyche. If you don't want me, you can say so."

He could make her back off. All he had to do was convince her that he looked at her as a sister. Sadly, it would take a hell of a better man than he was to sell that lie.

He curled his fingers around her wrist, removing her hand from his chest. "I'll give you whatever you want, Ellie, I swear. But we have to start slowly."

She nodded, still with that curious light in her eyes… as if she were already imagining the two of them naked and entwined in the sheets. "That's fair. So a kiss, then?"

She made it a question even as she moved against him, heedless of his damp nakedness. Lifting her face to his, she put her hand on the back of his head. "Kiss me."

A very long time ago he had danced with her and wondered how it would be to kiss a girl like Ellie. But this was different. In the interim, she'd been married…had given birth to a child. Conor was not into one-night stands, though he'd had his share of relationships.

Slowly, he lowered his mouth to hers. He'd never really thought of her as a short woman, but they were both barefoot and Ellie seemed small and vulnerable. That vulnerability gave him pause. Should he walk away from temptation?

When his lips touched hers, the internal discussion ended. His brain shut down instantly and his body took over. God, she felt amazing. His hands roved over her back. He badly wanted to feel her curvy butt in his palms, but protecting her had to come before his own base urges. He had to keep a tight rein on his hunger or it would consume them both.

"Ellie," he muttered. "Ah, God, Ellie."

Her arms went around his neck. "Hold me, Conor." Her voice broke. "I need you so much."

The need went both ways. He'd always assumed what he felt for one of his two best friends was a crush. Puppy love. The infatuation of a hormonal teenage boy for a beautiful girl. But what if it had been more? What if that emotion had lain dormant all these years? What if every woman he'd met had been judged by the yardstick that was Ellie?

Her lips were soft and sweet. At first, the kiss was chaste. He wasn't willing to torment either of them with a prelude that had no second act. In moments, though, her restrained enthusiasm sparked a naughty demon in his gut. A devil's advocate that said he would cherish her in bed. Make her feel like a queen. A goddess. Where was the harm in that?

When Ellie parted her lips, he slid his tongue into the recesses of her mouth. The kiss deepened. At some level he was aware that he was hot and sweaty and less than prepared for romance.

But against all odds, this was something more. Visceral. Honest. Intense. They met as equals. Haunted by the past. Yearning for a future. He wrapped his arms around her back, lifting her onto her tiptoes to better reach her mouth.

"Are you okay, Ellie?" he asked, the words hoarse.

Her answer was to press even closer. "Tell me you want me," she said. "Make me believe it."

If that was all he needed to do to please her, the job was easy. "Every damn day since you came back." He nibbled the side of her neck. "I used to dream about this," he muttered. "When we were kids. But you were dating your way through half of the boys in our sophomore class."

He felt her smile. "That's not very complimentary."

"Of course it is. Every guy I knew would have killed for the chance to be your boyfriend."

"Not you."

That silenced him. It was true. He'd been too afraid of

losing her altogether to risk anything intimate. At least not until the very end, right before his accident. And then afterward, Ellie had asked for what he couldn't or wouldn't give. Even now, the secret he was keeping from her gnawed away at him.

Ellie gasped, probably because he barely gave her a chance to breathe in between kisses. His body was taut and hungry, all the blood racing south. His sex was hard and ready. The evidence was impossible to hide in his current clothing.

"Ellie, sweetheart. Enough."

She clung to him, shaking her head vehemently. "Don't stop me. I might have an episode."

"Brat." He chuckled helplessly, even as he felt her fingernails scrape over his nipples. "We can't do this. Not now, anyway. It's too risky. Too soon."

Nine

Ellie knew he was right. But she was so aroused that she shivered with wanting him. He made her feel alive and whole and happy. And it had been so long, so very long since she had felt any of those things.

But she wasn't being fair to Conor. He was a man. With a powerful libido. What she was asking for was something he wasn't willing to give her. Not because he wasn't interested, but because he cared. That knowledge healed a jagged hurt in her soul. A raw, angry wound that had existed for a very long time.

Forcing herself to release Conor, she stepped back, cupping her hot cheeks with her hands. "I'm sorry."

He shook his head. "I don't want to hear those words anymore. Whatever we have…whatever we are…we'll figure it out."

"You sound so sure."

"Maybe I'm good at bluffing."

His wry grin threatened to melt her into a puddle. Her

heart felt more serene than it had in a long time. She was willing to wait, content in the knowledge that the world wasn't going to cave in on her if she didn't hold everything together.

Still, they were both only seconds away from doing something they might regret. Especially given the fact that Emory would soon be wailing for attention. To lighten the mood, she shoved her hands in her back pockets. "What does a girl have to do to get fed around here?"

The relief on Conor's face was almost comical. To give the man his due, he was walking on eggshells around her. Who knew what the doctors had told him and Kirby.

"I will talk about things," she said impulsively. "I swear. I just need time."

Conor's smile didn't quite reach his eyes. "Take all the time you need."

Considering how the day had begun, Ellie's first evening at Conor's home passed extremely well. Emory enjoyed exploring his new environment. The baby kept the dinner hour from being awkward. Afterward, Conor insisted on helping with the very physical parts of Emory's nighttime routine.

Ellie stood in the doorway of the bathroom watching the big, muscular man juggle the slippery little naked boy. It was comical and sweet and totally unfair. How was a woman supposed to keep her senses when faced with such a scene of domesticity?

Emory's gurgles of laughter when Conor made faces at him were precious and wonderful. She had missed her baby terribly. The hours she spent in Silver Glen's hospital were the first time she had ever been away from him overnight.

She had been sobered and abashed when the doctor explained her situation. She'd also been embarrassed. She was a normal, competent, well-educated woman. It was hard to accept that she had let herself get so close to the edge that her reason had momentarily snapped.

Conor shot her a glance over his shoulder. "Grab me his towel, will you?"

Reaching for the turquoise terry-cloth wrap with the doggy ears, she held it open in her arms while Conor lifted Emory out of the tub and handed him to her. Emory gave her the sweetest smile as she bundled him up and dried his little body. No matter what happened in her life, this helpless baby was her responsibility.

Conor glanced down at himself ruefully. "I'm soaked through to the skin. Let me change and I'll be back."

She nodded, heading for the small room that had become Emory's nursery. Conor had spared no expense in outfitting it. The light maple changing table and rocker matched the bed and dresser. The bedding was blue and green with circus animals gamboling across the fabric.

As she diapered Emory and rubbed his chubby arms and legs with lotion, she pondered the reasons a man might go to such expense for a woman who held no special place in his life. She and Conor were childhood friends. Nothing more. Even upon her return, their relationship had existed primarily because of Kirby and his situation.

The money wasn't really an issue. Conor had plenty of it. But to put all of this together so quickly, he had committed time, as well. And thoughtfulness. Was it because he felt guilty that they had argued?

Emory was old enough now to hold a cup with help. So she sat with him in the rocker and sang songs as he drank his milk. Soon his eyelids were drooping. She laid him in his crib, picked up the monitor, and tiptoed out of the room.

Fabulous smells wafted through the air as she stepped out into the hall. Following her nose, she made her way to the kitchen where she found Conor unpacking restaurant cartons.

His hair was rumpled and he wore an old gray Silver Slopes T-shirt untucked over wrinkled khakis. The Kavanaghs were wealthy. She knew that. She'd seen Conor in a tux and Conor half-naked. But whoever said that clothes made the man was dead wrong.

Conor was Conor. He was comfortable in his own skin. He was strong, both mentally and physically, and though he was powerful and extremely masculine, he had the gift of tenderness.

She knew how easy it would be to fall in love with him. Too easy. But she had Emory to consider. And there were things Conor didn't know. Things she hadn't told anyone.

Maybe it was cowardly, but for now all she wanted to do was live in the moment. The doctors had prescribed rest. So she would rest. And wallow in Conor's careful attention.

It would be wrong to seduce him. He was determined to do the honorable thing. And maybe he was right. Because if he learned her guilty secrets, he might turn away in disgust.

Chastened by that realization, she was careful to keep her distance as they carried dinner into the dining room.

"Good grief," she said. "You have enough food here for six people. Are we expecting a party?" Conor shook his head. "No. But I'm a fan of good leftovers, and I don't know what you like anymore." He sat down beside her.

As she dug into her teriyaki chicken, she tried not to notice the fact that his hip almost touched hers. Occasionally his arm brushed hers as he reached for a second helping or tried something new. It took an effort not to flinch or move away.

I don't know what you like anymore. It was true. The attraction that simmered between them was likely nothing more than the remnants of a teenage relationship that was long gone. She and Conor didn't really even know each other at all. She had secrets. No doubt he did, as well.

Secrets made a bad foundation.

On the other hand, if all she wanted…all *he* wanted…
was to scratch an itch, did it really matter if they bared
their souls? People indulged in purely physical encounters
all the time. Maybe she and Conor could have sex and that
would be it.

When he leaned forward to snag a dinner roll, she inhaled his scent. Not something as easily identifiable as aftershave, but a subtle fragrance, a mix of laundry detergent
and warm skin.

As unobtrusively as possible, she put a few more inches
between them. Suddenly, the idea of spending a few weeks
in this house, much less a few days, seemed daunting. She
finished up her meal and stood to carry her plate to the
kitchen. "I think I'll go to bed and read," she said, feeling
panicky for no discernible reason.

Conor stood, as well. "Are you feeling okay?" he asked,
concern etched on his face.

"I'm fine. A little tired."

He followed her to the kitchen, a silent presence at her
back. Once she had deposited her things in the dishwasher,
she gave him a small smile. "I'll see you in the morning."

She fled to her room and closed the door behind her,
leaning back against it and putting her hands over her face.
Maybe she *was* losing her mind. She didn't know what
she wanted. Part of her craved the physical oblivion of
Conor's lovemaking. The other part, the more rational part,
reminded her that she was a responsible parent…and that
she didn't deserve to be happy.

After a hot shower, she went through her nightly rituals.
At the vanity, she sat and brushed her hair the obligatory
one hundred strokes. The ends needed a good trimming.
But when was she supposed to find the time? Being a mom
meant squeezing every available moment out of the day.

She called Kirby to reassure him that she was fine. He
questioned her with a doctor's thoroughness, but when he

told her he was worried about her, it was her brother speaking, her twin. Convincing him she was well and happy was not easy, particularly since she wasn't at all sure she was telling the whole truth.

When she climbed into bed and plucked a book off the nightstand, it was still not even nine o'clock. The historical novel she was reading was good, but it had been more than a week since she last picked it up and she had lost the threads of the story. Tossing it aside, she hunkered down in the covers and turned out the light.

Exhaustion rolled over her in suffocating waves. Her head ached. Jangled emotions kept her brain spinning. She needed to make sense of her life. And leaning on Conor wasn't the answer.

But she felt so alone…

Conor flipped channels on the TV, wishing he could go for a walk. But he was reluctant to leave the house with guests under his roof. When his cell phone buzzed, he wasn't surprised to recognize Kirby's number.

He answered on the first ring. "Hey, Kirby. What's up?"

"How is she really?"

"I take it you talked to her?"

"For five minutes. She put on a good show. But I've known my sister a very long time. She doesn't like showing weakness."

"She headed off to bed early. I couldn't decide if it was because she felt bad or because she doesn't feel comfortable with me."

"Maybe she thinks her attraction to you is being disloyal to Kevin."

Conor's stomach clenched. He'd had the same thought. "I wouldn't say this to anyone else, but honestly, Kirby, I feel like I'm damned if I do and damned if I don't."

"I trust you."

"Great." Conor snorted. "I don't know whether to be flattered or creeped out. I'm not in the habit of discussing my intimate relationships with *anyone*, much less a family member of the female in question."

"At least you're contemplating sex. I haven't been with a woman since before my accident."

Conor gripped the phone, almost sure that his buddy hadn't meant to blurt that out. After a long moment of silence, he sighed. "That bites."

"Yeah. Tell me about it." Kirby's voice was a combination of resignation and frustration. "What am I supposed to do? Tell her to wait a minute while I pop off my foot? Or leave it on and hope it doesn't feel weird to her? I'm screwed."

"Or not."

Kirby burst out laughing. "Thanks for the help."

"Anytime, man. Anytime. But seriously, Kirby. When the right woman comes along, it won't matter."

"You sound awfully sure of that for a guy who's single and sleeping alone."

"Fine. I'll take my pep talks elsewhere. And for the record, I'm single *by choice*. Has anyone ever told you your bedside manner sucks?"

"If you end up in my hospital, I swear I'll be nice to you. But until then…"

"Promises. Promises."

They talked a little longer and then agreed that Kirby would drop by in the morning. Conor ended the call with a smile on his face. He had plenty of friends. Lots of friends, actually. But there was something about a guy who had known you since you were a snotty-nosed kid. Kirby understood Conor and vice versa.

It was wonderful to have him back in Silver Glen, even if for only a little while.

At ten, Conor walked in his sock feet to Ellie's door and

stood there quietly. He couldn't detect any sounds at all. Not that silence was a guarantee she was asleep.

He then moved a few steps down the hall to the other door that accessed the suite…the door to Emory's temporary nursery. All was quiet. He was determined to deal with Emory if the baby awoke during the night.

The most straightforward approach would have been to ask Ellie for the baby monitor. But she was stubborn, and despite doctor's suggestions, she was intent on caring for the baby all on her own. The chances of her surrendering the monitor so she could get a good night's sleep were slim to none.

With a sigh, he returned to the living room, knowing that he would never be able to sleep at this hour. He sat on the sofa, elbows on his knees, and dropped his head in his hands. What was he going to do about Ellie?

Maeve Kavanagh had started from an early age teaching her boys how to respect women. Perhaps because their father, Reggie, had been feckless and selfish, Maeve had instilled in her sons the two *R*s—responsibility and respect. That last one covered a multitude of sins. Respect for the environment. Respect for the less fortunate. Respect for your fellow man in general. But, most of all, respect for feminine vulnerability when it came to physical relationships.

Conor would never under any circumstances coerce a woman who said no. But what about a woman who said yes? A woman who had borne more than her share of tragedy and heartache recently. Who was strong in every way, but momentarily needed protection and support.

What was a man supposed to do in that situation?

A faint noise alerted him to the fact that he was no longer alone. Standing in the arched doorway was Ellie. Hair mussed. Feet bare. Eyes shadowed with dark smudges. Her expression was a cross between distress and defiance.

"Ellie." Great. His speech had been reduced to single-word sentences.

She tugged her thin turquoise robe tightly across her chest, perhaps unaware that she was giving him an even nicer view of her breasts. Particularly the way the nipples thrust against the soft fabric.

"I can't sleep," she said.

Was that a statement? Complaint? Request for help?

He stood and rubbed his chin, realizing that he had forgotten to shave that morning. In the hustle and hurry of making sure the house was ready before he dashed off to the hospital, he'd been focused on his concern for Ellie.

"Would you like some warm milk?" Great. Now he sounded like an old geezer.

Her golden-red hair seemed to glow, making her lack of color more pronounced. She shook her head. "No. Thank you."

"A shot of whiskey?"

Again she declined. "I can't. Because of the medication I'm taking."

"Ah." He'd exhausted his repertoire of sleep aids. Except for heart-pounding, wildly orgasmic, hot-monkey sex. And that was not on the list of approved rehabilitative activities for a woman who had suffered a blow to the head.

"Would you like to sit down?" He couldn't read her.

Ellie shook her head, still glued in the doorway, her lower lip trembling.

A flash of genuine anxiety drew him across the room. "Talk to me, Ellie. Tell me what's wrong. What do you want me to do for you?" He unfolded her arms and took both her hands in his. Her fingers were cold.

Without overthinking it, he drew her into his embrace, ruefully aware that his body instantly responded to hers.

She buried her face in his chest. "It's stupid," she muttered.

Her hair smelled like flowers. "Tell me, anyway." Why did she have to feel like perfection when he held her? The physical connection couldn't make up for all the unspoken realities that lurked between them with the deceptive nature of quicksand.

"I had nightmares," she whispered. "In the hospital. Kirby and Kevin were falling off the mountain. Again and again. I'm afraid to go to sleep." She paused. "Come to bed with me, Conor. Please. Not for sex, I swear."

Ten

Conor wondered what he had done in a prior life to deserve this kind of torture. But denying her was not an option.

"Of course," he said quickly. He suspected that her toes were as cold as her fingers. So he scooped her up in his arms and carried her to the bedroom. The large bed was mostly untouched. On Ellie's side, though, it was easy to see that she had been restless.

Tossing back the sheet and spread, he laid her down gently and covered her up. After kicking off his shoes, he climbed onto the mattress, scooted past her, and leaned against the headboard with a sigh. The room was dimly lit. He yawned, feeling peace envelop him, despite his acute awareness of the woman at his side.

As always, the paradox perplexed him. How could he want her so badly and yet be soothed simply to lie by her side?

Out of the corner of his eye he saw Ellie wriggling to

remove her robe. He held one sleeve until she managed the exercise. Now she was clad in nothing more than a sheer gown that was half-a-dozen shades lighter in color and a hundred times more provocative.

Though he could only see her from the waist up, that was enough.

He closed his eyes. "I would sing to you if I could," he joked. "But we'd both regret that."

"I don't know that regret is such a bad thing. At least it means we've lived." She took his attempt at humor and tossed it back in his court.

"I've lost a lot of things I've cared about, Ellie. And believe me, I've lived and breathed regret."

"Your career?"

He stared straight ahead, his brows drawn tight. "Yeah."

"I'm sorry about that," she said quietly. "I feel like Kirby and I let you down. You'd barely been home from the hospital two weeks when we moved away. But most of all, I'm sorry for breaking up with you after your accident. I was so damned scared, and I thought if I gave you a choice of skiing or me, you would pick me."

"We weren't even really a couple," he said, his throat tight. "No apologies necessary." Those had been dark days. Though he'd never admitted it to anyone, when he'd been trussed up in that hospital—his body broken and in jaw-clenching pain—there had been a second or two when he hadn't wanted to live. Even now it was hard to talk about it. "Tell me what you think Kirby will do in terms of picking a place to practice."

It was a clumsy change, of course, but he hated the feeling that she was poking around in his psyche.

Ellie inched closer to him, though they were still divided, her below the covers and him above. "I think he's leaning toward Miami. We've talked recently about buying a house together. I don't want to go back to work until

Emory is in school, but when I'm ready, Miami has a big enough international population to make my skill set valuable."

"And in the meantime?"

"Kirby will be working long hours. It will be nice for him to come home to a hot meal and an organized household."

"I doubt he expects you to wait on him hand and foot."

"Of course not. But the arrangement will be good for both of us. Emory is going to need a strong male influence in his life."

"And if Kirby falls in love?"

He felt Ellie go still. "Then I'll find my own place, of course."

Her voice was small and hurt. He was goading her deliberately, because the thought of her moving so far away a second time made him want to punch something. "Go to sleep," he said gruffly. "I won't leave you."

Ellie trembled, though she was plenty warm. What did Conor want from her? He'd made it sound as if a move to Miami was a personal betrayal. Was that how he'd felt when all three of them were only sixteen?

She closed her eyes, desperate for rest, but more desperate to crack the code that accessed Conor Kavanagh's protective shield. One moment he treated her with the avuncular platonic attention of a relative. The next he exuded an unmistakable vibe of sexual need.

Pretending to be asleep, she counted the cadence of his breathing. Out of the corner of her eye she could see that he had his hands folded across his abdomen. He had snagged two of the extra pillows and tucked them behind his back.

What was he thinking?

She was curled on her side, facing him. If she moved her hand, she could touch his hard thigh.

"Conor," she whispered.

He never flinched. "Yes?"

"Will you get under the covers and hold me?"

The seconds that ticked away before he answered were crushing.

When Emory made it to his six-month birthday and when Kirby finally finished all his surgeries, she'd naively thought she had reached her lowest point and was on the way back up, but this week had taught her differently.

Conor nodded. "Sure."

He rolled off the bed, folded the covers back and climbed in beside her. Instantly, she felt his body heat, as hot and wonderful as a furnace on an icy winter night. Still, he made no move to get any closer.

Knowing his scruples, she took the initiative. He was on his back. Scooting against him, she rested her bent knee across his leg and put her head on his arm.

When he shifted to wrap that same arm around her, she wanted to cry. Her parents had been with her after Kevin's death. And they'd stayed for a month until Kirby was past the danger point. But then they had returned to the jungle and to their work.

Kirby had been too ill to hold his sister and comfort her. Emory was yet to be born. Friends didn't know what to say to a woman who had lost so much. So she pretended she was strong. She had moved from one day to the next, doggedly doing what had to be done.

She would never forget Kirby sleeping in a chair during her labor and delivery. He'd been on crutches at that point, twenty pounds lighter and still recovering from a recent surgery. Mrs. Porter had missed the baby's birth. She'd contracted malaria in the jungle, and her husband had stayed in Bolivia to care for her.

After Ellie had been in labor for twenty-six hours, Kirby had passed out on the floor beside Ellie's bed and been admitted to a hospital room of his own. A night nurse with a drill sergeant attitude had coached Ellie through the final hours, smiling triumphantly alongside the exhausted mother when little Emory emerged, healthy and whole.

Now, in Conor's arms, all of that seemed like a dream. Ellie's eyes grew heavy. "This is nice," she said, the words slurred.

He kissed her forehead. "Sleep, Ellie. Just sleep."

When she surfaced the next time, the room was filled with the gray light of predawn. And it was raining. Hard. The steady drumming on the roof brought with it a sensation of coziness and safety.

Conor snored softly beside her. For a moment, she barely recognized the sensation that slid through her veins in a drowsy river. Happiness. Contentment. Hope.

Big emotions to hang on one brief moment in time. Conor was being nice to her, that's all. The challenges she faced still existed outside this bed. Even so, she was prepared to live in the now.

With her eyes closed, she inhaled the scent of him. Conor. Friend. Confidant. *And lover?*

Carefully, she slid her right hand beneath his warm cotton shirt where it had rucked up at his waist. His taut, flat abdomen invited a woman's touch. He was so real. So alive.

He moved restlessly in his sleep. Chagrined, she rolled away.

Though she was very still in the aftermath of her impulsive behavior, she had awakened the beast. He snagged her wrist and dragged her close.

His eyes heavy lidded, he gazed at her. "I can't say no to this anymore, Ellie. Because I want you more than my next breath. I'm not the man you need forever... But I could be the guy you need today...if that's all you want."

He would never know the courage it took to answer.

"Yes." As he rolled on his side to face her, her fingertips found his collarbone, his sternum, the soft trail of hair that bisected his chest and led to his belt buckle.

Conor's lopsided smile encompassed a wry awareness of all the reasons this was a bad idea. "I've wanted you since I was fifteen."

"With an extensive time-out in between," she pointed out.

Her heart pounded in a jerky rhythm as she deftly unbuttoned the single fastening at his waistband.

"Years. Minutes. Who cares?" He kissed her hard, his hips moving restlessly against hers. His breathing was harsh and his movements jerky as his hands caressed her breasts through a layer of fabric.

"Conor…" She whispered his name, caught up in a wave of desire so intense it left her dizzy and disoriented.

He bit her earlobe, the little spritz of pain sparking through her nervous system. "I'm here."

She pressed her hand, palm flat, against his sex…only a couple of layers of fabric between her skin and his. Guilt and pleasure and anticipation jostled for position in her few remaining brain cells.

Beneath her fingertips, he flexed and hardened. He groaned as she stroked him. The erection that rose hot and hard beneath her touch was not shy. Conor shifted in the bed. "Ellie…"

The way he said her name, all gruff and demanding, made her hot. She slid her fingers beneath the edge of his pants, not far enough to touch the evidence of his excitement, but enough to toy with the sensitive skin around his navel.

She moved half on top of him so she could nibble the side of his neck. "The doctor said exercise would be good for me…as a stress reliever." So far he was letting her set the pace, but she had no illusions. His whole body was tensed for action.

Lowering his zipper slowly, she heard his sharp intake of breath. Her hand closed around him, feeling the urgency in his sex. Warm skin over hot male need. Elemental. Timeless.

He cursed softly, even as he swelled in her grasp. "There's no going back, Ellie. Not after this." It was a warning, but since his hands kneaded her bottom as he said it, she didn't put much stock in the words.

She kissed him full on the mouth, exulting when he took control and pulled her tight against his chest. "I don't want to go back," she panted. "The past is over. I want to be selfish and irresponsible."

"You don't know how."

He kissed like a dream. For a split second, she hated all the faceless women he'd practiced with. But then his tongue stroked her lower lip and she forgot to care. He held her chin with one big hand, tilting her face toward his, sliding a finger around her jaw to play with her tiny gold hoop earring.

It would be really embarrassing to come from nothing more than a man touching her earlobe.

"Um, Conor?" she panted.

"Yeah?" He released her and levered upward to rip his shirt over his head.

"I'm on the pill. For medical reasons. And I haven't slept around."

He chuckled hoarsely, kissing the spot where her neck and shoulder met. "I think I knew that. The last part, I mean. You don't have to worry about me, Ellie."

When his teeth raked her skin, she thought she might swoon. Did women do that anymore? Or only ones that slept with Conor?

Her gown was strangling her. And she was hot. So hot.

Conor gripped the thin fabric. "Are you attached to this?"

Her nightwear was made of sheer Swiss cotton. Imported. Very expensive. Something she'd bought last year to remind herself she was still a woman and not only a mom. "Not particularly."

Two big hands ripped the batiste from stem to stern. "I've always wanted to do that." She thought he was joking until she saw the intent look on his face. He zeroed in on her breasts, his gaze slightly awed. "You're beautiful, Ellie…so damned beautiful it makes me ache."

She wanted to say *thank you* or *that's sweet*, but all she could do was close her eyes and feel. His touch was reverent but determined. Each of his hands was large enough to cup one of her full breasts.

Torn between wanting to savor his tenderness and needing to hurry him along, she hung teetering on the edge of something amazing…something she had wanted for a very long time.

She bit her lip. Speaking seemed unnecessary under the current conditions, but if she didn't say something, she was worried that Conor might linger too long. "Foreplay is great and all that," she said, "but I wouldn't mind if you moved on to the main course." Her comment was a masterpiece of rational, polite discourse.

Conor raised a single eyebrow. "Impatient much?"

She kicked his ankle. "I've waited a long time for this."

"Not as long as me," he muttered, finally understanding the urgency of the situation. Lifting his hips, he shed his pants and cotton boxers with the efficiency and speed of a seasoned athlete.

Now they were both naked.

He tossed back the covers and reclined on his side. "I think we should savor this."

"No." She lurched at him, managing to bump into a rather impressive body part. "Please tell me you're joking."

"I was." He laughed, wincing when she climbed on top of him to smother his face with kisses. "But then again, anticipation is half the pleasure."

Ellie placed her hands, palm flat, on his shoulders. "No. It's not. Pleasure me, Conor. Prove me wrong."

It was difficult for a man to make smart decisions when his brain was oxygen deprived. He *could* blame it on the fact that Ellie sat on his chest squashing the air out of him. Or on the fact that his erection was as rigid and solid as the proverbial iron spike because all the available O2 had rushed south in his bloodstream.

But the truth was, when he looked at Ellie naked, he forgot how to breathe.

Pleasure me, Conor. He wanted to. God knew he wanted to. Despite his arousal, some nasty little portion of his brain reminded him that this was likely the first time she'd had sex since her husband died.

What if he couldn't make her climax? What if she became so distraught in the midst of physically connecting that she had another breakdown? What if she cried because she missed her husband?

Damn it to hell and back.

He could pretend Ellie was his teenage fantasy. Maybe that would erase the troubling questions. But he wanted the adult Ellie. The accomplished, beautiful, multidimensional woman who spoke several languages and had a baby and smiled at him with the sweet openness that told him some things *never* change.

He gripped her hips. "You mean the world to me, Ellie." He laid it out there, not wanting her to think this was a toss away…an insignificant moment in the midst of a rough time in her life.

Above him, her hair fell like silken rain. "I want you, Conor," she said, her smile both tremulous and confident. "Both the boy I knew and the man you are."

Unwittingly, her words echoed his thoughts. "Did you ever wonder?" he asked. "About us being intimate?"

She grinned. "Of course. I was jealous of you and Kirby. You were both so close, and I wanted that with you."

"But the one time you and I tried to be more than friends, you said I wasn't the kind of guy you wanted."

"I was wrong." Her little wiggle scalded his nerve endings.

He shifted her, lifting her upward only to pull her down as he joined their bodies. When she slid onto his sex, taking him deep, he closed his eyes. Little flashes of light pulsed with the beat of his heart.

She was tight and hot and utterly perfect.

Ellie leaned back on her hands, driving him the slightest bit crazy. She placed her feet flat on the bed and used the purchase to ride him slowly. "I'll bet you know a lot of kinky stuff about sex. Admit it."

He gasped, already on the cusp of coming. "Don't talk," he begged.

Up. And down. "I thought men liked talking. At least during sex."

"I like it." His jaw ached from clenching his teeth. "But I don't need any more stimulation at the moment."

Inward muscles gripped his shaft. "Are you saying we're good together?"

"No."

She pretended to be hurt, when he knew damned well that she could tell he was straining to keep from crossing the finish line. "That's not very gallant." Leaning forward, she nipped one of his flat nipples with sharp teeth. "I'm doing the best I can."

From somewhere he found the presence of mind to touch

her where it mattered. His targeted caress turned his smart-mouthed tormentor into a needy beggar. Sprawling on his chest, she cried out. "Do something, Conor. I'm dying."

He rolled them instantly, shoving her onto her back, driving so deep he saw a red haze. Primal male urges took over. "Whatever you want, Ellie. Whatever you need."

After that, there were no words, no time-out, no playful sex talk.

There was only Ellie.

Eleven

Conor surfaced groggily, feeling as if he had finished a
challenging downhill slope. His muscles quivered. His body
was lax. His breathing struggled to find a normal rhythm.

And then it came again. The sound that had awakened
him. Emory.

It was seven-thirty. The kid was probably starving.

Conor moved surreptitiously, sliding out of bed and pulling on his underwear and pants. Ellie slept like the dead,
on her back, both arms flung over her head. She had whis-
ker burn on her throat.

Her naked body was mesmerizing. A painter or sculptor
would find her an irresistible subject. Though Ellie complained about her weight, Conor loved her curves. Full
breasts, shapely thighs, a butt that was made for a man's
hands.

She was real and warm and feminine in every way.

When Emory's babbles escalated, Conor knew he had to
move fast if he wanted Ellie to get more sleep. In the baby's

room, he scooped up the warm, sweetly scented toddler and nuzzled his belly. "Hey, little man. Let's get you a clean diaper, and Uncle Conor will find you something to eat."

Emory's eyes were huge as he sucked his fist. Conor managed the diaper change without incident. Once the soft pajamas were re-snapped in the careful sequence that required an engineering degree, the two of them escaped down the hall.

Tucking Emory into the newly purchased high chair, Conor grinned. "You're a cute kid."

Emory's response was a babbling string of syllables accompanied by drool. His sunny smile made a guy wonder if kids weren't worth the hassle after all.

Breakfast was easy. Dry Cheerios. Milk. Chopped up banana. At this rate, Conor would qualify as a baby nutritionist. While Emory polished off the food on his tray, Conor started the coffeepot. Yawning and rubbing a hand over his bare chest, he thought about the woman he'd left behind in the bed. Soft skin. Soft body. Soft everything.

Bad mistake. Now he had a boner. And it was going to be a very long day. Unless Emory took a nap. That had possibilities.

When Ellie appeared in the kitchen doorway a half hour later, she was wearing Conor's T-shirt. It had never looked so good. The neckline gaped, exposing the very spot he had nibbled only hours before.

The fact that she had supplemented the outfit with a pair of khaki shorts was not a great fashion choice in his opinion. He would have been fine with undies only. Or nothing at all beneath. But since Kirby was coming over at an unspecified time, it was probably a good thing that his sister had shown decorum.

Ellie's expression was hard to read. He'd hoped for a smile. Instead, she seemed abashed. Reluctant to meet his eyes. Keeping his face in neutral, he masked his disappointment. Mornings after were not always easy, especially since he and Ellie had made a big change in their relationship last night.

"I cook a mean waffle," he said. "Are you hungry?"

She nodded. "With eggs and bacon?"

He grinned. "Of course."

While Ellie sat with Emory and entertained her son, Conor threw together the meal. He'd built this house for the solitude and the peace. It was disconcerting to realize that having Ellie and Emory here exposed the fact there might be other more important things to consider.

Family. He was one of seven kids. And he loved his brothers. His mom was a sweetheart, and his dad, despite his many faults, had been a fun parent until he disappeared.

Conor had never really contemplated building a nest. He played hard and worked hard, and his recreational choices involved the kind of risk-taking adrenaline that made him feel alive. Ellie's rejection early on had taught him that few women wanted a long-term relationship with a man like him. He was okay with that. Mostly. Responsibilities tied a man down. He wasn't opposed to that lifestyle. Someday.

When he set a plate in front of Ellie, she put her hand on his arm. "Thank you, Conor." She looked up at him with a smile, a smile that knocked him off kilter.

"For the food?"

"Of course." But the mischief dancing in her eyes told a different story. Suddenly, every second of their predawn romp played in his head in vivid color.

"You're welcome," he muttered. "Eat your eggs before they get cold." He fixed his own plate and took the seat across from her, on the other side of Emory's high chair.

Silence reigned in the pleasant, sunny kitchen as they made short work of their meals.

Emory served as an innocent buffer. It was easier to interact with him than to deal with the fallout from what had happened. And damn it, what *had* happened? A change in the status quo for sure, but it was no big deal. He and Ellie had always enjoyed each other's company. They had merely taken their friendship one step farther.

It was late morning when Kirby made an appearance. In the meantime, Ellie had disappeared into her suite, ostensibly to bathe Emory and get him dressed for the day. As far as Conor could tell, she was hiding out.

Kirby looked good when Conor answered the front door. His buddy's shoulders were straight, his eyes clear and some of the lines around his mouth had disappeared.

"Come on in."

Kirby sprawled on the sofa, his legs propped on the coffee table. At first glance, you would never know that he wore a prosthesis. He lifted an eyebrow. "Is Ellie here? Or did you run her off?"

Conor had put on a shirt, but other than that, he was still in climb-out-of-bed mode. He shrugged, dropping onto the love seat across from Kirby. "She's doing something with the baby."

"Did she sleep well?"

Conor kept his gaze steady. "How should I know? She looked okay at breakfast." It was up to Ellie to decide who she told about her physical relationship with Conor. She and her twin shared most everything, but Conor wasn't going to make that call when the subject was such a private one.

"Hey, guys. Emory wants to say hello."

When Ellie walked into the room, Conor had to wonder if she had overheard the conversation.

Kirby patted the seat beside him. "Here, sis. Let me hold my handsome and superintelligent nephew."

Ellie handed him the baby and sat down, curling her legs beneath her. "Your nephew just smeared poo on his changing table."

* * *

She grinned as both men winced in unison. They were each so very masculine and assured. But like most bachelors, there were certain aspects of babyhood that stymied them.

As Kirby played a game of peek-a-boo with Emory, Ellie elbowed her brother gently. "How's Grandpa?" she asked. "Is he wondering where I am?"

"I thought he might ask, but he's been pretty fuzzy the last couple of days. The neighbor, Mrs. Perry, offered to check on him a couple of times while I'm up here."

"I should come home," Ellie said, the words impulsive. "You both need me."

Kirby took her hand in his. "I love you, sis. But you're not indispensable. I'm doing better every day. And you need to take it easy. Has Conor been looking after you?"

She felt her face turning red, but Kirby didn't seem to notice. "Of course. He fed Emory and me breakfast, and his housekeeper dropped by earlier to put a pot of chili on the stove. I know it's summer, but Conor and I agreed that it was a *chili* kind of day."

Kirby's face lit up. "Count me in." He glanced at Conor. "Ellie and I grew to appreciate all manner of South American cuisine, but there's nothing like home-cooked comfort food."

Ellie kissed her brother on the cheek and stood. "If you gentleman have the situation under control, I'd love to take a shower."

Kirby looked up at her. "You feeling okay this morning? You look good. You've got some color in your cheeks."

"I'm doing very well. Thank you for asking. Now can we quit referencing my unfortunate meltdown?"

"Did you ever talk to Mom and Dad?"

She nodded. In the hospital she had refused to call them, not wanting to interrupt their work, but once she was about to be released, she had phoned them, playing down the severity of her episode. It still made her uncomfortable to admit that she had been temporarily addled.

In her luxurious bathroom, she locked the door and stepped into the shower. The water was hot and strong and reviving. She hadn't gotten quite as much sleep as she would have liked.

Standing beneath the pelting spray, it was easy to remember why. There wasn't an inch of her skin Conor hadn't touched. He had made love to her as if they were the last two people on the earth. Out of control. Desperate. As if they might never have another chance.

And she had been equally urgent.

The whole tenor of their coming together really made no sense. Unless both of them, deep down, thought the relationship had an expiration date. She ran a washcloth over her breasts. They were sensitive, the swollen tips almost painful.

For months she had tried to pretend she was a mother first and a woman second. But sooner or later, her body was going to betray her. In fact, it already had...when she'd hit her head on a rock and imagined for a few hours that she was sixteen again.

Is that what she really wanted? To go back in time and be Conor Kavanagh's girlfriend? Or did she want something real? Something lasting? Something that meant growing and changing and allowing another person into her life?

She was chastened and thoughtful when she rejoined the men. All three males were on the living room floor, Conor and Kirby letting Emory ride them like horses. The baby was ecstatic, chortling and laughing. He grabbed a handful of Conor's hair and pulled.

"Ow!" Conor howled. His pretend indignation made the toddler do it again. Kirby tugged Emory's foot. "Be careful, love. The monster man is gonna get you."

Hovering in the doorway, Ellie watched them play. To see Kirby so happy and engaged was more than she ever could have wished for. Much of the thanks and credit for that transformation went to the man beside him.

Conor had brought such healing to their little circle of three. He'd made Kirby feel whole again. He'd given Ellie the certainty that her future was brighter than her past. He'd proved to Emory that he was an adult to be trusted.

Conor had moved seamlessly into their lives and worked his magic without fanfare. Was it any wonder that she was falling in love with him? She put a hand to her chest, feeling an odd little twinge. Love wasn't in the cards for her. She thought she had it once, and she lost it. So why try again? Why risk more pain?

Forcing herself to join the playgroup, she dropped onto her knees and tickled Emory's belly. "How's my sweetheart?"

Conor and Kirby exchanged droll looks. "We're fine," Kirby said.

She plucked Emory from Conor's back. "Very funny. There's only one man who has my heart." She kissed her son's head. "How about lunch, munchkin?"

"Yes, please." Conor touched arm lightly. "You stay here. Kirby and I will set everything out."

His fingers lingered, caressing the inside of her elbow. Kirby was already headed toward the kitchen, so the little byplay was private.

"I'm not an invalid," she muttered.

"Let me pamper you, Ellie. It makes me happy." He kissed her quickly, glancing over his shoulder to make sure they were alone.

Though the caress of his lips was brief, the light touch packed a punch. Or maybe she was already reeling from this morning. "By all means," she said. "Anything to make you happy."

"Anything?" His grin was devilish.

"Go find my brother. Before he eats our share."

To Conor's relief, lunch was fun and happy and bless-edly normal. Emory was in a good mood. Kirby's appetite was almost back to normal. Ellie smiled and relaxed. Conor played the clown until he had them all laughing and squab-bling like they had as kids and teenagers.

After they finished eating, Kirby grabbed an envelope he'd brought with him handed it to Ellie. "Here are the pictures you wanted me to get printed for Mom and Dad."

"Printed?" In this digital age, Conor was surprised.

Ellie opened the flap of the large brown mailer and flipped through the images. "Mom and Dad don't always have internet service, especially now that they're even deeper in the jungle to open this new clinic. So they like me to send photos they can hang up." She shook her head. "These are only four weeks old, but Emory changes every day."

While Conor took a look, she glanced at Kirby. "If I ad-dress this and put a note in, would you have time to mail it on your way back home?"

"Sure. Not a problem."

"Do you have packing tape and scissors, Conor?"

"Yep. My office is just past my bedroom on the same side of the hall. I've got a big rolltop desk. Try the left side, top drawer."

When Ellie disappeared, Kirby sighed. "She looks happy."

"I think you're right. At least I hope so. How long do you think we can keep her here?"

"As long as you and I can convince her it's for the best. My sister is stubborn."

"As are you and I."

Kirby grinned in agreement and opened his mouth to say

something, but whatever it was went unsaid. Ellie stormed into the kitchen, her face white…two spots of color high on her cheekbones.

She kicked the leg of Conor's chair, fury in every hair follicle. "You're going to climb Aconcagua?"

Belatedly, he realized that she held a familiar turquoise-and-yellow travel folder. One that he should have hidden far, far away. "Yes." What else could he say? He wasn't going to lie.

"When?"

"Next winter."

She whirled to face her brother. "*You* put him up to this."

Slowly, Kirby stood, a look of consternation on his face. "No."

Conor spoke softly, gauging her reaction with alarm. "I made those arrangements six months ago. Kirby had nothing to do with it."

She wilted suddenly, her anger morphing into perplexed pain as she gazed from one man to the other. "But Kirby must have egged you on, because you haven't cancelled."

Kirby spoke up, shooting Conor a warning look. "This kind of trip costs thousands of dollars. Prepayments that Conor wouldn't get back. Aconcagua is a fabulous adventure. Dozens of people climb it successfully year after year. What happened to Kevin and me was a freak accident. Conor will be fine."

"You don't know that."

Conor remained silent, feeling unaccountably guilty. He'd done nothing wrong, but *damn it to hell*…this wasn't how he wanted Ellie to find out. He'd planned to tell her himself. When the time was right.

Kirby put his arms around Ellie, hugging her close. "Conor is an experienced climber. He's done Kilimanjaro already. He knows what he's doing."

She looked over Kirby's shoulder at Conor, her eyes damp with emotion. "Is this true?"

Conor nodded grimly.

Ellie jerked away from her brother and backed up against the kitchen wall. "It's *both* of you," she said dully. "You don't feel alive unless you're risking your lives. But why don't you think about what it does to the people who love you?"

Kirby scowled. "That's not fair, Ell. I was a single man with all my affairs in order."

"What about me? You had me."

This time it was Kirby who paled. The standoff between siblings lasted for what seemed like hours. Ellie clutched the damning folder to her chest as if it were Pandora's box that couldn't be opened.

Kirby ran both hands through his hair. "I understand what you're feeling. I really do. But driving a car is dangerous. As is climbing into a plane. Life includes risk, Ellie. Just because you lost Kevin doesn't mean that Conor is doomed."

Now she was gray…haunted. "I don't want to talk about Kevin." Her jaw was so tight it must be giving her a headache. Her gaze was stony.

Kirby shook his head, his expression weary. "No. You never do. And that's the problem. That's why you snapped this week, Ell. If you don't deal with what happened, you'll never get past this."

For a moment, Conor thought she might bolt. She reminded him of a doe caught in the woods, not sure which way to run to avoid disaster.

He went to her instinctively, putting himself physically between the twins. The situation had escalated rapidly, and he was afraid one of them might say something that he or she would regret. He'd never forgive himself if his trip caused a permanent rift between his two best friends.

"That's enough, Kirby," he said. "Ellie has had a rough week." Gently, he pried the folder from Ellie's death grip and tossed it on top of the fridge. Taking her hands in his, he chafed them carefully. "Why don't you go put Emory down for his nap? He's falling asleep in his high chair. And you need to rest, too."

She shook her head, evading his grasp. "I'm leaving." Her voice was a low monotone. "As soon as I pack our things."

Kirby bristled, flushing with anger. "You sure as hell are not. My professional reputation is on the line here. The only reason you were released from the hospital is because I'm a doctor and because Conor promised to keep an eye on you."

"You can't keep me prisoner."

He brother was adamant. "I can for the next six days. After your checkup next week, as long as they clear you, you'll be free to do whatever you want. But until then, you're staying here in this house. End of story."

Conor suspected that if Ellie had been a hundred percent she would have gone head-to-head with her brother in a defiant showdown. But, given her current emotions, she couldn't manage it.

"I hate both of you," she said, her voice breaking.

Twelve

"That went well."

Kirby's moody scowl reflected Conor's feelings exactly. "She must have loved him very much."

"Yeah. I guess she did. But she can't grieve forever. It isn't healthy."

"Everyone faces loss differently. When my father disappeared, the end wasn't clean. First there were the months of not knowing. Then finally, a court order declaring him dead. My mother held it together because she had seven children. I'm sure I was too young to fully appreciate what she went through. But all I remember is the way she smiled and hugged us and swore that everything would be okay."

"I failed Ellie," Kirby said. "I should have been able to help her through Kevin's death."

"You were fighting a battle of your own. It's my turn to help her."

Kirby left soon afterward. Conor found himself alone and angry. A cloud settled over the house...as if someone had died. And in fact, that was pretty much the situation at hand. Even if it *had* been a long time ago. In the grand scheme of things, eighteen months could seem like the blink of an eye.

For Ellie, the pain of losing Kevin must be as raw and fresh as if it had happened yesterday. Finding Conor's travel plans would have brought it all back. She was suffering. And he wanted to comfort her. But, ironically, he was the person least qualified to do that.

The day was a thousand hours long. He felt honor-bound to stay close. Perhaps to help with the baby. Perhaps to look after Ellie if today's confrontation caused her to relapse.

He was no shrink, but he wondered if the fact that Kirby was finally on the road to recovery, both physically and mentally, had somehow given Ellie's subconscious permission to drop her heavy load. For months and months she'd had to be strong for her brother while at the same time undergoing unbelievable stress of her own.

Now that Kirby was better, Ellie had frayed a bit at the seams. And, unwittingly, Conor had weakened the very fabric of her existence.

What was his next move? He wasn't a fan of the sit-and-wait approach. He liked to plan a course of action and go with it.

But Ellie made that hard. She literally hid out in her suite with the baby. Though Conor felt foolish for doing so, he listened at the door every half hour to make sure he could hear her voice. That was a great plan in theory. But with the baby napping—Conor peeked in the nursery to make sure—there was no need for Ellie to converse.

When his overactive imagination got the better of him, Conor cracked *her* bedroom door, as well, and spied to see if she was okay. The sight that met his gaze wrenched his heart. Ellie was curled up in a ball on top of the covers, her hand pressed against her mouth.

He thought she was asleep, but he couldn't be sure. Quietly, he eased the door shut and walked away.

Ellie knew the exact moment that Conor looked in on her. And she knew when he closed the door and retreated. Though it was stupid, she couldn't bring herself to get into the bed properly. She and Conor had made love on those sheets. The experience had been wonderful. Poignant. Utterly satisfying.

And then he had betrayed her.

If you surveyed a hundred people and told them the tale, ninety-nine of them would probably say she had overreacted. But the hundredth one would understand. She had trusted Conor with her body and with her heart, though he didn't know that. To hear that he planned to climb the very mountain that had taken so much from her and from Kirby was unfathomable.

She wanted to rail at him and beat her fists on his chest. But Conor owed her no explanations. He was a free agent. One who knew that Ellie and Kirby were only passing through Silver Glen.

Why should Ellie's opinions or feelings bring any weight to bear on his actions?

Nevertheless, she felt the rip in her heart and filed it away with all the other pain. Pretty soon she was going to suck it up and admit that life in general was like playing the roulette wheel. The house always won.

She could beg Conor not to go, but she had tried that approach half a lifetime ago and failed. Even if she told him how she felt, there was still the matter of her guilty secret. The truth ate away at her, eroding her confidence.

Giving a man the silent treatment was a lot more effective when you weren't living in his house. By five o'clock, the walls of the suite, lovely though they were, began to close in on her. Emory was fractious and not to be consoled. They were both hungry.

With a mental white flag of surrender, Ellie put on a clean outfit, changed the baby and his clothes, and went in search of her host. She found him sitting on the front porch, his boot-shod feet propped on the railing, hands tucked behind his head.

She propped the baby on her hip. "I'm sorry I got so upset. Your life is your life. I don't have any right to criticize or pass judgment."

His feet dropped to the floor and he sat up straight. "And last night?"

"What about last night?" She kept her expression impassive, but it was an effort.

"When a man and a woman do what we did, it gives each of them implied rights."

She shrugged. "I don't think so. We were curious. We wanted to see if there was more than a spark."

"And was there?"

His eyes were dark and turbulent. Despite his seemingly relaxed pose when she stepped outside, his big frame vibrated with a combative edge.

She chose her words carefully. "Of course there was. We've shared a friendship that made us almost family."

"You're Kirby's sister, not mine. I *wanted* you, Ellie. I still do. Even knowing there's a good chance you're in love with another man. But if all you're doing is killing time until you jet off to some exotic city to start a new life with your brother and your kid, then I'd just as soon pass."

"That's not what you said this morning."

"As I recall, we didn't do a lot of talking."

"What do you want from me?" she cried, her chest tight and her eyes gritty.

Conor shook his head wearily. "Something you aren't willing or able to give, Ellie. Let's chalk last night up to an impulsive mistake. You've got your own demons to battle. I have a few of my own. We'd just make each other miserable. And life's too short for that."

"Where are you going?" she asked as he strode down the steps and around the side of the house.

The rustle of leaves in the summer breeze was her only answer.

Conor didn't know what to do about Ellie. All his life he'd been a smooth operator when it came to women. Flirt with them. Spoil them. Take a few to bed. But until now he hadn't realized how little those relationships had meant. He'd always been monogamous while involved with someone seriously. When the time came to end it, though, he'd never had his heart broken.

More importantly, he'd done his best to make sure *he* hadn't broken any hearts. He was always up-front with women. If they indicated an interest in home and hearth, he let them down gently and moved on.

Ellie created a whole new category. He was falling for her. And it wasn't some nostalgia-driven emotion from the past, although it was becoming more and more clear that his adolescent feelings for his best friend's sister had been more serious than he knew.

As a teenager he'd been confused by his response to Ellie. He enjoyed her company and considered her as much a friend as Kirby. But he hadn't recognized the sexual undercurrent as an indication of something deeper.

Now, with Ellie back in his life, albeit temporarily, everything clicked. Maybe because he was older and knew what he wanted and needed. Maybe because it was no longer taboo to woo her into his bed.

Sweat trickled down his back as he swung his ax to split a log. The pile of firewood at his side grew rapidly, ready for a season that was still weeks in the future. He liked the physical labor. It helped clear his head. It burned off some of the restless energy that plagued him.

What it didn't do was reveal answers.

Tonight, when Emory was in bed, it was time for Conor to talk straight with his tempestuous houseguest.

Ellie was both intrigued and on edge when Conor asked her to dress for dinner. She chose a sleeveless champagne silk tank dress that was entirely plain in the front but cut almost to her waist in back. The style made it impossible to wear a bra. Thankfully, her full breasts were firm and high.

She owned a small collection of good jewelry she had inherited from her grandmother Porter. From a glittery pile of bracelets and pendants, she chose a single long strand of pearls. They had been her grandmother's wedding gift from her husband. In today's market, the necklace would be obscenely expensive. To Ellie, the perfectly matched pearls were priceless.

Emory went to bed at seven most nights, so the adults were able to eat in peace. Over the elegant meal served in Conor's seldom-used dining room, they managed civil conversation. It helped that his housekeeper was present. The older woman had prepared a sophisticated version of baked pheasant with fresh summer vegetables as accompaniments.

The table was a work of art. Cream linen cloth, handmade dishes in shades of saffron and dark brown. Matching chunky candlesticks with beeswax tapers. The silverware was heavy and looked old. In deference to Ellie's concussion, water, not wine, flowed freely throughout the evening, served in amber goblets that surely weighed at least a pound each.

When she complimented the presentation, Conor grimaced. "Not long after I finished the house, my four sisters-in-law took it upon themselves to add what they said were necessary touches. It seemed to make them happy, so I gave them free rein."

"I think they did a great job. The house suits you…and the extra touches, too."

Making small talk with Conor was not easy. Their earlier argument had left them both on edge. Maybe they should always have one of Conor's employees nearby to act as referee or to keep the erotic subtext at bay.

Ellie had deliberately chosen to tamp down her pain and her frustration. Some wild part of her decided to live recklessly. If life was going to continually slap her in the face, she might as well enjoy the bright spots. And Conor Kavanagh was definitely a bright spot.

His dark suit was a masterpiece of understatement. He wore it as comfortably as he did everything else. Perhaps it was his animal grace that made him seem so at home in his own skin. He moved with confidence and concealed power, a beautifully masculine creature, incapable of being tamed.

To her credit, she understood his pursuit of adventure, even if she didn't like it.

After the main course was cleared, they feasted on strawberry shortcake. Ellie groaned, pushing hers aside, half-eaten. "You can finish mine," she said. "I'm stuffed, and besides, I happen to know you have an enviable metabolism."

"I'm shocked, Ellie. Was that an oblique compliment? I should ply you with wine more often."

"It was water, remember?" She knew he was teasing her, but in truth, the room spun ever so slightly. Was she trying to bolster her courage for what might seem an outrageous request?

At last, the quiet, efficient employee said her goodbyes and drove away. The house fell silent. Somewhere outside, a coyote howled in the distance. The sound sent a shiver down Ellie's spine. She was alone with Conor, absolutely alone. His property was so secluded they would have no interruptions.

He tapped a fork on the tablecloth absentmindedly, gazing down at a cup of coffee he hadn't bothered to drink.

Her skin felt hot and tight. She recognized her need for his touch even as she loathed her weakness. She was angry with him. Furious, in fact. For taking his precious life so lightly.

But apparently her libido was not so judgmental.

She wanted to clear the table or wash dishes or put away food…anything to occupy her hands and shatter the bubble of intimacy created by candlelight. But Conor's housekeeper had taken care of every detail. There was nothing for Ellie to do. Nothing but ache for Conor.

"I should go to bed," she said. "Emory will be up early."

Conor lifted his head, his heavy-lidded eyes world-weary and determined. "No games, Ellie. You and I have some things to discuss."

She lifted a shoulder, making the pearls slide across her chest. "I think we've said it all." It didn't escape her notice that Conor's gaze lingered a moment too long on the movement of the necklace and the way it curved around one breast.

Paradoxically, his urbane clothing and suave manners reminded her that beneath the trappings of civilization lay the man who had made love to her with single-minded abandon. She could see the evidence in his tight jaw and arrogant posture.

He was not happy with her.

Well, that was too damn bad. She wasn't happy with him, either.

He leaned back in his chair, lifting his water glass and taking a slow sip, eyeing her over the rim. When he put his drink back on the table, she wanted to crawl across the four feet that separated them and lick the moisture from his beautiful sculpted lips.

Bad girl. Bad Ellie.

Perhaps he could read her mind. Because a glint of amusement broke through his solemn regard. "Here's the thing, Ellie. You and I aren't exactly a match made in heaven. I think we could go further with this if either of us was willing to bend. But since that doesn't seem to be the case, I propose détente."

"Under what conditions?" Her legs quivered. Beneath the concealing edge of the tablecloth, she pressed a hand to her abdomen, striving unsuccessfully to control the swarm of butterflies that had taken residence there.

"Sex," he said bluntly. "Any way you want it."

"And nothing else?"

"I'm not willing to get serious with a woman who still lives with a ghost in her bed and who won't have me as I am."

The blunt criticism brought quick tears to her eyes. "You don't know what you're talking about," she snapped. "But it's just as well, because I'm not willing to get serious with a man who's a reckless lunatic."

"Thank God we're both on the same page." His sarcasm was biting.

"You don't have to make such a noble sacrifice," she snapped. "I won't be here much longer. Surely you can sublimate your need for sex."

He shrugged. "It's not a need for sex, Ellie. It's a need for you."

Ellie shouldn't have been surprised, but Conor saw shock flicker in her eyes. Tonight she looked like a princess. Her dress managed to conceal just enough to make a man go insane. He wanted to slide his hands over that silk and mold it to her curves and valleys.

Then he wanted to strip her bare.

The pearls were a nice touch. Perhaps he would let her wear those and nothing else.

His collar choked him. His heart racketed away in his chest, belying the fact that his aerobic capabilities were above average. Rising to his feet, he put one hand on the table to steady himself. "Come here," he demanded.

When she stood, he inhaled sharply. "Closer," he said.

She came to within inches of where he was standing, so near he could smell the faint perfume on her skin. "I'm here," she said quietly. "Now what?"

How far would she let him go? "Unbutton my shirt."

One blink of those long, thick eyelashes was her only reaction. Her fingers went to the buttons at his chest and slid them, one at a time, through the buttonholes. When she touched his bare skin in passing, his erection grew harder and his knees grew weak.

When she was done, her hands fell to her sides. She lifted an eyebrow as if to mock him. "Next?"

"Remove my tie."

Her hair brushed his chin when she reached up to struggle with the knot. At last, she managed to undo it, and then slid the expensive strip of red paisley from around his neck. She held it for a moment, her expression indecisive. Then she reached out and stuffed it in his hip pocket.

Neither of them acknowledged the fact that her fingers made indirect contact with his sex. But Ellie's cheeks flushed.

He swallowed. "Take off your shoes and bend over the table." He didn't really think she would do it. Any second now she would balk.

But he was wrong.

After only a moment's hesitation, she kicked off her sexy heels and turned her back to him. Carefully sliding the candles and the few remaining cups and glasses to the far end of the table, she then did as he had commanded. Her legs were splayed eight inches or so to keep her balance. She spread her arms above her head, palms down.

Sweet God in heaven.

The couture garment gaped now, the fabric almost sliding off her shoulders. He put one hand at the top of her spine and caressed her from nape to ass. "I like the view," he muttered.

They were both fully clothed, except for her shoes. But he was more aroused than he had ever been in his life. He cleared his throat. "I know you aren't wearing a bra. Is there any other underwear I should know about?"

She gave him a sizzling glance over her shoulder. "Feel free to find out."

The little tease wasn't going to get the upper hand. He planned to drive her wild. Just as soon as he remembered how to breathe.

Carefully, he lifted the silky hem of her dress and crumpled it in his left hand. With his right, he stroked the backs of her thighs. Ellie made a garbled noise and crossed her arms, burying her face.

"Problem?" he asked. This position stoked his desire, sending it spiraling higher.

Ellie shook her head but didn't speak.

He took that as license to continue. With his thumb, he traced the creases at the backs of her knees. Her skin was softer than the fabric in his hand. Releasing the dress, he put both hands on her legs. Her thighs were firm and womanly.

"Don't move," he groaned. "I'm about to discover what's under this dress."

Thirteen

Ellie whimpered and bit down hard on her bottom lip to keep from repeating such an embarrassing sound. She knew Conor had a playful side. But this kinky stuff was a facet of him she hadn't anticipated. He deserved to know the truth about her feelings for Kevin, but she couldn't bring herself to talk about it. Kevin was Emory's father. Conor was Ellie's lover. How had she let her life get so complicated?

When she felt the brush of Conor's fingers between her thighs, she gave up soul-searching. She had spent too many hours thinking and worrying and not enough time enjoying life.

With Conor, that was not going to be a problem.

Scalding heat spread from everywhere he touched. His fingertips were gentle as he explored the center panel of her undies. The satin underpants were bikini cut but not particularly daring. Nevertheless, she suddenly felt like the sexiest woman on the planet.

He pressed gently as he leaned over her and kissed the

center of her spine. "This is so much better than fighting," he muttered.

The weight of him on her back stole her breath but in a good way. "Don't bring up touchy subjects," she said, only half joking. "I'm trying to pretend you're my knight in shining armor."

Now, a single finger trespassed beneath the edge of her underwear and stroked gently. She was damp. And needy.

Conor's voice came hoarse and rough, his breath hot on the bare skin of her back. "I've never seen a woman less in need of rescuing. You're strong enough and brave enough to storm any castle. But I'd like to help if you'll let me."

He'd caught her at her weakest moment and said something so damned sweet she wanted to cry. To talk about Kevin's death would make her so vulnerable and naked she was afraid she might shatter and never find all the pieces.

"You *have* helped," she whispered. "You *are* helping."

Conversation ended as he thrust inside her body with first a single finger and then two. She moaned and moved against his hand, caught up in the magic that was Conor.

Suddenly, the weight at her back disappeared. She felt him drag the panties down her legs. He helped her step out of the small piece of cloth.

This morning he had ripped her nightgown. Now he was unbearably tender and gentle with her. Taking her by the shoulders, he brought her upright and turned her to face him. "You can trust me, Ellie."

His face was so serious, so dear. In his eyes she saw echoes of the boy who had been her best friend, along with Kirby. She *did* trust Conor. In almost every way that mattered. But she couldn't trust him not to die.

Lifting onto her tiptoes, she kissed him. His lips were firm and tasted of strawberries. "Take me to bed, Conor."

She wondered if he would have preferred his own room, but he didn't ask. They could have moved the baby monitor down the hall, but she had to admit that being close to her son made her feel more secure.

They walked hand in hand the short distance to the guest suite. Once inside her bedroom, Conor closed the door and kicked off his shoes. When she would have removed her dress, he stopped her. "Let me."

A short zipper at the base of her spine was designed to allow the dress to slide down over her hips. Conor lowered the tab but went no farther. He faced her, arms loosely around her waist. He kissed her nose, her eyebrows, the spot beneath her ear that made her shiver.

Ellie looked up at him, searching his face for answers. Why did being with Conor seem so very natural and right? She sighed, resting her cheek on his chest. "I wonder what would have happened all those years ago if I had kissed you more than that one time when we were both sixteen."

His hand tangled in her hair. She felt the rumble of his laughter. "Probably something we both would have regretted. I thought about you night and day. If we had done any serious fooling around, I might have imploded. Teenage boys aren't known for their self-control."

"I like the man you've become."

"Careful, sweetheart. All this praise will go to my head."

"I'm serious." She slid her hands inside his shirt. His skin was hot and smooth over hard muscle. There was a part of her that wanted to let Conor erase all of her worries. To lean on him and let him fight her battles. To play the helpless female.

But that was a role she'd never embraced in her life. She and Kirby had been treated as equals by their parents. No special favors for being a girl. She had learned at an early age that tears were unacceptable as a means of getting her way.

In college she had been stunned to watch so many young women manipulate guys with sex. Even as an eighteen-year-old, she had known that was wrong. A man and a woman should stand on equal footing in a relationship. Sex shouldn't be a bargaining chip.

"I'm still dressed," she said, leaning into him and stroking his back. When she slid her fingers into the waistband of his pants, she felt him shudder.

"Is that a complaint?"

"More of an observation."

"I can remedy that."

Carefully, he slid the dress from her shoulders and down her legs, holding her hand so she could step out of it. While she stood naked, he draped the silk over a nearby chair.

He took a step backward and leaned against the dresser, his hot gaze roving from her candy-apple-red toenails to the pulse that beat in her throat. The heat in his regard scalded her. She put her hands over her belly. "Don't stare. I've still got baby weight. I won't ever again be that teenage girl you wanted."

Now he scowled. "Stop it. You have no idea what you're saying. Hell, Ellie." He took her by the wrist and dragged her in front of the mirror. "Look at what I see."

She did look. And her eyes widened at the image of the man in crisp black-and-white. He was sophisticated. Handsome. Compelling. His smile held a dollop of arrogance mixed with the trademark humor that was Conor. "I feel a little at a disadvantage," she croaked.

It was disconcerting to see her nipples furled tightly, as if eagerly awaiting a lover's touch.

Conor moved behind her and encircled her with his arms. When his hands settled on her soft belly, she flinched and tried to shrug free. But he held her easily. "You have a woman's body, Ellie. A body that created and nurtured life. Do you know how magical that is? Don't ever apologize for the evidence of your sacrifice. To me, it's extraordinary."

She felt the sting of tears and blinked them away, ruefully aware that her emotions were still far too near the surface. "Thank you." She could barely speak the words.

"Enough serious talk," he said lightly. But in his eyes she saw a reflection of her own struggle to understand what was happening between them. He scooped her into his arms and carried her to the bed. "Don't move. I'm coming in after you."

Laughing softly, she acknowledged something that seemed so simple and yet was so very profound. Conor was fun. With him she felt pieces of her old self coming back. The young woman who had taken Buenos Aires by storm. Studied a handful of languages. Learned about political issues. Snagged fascinating internships. Graduated at the top of her class.

She'd had six job offers on her twenty-second birthday.

All of that seemed like a dream now. She wouldn't trade Emory for all the employment opportunities in the world. But she did want to reclaim her confidence. That—along with her ability to hope—had been decimated in the accident on Aconcagua.

She hadn't been on the mountain that day to witness the freak storm and to see the frantic efforts at search and rescue. But she had a good imagination. Those were the scenes that replayed again and again in her nightmares.

Dragging her thoughts from the grim reality that couldn't be changed, she gave herself up to the pleasure of watching Conor undress. Men did it so differently than women. First the jacket tossed carelessly aside. Then the shirt jerked free of the trousers and the sleeves ripped down the arms.

Conor was clearly impatient, but she wouldn't have minded if the striptease lasted a little longer. Her fascination must have penetrated his focus, because he stopped suddenly. "What?"

She lifted her arms over her head and linked her hands behind her neck. "Nothing. Just enjoying the show."

His hands went to his fly, unfastening it with a cocky flourish. "I've never been an exhibitionist, but if it turns you on, I'm sure I could drag this out for another half hour."

Sitting straight up in bed, she held out her hand and crooked her finger. "Don't you dare!"

Laughing, he finished the job without ceremony, never even noticing when Ellie's cheeks turned red and her breathing quickened. Once he had dispensed with pants, shoes, socks and underwear, he joined her under the covers, grabbing her up in a bear hug and rolling onto his back with her in his arms, one of his big thighs lodged between hers.

He pulled her head down for a kiss. "I'm sorry I upset you this morning, Ellie."

She noticed he wouldn't say he was sorry that he was going to climb the mountain that had killed her husband and maimed her brother. It was a lie, and Conor never lied. "I'm fine," she said. She didn't want to ruin the mood, and if she told him how much she hated the idea of him putting himself in danger, that's what would happen. "Have I mentioned what a fine specimen of manhood you are? I'm surprised I didn't have to fight off hordes of eager women to make it to your bed."

"The tales of my exploits are greatly exaggerated." His big hands palmed her bottom, squeezing gently. "I'm pure as the driven snow."

"Uh-huh."

He grinned at her, and her heart stopped. *Oh, God. She was so in love with him.* How much more self-destructive could she be?

Conor sobered as if he could read her mind. "Relax, Ellie." He tangled his fingers in her hair. During dinner she'd had it caught up in an antique hair clasp, but somewhere along the way, the delicate ornament had disappeared...right along with her sense of self-preservation.

"I'm relaxed," she said. "Really, I am."

He didn't seem convinced, but when she wiggled against him, his eyes glazed over. He grabbed her knee. "Easy there, darlin'."

"Sorry. Apparently, I'm eager. Or easy. I can't decide which."

"I'll take either. Or both." He palmed her nape. "Close your eyes, Ellie. Let me enjoy you."

His syntax must be wrong, because when he eased her gently onto her back and touched her intimately, *she* was definitely the one enjoying the caress. Conor had gifted fingers. He stroked and petted and plucked until her back arched off the mattress and she slid into an orgasm as sweet and pure as honey.

When she caught her breath and opened her eyes, Conor had fallen onto his back, his gaze trained on the ceiling. It was a very nice ceiling, but surely he had seen it before.

She swallowed, her throat dry. "Um, that was…"

"Maybe not my best work. I should probably try again."

Conor reeled from an extraordinary revelation. He was in love with Ellie. Not *falling* or *on the way* or any other euphemism. He was ass over heels, drowning and reaching for a life raft, crazily, wonderfully in love.

He slung an arm over his face, stunned and trying not to let on.

Ellie was still catching her breath. "You're good at that," she said, the words slurred.

"You inspire me."

"Very funny."

He'd never been more serious in his life. And never in his life had he been so afraid. He could stand at the top of a wicked European black diamond slope and feel no fear at all. The prospect of plunging into the course was nothing but exhilaration.

For years he had relished proving to himself that he was

no longer the kid who had to stay inside and watch as his brothers had all the fun. Each time he accomplished some physical goal, he managed to erase more and more of his constrained childhood. Even now with a bum knee and orders not to ski like a crazy man, he was still tempted to try, just for the fun of it.

But this thing with Ellie…that was another story. He wanted all of her. Not just her body, but her sharp mind, her clever wit, her unwavering loyalty and her love. Lord help him, he wanted her love. But that was the one thing he couldn't have, because that gift had been buried with her dead husband.

He had to pull himself together, or any minute now Ellie was going to see that there was something going on here besides a night of carnal enjoyment.

"Come here, little Ellie. You're too far away."

She scooted against him, curling into his embrace as if they had been doing this for months or years. He held her for long minutes, savoring the sense of peace. He wanted to make love to her. And he would, but he wanted a moment to pretend that she was his to keep.

At last, he ran a hand over her flank. "I need you," he said, the words unvarnished. "It eats me up. I can't stop thinking about you." Later he might regret his blunt honesty, but he wanted her to know how much he cared.

"I need you, too, Conor. Make love to me."

Sometimes sex was playful and sometimes it was erotic and sensuous. Tonight it was almost sacred. He moved into her, closing his eyes at the indescribable feeling of her tight passage clasping him and holding him and making wordless demands.

He would give her everything he had. But it might not be enough. Not enough to make her understand that life moved on and he wanted to move on with her. "Put your legs around my waist," he whispered. "I want more."

When she did as he asked, the resultant fit was perfect. He thrust again and again, as deeply as he could go, hard and fast, riding a wave he had no hope of beating. He heard Ellie cry out and knew he was free to take his own pleasure. But he held off a moment more. So he could imagine forever.

In the end, his climax caught him by surprise, ripping through his gut and demanding release.

He came forever, it seemed. And then everything was quiet.

What time was it? He had no clue. An hour might have passed. Or two. He was in heaven...floating on a cloud of bliss that would dissipate as soon as he opened his eyes.

Ellie was under him, their bodies still joined. He cleared his throat. "I can't feel my legs," he muttered. That fact might have been more alarming had he been less physically replete.

She pinched his thigh just below the buttock. Hard. "Still there," she said.

He tried to summon the will to move, but it was a no-go. "Am I crushing you?"

"I'm tough. I can handle it." Laughter lent wings to her words.

He smiled into her neck, inhaling her scent. "I hope you know CPR. If we do this again, I may black out from overexertion."

"I thought you were the big, tough athlete."

He felt her fingers comb through his hair. He was in a bad way if such a simply, nonsexual touch could turn him inside out. "We all have our weak spots," he said. "Apparently, mine is you."

Fourteen

Apparently, mine is you. Ellie replayed his words in her head. What did they mean? Here she went again, over-thinking things.

Deliberately, she let her mind wander, concentrating on each little piece of her current situation. The sheets on Conor's guest bed were top quality, smooth and cool even in summer. Conor's weight was comforting. She loved the feeling of connection, both mental and physical.

For this one moment in time, the two of them were in perfect accord. She was pretty sure she could feel his heart thumping against her breasts.

His hairy legs rubbed lazily against hers as if he might accidentally restart the fire. It wouldn't take much. Every time he gave her an orgasm, her greedy body started plotting for the next one.

"Are you sleepy?" she asked.

At last he shifted onto his back, yawning, leaving her bereft. "Give me fifteen minutes," he said, the words rough and low. He had one arm flung over his face. "And I'll be good to go again."

He was as good as his word. Twice…and once more during the night. The last time was somewhere around three in the morning. They finally decided they had to sleep, given that a baby was going to wake them up in a matter of hours.

Conor didn't bother asking her which half of the bed she wanted. He dragged her against his side, cuddling her close with one muscular arm.

She was sated and exhausted, but she didn't want to close her eyes when she had Conor all to herself. His breathing was slow and steady. She couldn't tell if he was actually asleep.

Was she ever going to tell him about Kevin? She knew there was no hope of anything serious unless she bared her soul. But a bared soul was so very raw and easily hurt. Conor's reaction was something she couldn't calculate.

He tugged a strand of her hair. "Go to sleep, Ell." The command was gravelly, his voice rough with fatigue. "Your son is not going to care that his mother has been awake all night."

"I know."

After another long silence, when she thought that surely Conor was asleep, he surprised her. "I wish Emory was mine. I wish I had been the first man to love you."

The giant boulder in her throat made it hard to speak. "Well, in a way you were," she said, tracing the silky line of hair near his navel. "It was puppy love, maybe. But still love, according to you."

"You know what I mean."

"Yes." He wished Kevin had never existed…had never wooed and married Ellie.

Conor tugged the light blanket over their shoulders. "Will you tell me about him…please? I want to know what he was like. He clearly had good taste in women."

The irony choked her. "I can't," she said, feeling the familiar tug of despair. "I can't, Conor. I'm sorry." Because if she told him the truth, he would walk away from her and never come back.

Conor slept in snatches until he heard the first sounds from Emory via the baby monitor. The toddler was used to him now and gave him a happy smile as Conor picked him up. After a clean diaper, the two men went in search of milk and cereal. Emory was hungry, so the meal was quick.

Conor, on the other hand, had no appetite at all. Until the middle of the night, he'd cruised on a high of endorphins, sure that he was winning Ellie over to his camp.

But it wasn't so. Things were the same as they had always been. Ellie couldn't bear to talk about her dead husband, and especially not to Conor.

When Emory's belly was full, Conor took him back to the bedroom and slid into bed beside Ellie. She stirred and lifted up on one elbow, swiping her hair from her face. She looked young and beautiful and confused.

"Why didn't you wake me?"

He shrugged. "I thought you could use the sleep. I'm always up early no matter how late I go to bed."

His oblique reference to their lovemaking was deliberate. He wanted to remind her they were good together. Incredibly incendiary, to be exact.

Ellie didn't appear to notice. She took Emory in her arms and nuzzled his neck. Suddenly, she must have realized that she was naked. "Ohmigosh, Conor. Bring me my robe."

"I'm sure he's seen you au naturel."

"Yes. But he was too young to understand. I don't want to scar him for life."

Conor rolled his eyes. "Do you worry about everything?"

"It's what mothers do. Comes with the territory."

He touched her arm. "My mother adores babies. And she knows you've had a difficult week. When I spoke to her yesterday, she offered to keep Emory for the morning so you and I can get away. Go for a drive. Walk in the mountains. Swim at Blackwoods Lake."

Ellie's mouth curved. "I'd forgotten about that. You and Kirby went skinny-dipping and left me on the shore. I was so mad at both of you."

"Well, it wasn't exactly appropriate as a group activity. But nothing's stopping us now."

"True. Does your mother really have time to babysit? Isn't Silver Beeches super busy this time of year?"

"It is. But Liam has insisted that Mom start taking some time off. She ran this family and the family business solo for a great many years. She deserves to have some fun."

Ellie lifted an eyebrow. "Changing diapers is fun?"

Conor bumped noses with Emory, making him chortle with glee. "I think your mama's insulting you, little man."

Ellie hugged her son close. "I am not. But babies aren't easy."

"Trust me. Mom suggested a visit to Gavin and Cassidy's house so he can play with the twins. It will be an epic playdate. If you don't object, we'll let Mom take your car so we won't have to move the seat."

"It's lovely of her to offer, and I accept."

He cocked his head, studying her face in silence.

"What?" she asked. "What's the big deal?"

"I expected to get the Silver Glen version of the Spanish Inquisition. I had my answers all ready."

"Are you disappointed that I'm being amenable?"

He leaned over her and kissed the shell of her ear. "I *love* it when you're amenable." His lips found hers, and despite the squirmy bundle in her arms, they managed a breath-stealing kiss.

"Can you juggle him while I take a shower?"

Conor sighed inwardly. What he wanted was to climb back into bed with a naked delicious Ellie. "Sure. Hand him over."

An hour later, they headed out. With a list of instructions and a bulging diaper bag, Maeve Kavanagh drove away in Ellie's car, leaving her own at Conor's house. She was tickled pink to have the social and outgoing Emory in her care.

Conor pointed his vehicle in the opposite direction from town, soon accessing a narrow road he hadn't followed since he was a teenager. Ellie glanced around the leafy lane with a smile. "It's just like I remember it," she said. Two deep tire tracks in the dirt required all of his concentration to keep his low-slung car from getting hung up in the weeds.

When they rounded a curve, the tiny lake came into view, more of a pond really. A long-ago property owner had damned up the creek to create a swimming hole. The water was smooth, the mirrored surface reflecting a cloudless sky. Weeping willows fringed the entire oval except for a small area where someone had dumped a truckload of white sand to make a beach.

Conor hadn't kept up with who owned the acreage currently. But high school kids had come up here for years, making out and taking midnight swims. With an absence of No Trespassing signs, it was a harmless enough pursuit.

On the other hand, when two full-grown adults decided to ignore the fact that they had no right to be here, the law might be fuzzy. Conor parked in the shade of the largest willow and rolled down the windows. Though it wasn't yet noon, the temperature was merciless. The mountains of North Carolina were normally cool and pleasant even in summer, but a record heat wave had moved in with no relief in sight.

He and Ellie got out of the car and stood side by side, staring at the beckoning water.

Ellie wrinkled her nose. "I don't like the idea of wading in not knowing what I'm going to find underfoot."

"Then leave your sneakers on." He already wore his swim trunks. All he had to take off was his shirt.

Ellie, on the other hand, had donned a simple cotton sundress with an elastic waist. Presumably, her swimsuit was underneath. "I will."

He ruffled the ends of her ponytail. "I don't suppose I could get you to try the skinny-dipping thing…" He brushed the nape of her neck deliberately.

Ellie took a deep breath and closed her eyes. "Um, no. I have a healthy aversion to being arrested."

"Spoilsport." He opened the trunk of the car to take out their beach towels and a small cooler. When he turned back around, Ellie was standing there in a black bikini.

He dropped the cooler on his toe.

While he danced around and cursed under his breath, Ellie laughed at him, her face lit up from within. It struck him then, just how much this past year and a half had taken away her glow. Though he hadn't seen her in years, he knew that the adult Ellie would have possessed the same *joie de vivre* that had made young Ellie so irresistible.

Conor had never understood the point of putting a rail-thin woman in a bikini. To him, curves were far more appealing. Ellie had an hourglass figure that did full justice to her swimsuit.

He tried to hide his reaction, though if she peered too closely at the front of his trunks, she wouldn't have any doubts. After putting their things beneath the shade tree, he held out his hand. "Ready?"

Ellie gazed at him with a half smile. "Tell me the truth. Are we really trespassing?"

He put a hand over his heart. "I wouldn't lie to you. We're being wild and bad and totally irresponsible."

Her grin widened. "Exactly what the doctor ordered."

They waded hand in hand out into the deep. Ellie squealed and tried to turn back when the water felt cold against her hot skin. But Conor made her go the distance. When they were in up to their necks, he leaned into a backstroke and turned lazy circles around her. "Is that all you're going to do? Just stand there?"

She narrowed her eyes. "I'm getting acclimated," she said primly.

"Or you're being chicken." He splashed water in her face. "Are you chicken, Ellie?"

The flash of her eyes could have boiled the pond. "I am *not* chicken," she declared. "I'm here, aren't I?"

Were they still talking about swimming, or was their subconscious meandering around the subject of why Ellie trusted him with her body but not her secrets? "Yes," he said huskily. "You are. Come here, Ellie. Lean on me."

He tugged her by the hands out into the center of the pond. It was too deep to touch bottom, but he was a good swimmer. He moved his arms back and forth and kicked his legs strongly, keeping them afloat.

Ellie linked her wrists behind his neck. She was so close, he could see shades of amber in her irises. And the tiny white scar on her chin from where she wrecked her bike in fifth grade.

She destroyed him completely when she rested her head on his shoulder. "This was a wonderful idea. There's something about water that washes away everything bad."

"Are things still bad for you?" he asked quietly.

"No. Not especially. But life is complicated."

"Not like when we were kids."

"No."

He hesitated, belatedly realizing that he had wanted Ellie

to share her darkest secrets with him, when he certainly hadn't been forthcoming about his. "I have a confession to make," he said. Beneath the water, their legs tangled, separated and tangled again.

With her breasts pressed up against him, it was difficult to focus, but this was important.

Ellie nuzzled his neck. "So serious. Is there a body buried up here somewhere?"

"You have a ghoulish imagination. Did anyone ever tell you that?"

She chuckled. "Maybe."

"No bodies," he said. The sun beat down on his head, making him dizzy. Or maybe it was the way Ellie clung to him as if she never wanted to let him go. He needed to hold her, but if he quit moving his arms, they would sink.

"You're being awfully mysterious," she said.

"It's no big secret, really. But when you asked me to help Kirby, I felt like a fraud."

She lifted her head, their lips almost touching. "I don't understand."

"You said I handled my disappointment about my ski career very well. But I didn't. I was angry as hell. And I spent a long time feeling sorry for myself."

"That's not what your family says."

"I'm a good actor. I was too proud to let anyone see how messed up I was."

"Oh, Conor. I didn't know."

"All I wanted to do was ski. I was such a cocky kid. I *knew* I was going to be the best in the world." Even now, the subject caught him in the throat. "I couldn't believe it when the doctor told me I couldn't compete anymore. Flying downhill was all I knew how to do. All I *wanted* to do."

"And then Kirby and I left." Her eyes were stricken.

"Yeah." He closed his eyes for a moment, afraid she would see how much he had suffered. A man didn't share those kinds of things. "So it hit me hard. I finished school and went on to college, but I was drifting. Taking over the ski lodge here at home was supposed to be a stopgap until I decided what I wanted to do with my life."

"And has it worked?"

When she looked into his eyes, it was as if she could see his sorry soul. Briefly, he regretted his revelation. But he wanted her to know that she was not the only one who had faced a loss of identity.

His arms were starting to tire, but his legs kept them afloat. "Turns out, I liked it. And being a part of Silver Glen, a part of the Kavanagh clan, has taught me what's important."

"But you still need to climb mountains to feel alive?"

He hadn't expected an outright attack. Then again, he of all people should know never to underestimate Ellie. She'd never let Kirby and Conor ride roughshod over her. And clearly, no one had ever told her that females were supposed to be the weaker sex.

"Low blow, Ell."

She nodded. "Yes. It was. But I'm trying to understand. You. My brother. You're smart men. It makes no sense."

"Life doesn't always make sense."

"Did you read that on a coffee mug somewhere?"

Conor was too relaxed to let her prod him. "Are we fighting?" he asked.

Her cute nose scrunched up in a suspicious frown. "Why do you want to know?"

"If we're fighting, it means we get to have makeup sex under that tree over there."

"Ah." Keeping one hand on his shoulder, she took the other one, slid it underwater and placed it smack on his goods. "Seems like we're on pretty good terms right now."

Conor choked and nearly drowned them both. "Um…"

"Um, what?" Her fingers were up to mischief.

"There's one big problem," he said.

"Oh?"

Less than sixty seconds of her brand of trouble and already she had him up and running. "*I* can't touch *you*," he complained. "Hardly seems fair."

She moved closer, wrapping her legs around his waist and kissing his chin and his neck. "I could do all the work."

He was tempted. Really tempted. But although he had spent three years on his high school swim team, he'd bet his last dime there wasn't a man alive who could keep his woman afloat while she was attacking him.

"How about a compromise?"

Fifteen

Ellie loved teasing Conor. Especially when he wanted the same thing she wanted. "I'm listening," she said.

"What if we move closer to shore so I can touch bottom?"

The buoyancy of the water made her feel light and free, but she was willing to be persuaded. "I like the idea of Conor Kavanagh being in over his head, but sure," she said.

He held her with one arm and swam with the other… only five or six strokes. When his feet found purchase, he kissed her. "Better. Much better," he said.

Beneath her fingertips, his skin was hot and smooth. The sun shone down on them mercilessly. Feelings swamped her. So many feelings. Nostalgia hardly even made the list, though this was a spot she and Kirby and Conor had visited many times.

But it was more than that. Here, she felt closer to the essence of life. In some ways, this secluded miniature lake reminded her of the jungle. Not the specific features, but the scent of hot earth and the sensation of being one with nature.

She cried out when Conor slid a hand underneath her swimsuit bottom and touched her. Intimately. Where her body recognized him as a lover. "You said *under the tree*," she panted as he played with her devilishly.

Resting his forehead against hers, he muttered, "Decided it was too far. Can't wait. This works."

They were standing out in the pond in full view of anyone who happened to walk by. "But, Conor…"

He brushed her clitoris with his thumb as he read her mind. "No one's anywhere around. We'd hear a car driving down the lane. And worst-case scenario, if someone shows up out of the woods, he or she wouldn't really be able to see a thing."

Self-indulgence won out over prudishness. Barely.

Conor bit her earlobe. "Trust me, Ellie. I won't let you go."

"But how are we going to…"

He did some kind of contortion that allowed him to free his shaft. Taking her hand, he guided it to where he pulsed hard and ready. "I need you, Ell."

The fact that he didn't dress it up—that, and the raw urgency in his plea—destroyed her. "I'm here," she whispered.

When she played with him gently, his eyes squeezed shut and his face flushed. He made a noise. The guttural sound went straight to her sex, leaving her swollen and ready.

Conor didn't even remove her bikini bottom. Instead, he shoved aside the strip of fabric between her legs and pushed inside her. He seemed beyond speech, and that was okay with her, because mere words couldn't really capture the elemental joining.

Standing, and with the water as a buoyant cushion, he

filled her completely, almost to the point of discomfort. His big hands cupped her bottom, lifting her into his thrusts.

She clung to him, dazed and crazed. Suddenly, it didn't matter if an entire brigade of onlookers appeared. The only thing that was real was Conor and his forceful possession.

They were wet and half-naked. Her fingernails dug into his shoulders. Arching her back, she moved with him, feeling his strength, his power, his utter focus on her and their joining.

She wanted to say *I love you.* To tell him how special he was. And how much he had healed the broken places in her heart. But instead, she buried her face in his neck and cried out when he sent her over the edge. The orgasm lasted for peak after peak. The pleasure was sharp and vicious, stripping away pretense.

Even as Conor found release in her body, she knew he had carved out a place in her heart and in her life. But in her future? The unlikelihood of that made her cling to him all the more. One more chance for bliss. One more day when she could pretend that their sexual chemistry was enough to erase everything else.

At last, when they were both breathing heavily and their muscles quivered, he staggered toward shore. At the last instant, he remembered to adjust their swimwear to a more modest orientation.

While Ellie stood, stunned and dripping in her sodden tennis shoes, Conor flipped out both of the big towels in a patch of grass and took her by the hand. "Five minutes," he begged. "And then we'll eat."

They napped like children. Conor spooned her, his strong arms wrapped around her. It was the safest and most secure she had felt in a long, long time.

Eventually, hunger won out. They ate their picnic ravenously, laughing and talking and exchanging barbs. Beneath it all, sexual tension lurked. After another swim—a real swim this time—they made love on dry land. Ellie ended up on top. When she leaned forward to kiss him, Conor grabbed a handful of her damp hair, hair that was already drying in the hot sun.

He played with it, brushing it over her breasts, over his eyes. Inside her, he was big and hard. Physically, they were a perfect match, each intensely attuned to the other's wants and desires.

"Conor," she said impulsively. "I need to tell you something."

His eyes darkened. "Not now, Ellie. Please. Today is about existing in the moment. No past. No future. Let's give ourselves a pass on real life. For once. You need a break. So do I."

With her hands on his taut shoulders, she nodded. "I'm going to be okay, Conor. You don't have to worry about me."

He grinned, lightening the mood. "You're way beyond okay, Ellie Porter. I give you a 9.7."

"How in the heck did I lose three tenths of a point?" She frowned.

Conor rolled them onto their sides, lifting her leg over his thigh as he thrust lazily. "One-tenth for stubbornness." He panted as time ran out for their spectacular finish. "One-tenth for being uptight."

She never did hear the last deduction. Conor groaned and came, taking her with him as he used his finger where their bodies joined to drive her wild.

In the aftermath, the afternoon was broken only by the sounds of their breathing and nature's chorus. Bird calls. The wind in the trees overhead. Bullfrogs. Even the quick, distinctive visit of hummingbird wings.

It was one of those perfect moments when you want to distill time in a bottle and keep it forever. She stroked

Conor's arm. "This has been a wonderful day. But I'm feeling the need to get home and see Emory."

"I understand."

They dressed in their original clothes, both of them damp and messy and definitely rumpled. Ellie grimaced. "I should have brought dry underwear. This swimsuit feels nasty."

Conor pulled a piece of grass from her hair. "Maybe we can snag a quick shower before we retrieve your son."

She punched his arm. "I know what you're thinking. And the answer is no. Separate showers. Short ones."

"Spoilsport." When he bent to gather up the towels he was smiling.

She finally remembered that Maeve would have to return Ellie's car. They couldn't pick up the baby in Conor's. So he sent his mother a text asking her to bring Emory home in a couple of hours and stay for dinner. Another quick text to the housekeeper, and the plans were set.

Ellie rested her head against the seat back as they drove home. "It was a magical afternoon. I'll have to send your mother some flowers as a thank-you."

"When you get to know her better, you'll see that she's the one to thank you. My brothers have begun producing offspring, but slowly...too slowly for Mom. She probably won't be happy until each one of us has three or four."

"And do you want a lot of kids?"

"Hard to say. I was one of seven, but that's a tall order for the twenty-first century."

"It must have been fun...growing up in the Kavanagh family."

"Yeah. But it would have been even better if my dad had pulled his weight. And then when he disappeared..."

"Your mom had to do it all."

"I've never heard her complain."

"Because she's your mother. I'd love to have a big family, but not as a single mom. I don't know how she did it."

At Conor's house, they parked and unloaded things from the trunk. As they walked up the front steps, he put an arm around her waist. "I had fun today, Ellie."

Her feelings were close to the surface, but she managed a smile. "Me, too." Happiness was a beautiful thing.

Kirby was waiting for them in the living room. He must have parked on the other side of the house.

"Hey, there," she said. She went to hug him but stopped. Not because of her wet clothes, but because of the look on his face. "What's wrong, Kirby?"

He didn't rise when they walked into the room. That in itself alarmed her. Kirby had been a different man since Conor came back into their lives. Calmer. Happier. Now, her brother was white-faced, his hair unkempt, his hand fisted on the arm of the sofa.

She sat beside him and touched his knee. "Talk to me, Kirby. You're scaring me."

"It's Grandpa," he said. "He's dead."

Ellie's vision grayed around the edges and she heard a buzzing in her ears. *Dead. Dead. Dead.* "I just spoke to him this morning. He was fine." Her lips were numb. She had trouble forming the words.

Kirby scrubbed his hands over his face. "He was watching TV in the recliner. We were chatting back and forth while I fixed his lunch. When I went into the den to tell him the meal was ready, he was gone."

"Oh, Kirby."

Conor watched, grim and incredulous as the twin siblings hugged each other. He wanted to go to Ellie and hold her, but now was not the time. She and Kirby were sharing their grief.

At last they separated. Conor handed Ellie a tissue but

didn't say anything. He didn't know *what* to say. How was it fair for one woman to lose so much?

Kirby sat back, his head resting on the sofa. "They've taken his body to the funeral home. When they have him ready we'll go down there for you to say goodbye."

"And Mom and Dad?"

"They were both stunned. Dad got choked up on the phone. He's kicking himself for not coming home when we did. Now it's too late."

"Poor Daddy. What about the funeral? Will they fly home?"

"They're still discussing it, but my guess is no. The logistics are phenomenally time-consuming, and as Dad said, it doesn't make sense to tackle those hurdles now when Grandpa is dead. I imagine they'll stay in Bolivia and when they finally move back next spring, we can have a brief private memorial service at the graveside."

Conor sat down across from them. "I am so very sorry. I liked Mr. Porter."

Kirby seemed more shaken than the situation warranted. "I'm a doctor, damn it. I keep asking myself if I missed something…if I should have taken him to the hospital this morning."

Conor stared at his two friends, hurting for them, feeling as if he were on shaky ground. "He died in his chair, Kirby. It sounds like a heart attack or a stroke. I know it's hard for you and your family, but if you think about it, we should all be so lucky to go that peacefully."

Neither sibling said much after that. He wondered if he had been too blunt with them. Conor stepped out of the room briefly to check in with his mom. She said Emory was waking from his nap and they would be on their way soon. Conor told Maeve what had happened and asked her to keep Emory a little longer.

When Conor returned to the dining room, Kirby was holding Ellie in his arms and they were both crying. Hell.

Quietly, he backed away and went to sit on the front porch.

When Ellie at last came to find him, almost two hours had passed. "We're going to the funeral home," she said. "But I don't know what to do about Emory."

"It's all taken care of. No worries. Would you like me to come with you?"

Ellie seemed smaller and quieter, as if a light had been snuffed out. "It's not necessary."

He stood up and cradled her to his chest. "I phrased that wrong. *May* I come with you? I really want to."

She nodded, sniffing against chest. "I'd like that."

They took separate cars to the funeral home. Conor had convinced Kirby to pack a bag and come up to Conor's house afterward. There was no reason for Kirby to stay alone down at Mr. Porter's house and grieve.

None of them felt much like eating dinner, but there was a little café in town where they could get soup and a sandwich afterward.

Conor had known the funeral home director most of his life. The man was professional and kind. Luckily, there were no other services that evening, so the place was quiet. Too quiet, maybe. It was hard to escape the aura of death and sadness.

Mr. Porter's body was draped in a sheet. Kirby and Ellie would have to make decisions about clothes and caskets and everything else in the morning. For now, it was time for a very private farewell.

Ellie touched the old man's forehead. "Goodbye, Grandpa. I'll miss you."

Conor had his left arm around her waist. Kirby held her left hand. As a trio, they had seen and survived a lot of ups and downs. Conor wished he could spare both of them this pain. They had survived so much. But it wasn't his call.

Ellie cried, silent tears that ran down her face and dripped onto her dress. "We should have come home sooner. We knew he wasn't doing well."

Her words made Kirby blanch.

Conor shook his head. "You didn't really have that choice. And your grandfather knew that. Until Kirby was on the mend, your grandfather would have wanted the two of you to spend time together."

"I suppose." She touched the body again, smoothing a lock of white hair. "He was so much fun when we were kids. After my grandmother died, he came to Bolivia a few times. He liked to travel, but he used to laugh and say that his old body didn't."

Conor had to take his cues from Kirby. At last Ellie's brother steered her away. "We have a lot to do tomorrow, Ell. Let's grab a bite to eat and go home to bed."

"Home?" She looked panicked.

"To Conor's, I mean."

"Oh…yes."

During the quick meal they consumed, the two men talked of generalities. Ellie said nothing, though she did eat all of her tomato soup and chicken sandwich.

Afterward, Kirby went to the empty Porter house to pack up his things.

When Ellie and Conor got to Conor's house, Maeve was already there with Emory. Conor's mother extracted Emory from his car seat and handed him over to Ellie. Then she hugged both Ellie and Emory. "Your son is a delight. And he's so smart."

For the first time that day, Ellie smiled. "Well, I think so, but I'm his mom, so I'm supposed to say that."

Maeve sobered. "I am so sorry to hear about your grandfather. I knew Mr. Porter. Most of Silver Glen did. He was well respected and much loved. Please accept my sympathies."

Ellie hugged Emory, her eyes damp. "Thank you, Mrs. Kavanagh. If you all will excuse me, I need to get Emory ready for bed."

When she walked into the house, Conor shrugged. Maeve was the first to speak. "Are you in love with that girl?"

"Mom!" Conor actually felt his ears turning red.

"Okay," she said, sighing. "I'll wait until you want to talk about her. I'm headed home."

Conor nodded in relief. "Kirby will be here in a few minutes. He and Ellie have some decisions to make. I'll keep you posted."

Maeve had no sooner driven away than Kirby showed up. He got out of his car with only a slight limp, perhaps due to stress and fatigue. In one hand he carried a small suitcase. He couldn't manage a smile as he walked up the front steps with Conor. "Where's Ellie?" he asked.

Conor held the door for him. "Putting the baby to bed. You want a beer?"

Kirby shook his head. "I'd like a shower if you don't mind."

"I'll show you the other guest room." Once Conor had pointed out all the amenities to his friend, he stopped in the open door on his way out. "I'm sorry, Kirby. Really sorry."

Kirby shook his head. "I never saw it coming down like this. I guess I need to make up my mind about those job offers."

Conor's stomach pitched at the implications of that statement. "Won't you have to deal with the house?"

"No. Dad and Mom will do that when they come back in the spring. I'll turn the utilities off, pay bills, you know… none of that will take more than a few days."

"What are you telling me, Kirby?"

"Ellie and I will be leaving Silver Glen sooner rather than later."

Sixteen

Conor lay awake for hours. He wanted Ellie in his bed, or he wanted to be in hers. Not for sex, though he thought about that with every other breath. He wanted to comfort her…to hold her…to promise her that she was going to get through this.

He and Kirby had stayed up until the wee hours… talking…occasionally laughing…cementing the bond that had grown since Kirby's return. They both shared a concern for Ellie's well-being. Though Ellie hadn't exhibited any lasting signs from her hospital stay, Mr. Porter's death was the emotional equivalent of "piling on."

Ellie was strong. But even the strongest trees break when the storms are bad.

Conor had made arrangements with his housekeeper to have a hearty breakfast ready at nine o'clock. Kirby and Ellie and Emory beat Conor to the table and were waiting for him.

Kirby looked pretty good for a man who hadn't slept much. "Thanks for the bed and the meal, Conor."

"It's the least I can do."

Ellie looked at him beseechingly. "I don't want to leave Emory again today. Would you mind coming with us to the funeral home and playing with him in the lobby?"

"Of course not." He reached across the table and touched her hand, not caring that Kirby was watching. "Did you sleep?"

Ellie nodded. "Yes." She looked at her brother and at Conor. "I'm okay, guys. You can stand down." Her smile reassured him, but he noticed she was paler than usual. And in her eyes he saw traces of that same vulnerability that worried him.

Fortunately, the decisions at the funeral home didn't take long. Ellie's eyes were red rimmed when they came out of the consultation room, but she seemed calm. "We're done," she said, taking Emory from him.

"What now?"

"The funeral will be tomorrow evening. The notice has already gone to the newspaper. We planned a very simple service."

Kirby took Ellie's arm. "Will it bother you if we all go over to Grandpa's house? We both could pack up our things. Conor says we're welcome to stay with him and, frankly, I want to, because the house without Grandpa is way too sad and empty."

"I agree."

While Kirby took care of a few last details with the funeral home concerning payment, Ellie and Emory sat in a nearby conversation area furnished with comfortable chairs. Emory was beginning to fuss, no doubt because he was hungry.

Conor leaned forward with his elbows on his knees and

forced Ellie to look him straight in the eyes. "I'm sorry, Ellie. Really sorry."

Her smile this time was more of a grimace. "We were having such a beautiful day…"

He caressed her cheek with the back of his hand. "We were. I hope you won't let what happened ruin your memories of yesterday. I won't forget it. Ever."

"Why?" Her eyes were huge.

"Because it was fun and crazy and amazing."

"It was, wasn't it?"

He leaned forward, almost kissing her, when they both remembered where they were.

He jerked backward.

Ellie turned red. "Bad timing," she muttered.

"Sorry." He was chagrined that his need for her could make him stupid. "I don't know what I was thinking."

"The same thing I was, I suppose. That we're damned good together in bed."

He clapped his hands over Emory's ears. "Ellie. Watch your mouth."

"Kirby's his uncle. I'm sure he's heard worse."

Kirby walked up and sat down beside them. "I heard my name being taken in vain. Not fair when I can't defend myself."

Ellie jumped to her feet. "Don't get comfortable. I don't know about you, but funeral homes give me the creeps. Let's get out of here."

By nine that evening, Kirby and Ellie were firmly ensconced in Conor's home. He found himself smiling for no particular reason except that he liked having them all beneath his roof.

Kirby took himself off to bed early. When Ellie disappeared with the baby to put him to bed, Conor grabbed a shower and changed into a pair of cotton sleep pants.

Under the circumstances, he wasn't going to wander nude around his house.

He had a feeling that his troubled thoughts were going to keep him awake yet again. Knowing that Kirby and Ellie no longer had a reason to stay in Silver Glen was both disturbing and galvanizing. He needed to do something. Say something.

But he kept coming back to his original stumbling block. Once before, Ellie had asked him to choose her over his skiing and he hadn't been able to do it. Would she expect him now to give up everything he loved to be with her?

Could he push for some kind of relationship with her knowing that Kevin's memory would always linger between them like an unwelcome third wheel? It was natural for a wife to grieve her husband. But for how long? Forever? Would Conor regret pushing the issue if all he could have was her body and her friendship?

Staring into a cup of decaf coffee, he made a decision. He and Ellie were friends. Good friends. Better than they had been in the last decade. Though it would be incredibly hard, he was going to let her go without a fight.

He wanted a woman whose heart was hers to give. He needed the kind of relationship his four older brothers had found. Ellie was one in a million. One day, when she managed to forget the tragedies of the past, she would be ready to move on.

But that time had not yet come.

With a splitting headache and a crushing pain in his chest, he placed the empty cup in the sink and turned out all the lights.

Padding barefoot down the hall to his bedroom, he stopped in shock just inside the door. Ellie was waiting for him. She perched on the side of his bed wearing a chaste blue knit gown that was not designed to be remotely sexy.

Even the conventional garment flattered her. Her hair

fell around her shoulders, making her look young and vulnerable.

"Ellie." That was smooth. But he was off his game. How was he supposed to act around the woman he wanted with every cell in his body?

Her hands twisted in her lap. "I missed you last night," she said, her gaze dark and, for once, impossible to read. "Will you sleep with me?"

Hell, yes. "Of course." He sat down beside her and took one of her hands in his. "Do you need anything? Warm milk? Hot cocoa? A snack?"

She managed a smile. "All I need is you."

He slid a hand behind her neck and pulled her in for a slow kiss. He tried to give her gentleness and patience. What he received in return was a kick to the gut. Raw passion. Unbridled desire.

Hand in hand, they returned to her room. "I'll hold you while you sleep."

She faced him, the broad expanse of the mattress between them. "That isn't enough."

"Ellie, I…" He ran his hands through his hair. Surely he deserved this one last time with her before she went away. But was it right? "You're in the midst of a crisis," he said.

"Life and death and change, Conor. What else is there? I'd rather be with you tonight than anywhere else in the world."

She stood there, bold and brave, breaking his heart with her almost visible aura of valor in the face of overwhelming odds.

"Then you have me," he said. "Take off your gown."

Ellie spared a moment to wonder if Conor thought she was being flippant about her grandfather's passing. She wasn't. Losing her only surviving grandparent was inevitable, but she hadn't been ready. No one ever was. She'd thought they had months, not days, to hear stories and swap hugs and be a family.

Now there was one less piece of her. One more broken spot that had to be glued back together.

She undressed, not because Conor had demanded it, but because she wanted to feel his naked skin against hers. Grief hovered in the wings, crushing and undeniable. But tonight she would hold it at bay, sheltered in Conor's embrace.

With the lights out, pale moonlight streamed through a crack in the drapes. She went to the window and pushed back the heavy fabric, needing to see evidence of eternity. "Do you mind?" she asked.

"No. We're invisible in the dark and, besides, there's no one around. Come to bed, Ellie."

They met in the center of the mattress on their knees. He smoothed her hair, his breath warm on her cheek.

"You make me happy, Conor," she whispered. There was so much more to say than that, but for tonight it was enough.

"I'm glad."

She felt him pressed close to her, chest to breasts, thigh to thigh. His rigid sex thrust against her belly, eager and importunate. Reaching between them, she took him in her hand, noting the sharp hiss of his breath.

"I love how you feel," she murmured, still dazzled by the rightness of being with him this way.

He groaned and laughed. "It's pretty good from this side, too." He cupped her breasts. "You have the most amazing body, Ellie. Not that I'm not crazy about your mind, but damn, woman."

When he pinched her nipples, she moved into him, wanting to be closer and closer still. "Don't make me wait tonight," she pleaded.

"Not a problem."

After that, words became unnecessary. They fell onto

the bed with soft mutters and choked laughter, so attuned to each other that she knew when he paused to debate the logistics. "Do you need a map?"

He moved behind her instantly and dragged a couple of pillows beneath her as she moved onto her hands and knees. "You're such a smart-ass, Ellie."

The laughter in his voice relaxed her, made her soft with yearning. As he entered her from behind, she felt his fingers on the nape of her neck. The innocent caress was in counterpoint with the primeval way he possessed her. His body staked a claim.

Closing her eyes, she buried her face in the pillow. Yesterday she had been on the brink of taking a chance…of telling him that she loved him…of confessing her secrets and her pain. But she'd thought she had more time. It was a hard lesson to learn. The only certain moments were in the now.

In the past few weeks, Kirby had spent numerous hours narrowing down his choice of hospitals. He was ready to make a decision. Which meant that soon, he and Ellie and Emory would be moving.

Her heart was breaking.

Conor eased out of her body and suddenly flipped her onto her back. "I need to see your face. You left me, didn't you?"

"I'm sorry," she said. "I was thinking about things."

He moved between her thighs and entered her a second time. "Don't think. Just feel."

Conor loved her gently and thoroughly, shuddering in her arms as he finished. Ellie's climax was more of a gentle swell and a gasped breath. In the aftermath, he wrapped her in his arms and kissed her temple. "I've got you, Ellie. Go to sleep."

The funeral was both a pleasure and an endurance test. Many more people showed up than she and Kirby had expected. Her grandfather had lived in Silver Glen most of his life. Townspeople came by, even those who didn't know Kirby and Ellie personally.

The Kavanagh clan turned out in full force, demonstrating their support. Since Emory wasn't the only child needing to be entertained, two college students home for the summer had been commandeered to babysit in a small room near the chapel where the service was to be held.

Through it all, Conor stood at Ellie's side. His comforting presence gave her strength. He introduced her to strangers and brought her water and tissues and generally made himself indispensable.

Kirby held court in an opposite corner. They had decided it made sense to divide and conquer. They had been receiving friends for over two hours, and she worried about her brother's stamina.

When she mentioned as much to Conor in a low voice, he shook his head and muttered in her ear. "I know Kirby. He won't sit down even if you ask him to. But don't worry. I'll keep an eye on him."

At last, it was time for the service. Ellie sat in the front row, Kirby and Conor flanking her. Though the minister was articulate and kind and had lovely things to say about Mr. Porter, Ellie blanked out.

Until that instant, she hadn't taken stock of the fact that this was her first funeral since Kevin's. It hit her suddenly, an overwhelming feeling as if she were drowning.

Sweat dampened her forehead and she wanted to gasp for breath. But there were rows and rows of people behind her. She could feel their eyes on her back. She gripped Conor's hand until her fingernails dug into his palm.

At last, it was over. The family was escorted out a side door. Ellie saw the black hearse, the black limo. The one she had ridden in with Kevin's parents on the way to the cemetery.

She tried to speak. But nausea rose in her throat. "I… Conor…"

Blackness swirled and shrouded her until the world disappeared.

Seventeen

Conor caught her before she hit the ground.

Kirby cursed.

"I'll take her home," Conor said.

Kirby nodded, his worried gaze on his sister's limp body in Conor's arms. "The graveside service won't take long. I'll be right behind you...or as soon as I can."

Conor's car was parked not far away. Opening the passenger door, he reclined the seat, set Ellie down carefully and belted her in after smoothing the skirt of her knee-length black dress. Moments later, when he started the engine, Ellie roused and sat up.

She put her hand over his on the gearshift. "Conor. Tell me what happened."

"You fainted. I'm taking you home."

"No, you're not." She reached for the door handle, unlocking it before he could stop her. "I can't let Kirby go to the cemetery on his own."

Fury blasted through Conor's calm. "Hell, Ellie. You

don't have to take care of the whole entire world. Somebody needs to take care of *you* for a change. And like it or not, today, that somebody is me."

She gaped at him as if he had sprouted an extra head. "You're yelling at me."

"Damn straight I am. Now sit still and do what I tell you to do."

Ellie collapsed in her seat, tearing leaking from the corners of her eyes.

Shit. "I'm sorry," he said hoarsely. "I know this is a tough day. But you're scaring me to death. People have heart attacks from stress, Ellie. Or complete mental breakdowns."

She didn't say a word.

He leaned his forehead on the steering wheel and said a prayer for patience. "I won't make you leave," he muttered. "If you're set on going to the cemetery."

Still the tears fell, slowly, painfully. As if something had broken and couldn't be fixed.

She turned her head toward him, face wet, expression quietly determined. "I want to go to the cemetery. But not in the limo. In your car. Will you go tell Kirby?"

"Do you want him to ride with us?"

She nodded, sniffing. "Yes, please."

Conor fetched Kirby and the two men climbed into the car without speaking, Conor behind the steering wheel, Kirby in the backseat. The cemetery wasn't far. A much smaller subset of mourners had come for this portion of the service. Many of them were Kavanaghs.

The day was warm but drizzly. Most people huddled beneath the green awning that flanked the burial spot. Conor kept a hand on Ellie the entire time. Her gaze was fixed on the flower-draped casket.

As promised, the ceremony was brief. Soon, after shaking hands and speaking with a few more people, it was time to go. Maeve had taken Emory with her to give Kirby and Ellie some time to change clothes and regroup.

Conor drove home, his gut in turmoil. Neither of his passengers spoke. When they reached the house, Ellie fled from the car. There was no other word for it.

Kirby and Conor climbed out and stared at each other.

"She'll be fine," Kirby said.

For the first time, Conor could tell he was lying.

After changing into jeans and a comfortable cotton button-down, Conor grabbed a sandwich. People had brought food to the house...enough to feed a small country. Conor liked living in a place where community was important. He'd watched as Kirby and Ellie reminisced with old friends and met cordial strangers. The Porter twins were wrapped in a cocoon of concern whether they realized it or not.

At last, he couldn't stand it. He had to check on Ellie. Giving her space seemed like the smart thing to do right now, but his gut was telling him there was more going on with Ellie than met the eye. Sadly, he had a feeling he knew what it was. All of the funeral stuff must have brought back Kevin's death.

Her bedroom door was open. No Ellie. She wasn't in the living room, either. Kirby, however, was sacked out face-down on the sofa. Conor exited as silently as he had come. His buddy needed the rest.

It was another ten minutes before he found Ellie...on the deck that extended from the back of the house. Conor had plans to put in a swimming pool and hot tub, but he hadn't gotten that far yet.

He had, however, invested in a collection of cushioned deck furniture. Some nights, he and a few poker buddies played out here and watched the sunset. Other times, Conor simply liked to sit as the evening waned and be alone with his thoughts.

Ellie had chosen a lounge chair, though it was a good bet she wasn't relaxed. She had her knees pulled up to her chest with her arms circling them. To Conor, the posture looked defensive.

Dragging a chair closer without an invitation, he felt his heart break when he saw that she was crying, sobbing, in fact.

He picked her up and sat back down on the chaise with her, his legs outstretched, Ellie curled in a ball of misery against this chest.

For a long time, he let her cry it out. They had nowhere to go, and tears were often cathartic. Eventually, however, he felt her go soft in his arms…heard the ragged cadence of her breathing as she exhausted herself.

Choosing his words carefully, he stroked her hair as he spoke. "Your grandfather wouldn't want you to do this, Ell. He'd want you to be happy."

She scrubbed a hand over her face and gave a little hiccupping sigh. "I'm not crying for Grandpa," she said.

"You're not?" Conor frowned.

"Well, I'm sad. I'll miss him a lot. But he lived a good life, and with the dementia accelerating, he faced a difficult road ahead. Now he's whole. And with my grandmother."

"Then why are you so upset? Why the tears, Ell? For Kevin? Did today bring it all back? Is that it?"

She stared at him, her expression guarded. "Yes. But not in the way you're thinking."

"It's understandable," he said gruffly, almost unable to look at her, because it hurt so damned much to know she still loved her dead husband. "It hasn't been that long since you buried him. Healing takes time." More time than Conor had.

Shaking her head, she flipped her hair behind her shoulders. The simple navy top she wore emphasized her pallor. "I shed all my tears for Kevin a long time ago. Today I was crying for you."

He stared at her. "I don't know what you mean."

"When we came home from the lake and Kirby was sitting there with such a terrible look on his face…waiting to tell me bad news… I realized that one day that same scenario may unfold. Only Kirby will be telling me about you. I've been strong and resilient and all those things they tell me I'm supposed to be. But, oh, Conor…if you died, I couldn't bear it."

She used the hem of her shirt to dry her face. The childish action made him want to smile, but this confrontation was too important.

"That won't happen," he said firmly.

Her jaw firmed mutinously. "You don't know for certain."

"I do," he said. "Because I canceled my trip yesterday."

She gaped at him. "Why?"

Why, indeed. Here came the hard part. In fact, he couldn't be this close to her and say it. So he levered himself up from the lounger and paced the deck. "You and I have differing opinions on the mountain-climbing thing, Ellie. I see it as an adventure. You see it as a death sentence. I may not agree with you, but I certainly understand why you feel that way."

She scooted back into her original position, resting her chin on her knees. "I still don't get why you canceled."

He shrugged. "Because I love you." The words fell like stones from his mouth. He held up a hand. "Don't say anything. Not a word. I know it's too soon and you still love Kevin. I know all that. But I love you too much to put you through any more pain. So the trip is off."

* * *

Ellie was astonished and deeply moved. To hear that Conor cared enough about her to give up something so important to him was utterly precious and very emotional.

But she had used up her tears.

The time had come to be honest with Conor. He deserved the truth, even if it put her in a bad light…even if it changed his opinion of her.

She wouldn't tell him she loved him. Not yet. Because he needed to understand the whole picture. She had kept things from him intentionally. To protect herself. To survive. To keep him at a distance.

But Conor had thrown down the gauntlet. He had been as honest as a man can be. It was up to her to match his courage.

"You've asked me again and again to open up to you or to Kirby about my feelings. To talk about Kevin's death. Both of you believe that I haven't dealt with what happened, and you're right. I suppose my hospitalization last week proved that. I didn't completely snap, but I definitely came unglued. Lucky for me, I had very good care. Although it may surprise you, I did share things with the doctor."

Conor sat down in a chair, his hands on his knees. "I'm so glad."

"It was hard. I won't lie. But I knew that if I could tell a stranger, I could eventually tell you."

"You don't have to. It's been a difficult day."

"I *want* to," she said.

Conor sat and waited. She liked that about him. His calm strength. His utterly unbreakable commitment to those he loved.

She searched her brain, looking for the perfect place to start. But the story was fragmented and sad and ugly. So one spot was as good as another. "Kevin and I were having trouble," she said.

"I see."

"It had been going on for far too long. We'd been married four years when he died. The first two were good... the last two not so much."

"Where did you meet?"

"In Buenos Aires. His father was Argentinian, his mother American. So Kevin straddled both cultures. He was sophisticated and well-traveled and never met a stranger. I was twenty-four. He was seven years older. He dazzled me."

"Did your parents approve?"

"I think so. He came from a good family. Had a great job. The two of us were head over heels in love."

"So what happened?"

"He wasn't cut out to be monogamous...or that's what he told me. When the cheating started, I questioned myself. I know, looking back, that I was not thinking clearly. But all I had to go by was my parents' marriage. They were— and still are—devoted to each other. I began to ask myself if I had failed Kevin somehow."

"Please tell me you know that's a pile of crap."

Conor's indignation soothed her nerves.

"I do now. But instead of addressing the infidelity directly, I begged him to go to marriage counseling." Remembering those sessions made her cringe inside. "Kevin was an amazing chameleon. He could wring emotion from an audience with a bald-faced lie and no one ever questioned him. The therapist we were seeing told me I was young and naive and I needed to learn how to trust my husband and not be so insecure."

Conor's vicious curse and look of incredulity was satisfying. Though the worst was yet to come. He shook his head. "That's almost criminal."

"You can see why I began to wonder if the problem was me. But in the end, I discovered that Kevin was a serial cheater. Things came to a head when I found out that one woman he'd been seeing regularly was also going on the Aconcagua trip."

"Damn."

"Yep. I told him I was finished. That I was going to file for divorce."

"And he agreed?"

"No. He said I was being childish and that there was no need for us to break up our marriage. That men were different from women and they needed variety. But I was still his wife. Blah, blah, blah…"

"Please tell me you punched the guy."

"Maybe if I had, I would feel better about all this. But no."

"And you didn't tell anyone?"

"I was too ashamed. I had always been the *smart* girl. It was humbling to know I had been taken in by a man whose personality and integrity were nothing more than smoke and mirrors." She paused, her throat tightening. "I moved out."

Conor was confused. Foreboding settled in his gut. By all rights, this story should be making him feel relieved. Instead, his skin crawled.

"So you moved out," he said slowly. "Good for you."

Ellie nibbled one of her fingernails. He'd never seen her do that. "Good in theory. Kevin was furious. I packed my things while he was at work one day. When he came home to an empty house, he went ballistic. He hired a detective, and in less than twenty-four hours Kevin was on my doorstep."

"What did he say?"

"His performance was Oscar-worthy. Contrition. Repentance. Begging for another chance."

"You didn't."

"I did. To me, marriage vows were sacred. If he was genuinely willing to change, I felt duty-bound to try again."

"Aw, hell, Ellie." He knew something was coming he didn't want to hear. "What did you do?"

"He asked to come in. I let him. And he forced himself on me. Repeatedly."

Conor felt nausea rise in his throat. "He raped you."

"He was my husband." She was so pale he was worried that she might faint again.

"Husband or not, Ellie, Kevin had no right to your body if you said no."

"He didn't see it that way. And he had an ace in the hole. He knew if I got pregnant that I would never leave him. So he didn't use protection."

Conor felt as if he were being ripped apart from the inside out. He didn't want the rest of Ellie's halting confession. He couldn't handle it. But he had no choice.

"What happened then?"

"When he fell asleep, I ran away."

"To Kirby's place?"

"I wanted to…so badly. But Kirby and Kevin were going on the Aconcagua trip together in little over a week. I didn't want there to be bad blood between them. A girlfriend offered me her couch. Since her boyfriend was a policeman, I felt relatively safe."

"And Kevin?"

"I have no idea if he tried to find me or not. I didn't go to work. I didn't go out. My friend wanted me to press charges. But I wouldn't agree. I'm not sure what I thought I was going to do. I was in shock, I guess."

"Thank God, you had someone looking out for you."

"Yes. I was lucky."

"What happened next?"

"I never saw Kevin again. The next I knew of him was

when I got word that he had fallen and died. And that Kirby was stranded."

Holy God. This was far worse than finding out Ellie was pining for a lost love. He was dumbfounded and struggling to process the dreadful details. She'd been raped, widowed and almost lost her brother.

"Who got in touch with you?"

"I felt safe because Kevin was on the mountain. So I went home to get some more clothes and larger items I'd had to leave behind. I had recovered enough mentally to know what he had done to me. I was prepared to go back to my apartment and press charges as soon as he returned. While I was at the house, the phone rang and rang. I finally answered it. That's when I heard what had happened." She shook her head, her expression bemused. "Three weeks later I found out I was pregnant."

Conor hunched his shoulders and searched for words. No wonder she hadn't wanted to talk about it. "Did you ever tell Kirby and your parents?"

She shrugged. "No. Kirby has had enough to deal with without juggling my problems. And the truth would have killed my parents."

"I don't know what to say, Ellie. I wish he was alive so I could throttle him."

Her smile was weak. "You said you loved me. But you need to hear me out before you say it again."

"It's not the kind of thing a man takes back in fifteen minutes."

His humor was lost on her. "Conor." She looked out over the valley, almost as if she had forgotten he was there.

"Yes, Ellie?"

"When I hung up the phone…after hearing that Kevin was dead, I did something terrible."

He couldn't let her go on. Not without touching her. Returning to where she sat, he picked her up, even as she struggled to get free, and sat down, pulling her between the vee of his thighs so her back was against his chest.

"Okay, my love. Tell me this terrible thing you did."

She waited so long he thought she had changed her mind. Her fingers linked with his, playing with the gold signet ring on his right hand. Finally, she spoke. "I stood there in our house…the place I never wanted to see again, and I wasn't sad. I wasn't devastated. I wasn't even upset."

He kissed the back of her hair. "You were likely in shock, but go ahead."

She half turned, staring up at him with tragic eyes. "I was relieved, Conor. What kind of person is *relieved* to hear someone has died?"

A year and a half. Eighteen months. Longer by now. All this time she had borne the weight of her guilt. Even as she nursed her brother back to health…even as she endured labor and sleep deprivation and learned how to be a good mother…all that time his sweet Ellie had tortured herself.

He cupped her face in his hands and kissed her nose. "You are such a drama queen. If you were expecting me to throw you out of my house or demand that you dress in sackcloth and ashes, you're going to be sadly disappointed."

The look of shock on her face was priceless. Not for anything in the world would he let her know how horrified he was by what she had experienced. His job was to give her normalcy…and indirect absolution. Smiling, though it was an effort to tamp down his anger at her worthless dead husband, he pulled her to her feet.

"I love you," he said, the words steady. "Nothing you told me just now changes that. Nothing ever will."

Ellie gazed at him with an expression that defied description. She had kept her emotions under such tight lock and key it was no wonder she'd stumbled recently. No one could keep such painful secrets indefinitely. But Ellie had tried.

Her arms hung at her sides, though his were around her shoulders. "I made a terrible mistake, Conor. How can I ever trust my judgment again?"

Her question was valid. But he had the answer.

"Tell me something, Ellie. When you and Kirby came back to Silver Glen, what did you think when you saw me?"

"Ah..." The muscles in her throat worked. "I...uh..."

"You felt a spark, didn't you? A small, warm remembrance of the past."

She licked her lips. "Yes."

He could barely hear the syllable. Gathering her into his arms, he lifted her onto her toes and kissed her until they were both breathless. "We had something, Ellie. All those years ago. It was a seed, I think. A seed that contained the possibility of something pretty wonderful. But things happened. Life separated us. So the seed never germinated."

"Are you sure you aren't a botanist?"

Her sass reassured him. If she could spar with him, she was going to be okay. "I'm serious. If you had stayed in South America...if you'd had a happy marriage...you and I would have been nothing but a memory."

"And now?"

Joy rose in his chest. And a surge of adrenaline stronger than any he'd ever experienced while skiing or climbing a mountain. "Now, I'm going to fertilize the hell out of that thing. I'm going to tell you I love you every day of your life. I'm going to make love to you every night so that we're both haggard from lack of sleep. God willing, and with your agreement, I'm going to give little Emory a few siblings."

"All that from a seed?" Her eyes were shining with happiness, not tears.

"It's our own little miracle."

She slid her hands around his neck, playing with his ears, stroking his nape. "I don't think Kirby really wants to go to Miami. He asked me what I thought about him opening a clinic here…one that caters to children with special needs. And I've been thinking that Silver Glen might need an international visitor center." She rested her head on his shoulder. "I love you with all my heart, Conor Kavanagh."

He had waited a long time to hear it. Now that the moment had come, his knees were embarrassingly weak. "No take backs."

Lifting her by the waist, he set her on the teak picnic table so he could better reach her mouth. He kissed her hard, his hands tangled in her beautiful hair as he held her head and angled her lips to his.

"Marry me," he muttered. "Let me adopt Emory."

"Yes." She smothered his face with kisses, her light happy laughter more gratifying to him than all the gold medals in the world.

"I wonder if we could send Kirby up to the Silver Beeches Lodge to spend the night."

"Conor!" She punched his arm. "You'd throw your best friend to the wolves just to have sex with me?"

"Loud sex. Noisy sex. Kitchen-table sex. And yes, I would. Though a room at a five-star hotel is hardly a punishment."

She wrapped her legs around his waist, leaning back on her hands. "If we're nice to him, he might be willing to keep Emory while we go on our honeymoon."

Conor's eyes glazed over. He was hard and ready. And he wanted Ellie. When he got her in bed, he'd never let her go. "Works for me," he said.

"I love you, Conor."

It was only the second time she had said it. He didn't think the words would ever get old. Her smile was everything that was Ellie. Sweet. Sexy. Funny. And his. No shadows. No ghosts. Only a future for them to explore together.

"I love you, too, my gorgeous, wonderful best friend." He kissed the spot beneath her ear that was supersensitive.

"Do you think Kirby will be surprised?"

"I doubt it. Your brother is a very smart man." He pulled her to her feet. "Let's go tell him the good news."

As they walked into the house, it hit him hard. Happiness. Contentment. Sheer euphoria. He was *home*. And Ellie Porter was finally his.

She looked up at him, mischief on her face. "But we're still having sex later, right? Even if we have to be quiet?"

"You can count on it, Ellie. You can count on it."

* * * * *

"I'm the one at a disadvantage, if you were hoping I was Will.

"I'm James. The other Rowling. Will is my brother."

"Brother? Oh," Bella drawled as it hit her. "You and Will are twins."

"Guilty." His eyes twinkled, sucking her under his spell for a moment.

"Then I'm doubly sorry." With no small amount of regret, she reeled back her less-than-innocent interest. "It's fine, really."

It was not fine. It was so the opposite of fine, she couldn't even wrap her head around how not fine it was. Because she'd just realized this sensually intriguing man she'd accidentally tripped over was the brother of the man her father wanted her to marry.

If that didn't complicate her life a million times over, she didn't know what would.

Her hand was still gripped tightly in his and he didn't seem in any hurry to let her go. But he should. She pulled free and crossed her arms, wishing for a cover-up. Why did that glint in James's eye cause her to feel so exposed all at once?

* * *

The Princess and the Player is part of the series Dynasties: The Montoros—One royal family must choose between love and destiny!

THE PRINCESS
AND THE PLAYER

BY
KAT CANTRELL

MILLS &
BOON

Published in Great Britain 2015
by Mills & Boon, an imprint of Harlequin (UK) Limited,
Eton House, 18-24 Paradise Road, Richmond, Surrey, TW9 1SR

© 2015 Harlequin Books S.A.

Special thanks and acknowledgement are given to Kat Cantrell for her contribution to the Dynasties: The Montoros series.

ISBN: 978-0-263-25272-9

51-0815

Harlequin (UK) Limited's policy is to use papers that are natural, renewable and recyclable products and made from wood grown in sustainable forests. The logging and manufacturing processes conform to the legal environmental regulations of the country of origin.

Printed and bound in Spain
by CPI, Barcelona

Kat Cantrell read her first Mills & Boon® novel in third grade and has been scribbling in notebooks since she learned to spell. What else would she write but romance? She majored in literature, officially with the intent to teach, but somehow ended up buried in middle management in corporate America, until she became a stay-at-home mum and full-time writer.

Kat, her husband and their two boys live in north Texas. When she's not writing about characters on the journey to happily-ever-after, she can be found at a soccer game, watching the TV show *Friends* or listening to '80s music.

Kat was the 2011 Mills & Boon So You Think You Can Write winner and a 2012 RWA Golden Heart Award finalist for best unpublished series contemporary manuscript.

One

Auwck. Auwck.

Bella Montoro's eyelids flew open at the raucous and unwelcome alarm clock. One of the pair of feral blue-and-gold macaws who lived in the tree outside the window of her Coral Gables mansion had chosen today, of all days, to wake her early.

Miami was full of wild macaws and normally, she loved them. Today, not so much.

Groaning, she smooshed a pillow over her head but the pressure didn't ease her champagne headache and the barrier didn't muffle the happy squawks of her feathered friend. Fine. It was time to drag herself out of bed anyway.

She sat up. A glance through the bay window confirmed which bird it was.

"Good morning, Buttercup," she muttered sarcastically, but with the window closed, the macaw couldn't hear her.

She didn't dare open the window for fear she'd frighten her away. Both Buttercup and her mate, Wesley, were as wild as the day was long, and Bella enjoyed it when they deigned to hang out with her. She watched them groom themselves for as long as she dared since she wouldn't get to see them for a while once she left Miami for the small country of Alma—today's destination.

Bella had always known she was descended from royalty, but a dictator had been ruling her ancestor's country for ages. She'd never expected the political climate to shift. Or for the Montoros to reclaim the throne. But it had happened and though her father was first in line to become king, his divorce rendered him ineligible for the crown due to Alma's strict laws. Then her oldest brother, Rafe, had abdicated his place so he could focus on the new baby he and his fiancée, Emily, were expecting.

Her other brother, Gabriel, had stepped up, adopting his new role with an ease Bella admired. And while she liked the tiny island country of Alma well enough to go back for her brother's coronation as the new king, the promise of bigger and better parties didn't fully make up for having to leave behind the things she loved in Miami.

She was also leaving behind her great-aunt Isabella, who might draw her last breath any day now. Rafe would check in on her of course, and Bella could call. But still. It wasn't the same as having daily access to the woman who always had a kind word and gentle piece of advice, no matter what the occasion. Bella had been named for her father's aunt, and they shared a kinship that transcended age.

Her father owed her for agreeing to this move to Alma. Big time.

Bella watched Buttercup groom her feathers for a moment, and then turned away from the beautiful view of the grounds. She might not see this house again either, and she'd taken for granted how much she loved living here. Now that the day of her departure had arrived, everything had gotten real, really fast. She'd been an American her whole life and while she'd always enjoyed the privileges of being a Montoro, becoming a member of Alma's royal family carried heavy responsibilities with few tangible rewards.

Not that anyone had asked her opinion.

With far too much racket for Bella's taste, her maid, Celia, bustled into the bedroom and frowned at the crumpled, glittery dress on the floor as she stepped over it. "They have plenty more hangers at the store if you've run out, Miss Bella."

Bella grinned at the woman who'd been her friend, confidant and occasional strong shoulder for years, blessing her for sticking to their tried-and-true teasing instead of becoming maudlin over the irreversible changes that had ripped through the Montoro family recently.

"Got hangers," Bella informed her around an involuntary yawn. "Just not the will to use one at three a.m."

Celia sniffed as if displeased, but an indulgent smile tugged at her mouth nonetheless. "Seems like a gal about to get on a plane in a few hours might come home at a decent hour."

"Oh, but it was my last night in Miami!" Bella protested without any real heat and stretched with a moan. "I had lots of people to see. Lots of parties to attend."

"Hmpf. Lots of money to talk your friends out of, you mean."

Celia was one of the few people who recognized that Bella's involvement in wildlife conservation wasn't just a rich girl's cute hobby. It was Bella's passion and she used her connections. Shamelessly. And it wasn't an accident that she'd been named the top fund-raiser in Florida by two different conservation groups.

"You say that like it's a bad thing." Bella shook her head as Celia selected an outfit from the overflowing closet and held it out with a raised eyebrow. "Not that one. The blue pantsuit for the plane. With the cropped jacket."

Like a well-rehearsed ballet, Bella and Celia danced around each other as they navigated a bedroom that closely resembled a post-hurricane department store. Everyone joked that you could always tell when Bella had whirled through a scene because nothing was in one piece afterward. It was a reference to Bella's birth during the harrowing hours of Hurricane Andrew, before FEMA had started cracking down on evacuations.

Both mother and baby had emerged from the storm without incident, but Bella held the private belief that the experience had branded her soul with hurricane-like qualities she couldn't shake. Not the least of which was a particular talent for causing chaos.

Celia began packing Bella's suitcases while her mistress dressed and they laughed over Bella's account of the previous night's parties, as they'd done many a morning over the years. But this would be the last time for a long time. Maybe forever, depending on what happened in Alma.

Bella kept up the light banter, but she was pretty sure the shadows in Celia's eyes were reflected in her own. As the hour grew near for Bella to leave for the sun-drenched islands of Alma, she couldn't stand it any longer. "I wish you could go with me to Alma!"

And then to her mortification, Bella burst into tears.

Celia folded Bella into her arms and they clung to each other. When Adela, Bella's mom, had finally ditched her cold, unsatisfying marriage the day after Bella's eighteenth birthday, Celia had been the one who stuck around to make sure Bella didn't get into too much trouble. Best of both worlds—she had someone who cared, but who also couldn't tell her what to do. Bella did not like being told what to do.

"There, now. Your brother will look out for you and besides, you'll be having so much fun as the new princess, you won't even notice I'm not there."

"That's not true," Bella sniffed and hugged Celia tighter. "Gabriel will be busy with king stuff and spend all his free time with Serafia now that they're getting married. What if I'm banished to some out of the way place—*alone*?"

She wouldn't put it past her father to lock her up in the palace dungeon or do something else equally archaic since he seemed bent on rediscovering his old-fashioned side. That last photo of her to hit the tabloids? Totally not her fault. How was she supposed to know the paparazzi had hidden in the foliage surrounding Nicole's pool? Everyone else had shed their swimsuits, too, but Bella was the only one they'd targeted, of course.

Rafael Montoro the Third was not amused. Apparently it was problematic that her father's business associates and soon-to-be-king Gabriel's future subjects in Alma could easily access naked photos of Bella.

No one seemed to remember that she was the victim in that scandal.

Celia snorted. "With Gabriel about to take the throne, your father will want the whole family in the public eye, gaining support for your brother. You're the only princess Alma's got, sweetie. They'll love you and so will your fiancé. Your father can't lock you away *and* expect you to marry the man he's picked out."

"Yeah, I've been trying not to think about that." Her head started pounding again and that fourth glass of champagne last night started to feel like a bad idea. But her friends had been determined to send her off in style to her new life as the sister of the king of Alma, so how could she refuse?

Besides, anything that helped her forget the arranged marriage her father was trying to force down her throat was a plus in her book. Fine time for her father to remember he had a daughter—when it was important for the Montoro family to strengthen ties with Alma through marriage. How come Gabriel and Rafe didn't have to marry someone advantageous? Her brothers had chosen their own brides. It wasn't fair. But her father had made it clear she was to get on a plane and meet this man Will Rowling, who was the son of one of Alma's most powerful businessmen.

Maybe she should be thankful no one had thought to match her with Will's father. Seemed as if that might be more advantageous than marrying the son. She shuddered. *No* marriage sounded like fun, no matter who the guy was.

If Alma turned out to be horrible, she'd just come home. Rafe and Emily were going to make her an aunt soon, and she'd love to hang out in Key West with the baby. Nobody dictated Bella's life but her.

"Mr. Rafael isn't completely unreasonable. After all, he did agree to let you meet Will and see how things go. Just remember why you're doing this," Celia advised.

Bella's guilty conscience reared its ugly head and she eased out of Celia's embrace before the older woman sensed it. "It's my royal obligation to help Gabriel ascend to the throne," she mimicked in her father's deep voice. "The whole family needs to be in Alma to prepare for the coronation."

But that wasn't really why she'd agreed to go. Miami had grown too small to hold both Bella and Drew Honeycutt. Honestly, when you told a guy that you just wanted to have fun and not take a relationship seriously, he was supposed to breathe a sigh of relief.

He was not supposed to fall to one knee and propose after two months of casual dating. And then plaster his second proposal on twenty billboards around the city, along with Bella's picture and a cartoon heart around her face. The third proposal spread across the sky in the form of a "Will you marry me, Bella Montoro?" banner behind a small plane, which flew up and down South Beach for six hours while Bella was at a private cookout on the penthouse terrace of Ramone, the new guy she'd been seeing. A fan of drama Ramone was not. Thanks to Drew, he'd bowed out.

And Bella had really liked Ramone, dang it; the more

he drank, the more money he handed over for her wild-life charities.

Drew followed her around, popping up at parties and museum openings like a bad penny, espousing his love for Bella with horrific poetry and calf eyes galore. It would be great if she could tell him off, but Honeycutt Logistics did a lot of business with Montoro Enterprises and she couldn't afford to irritate her father further. Plus, she was 97 percent sure Drew was harmless and worse, he seemed genuinely baffled and brokenhearted over her continual rejection of his proposals.

Each Drew sighting was another kick to the stomach. Another reminder that she was the hurricane baby, destined to whirl through people's lives and leave havoc in her wake. If only she could find a way to *not* break everything into little pieces—even though it was always an accident—she'd feel a lot better. She hated hurting people.

It was probably not a bad plan to disappear from the Miami scene for a while.

Celia managed to get Bella into the car on time and with all her luggage. The gates parted and Bella waved goodbye to Buttercup, Wesley and the house she'd grown up in as the driver picked up speed and they exited the grounds. Sun sparkled across Biscayne Bay and her spirits rose with each mile marker along the highway to the private airstrip where the Montoro Enterprises jet waited to fly her to Alma.

This was an adventure no matter what and she was going to enjoy every second of the sun, sand and royal parties ahead. By the time she'd boarded the plane, buckled her seatbelt and accepted a mimosa from Jan—the same flight attendant who'd given her crayons and coloring books once upon a time—Bella's mood had turned downright cheerful. Cheerful enough to sneak a glance at the picture of Will Rowling her father had sent her.

He was classically handsome, with nice hair and a

pleasant smile. The serious glint in his eye might be a trick of the light. Serious she could do without and besides, this was the guy her *father* had picked. Chances were Will and Bella would get on like oil and water.

But she'd reserve judgment until she met him because first and foremost, Alma was about starting fresh and Will deserved a chance to prove they were meant for each other. If he came out strong with a fun-loving nature and swept her off her feet, she'd be okay with a fabulous love affair and passion to spare.

Though she couldn't deny that one of the big question marks was what kind of guy would agree to an arranged marriage in the twenty-first century. There was probably something really wrong with Will Rowling if he couldn't meet women on his own. She probably had a better chance of her plane flying into an alternate universe than finding her soul mate in Will Rowling.

For the fourth time, someone kicked sand in James Rowling's face and for the fourth time, he ignored it. If he let loose with a string of curses—the way he wanted to—he'd only alert someone to his presence here, and James was trying to be invisible.

Or at least as invisible as one of Alma's most notorious failures could be. Maybe in fifty years he could fade into the woodwork, but every single citizen of Alma—and probably most of the free world—had watched him miss that goal in the World Cup. Anonymity was scarce.

So far, no one had recognized him with Oakleys covering his eyes and a backward ball cap over his hair. The longer he kept it that way, the better. The last thing he wanted was a bunch of questions about why Real Madrid had dropped his contract. It wasn't hard to look that one up…along with pictures of James leaving a bar in Rio with a prostitute…not that she'd mentioned money to *him*. Or worse, questions about whether he planned to stick around his adopted homeland and play for Alma's reserve football team—*soccer* team if the questioner was American.

No comment.

A reserve team was for beginners. He would get a new professional league contract, period. If not around here, then maybe back in England, where he'd been born. There was no other alternative. Football was his life.

Peeling his shirt away from his sticky chest, he leaned back into his short-legged beach chair, stuck his legs straight out and closed his eyes, somehow sure the elusive measure of peace he sought would be within reach this time. He almost snorted. When had he turned into an optimist?

There was no peace to be had and if there was, it sure as hell wouldn't be found in Alma, the capital of boring. Not to mention his father's presence permeated the entire island, as if Patrick Rowling's soul lived in the bedrock, sending out vibrations of disapproval on a regularly scheduled basis.

That's why James was at the beach at Playa Del Onda, soaking up the sun instead of doing whatever it was his father thought he should be doing, which would never happen because James lacked the capacity to do what his father said. It was like a mutated gene: his father spoke and James's brain refused to obey. He automatically did the opposite.

"Ooof!" Air whooshed from his lungs as something heavy landed square on his chest.

Then his beach chair flipped, tossing him into the sand on top of something. It squealed.

Some*one*. When his vision cleared, the tangle of supplebodied woman and blond hair underneath him captured his complete attention.

He gazed down into the bluest set of eyes he'd seen in a while. Something shifted inside as the woman blinked back, her beautiful heart-shaped face reflecting not an iota of remorse over their risqué position. Her body had some-how slid into the grooves of his effortlessly and the slight-est incline of his head would fuse his lips to hers.

She'd fully gobsmacked him.

Their breath intermingled. She seemed in no hurry to unstick her skin from his and in about two and a half seconds, his own body would start getting into the moment in a huge and inappropriate way.

Sexy strangers signaled big-time problems and he had enough of those.

Reluctantly, he rolled off her and helped her sit up. "Sorry about that. You okay?"

"Totally." Her husky voice skittered across his skin and he was hooked on the sound of it instantly. American. His favorite. "My fault. I was focused on this thing instead of where I was going."

She kicked at a Frisbee he hadn't noticed lying in the sand two feet away. But who'd pay attention to a piece of plastic when a fit blonde in a tiny bikini landed in your lap? Not him.

"I like a girl who goes for the memorable introduction."

It was certainly a new one. And he'd experienced his share of inventive ploys for getting his attention. Knick-ers with cell phone numbers scrawled in marker across the crotch, which he discovered had been shoved into his pocket. Room keys slipped into drinks sent over by a knot of football groupies at a corner table. Once, he'd gone back to his hotel room after a press junket to find two naked women spread out across his bed. How they'd gotten in, he still didn't know.

The logistics question had sort of slipped his mind after ten minutes in their company.

"Oh, I wasn't angling for an introduction." She actually blushed a bit, which was oddly endearing. "I really didn't see you there. You kind of blend into the sand."

"Is that a crack about my British complexion?" he teased. "You're pretty pale yourself, darling."

She laughed and rearranged her hair, pulling it behind her back so it didn't conceal her cleavage. A move he thoroughly appreciated. This gorgeous klutz might be the best thing that had happened to him all week. Longer than that. The best thing since arriving in Alma for sure.

Maybe it wasn't so bad to be stuck here cooling his heels until a football club whose jersey he could stomach wearing knocked on his door.

"No, not at all. I wouldn't be so rude as to point out your flaws on our first meeting." She leaned forward, her vibe full of come-hither as she teased him back.

Intrigued, he angled his head toward her. "But on our second date, all bets are off?"

Glancing down coquettishly, she let loose a small smile. "I'm more of a third-date kind of girl."

His gut contracted as the full force of that promise hit him crossways. She was a unique breed of woman, the most fascinating one he'd met thus far on this stupid rock he was being forced to call home for the time being. The memory of her hot flesh against his was still fresh—it was enough to drive him mad. And he suspected she knew exactly what she was doing to him.

"I have a feeling you'd be worth the wait."

She picked that moment to stand and for some reason, the new angle cast her in a different light. It tickled his mind and he recognized her all at once. Pictures of the new princess had graced every news channel for the past couple of weeks, but she'd been clothed. Regardless, he should have recognized her sooner and maybe not disgraced himself by flirting with a woman who probably really had no clue she'd stumbled over a former football player for Real Madrid.

A princess—especially one as fit as Bella Montoro—wasn't running around the beach at Playa Del Onda looking to meet guys, whether they were semifamous or not. Which was a dirty shame.

He shoved his hat back onto his head and repositioned his sunglasses, both of which had flown off during the sand tango.

Ms. Montoro... Princess Bella... Your Royal Highness... What did you even call her when her brother hadn't been crowned yet? Whatever the form of address, she was way out of his league.

But that didn't mean she thought so. She hadn't bothered to hide the frank attraction in her gaze when she'd been in his arms earlier. If there was anything he knew, it was women, and she might be royalty but that didn't necessarily make her off-limits.

He quickly scrambled to his feet in case there was some protocol for standing when princesses stood...even if she was wearing a postage stamp–sized white bikini that somehow covered everything while leaving nothing to the imagination.

No point in beating around the bush. "Am I permitted to call you Bella or is there some other title you'd prefer?"

"What, like *Princess*?" She wrinkled her nose. "I'm not really used to all that yet. And besides, I think we're a little past that stage, don't you?"

The feel of her soft curves flush against his body flooded his mind and his board shorts probably wouldn't conceal his excitement much longer if he didn't cool his jets. "Yeah. Formality isn't my specialty anyway. Bella it is."

Strangely, calling her Bella ratcheted up the intimacy quotient by a thousand. He liked it. And he wanted to say it a bunch more times while she lay stretched out under him again. Without the bikini.

She smiled and glanced down, as if the heat roiling between them was affecting her, too, and she didn't know quite what to do with it. "This is all so awkward. I wasn't sure you knew who I was."

Shrugging, he stuck his hands behind his back because he had no clue what to do with them. It was the first time he'd been unsure around a woman since the age of fourteen. "I recognized you from your pictures."

She nodded and waved off her friend who'd most likely come to investigate the disappearance of her Frisbee partner. "Me, too. I wasn't expecting to run into you on the beach or I would have dressed for the occasion."

Ah, so she *did* know who he was—and dare he hope there was a hint of approval there? She'd gotten rid of the friend, a clear sign she planned to stick around for a while at least. Maybe he wasn't so far out of her league after all. "I'm a fan of your wardrobe choice."

Laughing, she glanced down. "I guess it is appropriate for the beach, isn't it? It's just not how I thought meeting you would go. The picture my father sent painted you as someone very serious."

"Um…you don't say?" He'd just completely lost the thread of the conversation. Why would her father be sending her pictures, unless… Of course. Had to make sure the precious princess didn't taint herself with the common riffraff. *Stay away from that Rowling boy. He's a boatload of trouble.*

His temper kicked up, but he smoothed it over with a wink and a wicked smile. "I'm every bit as bad as your father warned you. Probably worse. If your goal is to seriously irritate him, I'm on board with that."

He had no problem being her Rebel Against Daddy go-to guy, though he'd probably encourage her to be *really* bad and enjoy it far too much. Instantly, a few choice scenarios that would get them both into a lot of trouble filled his mind.

Her eyes widened. "He, uh, didn't warn me about you… Actually, I'm pretty sure he'd be happy if we went out. Isn't that the whole point of this? So we can see if we're suited?"

This conversation was going in circles. Her father wanted them to date? "He's a football fan, then?"

She shook her head, confusion clouding her gaze. "I don't think so. Does that matter to you, Will?"

"Will?" He groaned. This was so much worse than he'd anticipated. "You think I'm Will?"

More importantly, her father had sent her a picture of Will for some yet-to-be-determined reason, but it wasn't so she could flirt with Will's twin brother on the beach. And this little case of mistaken identity was about to come to an abrupt halt.

Two

Bella laced her fingers together as she got the impression all at once that she wasn't talking to the man she thought she was. "Aren't you Will Rowling?"

He had to be. She'd studied his picture enough on the plane and then again last night while she tried to go to sleep but couldn't, because she'd been wondering what in the world her father was thinking with this arranged marriage nonsense. And then she'd come to the beach with the daughter of one of the servants who was close to her age, only to trip over said man her father had selected.

Except he was staring at her strangely and the niggle of doubt wormed its way to the surface again. How could she have made such a mistake?

"Not Will. Not even close," he confirmed.

He grinned, and she let herself revel in his gorgeous aqua-colored eyes for a moment because she didn't have to fight an attraction to him if he wasn't the man her father picked out for her.

The sun shone a little brighter and the sea sparkled a bit

bluer. Digging her toes into the warm sand that suddenly felt heavenly against her bare feet, she breathed a sigh of relief and grinned back.

This was turning out better than she'd hoped. Geez, she'd been one heartbeat away from believing in love at first sight and trying for all she was worth to shut it down. Because she'd thought he was Will Rowling. Imagine *that*. Her father would be insufferable about it and demand they get married right away if she'd become smitten so fast. It would have been a disaster.

But if this extremely sexy man wasn't Will—*perfect*. She slid her gaze down his well-cut body, which a T-shirt and long shorts couldn't hide. Of course she'd felt every single one of his valleys and hard peaks. Intimately.

No. This was *not* perfect. She was supposed to be meeting Will and seeing if they got along, not flirting with some look-alike stranger who made her itch to accept the wicked invitation in his gaze, which promised if he got her naked, he'd rock her world.

With no small amount of regret, she reeled back her less-than-innocent interest.

"Well, sorry about that, then," she said and held out her hand. Might as well start over since this whole thing had blown up in her face. "Bella Montoro. I guess you already knew that, but I'm at a disadvantage."

His rich laugh hit her a moment before he clasped her hand in his and the combination heated her more than the bright sun or her embarrassment. "I'm the one at a disadvantage, if you were hoping I was Will. I'm James. The other Rowling. Will is my brother."

"Brother? Oh," she drawled as it hit her. "You and Will are twins."

"Guilty." His eyes twinkled, sucking her under his spell for a moment.

"Then I'm doubly sorry." Mortified, she racked her brain, but if her father had told her Will had a twin brother, she surely would have remembered that. "I've made a complete mess out of this, haven't I?"

"Not at all. People confuse us all the time. It's fine, really."

It was not fine. It was so the opposite of fine, she couldn't even wrap her head around how *not fine* it was. Because she'd just realized this sensually intriguing man she'd accidentally tripped over was the *brother* of the intended target of her father's archaic arranged marriage plan.

If that didn't complicate her life a million times over, she didn't know what would.

Her hand was still gripped tight in his and he didn't seem in any hurry to let her go. But he should. She pulled free and crossed her arms, wishing for a cover-up. Why did that glint in James's eye cause her to feel so exposed all at once?

"I'm curious," James said casually as if the vibe between them had just cooled, which it most definitely had not. "Why did your father send you a picture of Will?"

"Oh, so I would know what he looks like." Actually, she'd demanded he do so. There was no way she was getting on a plane to meet someone blind.

"I'm sensing there's more to the story." His raised eyebrows encouraged her to elaborate.

"Wouldn't you wonder about the appearance of a person your father wanted you to marry? I sure did."

Surprise flew across James's face. "Your father wants you to marry Will? Does Will know about this?"

"Of course he does. Your father was the instigator, actually. You didn't know our fathers cooked up this idea of an arranged marriage?"

His laugh was far more derisive this time. "The elder Rowling doesn't share much of what goes on his head. But somehow it doesn't shock me to discover dear old Dad wants his son married to a member of the royal family. Did you agree?"

"No! Well, not yet anyway. I only agreed to meet Will and see what happened. I'm not really in the market for a steady relationship, let alone one as permanent as marriage."

Groaning, she bit her lip. Too late to take that back, though it had been the God-honest truth. Regardless, spilling her guts to the brother of her potential fiancé wasn't the best plan. James would probably run off and tell Will his future bride had felt up his brother on the beach— totally not her fault!—flirted with him—maybe partially her fault—and then declared marriage to be worse than the plague.

Instead of falling to his knees in shock, James winked and dang, even that was sexy.

"Woman after my own heart. If you don't want to get married, why even agree to meet Will?"

Why was she still standing here talking to the wrong brother? She should go. There was nothing for her here. But she couldn't make herself walk away from the spark still kicking between them.

"It's complicated," she hedged.

She sighed and glanced over her shoulder, but there was no one in earshot. She didn't want to draw the attention of a camera lens, but surely it couldn't hurt to spend a few minutes chatting with the man who might become her brother-in-law...so she could keep reminding herself that's who he was to her. If nothing else, she could set the record straight in case he intended to repeat this conversation verbatim to his brother.

"I'm the king of uncomplicating things," James said with another laugh that curled her toes deeper into the sand. "Try me."

It wasn't as if anyone was expecting her back at the gargantuan house perched on the cliff behind them. Gabriel was never home and her father... Well, she wasn't dying to run into him again.

She shrugged. "We're all new at this royalty thing. I don't want to be the one to mess it up. What if I don't try with Will and it has horrible repercussions for my brother Gabriel? I can't be responsible for that."

"But if you meet Will and you don't like him, how is that different than not meeting him in the first place? Either way, you don't end up with him and the repercussions will be the same."

How come she'd never thought of that? "That's a good point."

"Told you. I can uncomplicate anything. It's a skill." James's smile widened as he swept her with an impossible to misinterpret look. "I just figure out what I want to do and justify it. Like...if I wanted to kiss you, I'd find a way."

As his gaze rested on her lips, heat flooded her cheeks. And other places. She could practically feel the weight of his kiss against her mouth and he hadn't even moved. A pang of lust zinged through her abdomen and she nearly gasped at the strength of it. What was it about him that lit her up so fiercely?

"You shouldn't be talking about kissing." She inwardly cursed. That should have come out much more sternly, instead of breathy with anticipation. "Flirting as a whole is completely off-limits."

A hint of challenge crept into his expression and then he leaned in, stopping just short of touching her earlobe with his mouth. "Says who?"

"Me," she murmured as the scent of male and heat coiled up low in her belly, nearly making her weep with want. "I'm weak and liable to give in. You have to be the strong one and stop presenting me with so much temptation."

He laughed softly. "I'm afraid you're in a lot of trouble, then."

"Why?"

"Because I have absolutely no reservations about giving in to temptation."

The wicked smile spreading across his face sealed it—she *was* in a lot of trouble. She was supposed to marry his brother. And the last thing she needed was to set herself up for a repeat of the Drew Debacle, where she accidentally broke James's heart because she ended up with Will. Better all around to stay away from James.

Why did the wrong Rowling have to be so alluring and so delicious?

Maybe she could find Will similarly attractive if she just gave him a chance.

"I'll keep that in mind." All right, then. She was going to have to be the one to step away. Noted.

So step away. Right now.

Through a supreme act of will, she somehow did. James's gorgeous aqua eyes tracked her movement as she put one foot, then two between them. He nodded once, apparently in understanding but definitely not in agreement.

"See you around, Princess."

He stood there, one hip cocked in a casual stance that screamed Bad Boy, and she half waved before she turned and fled.

As she climbed the stairs to the house, she resisted looking over her shoulder to see if she could pick out James's yellow T-shirt amidst the other sun worshippers lounging on the white sand. He wasn't for her and there was no getting around the fact that she wished otherwise.

James Rowling was forbidden. And that might be his most attractive quality.

Bella entered the Playa Del Onda house through the kitchen, and snagged a glass-bottled cola from the refrigerator and a piece of crusty bread from the pantry. Both the colas and the bread tasted different in Europe but she didn't mind. All part of the adventure.

Thoughts still on the sexy man she'd abandoned on the beach, Bella munched on the bread as she climbed the stairs to her bedroom. She almost made it before a dark shadow alerted her to the fact that her least favorite person in the house had found her.

"Isabella." Her father's sharp voice stopped her dead, four steps from the landing on the second floor.

"Yeah, Dad?" She didn't turn around. If you didn't stare him in the eye, he couldn't turn you to stone, right?

"Is that how you dress to go out?"

"Only when I go to the beach," she retorted. "Is there something new you'd like to discuss or shall we rehash the same subject from last night? You didn't like that outfit either, if I recall."

Ever since Adela, Bella's mother, had left, this is how it went. Her father only spoke to her when he wanted to tell her how to run her life. And she pretended to listen. Occasionally, when it suited her, she went along, but only if she got something out of it.

"We'll rehash it as many times as it takes to get it through your scattered brain. Gabriel is going to be *king*." Rafael stressed the word as if she might be confused about what was happening around her. "The least you can do is help smooth his ascension with a little common sense about how you dress. The Montoros have no credibility yet, especially not with that stunt your brother pulled."

"Rafe fell in love," she shot back and bit her tongue.

Old news. Her father cared nothing for love, only propriety. And horror of all horrors—his eldest son had gotten a bartender pregnant and then abdicated the throne so he could focus on his new family. In Daddy's mind, it fell squarely into the category of impropriety. Unforgivable.

It was a reminder that her father also cared little for his daughter's happiness either. Only royal protocol.

"Rafe is a disappointment. I'll not have another child

of mine follow his example." He cleared his throat. "Face me when we're speaking, please."

She complied, but only because the front view of her bikini was likely to give him apoplexy and she kind of wanted to see it.

He pursed his lips but, to her father's credit, that was his only reaction. "When have you arranged to meet Will Rowling?"

Ah, of course. Complaining about her bikini was a smoke screen—this was actually an ambush about her arranged marriage. With the scent of forbidden fruit lingering in her senses coupled with her father's bad attitude, she'd developed a sudden fierce desire to spend time with someone who had clearly never met a good time he didn't like.

And his name wasn't Will. "I haven't yet."

"What are you waiting for, an invitation? This is your match to make, Isabella. I'm giving you some latitude in the timing but I expect results. Soon." The severe lines around his mouth softened. "This alliance is very important. To the entire Montoro family and to the royal legacy of Alma. I'm not asking this for myself, but for Gabriel. Remember that."

She sighed. "I know. That's why I'm here. I do want to be a credit to the royal family."

Hurricane Bella couldn't whirl through Alma and disrupt the entire country. She knew that. Somehow, she had to be better than she'd been in Miami. The thought of Miami reminded her of Buttercup and Wesley, her feathered friends she'd left behind. Some said the wild macaws that nested in southern Florida were people's pets set free during Hurricane Andrew. She'd always felt an affinity with the birds because they'd all survived the storm. Buttercup and Wesley could continue to be her source of strength even from afar.

"Good. Then arrange to meet Will Rowling and do it soon. Patrick Rowling is one of the most influential men in Alma and the Montoros need his support. We cannot afford another misstep at this point."

It wasn't anything she hadn't heard before, but on the heels of meeting James, the warning weighed heavily on her shoulders. Gabriel hadn't wanted to be thrust suddenly into a starring role in the restoration of the monarchy to Alma's political landscape. But he'd stepped up nonetheless. She could do the same.

But why did it matter which Rowling she married anyway? Surely one was as good as the other. Perhaps she could turn this to her advantage by seeing where things went with James.

"I'll do my best not to mess this up," Bella promised.

If it didn't matter which Rowling she picked, that meant she didn't need to call Will anytime soon. The reprieve let her breathe a little easier.

Her father raised his eyebrows. "That would be a refreshing change. On that note, don't assume that you left all the tabloids behind in Miami. The paparazzi know no national boundaries. Stay out of scandalous situations, don't drink too much and for God's sake, keep your clothes on."

She saluted saucily to cover the sharp spike of hurt that she never could seem to stop no matter how many times she told herself this was just how he was. "Yes, Father."

Escaping to her room, Bella took a long shower but it didn't ease the ache from the showdown with Rafael.

Why did she still care that her father never hugged her or told her he was proud of her? Not for the first time, she wondered if the frosty temperature in her father's demeanor had caused her mother to leave. If so, Bella hardly blamed her. She hoped Adela had found happiness.

Happiness should be the most important factor in whom you married. The thought solidified Bella's resolve. If her father wanted a match between the Montoros and the Rowlings, great. Bella would comply—as long as the Rowling was James.

She'd rather see where that led than try to force a match with the right brother.

Why shouldn't she be allowed to be as happy as Rafe and Gabriel?

The loud, scornful whispering at the next table over started to annoy James about two bites into his paella. Couldn't a bloke get something to eat without someone publicly crucifying him? This time, the subject of choice was his lack of a decision on whether to take a spot on Alma's reserve team.

The two middle-aged men were in complete agreement: James should be happy to have *any* position, even though Alma wasn't a UEFA team. He should take his lumps and serve his penance, and then it would be acceptable to play for a premiere club again, once he'd redeemed himself. Or so the men opined, and not very quietly.

The paella turned to sawdust in his mouth. He was glad someone knew what he needed to do next in his stalled career.

Playing for Alma was a fine choice. For a beginner. But James had been playing football since he was seven, the same year his father had uprooted his two sons from their Guildford home and moved them to the tiny, nowhere island of Alma. Football had filled a void in his life after the death of his mother. James loved the game. Being dropped from Real Madrid had stung, worse than he'd let on to anyone.

Of course, whom would he tell? He and Will rarely talked about anything of note, usually by James's choice. Will was the perfect son who never messed up, while James spent as much effort as he possibly could on irritating his father. James and Will might be twins but the similarities ended there—and Will was a Manchester United fan from way back, so they couldn't even talk football without almost coming to blows.

And Will had first dibs on the woman James hadn't been able to forget. All without lifting a finger. Life just reeked sometimes.

Unable to eat even one more bite of the dish he'd found so tasty just minutes ago, James threw a few bills on the table and stalked out of the restaurant into the bright afternoon sun on the boardwalk at Playa Del Onda.

So much for hanging out at the beach where fewer people might recognize him. He might as well go back to Del Sol and let his father tell him again how much of a disappointment he was. Or he could swallow his bitterness and get started on finding another football club since none had come looking for him.

A flash of blond hair ahead of him caught his eye. Since Bella had been on his mind in one way or another since he'd met her the day before, it was no wonder he was imagining her around every corner.

He shouldn't, though. She'd been reserved for the "right" Rowling, the one who could do no wrong. James's black sheep status hadn't improved much. Frankly, she deserved a shot at the successful brother, though he had no clue if Will was even on board with the match their father had apparently orchestrated. When Bella mentioned it yesterday, that was the first he'd heard of it. Which didn't mean it wasn't legit.

The woman in front of him glanced into a shop window and her profile confirmed it. It *was* Bella.

Something expanded in his chest and he forgot why he wasn't supposed to think about her. Unable to help himself all of a sudden, James picked up his pace until he drew up alongside her. "Fancy meeting you here."

Tilting her head down, she looked at him over the top of her sunglasses and murmured something reassuring to the burly security detail trailing her. They backed off immediately.

"James Rowling, I presume?" she said to him.

He laughed. "The one and only. Getting in some shopping?"

"Nope. Waiting around for you to stroll by. It's about time. I was starting to think you'd ordered everything on El Gatito's menu." She nodded in the direction of the restaurant he'd just exited and leaned in to murmur, "I hope you skipped the cat."

She'd been waiting for him? The notion tripped him up even more than her wholly American, wholly sexy perfume, for some odd reason.

"I, uh, did. Skip the cat," he clarified as he caught her joke in reference to the restaurant's name. "They were fresh out."

Her smile set off a round of sparks he'd rather not have over his brother's intended match.

"Maybe next time."

"Maybe next time you'll just come inside and eat with me instead of skulking around outside like a stalker," he suggested and curled his lip. What was he *doing*—asking her out? Bad idea.

One of her eyebrows quirked up above the frame of her sunglasses. "I can say with absolute authority that me noticing you heading into a restaurant and accidentally-on-purpose hanging around hoping to run into you does not qualify as stalking. Trust me, I'm a bit of an expert. I have the police report to prove it."

He had a hard time keeping his own eyebrows from shooting up. "You're a convicted stalker?"

Her laugh was quite a bit more amused this time. "Not yet. Don't go and ruin my perfect record now either, okay?" She shrugged and slipped off her sunglasses. "I picked up a stalker in Miami a couple of years ago. So I'm pretty familiar with American law. I would hope it's reasonably similar in Alma."

Sobering immediately, he tamped down the sudden and violent urge to punch whomever had threatened Bella's peace of mind. She'd mentioned it so casually, as if it wasn't a big deal, but it bloody well *was*. "What do you mean, you picked up a stalker? Like you went to the market to get milk and you just couldn't resist selecting a nutter to shadow you all the way home? No more jokes. Is he in jail?"

That may have come out a little more fiercely than he'd intended, but oh, well. He didn't take it back.

Wide-eyed, she shook her head. "He was practically harmless. A little zealous with his affections, maybe. I was out for the evening and he broke into my bedroom, where he waited for me to come home, bouquet of flowers in hand, like we were a couple. Or at least that was his sworn testimony. When my father found out, he immediately called the police, the mayor of Miami and the CEO of the company who'd sold him the security system installed on the grounds. I'm afraid they were rather harsh with the intruder."

Harmless? Anyone who could bypass a security system was far from harmless.

"As well they should have been." James developed an instant liking for Bella's obviously very level-headed father. "Was that the extent of it? Do I need to worry about the nutter following you across the pond?"

James had had his share of negative attention, invasions of privacy and downright hostile encounters with truly disturbed people. But he had fifty pounds and eight inches on Bella, plus he knew how to take care of himself. Bella was delicate and gorgeous and worthy of being treated like the princess she was. The thought of a creepy mouth-breather following her through the streets of Alma in hopes of doing depraved things made him furious.

"I doubt it. I haven't heard a peep from him in two years." She contemplated James with a small smile and crossed her arms over the angular sundress she wore. "You seem rather fierce all of a sudden. Worried about me?"

"Yes," he growled and shook his head. She was not any

of his concern—or at least she shouldn't be. "No. I'm sure your security is perfectly adequate."

He waved at the pair of ex-military types who waited a discreet distance away.

"Oh, yeah. My father insisted." Her nose wrinkled up delicately. "I'm pretty sure they're half security and half babysitters."

"Why do you need a babysitter?"

He couldn't leave it alone, could he? He should be bidding her good afternoon and running very fast in the other direction. But she constantly provoked his interest, and it was oh-so-deliberate. She wasn't walking away either and he'd bet it was because she felt the attraction sizzling between them just as much as he did.

Hell, everything he'd learned about her thus far indicated she liked the hint of naughtiness to their encounters... because they weren't supposed to be attracted to each other.

"I have a tendency to get into trouble." She waggled her brows. "These guys are here to keep me honest. Remind me that I have royal blood in my veins and a responsibility to the crown."

That was too good of a segue to pass up. "Really? What kind of trouble?"

"Oh, the worst kind," she stressed and reached out to stroke his arm in deliberate provocation. "If you've got a reputation to uphold, you'd best steer clear."

The contact of her nails on his bare arm sang through him. This was the most fun he'd had all day. "Sweetheart, I hate to disillusion you, but I've managed to ruin my reputation quite nicely all by my own self. Hanging out with you might actually improve it."

"Huh." She gave him a wholly inappropriate once-over that raised the temperature a few thousand degrees. "I'm dying to know. What did you do?"

"You really don't know?" That would be a first.

When she shook her head, he thought about glossing

over it for a half second, but she'd find out soon enough anyway. "Mishap in Rio. Some unfortunate photographs starring me and a prostitute. I swear, money never came up, but there you go. The world didn't see it as an innocent mistake."

Gaze locked on his, she squeezed his arm. "Man after my own heart. Of all the things I thought we might have in common, that was not it. I'm recovering from my own photographer-in-the-bushes fiasco. Cretins."

"Oh, that's too bad. Sorry."

A moment of pure commiseration passed between them. And it spread into something dangerously affecting. They shared a complete lack of reverence for rules, their chemistry was off the charts and they were both in Alma trying to find their footing. It was practically criminal that he couldn't explore her gorgeous body and even more attractive mind to his heart's content.

But he couldn't. While he might have competed with Will over women in the past, this one was different. James wasn't in a good place to start anything with a woman anyway, especially not one who would live in the public eye for the foreseeable future. She needed to be with Will, who would take care of her and not sully her with failure.

Not to mention that his father seemed to have struck some kind of bargain with the Montoro family. Until James knew exactly what that entailed, he couldn't cross the line he so badly wanted to.

She'd flat out told him he'd have to be the strong one, that he should stop tempting her. So that was the way it had to be.

James smiled and slipped his own sunglasses over his eyes so she couldn't read how difficult this was going to be for him. "Nice to see you again, Bella. I've got an appointment I'm late for so I've got to dash."

Casual. No commitment to calling her later. Exactly the right tone to brush her off.

She frowned and opened her mouth, but before she could say something they'd both likely regret, he added, "You should ring Will. Cheers," and whirled to take off down the boardwalk as fast he could.

Being noble tasted more bitter than he would have ever anticipated.

Three

James's rebuff stayed with Bella into the evening.

Apparently he wasn't of the same mind that a match between the Rowlings and Montoros could work just as easily between James and Bella as it could with his brother.

Being forced into a stiff, formal dinner with her father didn't improve her mood. Gabriel and Serafia were supposed to be there, too, which was the only reason Bella agreed, but the couple had yet to show.

Five bucks said they'd lost track of time while indulging in a much more pleasurable activity than dinner with Little Sister and Frosty Father. Lucky dogs.

Bella spooned up another bite of Marta's gazpacho, one of the best things the chef had prepared so far, and murmured her appreciation in case her father was actually paying attention to her today. But her mind was back on the boardwalk outside El Gatito. She'd have sworn the encounter with James would end with at least a kiss in the shadows of a storefront. Just to take the edge off until they got behind closed doors and let the simmering heat between them explode.

"Isabella." Her father's voice startled her out of an X-rated fantasy that she shouldn't have envisioned at all, let alone at the dinner table.

Not because of the X factor, but because it had starred James, who had cast her off with the lovely parting gift of his brother. *Call Will.* As if James had already grown tired of her and wanted to be clear about what her next steps should be.

"Yeah, Dad?" He must have realized that they were actually sitting at the same table. For once. She couldn't remember the last time they'd eaten together.

"You should know your great-aunt Isabella has decided to spend her last days in Alma. She arrived this morning and is asking after you."

Sudden happy tears burned Bella's eyelids. "Oh, that's the best news ever. Isn't she going to stay here with us?"

"The restoration of the monarchy is topmost on your aunt's mind." Rafael's gaze bored into her; he was no doubt trying to instill the gravity of royal protocol. "Therefore, she is staying in Del Sol. She wished to be close to El Castillo del Arena, so that she may be involved in Gabriel's coronation to the extent she is able."

Bella swore. Del Sol was, what? An hour away? Fine time to realize she should have taken her father up on the offer of a car…except she hadn't wanted to learn all the new traffic laws and Spanish road signs. Too late now— she'd have to take the chauffeured town car in order to visit Tía Isabella.

"Playa Del Onda is practically like Miami." Bella grumbled, mostly to herself. "You'd think she'd prefer the coast."

Her father put his spoon by his plate even though his bowl of gazpacho was still almost full. It hadn't been long enough since the last time they'd dined together for her to forget that meant a subject of grave importance was afoot and it wasn't her aunt's preference of locale.

"I have another matter to discuss. How was your first meeting with Will Rowling?"

Biting back a groan, she kept eating in a small show of defiance. Then she swallowed and said, "I haven't scheduled it yet."

Her father frowned. "I have it on good authority that you spoke to him today. On the boardwalk."

Spies? Her father had stooped to a new low. "I wasn't talking to Will. That was James."

Oh, duh. Her brand new security-guards-slash-babysitters had spilled the beans. Too bad they were the wrong beans.

Rafael's brows snapped together. "I cannot make myself more clear. Will Rowling is the man you should be pursuing."

Bella abandoned her spoon and plunked her elbows on the table to lean forward, so her father didn't miss her game face. "What if I like James better?"

Never mind that James had washed his hands of her. Regardless, it was the principle of the thing. Her father liked to try and run her life but failed to recall that Bella's typical response was to tell him to go to hell.

"James Rowling is bad news wrapped with trouble," Rafael shot back with a scowl. "He is not good enough for my daughter."

It seemed as if James had quoted this exact conversation to her yesterday on the beach. What was he, psychic? James's comment about the photographs that had gotten him into trouble crossed her mind and she realized there must be more to the story. She actually knew very little about the man other than the way he made her feel when he looked at her.

She eyed her father. What if Rafael had *told* James to brush her off? Would James have listened? She wouldn't put it past her father to interfere and now she wished she'd chased James down so she could ask. Shoot. She'd have to arrange another accidental meeting in order to find out.

"Maybe I'd like to make that decision on my own."

"Perhaps you need a few more facts if you're determined to undo the work I've already done on your behalf." Her father rubbed his graying temple. "Will Rowling is the next CEO of Rowling Energy, and he will be of paramount importance to your brother's relationship with the entire European oil market. How do you suppose the Montoros will lead a country rich with oil if we do not have the appropriate alliances in place?"

"Gabriel's smart. He'll figure it out," she said, but it came out sounding a little sullen. As smart and capable as Gabriel may be, he'd never been king before and besides, Alma hadn't had a king in a long time, so her brother would be a bit of a trailblazer.

She owed it to Gabriel to give him a leg up.

"Have you given any thought to Will Rowling's feelings, Isabella? You haven't reached out to him in the three days since you've arrived. You could not have insulted him more if you tried."

No, she hadn't thought of that. She swore. Her father had a very small point. Miniscule. But a point nonetheless. How would she feel if Will had come to Miami to meet her and then didn't call her, choosing instead to flirt outrageously with her best friend, Nicole, for example?

She'd hunt Will down and tell him to his face what a dog he was. So why should she get a pass to do whatever pleased her? It didn't matter if her father had scared off James—this was about doing what she said she'd do.

"I'll meet Will. Tomorrow, if he's free," Bella promised and turned her attention to eating. The faster the gazpacho disappeared, the faster she could as well.

It didn't go down as well this time. Righteousness wasn't as fun as it looked in the brochure.

* * *

Will Rowling took Bella's call immediately, cleared his schedule for the next morning and agreed to take her on a tour of Alma. He'd been very pleasant on the phone, though his British accent sounded a bit too much like James's for her liking.

When Will picked her up at 10:30 a.m. on the dot, she flung the door open and actually had a bad Captain Obvious moment when she realized Will *looked* like James, too. *Duh.* As common as fraternal twins were among the moneyed set of Miami, she'd never actually met a set of identical twins.

She studied him for a long second, taking in the remarkable resemblance, until he cleared his throat and she found a dose of manners somewhere in her consciousness. "I'm so sorry! Hello. You must be Will."

"I don't know if I must be, but I am Will," he agreed.

Was that a joke? Trying not to be too obtrusive, she evaluated his expression but it was blank. With James, she never had to wonder. "I'm Bella, by the way."

"I assumed so. I have your picture."

Of course he did. And this was her house. Wasn't this fun? "Are you ready to go?"

"Yes, if you are." With a smile that didn't reach his eyes, he held out a hand toward his car, and waited until she left the house to follow her so he could help her into the passenger seat.

Will climbed into the driver's seat and buckled his seat belt carefully before starting the car, which guilted Bella into fastening hers as well. Seat belts. In an itty-bitty place like Alma, where nothing happened.

She sighed and pasted on a bright smile. "Safety first."

Usually she trotted that line out during a condom discussion. She almost cracked a joke along those lines, but something told her Will might not appreciate the parallel. Sinking down in her seat, she scouted for a topic of discussion. They were supposed to be seeing how they meshed, right?

Will must have had a similar thought process because he spoke first. "Thanks for arranging this, Bella. I'm chuffed to show you around Alma, but I'd like to know what you might be interested in seeing. Anything jump out at you? I'm at your command."

Did he mean that in the double-entendre way? A provocative rejoinder sprang to her lips that she'd have let fly if she'd been in the car with James. Should she flirt with Will, the way she normally did on a date, or would that just lead to him taking her up on it, when she wasn't even sure she wanted him to? Maybe she should just be herself, but what if Will hated her immediately? Would her father lay another guilt trip on her?

All of this second-guessing was making her nuts. She wasn't with James, and *everyone*—including James— wanted her to make nice with the proper Rowling. Yeah, she'd looked up James last night, finding far more information about him than she'd expected, and little of it would fit the definition of the word *proper*.

No one, not even James, had thought it relevant to mention the man was a professional soccer—*football* in Europe, apparently—player. Since he appeared to have quite a bit of fame, maybe he'd assumed she already knew. Regardless, bad press followed James around like it did her. No wonder her father had nearly had a heart attack when she mentioned James's name. He was the very opposite of the proper brother.

Proper pretty much covered Will's personality. Five minutes in, and judging by the stiff set of Will's shoulders, he wasn't as much of a fun time as his brother. Hopefully, she'd judged wrong and would soon discover otherwise.

"Thanks," she responded. "I've only seen the coast and a bit of Del Sol. Why don't you pick, since this is your home?"

"No problem." He shot her a small but pained smile, cluing her in that this whole set up might be as difficult for him as it was for her.

She should give him a break. "So, Will. How long have you lived in Alma?"

An innocuous enough subject, hopefully, and given the brothers' accents, it was a safe bet they hadn't been born here.

"Since I was seven. My father moved us here from England."

"Oh, that must have been quite an adventure."

She'd lived in Miami her whole life and living someplace new did have appeal for that reason alone. If only this arranged marriage business hadn't soured the experience of coming to Alma, she'd be having a blast. And that was why she still didn't think of it as her home... She still reserved the right to go back to Miami and play aunt instead of princess if the royal pressure grew too great.

Though with Tía Isabella's arrival in Alma, going home held much less appeal.

Will's face remained expressionless, but he tapped his pinky on the steering wheel in a staccato rhythm as he drove north out of Playa Del Onda along the coastal road that circled the main island.

"The move was difficult," he said shortly and paused so long, she wasn't sure he planned to continue. But then he said, "My mother had just died."

"I'm sorry," Bella murmured. "That *would* be difficult on young boys."

All at once, she realized this was James's history as well as Will's. And now she was absurdly interested in learning more. The gorgeous deep blues of the bay unfurled as far as the eye could see on her right but she ignored the spectacular view in favor of watching Will.

"Thanks." He glanced in the rearview mirror and double-checked the side mirrors before changing lanes. Will Rowling might very well be the most careful driver she'd ever met. "Look, let's just get all of it out on the table, shall we?"

"Depends on what you mean by *all* and *table*," she countered, a little puzzled by his abrupt change of subject.

Was this the part of the date where he expected her to air all her dirty laundry? She'd never had a long-term relationship, never wanted one, never thought about what went into establishing a foundation for one. Maybe they were supposed to spill deep, dark secrets right off the bat. She was *so* not on board with that.

"About the arranged marriage," he clarified. "We should clear the air."

"I'm not a lesbian looking for a fake husband and I don't have a crazy uncle chained up in the closet, if that's what you're fishing for."

He flashed a brief smile, the most genuine one yet, giving her a glimpse of what he might be like if he loosened up a little. "I wasn't fishing. I meant, I wanted to tell you that marriage wasn't my idea. I'm not after your title or your fortune."

"Oh. Then what are you after?"

The smile vanished as his expression smoothed out into the careful nothingness he'd worn since the first moment. "Aligning myself with the Montoros through marriage is advantageous for Rowling Energy. It would be fitting if we suited each other. That's the only reason I agreed to meet you."

Ouch. That was kind of painful. Was she actually disappointed his motives for this pseudo-date nearly matched hers word for word? Well, not really, but no woman liked to find out a man was only interested in her connections. At least he'd admitted it up front.

All on the table, indeed.

"Yeah. I get that. My father pretty much insisted that I get on a plane and fall in love. Not necessarily in that order." Her lips twisted into a grimace automatically.

"Since we're on the subject, would you really go through with it?"

"Marriage, you mean?" A shadow darkened his gaze though his eyes never left the road. "Rowling Energy is on the brink of gaining a starring role on the world's oil stage. Our alliance makes very good sense. My assumption is that you thought so as well."

"Wow." Bella blinked. Had he memorized that careful statement in one sitting or had he repeated it to himself in the shower for the past week so he could get it out without stumbling? "I bet you say that to all the girls."

If she'd ever had any shred of doubt about her ability to tolerate an arranged marriage, it had just been crushed under the heel of Will's ambition. There was no way she'd marry *anyone* unless the words *deliriously happy, scorching passion* and *eternal love* entered into the conversation about a hundred times first, and even then, vows would be far, far in the future.

His eyebrows rose slightly. "Meaning?"

She rolled her eyes. "I just hadn't pegged you for a romantic. That's all."

"It wasn't intended to be romantic," he explained, and she had the distinct impression he really thought she'd needed the clarification.

As nightmare dates went, this one hit the scale at about eleven point five. So much for being herself. *Check, please.*

"Will, I have a confession to make. Instead of seeing the sights, I'd really like a ride to Del Sol to visit my great-aunt Isabella." She blazed ahead before he could say no. "She's very sick and I'd like to see her. The timing is terrible, I realize, but my mind is just not where it should be for this outing."

Hitching a ride hadn't been her intent when she'd called him, but a savvy woman knew when to cut her losses and she might offend Will if she screamed bloody murder in his ear…which she might very well do if forced to spend five more minutes in his company.

This was not going to work out. Period. The last thing she wanted was to be stuck in a horrible marriage to a cold-hearted man, as her mother had been. If it didn't make you happy, why do it? Why do *anything* that didn't have fun written all over it?

"No problem." Will checked forty-seven points of the car's position and did a U-turn to head to the interior of the island. "I sensed that you were distracted. Glad to know the reason why."

Yet another reason they would never work—obviously Will read her about as well as she could read Spanish. She'd been the opposite of distracted, but only because she'd been hoping for a scrap of information about James, God knew why.

"Yeah, I'm a mess. My aunt has Parkinson's and her prognosis is…not good." Bella left it at that and choked back the wave of emotion for a situation she couldn't change and hated with all her heart.

Good thing Will wasn't her type. Now she had the morning free to visit Tía Isabella and she didn't even have to feel guilty about it because she'd gone out with Will, as ordered.

"I'm sorry," Will said earnestly. "You should definitely visit her. We can go out another time when you're feeling more in the mood for company and conversation."

Oh, so *she* was the problem in this equation? She scowled but didn't comment because then she might say something she couldn't take back about the stick up Will's butt. "Sure. That would be nice."

"Well, this may be an ill-timed invitation, then, but Rowling Energy is throwing a party tonight at my father's house for some of our elite associates. Would you care to attend as my date? Might be less pressure and more fun than being one-on-one like this, trapped in a small car."

How…reasonable. Oh, sure it was strictly an opportunity for Will to trot her out around his snobby business partners who only cared about whom he knew. She wasn't stupid. But a party was right up her ally and the magic word *fun* only sweetened the pot. With enough champagne, she might even forget the whole setup reeked of royal responsibility and actually have a good time. Less pressure, as advertised.

Maybe she'd misjudged Will Rowling. "I have the perfect dress."

"It's settled, then."

In no time and with only one internet map miscalculation, they found Tía Isabella's narrow cobblestone street in the heart of Del Sol. Like a true gentleman, Will helped Bella from the car at the door of her great aunt's rental house, and had a word with Tía Isabella's housekeeper to ensure Bella would have a return ride home. The housekeeper promised to have a car sent from Playa Del Onda, so Will took his leave.

All in all, Will seemed like a nice, upstanding guy. He was certainly handsome enough and had gorgeous aqua-colored eyes. Too bad she couldn't get the sexier, more exciting version she'd tripped over at the beach off her mind.

"Patrick James Rowling!"

James groaned and thought about ducking out the door of the sunroom and escaping Casa Rowling through the back gate. When his father three-named him, the outcome was never fun nor in his favor.

Actually, any time his father spoke to him it was unpleasant. Even being in the same room with Patrick Rowling reminded James that his mother was dead and it was his father's fault. Time healed all wounds—except the ones that never should have happened in the first place. If his father hadn't yelled at his mum, she wouldn't have left in tears that night back in Guildford. Then his mum's single-car accident would never have happened. He and

Will wouldn't have become motherless seven-year-old boys. The fractured Rowling family wouldn't have subsequently moved to Alma, where James didn't know anyone but Will, who was too shell-shocked to do anything other than mumble for nearly a year.

But all of that had happened and James would never forgive *or* forget.

As a result, James and Patrick gave each other a wide berth by mutual unspoken agreement, but it was harder to do when under the same roof. James should really get his own place, but he still wasn't sure if he planned to stay in Alma, so here he was.

Patrick Rowling, the man who'd named his first born after himself in a moment of pure narcissism, stormed into the sunroom and shoved a newspaper at James's chest with a great deal more force than necessary. "Explain this."

"This is commonly known as a newspaper." James drew out the syllables, ladening them with as much sarcasm as possible. "Many civilized nations employ this archaic method of communicating information and events to subscribers. Shall I delve into the finer points of journalism, or are we square on the purpose of this news vehicle?"

His father's face had grown a deeper, more satisfying shade of purple the longer James baited him. A thing of beauty. James moved his half-empty teacup out of the line of fire, in case of imminent explosion. It was Darjeeling and brewed perfectly.

"You can dispense with the smartass attitude. I've had more than enough of it from you to last a lifetime."

What he really meant was that he'd had enough of James doing the opposite of what Patrick commanded. But if James toed the line, how could he make his father pay for his sins? Of course, his father could never truly pay in a lifetime. The sad part was that James might have settled for an apology from his father for all the horrible things he'd caused. Or at least a confession. Instead, his father heaped praises on Will the Perfect Son and generally pretended James didn't exist.

Until James managed to get his attention by doing something beyond the pale. Like whatever had gotten the elder Rowling's dander up this time.

His father poked the paper again. "There's a rather risqué photo of you on the front page. Normally, I would brush it off as further proof you care nothing for propriety and only your own self-destruction. But as it's a photo of you with your brother's fiancée, I find it impossible to ignore."

"What?" His brother had a *fiancée*? "What are you talking about?"

James shoved his father's hand away and shifted the paper so he could see the front page. There it was, in full color. He whistled. What a gorgeous shot of Bella in his arms. Her hair all mussed and legs tangled in his. He might have to cut it out and frame it.

Wait… *Bella* was Will's fiancée? This was news to James. Last he'd heard, Bella planned to see how things went before committing to marriage. Had Will even *met* Bella yet?

"Your timing is impeccable, as always. Now that we're all caught up, please explain how you managed to create a scandal so quickly." Dear old Dad crossed his arms over the paunch he liked to pretend gave him a stately demeanor, but in reality, only made him look dumpy.

Obviously they were nowhere near caught up.

"Maybe that's Will—did you ever think of that?" James challenged mildly and went back to sipping his tea because he had a feeling he'd need the fortification.

"Your brother is with the Montoro princess as we speak and it's their first meeting."

Montoro princess. Really? James rolled his eyes. His father couldn't be more pretentious if he tried. "If they hadn't even met until today, how are they already engaged?"

Waving his hand with a snort, Patrick gave him a withering look. "Merely a formality. They will be engaged, mark my words. So as far as you're concerned, she's your brother's fiancée. Will is quite determined to woo her and I've never seen him fail at anything he set his mind to."

Despite what should be good news—his father had deliberately thrown the word *fiancée* in James's face even though it wasn't true—James's gut twisted at the thought of Will and Bella together. Why, he couldn't explain, when he'd been the one to suggest Bella should ring Will. Obviously, she'd taken his advice and rather quickly, too. He'd just run into her in town yesterday.

"Smashing. I hope they're having a fantastic time and fall madly in love so they can give you lots of royal babies, since that's the most important accomplishment a Rowling could hope to achieve." The sentiment had started out sincerely but halfway through, disappointment had tilted his mood. James lived his life with few regrets but stepping aside so Will had a fair shot with Bella ranked as a decision he'd questioned more than once.

"Don't change the subject. If you deliberately staged that picture with the princess to ruin your brother's chances, the consequences will be dire," his father warned.

James couldn't quite bite back the laugh that burst out. "Oh, please, no. Perhaps you'll disown me?"

What else could his father possibly do to him besides constantly express his displeasure in everything James did? Being signed with Real Madrid hadn't rated a mention. Being named captain of the Alma World Cup team wasn't worthy enough of a feat to get a comment.

Oh, but miss a goal—that had earned James an earful.

Patrick leaned forward, shoving his nose into James's space and into his business all at the same time. "If you don't stay away from the Montoro princess, I will personally ensure you never play football again."

James scoffed. "You're off your trolley. You have no power in my world."

And neither did James, not now. It pricked at his temper that his father would choose that method to strike at him. Patrick clearly failed to comprehend his son's life crisis if he didn't already know that James had managed to thoroughly subvert his own career with no help from anyone.

The threat gave him a perverse desire to prove he could come back from the twin failures of a missed goal and a dropped contract. He needed to play, if for no other reason than to show everyone James Rowling couldn't be kept down.

"Perhaps. Do you want to wager on that?"

James waved nonchalantly with one hand and clenched the other into a tight fist. What colossal nerve. A supreme act of will kept the fist in his lap, though letting it fly against the nearby wall might have ended the conversation quite effectively.

"Seems like pretty good odds to me, so don't be surprised if I roll the dice with Bella." He waggled his brows. "I think that picture is enough of an indicator that she fancies me, don't you think?"

Which might have been true when the picture was snapped, but probably wasn't now that he'd stepped aside. Will would be his charming self and Bella would realize that she could have the best of both worlds—the "right" Rowling and her father's blessing. Probably better for everyone, all the way around.

Deep down, James didn't believe that in the slightest. He and Bella had a spark between them, which wouldn't vanish with a hundred warnings from the old geezer.

"The monarchy is in its fledgling stages." Patrick hesitated for the first time since barging into the sunroom and James got the impression he was choosing his words carefully. "Rowling Energy has a unique opportunity to solidify our allegiance and favor through the tie of marriage. There is only one Montoro princess."

"And only one heir to the company," James said sourly. "I get it. Will's the only one good enough for her."

His father sighed. The weariness that carved lines into his face around his mouth had aged him quickly and added a vulnerability to his expression that James hadn't been prepared for. Patrick had never been anything other than formidable for as long as James could remember.

"I would welcome you at Rowling Energy if you expressed but a smidgen of determination and interest." Then his father hardened back into the corporate stooge he'd become since entering into the high stakes oil market. Dad had too many zeroes in his bank account balance to truly be in touch with his humanity. "Will has done both, with remarkable success. If you would think of someone other than yourself, you'd realize that Will has much to gain from this alliance. I will not be at the helm of Rowling forever. Will needs every advantage."

Guilt. The best weapon. And it might have worked if James truly believed all that drivel. Marrying into the royal family was about his father's ambition, not Will's.

"Maybe we should let Bella sort it on her own, eh?" James suggested mildly. He didn't mind losing to Will, as long as the contest was fair.

"There's nothing to sort," his father thundered, growing purple again. "Stay away from her. Period. No more risqué pictures. No more contact. Do not ruin this for your brother."

To put the cap on his mandate, Patrick Rowling stormed from the sun-room in much the same manner as he entered it. Except now Bella Montoro had been transformed into the ripest forbidden fruit.

James had never met a scandal he didn't want to dive headlong into, especially when it involved a gorgeous woman who clearly had the hots for him. Pissing his father off at the same time James introduced himself to the pleasures of Princess Bella was just a sweet bonus.

Four

Bella spent two wonderful hours catching up with her great aunt Isabella, but the sickly woman grew tired so easily. Coupled with the fact that Isabella's advanced Parkinson's disease meant she was bedridden, it was difficult for Bella to witness her once-vibrant aunt in this condition. Regardless, she kept a bright smile pasted on throughout their visit.

But even Bella could see it was time for her to leave lest she overtire Isabella.

Before she asked her aunt's nurse to call a cab, Bella took Isabella's hand and brought it to her cheek. "I'm glad you decided to come to Alma."

"This is where I choose to die," Isabella said simply with a half smile, the only facial expression she could still muster. "I will see Gabriel become king and my life will be complete."

"I wish you wouldn't say things like that."

It was depressing and wretched to think of the world spinning on without Isabella, whom Bella loved unconditionally and vice versa. Her throat burned with grief and unreconciled anger over a circumstance she couldn't change.

Geez, she'd been less upset when her mother had left. That had at least made sense. Parkinson's disease did not.

"It is but truth. All of us must make our lives what we can in the time allotted to us." Isabella paused, her voice catching. "Tell me. Have you visited the farmhouse yet?"

"What farmhouse?" Had her father mentioned something about a farmhouse and she'd been too busy ignoring him to remember? Shoot. She'd have done anything Isabella asked, even if the request came via her father.

"Oh, dear." Her aunt closed her eyes for a moment. "No, I don't believe I imagined it. It's white. In the country. Aldeia Dormer. Very important. My mother told me and Rafael of it. My brother is gone, God rest his soul, so I'm telling you. You must find it and…"

Trailing off with a blank expression, Isabella sat silent for a moment, her hand shaking uncontrollably inside Bella's as it often had even before her aunt's disease had progressed to include forgetfulness and the inability to walk.

"I'll find the farmhouse," Bella promised. "What should I do when I find it?"

"The countryside is lovely in the spring," her aunt said with bright cheer. "You take your young man with you and enjoy the ride."

"Yes, ma'am." Bella smiled. Wouldn't it be nice to actually have a "young man" in the sweet, old-fashioned sense that Isabella had meant? Bella had only mentioned Will because her father had apparently told Isabella all about the stupid arranged marriage. It was the first thing her aunt had asked after.

"Wear a red dress to the party tonight and take photographs." Isabella closed her eyes and just when Bella thought she'd fallen asleep, she murmured, "Remember we all have a responsibility to our blood. And to Alma. I wish Rafael could be here to see his grandson take the throne."

"Red dress it is," Bella said, skipping over the royal responsibility part because she'd had enough of that for a lifetime.

Wasn't it enough that she was going to the party as Will's date when she'd rather be meeting James there? And if James happened to show, would it be so much of a crime if she danced with him once or twice? She'd still be Will's date, just the way everyone wanted, but would also give herself the opportunity to find out if James had pawned her off on his brother because he didn't like her or because of some other reason.

Guilt cramped her stomach as her aunt remained silent. Yeah, so maybe Bella considered it a possible bonus that she might run into James at the party. Was that so bad?

"Isabella, I—" Bella bit her lip before she spilled all her angst and doubt over what her father had asked her to do by giving Will a chance. Her aunt was tired and didn't need to be burdened with Bella's problems.

"The farmhouse. It's part of the Montoro legacy, passed down from the original Rafael Montoro I, to his son Rafael II. And then to his son Rafael III. Remember the farmhouse, child," her aunt wheezed out in the pause.

"I will." Before she could change her mind again, Bella went for broke. "But I might take a different young man with me than the one my father wants me to marry. Would that be a bad thing?"

"You must make your own choices," her aunt advised softly. "But beware. All choices have consequences. Be sure you are prepared to face them."

Isabella's shaking hand went slack as she slipped off into sleep for real this time. Bella took her leave reluctantly and slid into the waiting car her father had sent for her, wishing her aunt wasn't so sick that they could only have half of a conversation.

What had Isabella meant by her warning? During the hour-long ride back to Playa Del Onda, Bella grappled with it. Unfortunately, she had a sinking feeling she knew precisely what her aunt had been attempting to tell her. Being born during a hurricane hadn't infused Bella with a curse that meant she'd always leave broken hearts in her wake. It was her own decisions that had consequences, and if she wanted to be a better person than she'd been in Miami, she had to make different, more conscious choices.

Hurricane Bella couldn't cut a swath through Alma, leaving broken pieces of her brother's reign in her wake. Or broken pieces of her father's agreement with Will's father. Mentioning all of Bella's ancestors hadn't been an accident—Isabella wanted her to remember her roots.

Either she had try for real with Will and then tell him firmly it wasn't going to work, or she had to skip the party. It wasn't fair to anyone to go with the intention of running into James for any reason.

By the time the party rolled around, Bella was second-guessing the red dress. She'd never worn it before but distinctly remembered loving it when she'd tried it on at the boutique in Bal Harbour. Now that she had it on… the plunging neckline and high slit in the skirt revealed a shocking amount of flesh. But she'd promised Isabella she'd wear red, and it was too late to find another dress.

And honestly, she looked divine in it, so… Sexy red dress got the thumbs up. If she and Will were going to get along, he'd have to accept that she liked to feel beautiful in what she wore. This dress filled the bill. And then some. If a neckline that plunged all the way to the dress's waistband caused a problem with Rowling's business associates, better she and Will both find out now they weren't a good match.

The chauffeur helped her into the back of the Montoro car. Thankfully, Will hadn't offered to pick her up so she had an easy escape if need be. *Please God, don't let me need an escape.*

Within ten minutes, the car had joined the line of Bentleys, Jaguars and limousines inching their way to the front steps of the Rowling mansion. Like the Montoros' house, the Rowlings' Playa Del Onda residence overlooked the bay. She smiled at the lovely sight of the darkened water dotted with lighted boats.

When Bella entered the double front doors, Will approached her immediately, as if he'd been waiting for her. His pleasant but slightly blank expression from earlier was still firmly in place and she bit back a groan. How long were they going to act like polite strangers?

Jaw set firmly, Will never glanced below her shoulders. Which sort of defeated the purpose of such a racy dress. What was the point of showing half her torso if a man wasn't even going to look at it?

"Bella, so nice to see you again," Will murmured and handed her a champagne flute. "That dress is stunning."

Okay, he'd just earned back all the points that he'd lost. "Thanks. Nice to see you, too."

His tuxedo, clearly custom-cut and very European, gave him a sophisticated look that set him slightly apart from the other male guests, most of whom were older and more portly. Will was easy on the eyes and commanded himself with confidence. She could do worse.

Will cleared his throat. "Did you have a nice afternoon?"

"Yes. You?"

"Dandy."

She sipped her champagne as the conversation ground to a halt. Painfully. Gah, normally she thrived on conversation and loved exchanging observations, jokes, witty repartee. Something.

The hushed crowd murmured around them and the tinkle of chamber music floated between the snippets of dialogue, some in English, some in Spanish. Or Portuguese.

Bella still couldn't tell the difference between the two despite hearing Spanish spoken by Miami residents of Cuban descent for most of her life.

She spotted her cousin Juan Carlos Salazar across the room and nearly groaned. While they'd grown up together after his parents died, he'd always been too serious. Why wasn't he in Del Sol managing something?

Of course, he looked up at that moment and their gazes met. He wove through the crowd to clasp Will's hand and murmur his appreciation for the party to his hosts. Juan Carlos was the kind of guy who always did the right thing and at the same time, made everyone else look as if they were doing the wrong thing. It was a skill.

"Bella, are you enjoying the party?" he asked politely.

"Very much," she lied, just as politely because she had skills, too, just not any that Juan Carlos would appreciate. "I saw Tía Isabella. I'm so glad she decided to come to Alma."

"I am as well. Though she probably shouldn't be traveling." Juan Carlos frowned over his grandmother's stubbornness, which Bella had always thought was one of her best traits. "Uncle Rafael tried to talk her out of it but she insisted."

The Montoros all had a stubborn streak but Bella's father took the cake. Time for a new subject. "How are things in the finance business?"

"Very well, thank you." He shot Will a cryptic glance. "Better now that you're in Alma working toward important alliances."

She kept her eyes from rolling. Barely. "Yes, let's hear it for alliances."

Juan Carlos and Will launched into a conversation with too many five-syllable words for normal humans to understand, so Bella amused herself by scrutinizing Will as he talked, hoping to gather more clues about his real personality.

As he spoke to Juan Carlos, his attention wandered, and Bella watched him watch a diminutive dark-haired woman in serviceable gray exit by a side door well away from the partygoers. An unfamiliar snap in Will's gaze had her wondering who the woman was. Or rather, who she was to Will. The woman's dress clearly marked her as the help.

Will didn't even seem to notice when Juan Carlos excused himself.

"Do you need to attend to a problem with the servants?" Bella inquired politely.

She'd gone to enough of her parents' parties to know that a good host kept one eye on the buffet and the other on the bar. Which was why she liked attending parties, not throwing them.

"No. No problem," Will said grimly and forced his gaze back to Bella's face. But his mind was clearly elsewhere.

Which told her quite a bit more about the situation than Will probably intended. Perhaps the dark-haired woman represented at least a partial answer for why Will seemed both pained by Bella's presence and alternatively agreeable to a marriage of convenience.

Bella had come to the party as requested by God and everyone and she deserved a chance with Will. He owed it to her, regardless of whether he had something going on with the diminutive maid.

"Look, Will—"

"Let's dance." He grabbed her hand and led her to the dance floor without waiting for an answer, off-loading their champagne glasses onto a waiter's tray as they passed by.

Okay, then. Dancing happened to be one of her favorite things about parties, along with dressing up and laughing in a private corner with someone she planned to let strip her naked afterward.

For some reason, the thought of getting naked with Will made her skin crawl. Two out of three wasn't bad, though, was it?

The quartet seated in the corner had switched from chamber music to a slightly less boring bossa nova–inspired piece. Not great, but she had half a chance of finding a groove at least.

Was this how the people of Alma partied? Or had the glitzy Miami social scene spoiled her? Surely not. Alma was one of the wealthiest countries in the European Union. What was she missing?

Halfway into the song, Will had yet to say a word and his impersonal hand at her waist might as well have belonged to an eighty-year-old grandfather. This might go down in history as the first time a man under thirty had danced with her and not used it as an excuse to pull her into his strong embrace. It was as if Will had actually wanted to *dance* or something.

None of this screamed, "I'm into you."

Perhaps the problem with this party lay with the host, not the country. Will might need a little encouragement to loosen up.

When the interminably long dance finally ended, Bella smiled and fanned herself as if she'd grown overheated. "My, it's a little warm in here."

Will nodded. "I'll get you another glass of champagne."

Before he could disappear, she stopped him with a hand on his arm, deliberately leaning into it to make the point. "That's okay. Let's go out on the terrace and talk."

The whole point was to get to know each other. The car trip hadn't worked. Dancing hadn't worked. They needed to try something else.

"Maybe in a few minutes," Will said with a glance around the room at large. "After I've played the proper host."

Disappointment pulled at her mouth but she refused to let a frown ruin her lipstick. "I hope you won't mind if I escape the heat for a bit by myself."

For a moment, she wondered if he'd really let her go.

He'd invited her, after all, and hadn't introduced her to one person yet. This was supposed to be a date, wasn't it?

"Certainly." Will inclined his head toward the double glass doors off the great room. "I'll find you later."

Fuming, Bella wound through the guests to the terrace—by herself!—and wondered when she'd lost her edge. Clearly a secluded terrace with a blonde American in half a dress didn't appeal to Will Rowling. What did—dark-haired housekeepers?

Great, she thought sourly. Bella had come to the party with the genuine intent of seeing where things might go with Will, because she said she would. Because she'd bought into the hoopla of being a princess, which came with responsibilities she'd never asked for nor wanted any part of.

But she'd done it, only to be hit over the head with the brutal truth yet again. The man her father wanted her to marry had less than zero interest in her as a person. She wouldn't be surprised to learn Will was perfectly okay with a hard-core marriage of convenience, complete with separate bedrooms and a paramour on the side.

Sounded an awful lot like her parents' marriage, and *that* she wanted no part of.

She shuddered, despondent all at once. Was it asking too much for someone to care what she would actually have to sacrifice with this mess her father had created?

The night was breathtaking, studded with stars and a crescent moon. Still, half the stone terrace lay in shadow, which went perfectly with her mood. Leaning on the railing, she glanced down into the crash of ocean against the cliff below.

"Thinking of jumping?"

The male voice emanating from behind her skittered down her spine, washing her in a myriad of emotions as her heart rolled and her pulse quickened. But she didn't turn to face him because she was afraid if she actually glimpsed

James for even a fraction of a second, all of her steely resolve to work things out with his brother would melt like gelato in the sun. And the leftover hot sticky mess would be difficult to clean up indeed.

"Would you stop me?" she murmured.

"No. I'd hold your hand all the way down, though."

Her eyelids fluttered closed. How had he managed to make that sound so daringly romantic?

The atmosphere shifted as he moved closer. She could feel him behind her, hear the intake of his breath. A sense of anticipation grew in the silence, peppering her skin with goose pimples and awareness.

Before it grew too intense, she blurted out, "I called Will."

James wasn't for her. She needed to keep reminding herself that.

"I gathered that." He sounded amused and reckless simultaneously. "I plan to personally drive him to the eye doctor tomorrow."

"Oh? Is he having problems with his eyes?"

"Obviously. Only a blind man would let you out of his sight, especially if he knew you planned to be alone on a moonlit terrace. Any plonker could be out here, waiting to ravish you."

She'd been so wrong. Other than a similar accent, James's voice was nothing like Will's. Will had yet to lose the ice while James breathed pure fire when he spoke.

"Good thing his moral, upstanding brother is the only one out here. He wouldn't dare lay a finger on me."

Maybe James needed a reminder that Bella and Will were supposed to get married, too. After all James had been the one to cool things off between the two of them, which had absolutely been the right thing to do.

"Yeah? While Will's having his eyes examined, maybe I'll get my IQ checked, then," James said silkily.

"Feeling a little brainless this evening?"

"I definitely feel like my brain has turned to mush. I think it's that dress. Your bare back framed by that little bit of fabric…it makes me imagine all sorts of things that probably aren't very smart." The frank appreciation in his voice floated through the still night, wrapping around her deliciously. "Let me see the front."

"No." Feeling exposed all at once, she crossed her arms. "I didn't wear this dress for you."

"Shame. I'm the only one here who fully appreciates what's underneath it."

In a flash, her core heated with the memory of being in James's arms on the beach, his hard body flush with hers.

"You shouldn't speak to me like that," she said primly, and nearly gasped as he drew achingly close to her back. She could sense his heat and it called to her.

"Because you don't like it?" he murmured, his mouth not two inches from her ear in a deliberate tease that shot sensation down the back of her throat.

Her breath caught and she gripped the railing lest her weak knees give out. "Because I do."

He laughed and it spiked through her with fingers of warmth.

"That's right," he said smoothly, as if recalling something critically important. "You're weak and liable to give in to temptation. Everything I've always wanted in a woman."

"That's so funny. I'd swear you brushed me off at our last meeting," she couldn't help but reply. It still stung, despite all the reasons why she suspected he'd done so.

"I did," he admitted in an unprecedented moment of honesty. Most men she'd ever met would have tried to pass it off, as if she'd been mistaken. "You know why."

"Because you're not interested."

The colorful curse he muttered made her smile for some reason. "You need *your* IQ checked if you believe that."

"Because my father scared you off?"

"Not even close."

"Because I'm supposed to be with Will," she said definitively and wished it hadn't come out sounding so bitter.

"Yes." James paused as if to let that sink in. "Trust me. It was not easy. But he's my brother."

"So you're okay with it if I marry Will?"

She imagined Christmas. That would be fun, to sit next to her boring husband who was screwing another woman on the side while the man she'd been dreaming about sat across the room. As Mr. Rowling carved the turkey, she could bask in the warm knowledge that she'd furthered a bunch of male ambition with her sacrifice to the royal cause.

"Is that what you want?" he asked quietly, his voice floating out on the still night air.

The question startled her. She had a choice. Of course she did. And now she needed to make it, once and for all.

The night seemed to hold its breath as it waited for her to speak. This was it, the moment of truth. She could end this dangerous attraction to the wrong brother forever by simply saying yes. James would walk away.

Something shifted inside, warring with all the sermons on responsibility and family obligations. And she couldn't stand it any longer.

She didn't want Will.

Whirling, she faced James, greedily drinking him, cataloguing the subtle differences in his features. He and Will weren't identical, not to her. The variances were in the way James looked at her, the way her body reacted. The heat in this man's gaze couldn't be mistaken. He was all James and 100 percent the object of her desire.

She let her gaze travel over his gorgeous body, clad in a tuxedo that fit like an extension of his skin, fluid and beautiful. And she wanted nothing more than to see the secrets it hid so carefully beneath the fabric.

He raked her with a once-over in kind that quickened her

core with delicious tightness. *That* was how a man should look at you in such a dress. As if he'd been presented with every last fantasy in one package.

"The back was good," he rasped, his voice clogged with undisguised desire. "But the front…"

Delighted that she'd complied with Isabella's fortuitous request to wear red, she smiled. "I do like a man at a loss for words."

Moonlight played over his features and glinted off the obscenely expensive watch on his wrist as he swept up her hand and drew her closer. So close, she could almost hear his heart beating.

"Actions speak louder and all that." His arm slid around her waist, pulling her to within a hairsbreadth of his body and she ached for him to close the distance. "Plus, I didn't want to miss your answer."

"Answer to what?"

He lowered his head to murmur in her ear, "What it is that you want."

If she wanted Will, Bella had about two seconds to say so, or James would be presenting the woman in his arms with some hot and heavy temptation. He preferred to get on the same page before that happened because he had a bad feeling *he* might be the weak one on this terrace.

With so much forbidden fruit decked out in a mouthwatering dress that screamed sin and sex, he'd rather not put his ability to resist Bella to the test. But he would resist if she said no, regardless of whether he'd been baiting her in hopes of getting her to break first. Because then he'd be in the clear if she came on to him, right?

The sharp intake of her breath and a sensuous lift of her lips gave him all the nonverbal communication he needed. Then she put the icing on it with a succinct, "Will who?"

The gap between their bodies slowly vanished until their torsos brushed, but he couldn't have said if he closed it or she did. This was not what he'd planned when Bella had inadvertently joined him on the terrace, but it was certainly what he'd fantasized might happen if she'd given him the slightest encouragement.

With her lithe little body teasing his, her curves scarcely contained by that outrageous dress, he could hardly get his mind in gear long enough to form complete sentences. "You could have just said that from the outset."

"You could have said *call me instead of Will* on the boardwalk."

Not if he'd hoped to sleep at night he couldn't have. Of course, he'd done little of that anyway, tossing and turning as he imagined this gorgeous, vibrant woman with his brother.

He nodded in concession, hardly breathing for fear of alerting her to how very turned on he was. "It was my one noble gesture for the decade. Don't expect another one."

She laughed and he felt it vibrate against his rock-hard lower half, which did not improve matters down below. Dangerous and forbidden did it for him in the worst way and when both came in a package like Bella, he might as well surrender to the moment right now. They were both aware of where this was headed, weren't they?

"You know, you spend a lot of time blabbing about how wicked you are, but I've yet to see evidence of it." Her brow arched saucily, turning silvery in the moonlight. "What happened to my man of action?"

"You wanna play?" he growled and slid his hand to the small of her back, pushing her deep into the crevices of his body. "Here's round one of How Bad Can James Be?"

Tipping up her head, he captured her smart mouth with his lips, molding them shut while tasting her simultaneously. What started as a shut-up kiss instantly transformed, becoming slow and sensuous and exploratory as he delved into her sweetness. She met him stroke for stroke, angle for angle, silently begging him to take her deeper.

He *finally* had Bella in his arms. Exactly as he'd ached to have her since releasing her from their first embrace.

Still in the throes of an amazing kiss he never wanted to end, he pinned her against the stone railing, wedging their bodies tight and leaving his hands free to roam where they pleased.

And that creamy expanse of flesh from neck to waist had been calling his name for an eternity. Almost groaning with the pleasure of her mouth under his, he slid a palm north to let his fingertips familiarize themselves with her bare back. Heated, smooth flesh greeted his touch. Greedily, he caressed it all and she moaned throatily, flattening her back against his palm, pleading for more.

He gave it to her.

Nearly mindless with the scent of Bella filling his head, he held her closer in his arms, sliding a knee between her legs to rub at her sweet spot. Heavenly. He wanted to touch every part of her, to taste what he'd touched. To take them both to nirvana again and again as the blistering, forbidden attraction between them was allowed free reign once and for all.

Suddenly, she tore her mouth free and moved out of reach, breathing heavily. "That was…um—"

"Yeah." Earthshaking. Unprecedented. Hotter than Brazil in the summer. "Come back so I can do it again."

He reached for her and for a second, he thought she was going to do it. Her body swayed toward him and his mouth tingled in anticipation of locking on to those lips of hers again.

But then she shook her head, backing up another step. "I can't be with you like this. It's not fair to Will. We have to straighten everything out first."

Bloody hell. Will hadn't crossed his mind once while James kissed his brother's date. Any of dear Father's business cronies could have come upon them on the terrace and there were few people in Alma who confused the twins.

Everyone knew James had inherited Grandfather Rowling's priceless antique watch—much to Patrick's chagrin. It was the first thing people looked for when in need of a handy way to identify the brothers.

"Yes, of course you're right." Though his body ached to yank her back into his arms, he gave her a pained smile instead. "This isn't over."

"Oh, no." She shot him an indecipherable look. "Not by half. The next time you and I are together, I will be naked and screaming your name."

His eyelids flew shut and he groaned. "Why can't that happen tonight?"

"Because as far as the rest of the world is concerned, Will is the Rowling I'm supposed to be with. I've had too many scandals mess up my life to knowingly create a preventable one. That's why it must be perfectly clear to everyone that Will and I are not getting married before you and I get naked."

Grimly, he nodded, the photo of the two of them on the front page fresh in his mind. They should probably address that, too, at some point, but he'd topped out on issues he could reasonably deal with.

"You should go. And go fast before I change my mind." Or lose it. "I'm fresh out of nobility *and* the capacity to resist you."

She whirled and fled. He watched her beautiful back as she disappeared inside the house, and then went in search of a bottle of Jameson to get him through what promised to be a long night indeed.

Five

James cornered Will in his Rowling Energy office at 9:05 a.m. This was the earliest James could recall being awake, dressed and out of the house in quite some time. But this cat-and-mouse game had grown tiresome, and the man who shared his last name, his blood and once upon a time, had even shared a womb, had the power to end it.

"Will."

James didn't cross the threshold out of respect for the fact that he was on his brother's turf. Instead, he waited for him to glance up from his report. Will's expression remained composed, though James caught a flash of surprise in the depths of his gaze, which the Master of Calm quickly banked.

"Yes?"

And now they'd officially exchanged two words this week. Actually, James couldn't remember the last time they *had* talked. They'd never been close. Hell, they were rarely on the same continent, but that wasn't really the reason. The divide had started the night their mum died and grown exponentially over the years.

"We have to talk. Can I come in?"

"Since you're here already, I suppose." Will's long-suffering sigh said he deserved a medal for seeing James on such short notice.

James bit back the sarcasm strictly because he was the one with the mission, though his brother's condescension pricked at his temper. The brothers would never see eye to eye, though why James cared was beyond him.

They'd taken different paths in dealing with the single most defining year of their lives, Will choosing to compensate for the loss of everything familiar by becoming whatever their father said, as long as the remaining parent paid attention to him.

James compensated for his mother's death by lashing out at his father, refusing to forgive the ultimate crime— though James could never run far enough or get into enough trouble to drown out the sound of his own conscience. While he'd never forgive his father for driving his mum out into the rainy night, back in the deepest reaches of his soul, he blamed himself more.

Because he'd heard them arguing and hadn't done anything. What if he'd run out of his hiding place to grab on to his mum and beg her not to leave? She wouldn't have. He knew she wouldn't have. But she'd probably assumed both her boys were asleep. One of them had been.

James took a deep, not at all calming breath as he settled into one of the wingback chairs flanking Will's desk. "It's about Bella."

"Ms. Montoro? What about her?"

James rolled his eyes. "Well, I was going to ask how serious you are about her, but that pretty much told me."

"How serious I…" Will's gaze narrowed. "You've got the hots for her."

That didn't begin to describe what had happened on the terrace last night. Or every moment since the princess had blinked up at him with those big eyes after upending his world. "If you're determined to see this arranged marriage through, I won't stand in your way."

Steepling his hands, Will sat back in his chair, contemplating James carefully. "Really? That's a first."

"What's that supposed to mean?"

"When was the last time you considered anyone above yourself? Especially when a woman is involved."

James was halfway out of his seat before he checked himself. Fisting his hand in his lap as he sat back down, he forced a smile. "I won't apologize for looking out for myself. No one else does. But I will concede the point. This woman is different."

He nearly choked on the words he hadn't consciously planned to say. But it was true. Bella wasn't like anyone else he'd ever met.

Smirking, Will nodded once. "Because she's earmarked for me."

Is that what he thought this was about? That James had come to Will in a fit of jealousy?

"Earmarked? Is that how you talk about her? Bella's a person, not a pile of money."

The nerve. Will had spent too much time in budget meetings if he equated a flesh-and-blood woman with reserve funds.

"Yes. But surely you realize we're talking about an arranged marriage. It's a form of currency, dating back to the dawn of time. No one is under a different impression."

James had a sick sort of realization that what Will described was probably quite right. Two fathers had struck a deal, bargaining away their children's future with no thought to what could or should go into a marriage decision. Namely, the desires of the bride and groom in question.

If he didn't miss his guess, Will accepted that. Embraced it. Thought it was a brilliant idea.

If James had known this was the case, he'd have taken

Bella straight to his room last night and skipped the formality of giving his brother a heads-up that things had changed. "Bella has a different impression. She's not interested in being bought *or* sold."

Will eyed him thoughtfully. "Why hasn't she come to me herself?"

"Because this is between you and me, brother. She didn't want to get into the middle of it." Which he fully appreciated, whether Will did or not. James had to look at himself in the mirror for the rest of his life and he'd prefer not to see his own guilty conscience staring back at him. "And she won't. Neither will I allow her to. If you say you're planning to pursue this ridiculous idea of aligning Rowling Energy to the Montoros through marriage, so be it. Just be sure you treat her like a princess."

Maybe James wasn't done being noble after all. He'd fully expected to walk in here and demand that Will release Bella from their fathers' agreement. But somehow he'd wound up caring more about Bella and how she was being marginalized than whether he'd cleared the way to sleep with her.

"I see." Comprehension dawned in Will's gaze. "You're the reason she left the party so quickly last night. Last I knew, she'd gone out on the terrace for some air, and the next, she'd begged off with a headache."

"I'm sorry," James said earnestly. "I didn't plan for any of this to happen. But Bella deserves better than to be thought of as currency. She's funny and incredible and—"

He broke off before he said something he couldn't take back, like *she's the hottest kisser I've ever met.* Somehow, he didn't think that would go over well.

"You've got it bad." Will didn't bother to hide his smirk. "Never would have thought I'd see the day. She's really got you wrapped, doesn't she?"

As if Bella called the shots or something? James tried to do the right thing one time and all he got was grief.

"She's important," James growled. "That's all."

Will grinned mischievously, looking more like Mum than he usually did. "Ha. I wouldn't be surprised if you proposed to her before her brother's coronation."

"Propose? You mean ask her to marry me?" Ice slid down James's spine and he threw up a hand to stave off the rest of Will's outpouring of madness. "That's not what's going on here. We're just… I'm not… It's that I didn't want to poach on your territory. It's not sporting."

"Gabriella. Paulinha. Abril." Ticking them off on his fingers, Will cocked his head. "I think there was another one, but her name escapes me."

Revisionist history of the worst kind. "If I recall, Abril went home with you. Despite the fact that I saw her first."

"But that's my point. We've competed over women in the past. But you have never come to me first." Will's phone rang, but he ignored the shrill buzz. "We've always subscribed to the may-the-best-man-win philosophy. So obviously Bella is the one."

Yeah, the one James wanted in his bed. That was it. Once they burned off the blinding attraction, they'd part amicably. "No way. You're reading into this."

An even worse thought occurred to him then. Did *Bella* think there was more going on here? Like maybe James wanted to take Will's place in the diabolical bridal bargain their fathers had struck? Surely not. There'd been plenty of flirting, and lots of use of the word *naked*. But no one had said anything about being serious.

Will shook his head, a smile still tugging at his lips. "I don't think so. Put your money where your mouth is."

"A bet? Seriously?" All the long hours in the service of Patrick Rowling's ego had obviously pickled his brother's brain.

"As a heart attack." Nodding at James's wrist, he pursed his lips for a beat. "Grandfather's watch. That's how bad I think you've got it. If you propose to Bella before Gabriel Montoro takes the throne, you give it to me, free and clear."

James laughed. "You are so on."

What a stupid thing to ask for. Will knew how much James loved his grandfather's watch. It was one of the few mementos from England that James had left, and Grandfather had given it to him on his eighteenth birthday. Losing it was not happening. Proposing to Bella was not happening, before the coronation or after.

Sucker's bet. James rubbed his hands together gleefully. "If I don't propose, then what? Make this worth my while."

"I'll come up with something."

James and Will shook on it.

"So this means the arranged marriage is totally off, right?" No point in going through all of this just to find out Will was toying with him.

"Totally off."

A glint in his brother's eye caught his crossways. "You were never interested in her."

"Never," Will confirmed solemnly. "Bella's got all the right parts and everything, and she would have opened up some interesting possibilities for Rowling. But she's not my type. I'm fine with cancelling the whole agreement."

Not his type. That was insane. How could Bella not be every red-blooded man's type? "You'll talk to Father?"

"Sure. It's better coming from me anyway. Now get out so I can run this company."

James got out. He had a naked princess in his future after all.

Bella's eyes started to ache after thirty minutes of trying to read the tiny map print.

"I give up," she muttered and switched off the lamp adorning her bedside table.

All of the words were in Spanish anyway. How was she

supposed to use this map Alex Ramon's assistant had given her to find the farmhouse Tía Isabella had mentioned?

When Bella had asked Rafael about it, he sent her to speak with Alex Ramon, Alma's deputy prime minister of commerce. His assistant helped her scour the royal archives until they found one solitary mention of the abandoned farmhouse in a long list of Montoro holdings. But there was little to go on location-wise other than *Aldeia Dormer*, the name of a tiny village.

At least Mr. Ramon's assistant had managed to find the key to the property tucked away in a filing cabinet, a real plus. Assuming the key still worked, that was.

Now she just had to find the farmhouse. Tía Isabella's urgency had taken root, not to mention a healthy dose of curiosity about how an old farmhouse counted as part of a legacy. There was no way Bella would actually give up.

Plus, finding the farmhouse was a project, her gift to Isabella. Bella needed a local with plenty of time on his hands and access to a vehicle to help her scour the countryside for this farmhouse. And who didn't mind ditching her babysitters-slash-security guys.

Her phone rang. She glanced at it and frowned at the unfamiliar number. That was the second time today and the first caller had been Will. Dare she hope this might be the brother she'd rather talk to? "Hello?"

"You haven't been to the beach all day." James's smooth voice slid through her like silk.

"Was I supposed to be at the beach?" With a wide grin, she flipped over on her back to stare at the ceiling above her bed, completely uninterested in cryptic maps now that she had a much better distraction.

"How else am I supposed to run into you?" he pointed out. "You never gave me your phone number."

Because he'd never asked. "Yet it appears I'm speaking to you on the phone at this very minute."

"A bloke has to be resourceful around this island if he wants to ask a princess out on a date. Apparently."

A little thrill burst through her midsection. After walking away from James at the party, she'd mentally prepared for any eventuality. A woman didn't get between brothers, and James, for all his squawking about being a bad boy, wouldn't have pursued her if Will had called dibs.

And then there was always the possibility James would grow weary of all the obstacles between them. She didn't have any guarantees she'd even hear from him again.

"This is your idea of resourceful? What did you do, hit up Will for my phone number?"

James cleared his throat. "I talked to him. About us."

That was pretty much an admission of how he'd gotten her number. "Yeah. He told me."

"Well, half my battle is won. My day will be complete if you would kindly get your gorgeous rear down to the beach."

Scrambling from the bed, Bella tore off her shorts as she dashed for the dresser and wedged the phone under her chin to pull out a bikini. "What if I'm busy?"

"Cancel. In fact, cancel everything for the rest of the day."

The rest of the day with James? She was so on board with that plan, she could hardly keep the giddiness in check. But she couldn't let *him* know how much she was into him. That was rule number one.

"You'll have to give me more than that in order for me to clear my schedule." She whipped her shirt off one-handed, knocking the phone to the floor. She cursed and dove for it. "I'm American. We invented high-maintenance dating. Make it worth my while."

Head tight to her shoulder so the phone didn't try another escape attempt, she wiggled out of her underwear.

"Trust me, sweetheart," he said with a chuckle. "I've been all over the world. I'm more than capable of handling one tiny American. If you want to find out how worth it I am, walk out the door."

"I'm not dressed," she informed him saucily. Even someone as fashion savvy as Bella couldn't tie a bikini with one hand. And for some reason, now that he knew she was naked, it was an oddly effective turn-on.

"Perfect," he purred. "I like a woman who can read my mind. What am I thinking right now?"

If it was anything close to what she was thinking, a public beach was not the best place for them to be together. "You're thinking that you'd better hang up so I can, you know, leave the house."

His laugh rolled through her and then cut off abruptly as the call ended. She hummed as she threw on her bikini and covered it with a short dress made of fishnet weave.

She hit the foyer in under three minutes and almost escaped without her security detail noticing her stealthy exit, when she heard the voice of doom call out behind her.

"Isabella."

Groaning, she turned to face her father since the cover up was just as see-through from the front as the back. The faster she withdrew from his clutches, the better. "Yeah, Dad."

"I understand you told Will Rowling you weren't interested in him. I'm very disappointed."

Of course he was. He'd have to smooth things over with Patrick Rowling and figure out another way to make everyone miserable.

"That's me. The disappointing daughter," she admitted lightly, hoping if she kept her cool, the extraction might go faster. She had a man waiting patiently for her on the beach.

"You cannot continue behaving this way. Marriage to Rowling will settle you and nothing else seems to work to that end. You must repair your relationship with him."

His hand flew up to staunch the protest she'd been about to voice.

"No, Isabella. This is a serious matter, among other serious matters I must discuss with you. However, I'm expected to accompany Gabriel to a royal function. Be here when I get back," her father commanded.

"Sure, Dad." She fled before he could tell her when he'd be back because then she could claim ignorance when she wasn't here.

Her stomach tightened as she walked down the narrow cliffside stairs to the beach. Why couldn't she have timed that better? The encounter put a damper on the joy she'd had since the moment she'd heard James's voice.

When her toes sank into the sand, she scoured the sun-worshippers for a glimpse of the whipcord physique she couldn't erase from her mind. James was easy to spot in a turquoise shirt that shielded his British complexion from the rays. Sunglasses covered his beautiful eyes and as always, he wore the expensive watch he never seemed to leave home without. He lay stretched out on a towel off to the side of the crowd, lounging in his own little cleared area.

"Thought you'd never get here," he commented when she flopped down next to him. He paused and whipped off his glasses to focus on her intently. "What's wrong?"

How bad was it that he made her so mushy just by noticing that she was a little upset? "Nothing. My father."

"Say no more." James shook his head and sat up to clasp her hand in his, squeezing it once. "I've been avoiding mine since the pictures hit."

"What pictures?"

"You don't know?" When she shook her head, he rubbed his face with his free hand. "Someone snapped us with me on top of you when you tripped over my chair the other day. We were on the front of the Playa Del Sol newspaper. And probably all the other ones, too. I'm sorry, I figured you'd seen them. Or had a confrontation with your father about them."

Oh, that explained a lot, especially Rafael's use of his boardroom voice. "I learned the hard way to never search my name on the internet, so no, I haven't seen the pictures. And I think I just narrowly missed that confrontation. The one I had was bad enough, but fortunately, he was too busy to give me a proper talking to. I'm supposed to be home when he gets back so I can obediently listen to his lecture. Oops."

James flashed a quick grin. "You're my kind of woman."

"We seem to have a flagrant disregard for authority in common, don't we?"

"When it makes sense," James corrected. "You're not sixteen. You're a grown woman who can make her own choices. If you want to be with me, you should get that opportunity, authority figures aside."

As much as she liked his point, she was still a member of the royal family and the idea of smarmy pictures floating around upset her, especially when the actual event had been so innocuous.

"So we're both rebels, but only when presented with pigheaded fathers?"

"Exactly." His thumb smoothed over hers and he had yet to return his sunglasses to their perch over his eyes. The way he was looking at her, as if he understood her so perfectly, they didn't even need words—it took a massive amount of willpower to not throw herself into his arms.

Why were they outside in plain sight again? Her babysitters could lumber down the stairs from the house at any moment, squelching what promised to be an adventurous day.

"This wasn't exactly what I had in mind for our first date," she remarked with an exaggerated glance around. "Too many people and I'm pretty sure I remember something about getting naked. I readily admit to bucking authority when called for, but I am not a fan of sand in certain places. What shall we do about that?"

James's blue eyes went sultry and he gripped her hand tighter. "A little bird told me you were high maintenance, so I was going to take you to dinner later at Casa Branca in Del Sol. But I see the huge gaping flaw in that plan since you would indeed have to be dressed for that."

"It's also pretty public. I'd love to escape prying eyes, security details and cameras for at least one night." She frowned. Was nowhere sacred enough to spend time with a man she was just getting to know without fear of creating a whole brand-new scandal? "Can we go back to your place?"

They certainly couldn't go to hers, not with the royal lecture pending.

"Ha." James rolled his eyes, turning them a myriad of blues in the sunlight. "I can only imagine dear old Dad's aneurism when I walk through the front door with you."

No, neither of them were sixteen but it felt that way when they couldn't even find a place to be alone without overbearing parents around. So it was time for an adult solution.

"New plan," Bella chirped. "I've heard a rumor of an abandoned farmhouse that's part of our family's royal property. But I don't know where it is. I need someone with a car and a good knowledge of the roads in Alma to help me find it. Know anyone like that who's also free to drive around with me?"

"James's Abandoned Farmhouse Locators, at your service." He bowed over her hand with mock ceremony. "Let's plan on making a night of it. We'll get some takeout. Do you want to run back upstairs to grab a few things?"

"Give me five minutes." She mentally packed an overnight bag. Had she brought that smoking hot lingerie set she hadn't worn yet?

"Four." He raised her hand to his lips and kissed it. "That bikini is killing me. I want to untie it with my teeth and take a good hard look at what's underneath. Then my mouth will be busy getting acquainted with every inch of your naked body."

She shuddered as his words lanced through her core with a long tug. "I'll be back in three."

Six

The small cockpit of James's car filled with the scent of Bella instantly. It was exotic, erotic and engaging, flipping switches in his body he'd have sworn were already wide open from the visual of Bella at the beach in that little bikini.

How was it possible to be even more turned on when you were already blind from lack of release?

She'd changed into a little white sundress that hugged her curves. The tiny straps begged for a man's hands to slip them off her shoulders, kiss the smooth flesh and then keep going into the deep V of her cleavage.

It was going to be a long, long drive through the interior of Alma as they looked for an abandoned farmhouse Bella insisted they could find. Problem was, he wanted her now, not in two hours after they crisscrossed the island in his green Lamborghini, which was hardly invisible.

As they clicked their seatbelts, his phone buzzed and he glanced at it out of habit, already planning to ignore whatever it was. Nothing could be more important than Bella.

Except it was a text message from Will. Who never texted him. Frowning, James tapped the screen of his phone and read the message.

I had nothing to do with this, but thought you should know.

Nothing good was going to come of clicking the link Will had sent, but forewarned was forearmed, so James did it anyway.

Montoro Princess to Wed the Heir to Rowling Energy.

The headline was enough. He didn't need to read the rest.

With a curse, he tilted his phone toward Bella. "Now taking bets on which of our fathers is behind this."

She glanced at it and repeated his curse, but substituted the vilest word with a more ladylike version, which put a smile on his face despite the ill-timed, fabricated announcement.

"Mine," she announced with a snort. "Control and dictate is exactly his style."

"Sure you're not describing my father?" James returned. "Because that's his MO all day long."

"No, it's my father. Definitely. But it doesn't matter." She grabbed his phone, switched it off and stuffed it in the bag at her feet. "You can't have that back. No more scandals, interfering fathers and marriage alliances. Just drive." She glanced over her shoulder. "And now. Before my babysitters figure out I'm not in the house."

Since that sounded fine to him, he backed out of his beachside parking place and floored the gas pedal, heading west out of Playa Del Onda.

"This is a gorgeous car," she commented with apparent appreciation as she caressed the dashboard lovingly in a way that immediately made him want her hand in his lap instead of on his car. "I dated a guy in Miami with an

Aventador, but it's so flashy without any real substance. The Gallardo is more refined and I love the color."

God, she *was* going to kill him before the day was over. "You know cars? I can't begin to tell you how hot that is."

She shrugged with a musical laugh, knocking one of the straps of her dress askew and drawing his attention away from the road. Dangerously.

"It's hard to live in a place like Miami without gaining at least some passing knowledge. I'll let you in on a secret, though. We girls always judge a man by his car. Mercedes-Benz? Too serious. Porsche? Works too hard. Corvette? Too worried about his hair."

James laughed in spite of the discomfort going on down below that likely wouldn't ease for an eternity. "So my Lamborghini is the only reason you wanted to go out with me?"

"The car test only works if you haven't met the guy yet. We're strictly talking about taking someone's measure in the parking lot."

He shifted to take a hairpin curve as they wound away from the beach into the more sparsely populated inland roads of Alma. Since he had no idea what they were looking for, he'd drive and let her do the surveying.

"Then I'll go with my second guess. You wanted to go out with me because I'm a witty conversationalist." He waggled his brows and shot her a sly smile. "Or door number three—I know a trick or two between the sheets."

He'd meant to be flirtatious, but now that it was out there, he realized the conversation with Will still bothered him a bit. Bella had said on numerous occasions that marriage wasn't her thing. Regardless, establishing the ground rules of what they were doing here couldn't hurt.

"Both." Blond hair swinging, she leaned on the emergency brake between them, so close he imagined he could hear her heart beating. "We have all night long and I do love a good conversation, especially in the dark. But if you forced me to choose, I'd go with door number three."

Brilliant. So they were both on the same page. They were hot for each other and wanted to burn it off with a wild night together. "Just so you know, with me, sheets are optional."

Awareness tightened the atmosphere as she let her gaze travel down his chest and rest on the bulge in his pants. He could hardly keep his attention on the road. Who wanted to watch the scraggly countryside of Alma when a goddess sat in the adjacent seat?

"By the way," she said. "I think we just passed the road we were supposed to take."

With a groan, he did a quick U-turn and drove down the street barely noticeable in the overgrowth of trees and groundcover. "I didn't know we had directions. Maybe you could speak up earlier next time?"

"Sorry, I'm a little distracted. Maybe you could stop being so sexy for a couple of minutes." Fanning herself as if he'd heated her up, she trailed a finger down his bicep muscle and toyed with the crook of his elbow.

"Me?" he growled. "You're the one in that knockout dress. All I can hear in my head is your voice on repeat, when you said the next time we were together, you'd be naked."

"Oh, did I forget to tell you?" She kissed the tip of her finger and pressed it to his lips, but she pulled away too quickly for him to suck the finger into his mouth the way he wanted to. "I'm naked under this dress. Wanna pull over?"

He nearly whimpered. "I cannot possibly explain how much I would like to do exactly that. But we are not getting it on in the car like a couple of horny teenagers. You deserve to be treated right and that includes a bed and me taking my time enjoying you."

Besides, they might be headed into the heart of rural Alma, but the roads were not deserted. They passed cars constantly. People knew who drove the only green Lamborghini on the island and all it would take was one idiot with a camera phone for another risqué picture of James and Bella together to land in the public eye. It was a dirty shame he hadn't tinted the windows on his car.

Until they straightened out the marriage announcement, it would create so much less of a jumble if they kept a low profile.

"Then drive faster," Bella suggested, and her hand wandered over to rest on his inner thigh, where she casually stroked him. Innocently, as if she touched him all the time, except she hadn't touched him like *that* before and his vision started to blur with unrequited lust.

He stepped on the gas. Hard.

"Where are we going?" Driving around until they stumbled over a farmhouse that may or may not exist had started to sound like the worst idea he'd ever agreed to.

"This is the main road to Aldeia Dormer, right?" When he nodded, she pointed at the horizon. "The assistant I talked to thought she remembered that the farmhouse was on the outskirts, before you hit the village. If you keep going, we'll find out."

"What if I just take you to a hotel and we check in under an assumed name?"

He had plenty of practice with parking in an obscure place and passing out discrete tips to the staff so he and his lady friend could duck through the kitchen entrance. Why hadn't he insisted on that in the first place? The text from Will had muddled him up, obviously. There was a former castillo-turned-four-star-bed-and-breakfast on the south side of Playa Del Onda that he wouldn't mind trying.

She shook her head with a sad smile and it was so much the opposite of her normal sunny demeanor, he immediately wanted to say something to lighten the mood. But what had caused such an instant mood shift?

"My aunt asked me to find the farmhouse. It's important to her and maybe to Gabriel. She said it was part of the Montoro legacy. We're already so close. I promise, if we don't find it soon, I'll reconsider the hotel."

Her earnestness dug under his skin and there was no way he could refuse. "Sure. We'll keep going."

Okay, maybe she was a little different from other women he'd dated. He certainly couldn't recall catering to one so readily before, but that was probably due to the degree of difficulty he'd experienced in getting this one undressed and under him.

They drove for a couple of miles, wrapped in tension. Just when James started to curse his flamboyant taste in cars, they crested a hill, and she gasped as a white farmhouse came into view.

Wonders of wonders. "Is that it?"

"I'm not sure." Bella pursed her lips as he drove off the main road onto the winding path to the farmhouse and parked under a dangerously dilapidated carport.

Would serve him right if this ill-conceived jaunt through Alma resulted in a hundred grand worth of bodywork repairs when the carport collapsed on the Lamborghini. "I thought you said it was off this road."

"Well, it's supposed to be. But I've never been here before," she pointed out. "Maybe there are a hundred white farmhouses between here and Aldeia Dormer."

"Only one way to find out." He helped her from the car and held her hand as they picked through the overgrown property. "Don't step in the tall weed patches. There might be something living in them you'd rather not tangle with."

She squeezed his hand. "I'm glad you're here, then. I'll let you deal with the creepy crawly stuff."

"I'll be your hero any day."

Her grateful smile made his chest tight with a foreign weight because he felt like a fraud all at once. The only heroic thing he'd ever done in his life was give Bella an opportunity to be with Will if she chose. When had he last expended any appreciable effort looking out for someone else's welfare?

He could start right now, if he wanted to. No reason he couldn't keep an eye out for opportunities to throw himself in front of a bullet—figuratively speaking—for an amazing woman like Bella. If she'd smile at him like that again, the payoff wasn't too shabby.

The farmhouse's original grandeur still shone through despite the years of neglect. Once, the two-story clapboard house had likely been the home of a large family, where they gathered around an old wooden table at supper to laugh and tell stories as dogs ran underfoot.

As if he knew anything about what a family did at supper. Especially a family whose members liked each other and spent time together on purpose. Did that kind of lovely fairy tale even exist outside of movies? He swallowed the stupid lump in his throat. Who cared? He had no roots and liked it that way.

The property spread beyond the house into a small valley. Chickens had probably clucked in the wide backyard, scolding fat pigs or horses that lived in the wooden pens just barely visible from the front of the house. The fences had long fallen to the weed-choked ground, succumbing to weathering and decay.

James nearly tripped over an equally weathered rectangular wooden board hidden by the grass and weeds. He kicked at it, but it was solid enough not to move much despite the force of his well-toned football muscles. Metal loops across the top caught his attention and he leaned down to ease the board up on its side.

"It's a sign," Bella whispered as her gaze lit on the opposite side.

James spun around to view the front. In bold, blocky letters, the sign read *Escondite Real*. "In more ways than one."

Unless he missed his guess, this was indeed the property of royalty. Or someone's idea of a joke.

"No one told me to brush up on my Spanish before I came here. What does it say?" Bella asked with a mock pout.

"Royal Hideaway. Is this where your ancestors came to indulge in illicit affairs?"

Mischievously, she winked at James. "If not, it's where the current generation will."

"Illicit affairs are my favorite." Taking her hand again, he guided her toward the house.

"Look. It's beautiful."

Bella pointed at a butterfly the size of his palm. It alighted on a purple bougainvillea that had thrived despite the lack of human attention, the butterfly's wings touching and separating slowly. But the sight couldn't keep his attention, not when Bella's face had taken on a glow in the late afternoon sunlight as she smiled at the butterfly.

God, she was the most exquisite woman he'd ever seen. And that was saying something when he'd been hit on by women renowned the world over for their beauty.

"Let's check out the inside." He cleared the catch from his throat, mystified by where it had come from. Women were a dime a dozen. Why didn't Bella seem like one of the legion he could have in his bed tomorrow?

It didn't matter. Will hadn't seen what he thought he'd seen when James cleared the air with him. The watch on his wrist wasn't going anywhere anytime soon.

Bella fished a set of keys from her bag. The second one turned the tumblers in the padlock on the splintered front door. It opened easily but the interior was dark and musty. Of course. There wouldn't be any electricity at an abandoned farmhouse. Or a cleaning crew.

"I guess we should have thought this through a little better," James said. "At least we know we're in the right place since the key worked."

Any hope of stripping Bella out of that little dress and spending the night in a haze of sensual pleasure vanished as something that sounded as if it had more feet than a football team scrabbled across the room.

"Yeah. It's a little more rustic than I was anticipating." She scowled at the gloom. "I'm not well versed in the art of abandoned farmhouses. Now what?"

Bella bit her lip to staunch the flow of frustrated tears. Which didn't exactly work.

This was all her fault. She'd envisioned a romantic rendezvous with a sexy, exciting man—one she'd looked forward to getting to know *very* well—and never once had it crossed her mind that "abandoned" didn't mean that someone had picked up and left a fully functioning house, ready and waiting for her and James to borrow for a night or two. The most strenuous thing she'd expected to do before letting James seduce her was kill a spider in the shower.

Graying sheets covered in cobwebs and dust obscured what she assumed must be furnishings underneath. The farmhouse hadn't been lived in for a long time. Decades maybe. The property may not even have running water. She shuddered. What had Isabella sent her into?

One tear shook loose and slid down her face.

Without speaking, James took her hand and drew her into his embrace, which immediately calmed her. How had he known that was what she needed? She slid her arms around his waist and laid her head on his strong chest.

Goodness. His athlete's physique did it for her in so many ways. He was shockingly solid and muscular for someone so lean and her own body woke up in a hurry. Sensation flooded her and she ached for him to kiss her again, as he'd done on the terrace—hot, commanding and so very sexy.

But then he drew back and tipped her chin up, his gaze serious and a bit endearing. "Here's what we're going to do. I'll drive into the village and pick up a few things. I hate to leave you here, but we can't be photographed together. While I'm gone, see if you can find a way to clean up at least one room."

His smile warmed her and she returned it, encouraged by his optimism. "You do have a gift for uncomplicating things. I'm a little jealous," she teased.

"It'll be smashing. I promise."

He left and she turned her attention to the great room of the farmhouse. Once she pulled the drapes aside, sunlight shafted into the room through the wide windows, catching on the dusty chandelier. So the house was wired for electricity. That was a plus. Maybe she could figure out how to get it activated—for next time, obviously, because there was a distinct possibility she and James might make long-term use out of this hideaway. Being a princess had to be worth something, didn't it?

Holding her breath, she pulled the sheets from the furnishings, raising a tornado of dust that made her sneeze. Once all the sheets were in a pile in the corner, she dashed from the room to give all the flurries a chance to settle. Using her phone as a flashlight, she found a broom in one of the closets of the old-fashioned kitchen.

"Cinderella, at your service," she muttered and carried the broom like a sword in front of her in case she ran into something crawly since her knight had left.

By the time he returned, the sun had started to set. She'd swept the majority of the dust from the room and whacked the cobwebs from the corners and chandelier. The throaty growl of the Lamborghini echoed through the great room as James came up the drive and parked. The car door slammed and James appeared in the open doorway, his arms weighted down with bags.

"Wow." He whistled. "This place was something back in the day, huh?"

She glanced around at the rich furnishings, which were clearly high-end, even for antiques, and still quite functional if you didn't mind the grime. "It's a property owned by royalty. I guess they didn't spare much expense, regard-less of the location. I wonder why no one has been here for so long?"

And why all these lovely antiques were still here, like ghosts frozen in time until someone broke the spell.

"Tantaberra liked Del Sol." James set his bags down carefully on the coffee table and began pulling out his bounty. "My guess is this was too far out of the limelight and too pedestrian for his taste."

A variety of candles appeared from the depths of the first bag. James scouted around until he found an empty three-pronged candelabra, screwed tapers into it and then flicked a lighter with his other hand. He shut the front door, plunging the room into full darkness. The soft glow of the candles bathed his face in mellow light and she forgot all about the mystery of this farmhouse as he set the cande-labra on the mantel behind the brocade couch.

"Nice. What else did you bring me?" Bella asked, in-trigued at the sheer number of bags James had returned with. She'd expected dinner and that was about it.

"The most important thing." He yanked a plaid blanket from the second bag and spread it out on the floor. "Can't have you dining on these rough plank floors, now can we?"

She shook her head with a smile and knelt down on the soft blanket to watch him continue unpacking. It seemed as if he'd thought of everything, down to such necessary but unique details as a blanket and candles. It was a qual-ity she would never have thought to admire or even notice. And in James, it was potently attractive.

"Second most important—wine." He plunked the bottle next to her and pulled out two plastic cups. "Not the finest stemware. Sorry. It was the best I could do."

His chagrin was heartbreakingly honest. Did he think she'd turn up her nose at his offering? Well, some women probably would, but not Bella.

"It's perfect," she said sincerely. "If you'll give me the

corkscrew, I'll pour while you show me what else you found in town."

He handed her a small black-cased device of some sort. It looked like a pocketknife and she eyed it curiously until he flicked out the corkscrew with a half laugh. "Never seen one of these before?"

"My wine is typically poured for me," she informed him pertly with a mock haughty sneer, lady-of-the-manor style. "Cut me some slack."

Instead of grinning back, he dropped to the blanket and took her hand. "This is a crappy first date. I wish I could have taken you to dinner in Del Sol, like I'd planned. You deserve to be waited on hand and foot and for me to make love to you on silk sheets. I'm sorry that things are so out of control for us right now. I'll make it up to you, I swear."

"Oh, James." Stricken, she stared into his gorgeous aqua eyes flickering in the candlelight. "This is exactly what I've been envisioning since I got in the car back at the beach. I don't need a three-hundred-euro dinner. I just want to be with you."

"You're a princess," he insisted fiercely. "I want to treat you like the royalty you are."

Good grief. Was all this because of the stupid joke she'd made about being high maintenance? Obviously he'd taken her at her word. Backpedaling time.

"You do that every time we're together. Encouraging me to make my own choices about who I date. Bringing me to the farmhouse simply because I asked, without telling me it was crazy. Holding me when I cry. Being my hero by making this night romantic with ingenuity and flair, despite the less than stellar accommodations. How could I possibly find fault in any of that?"

A little overcome, she stared at him, hoping to impart her sincerity by osmosis. Because he was amazing and somehow verbalizing it made it more real. Who else in her life had ever done such wonderful things for her? No one. Tender, fledgling feelings for James welled up and nearly splashed over.

He scowled. "I did those things because you needed me to. Not because you're a princess."

Silly man. He didn't get what she was saying at all. "But don't you see? I need someone to treat me like *me*. Because you *see* me and aren't wrapped up in all the royal trappings, which are essentially meaningless at the end of the day."

That was the mistake her father had made, trying to pawn her off on Will. And Will was nearly as bad. Everyone was far more impressed with her royal pedigree than she ever was. Everyone except James. And now he was being all weird about it.

Just as fiercely, she gripped his hand. "I wasn't a princess last year and if you'd met me then, wouldn't you have tried to give me what I needed instead of trying to cater to some idea you have about how a girl with royal blood should expect you to act?"

"Yeah." He blew out a breath. "I would. I just didn't want this to be so disappointing for you. Not our first time together."

Seriously? After the way he'd kissed her on the terrace? There was no freaking way he'd disappoint her, whether it was their first time or hundredth time. The location hardly mattered. She wanted the man, not some luxury vacation. If he thought dollar signs turned her on, she'd done something wrong.

"Our first time together cannot be disappointing, because you're half the equation," she chided gently. "I expect fireworks simply because you're the one setting them off. Okay?"

He searched her expression, brows drawn together. "If you're sure."

She caressed his arm soothingly, hoping to loosen him up a little. The romantic candlelit atmosphere was going to waste and that was a shame. "Yeah. Now show me what else is in your magic bag."

With a grin, he grabbed the last bag. He fished out a roll of salami, which he set by the wine, then lined up a wedge of cheese, boxed crackers and a string of grapes. "Dinner. I wish it—"

"Stop. It's food and I'm hungry. Sit down and let's eat it while you tell me stories about growing up in Alma." Patting the blanket, she concentrated on opening the wine, her one self-appointed task in the evening's preparations. It was tougher to pierce the cork than she'd anticipated.

Instead of complying with her suggestion, he took the bottle from her hands and expertly popped the cork in under fifteen seconds.

"You've done that before," she accused with a laugh as he poured two very full glasses of the chilled white wine. It was pretty good for a no-name label and she swallowed a healthy bit.

"Yep. I'm a master of all things decadent." He arched a brow and plucked a grape from the bunch to run it across her lips with slow sensuality that fanned heat across her skin instantly. "Hurry up and eat so I can show you."

Watching him with unabashed invitation, she let him ease the grape between her lips and accepted it with a swirl of her tongue across the tips of his fingers. His eyelids lowered, fluttering slightly, and he deliberately set his glass of wine on the coffee table, as if to silently announce he planned to use both hands in very short order.

She shuddered as all the newly-awakened feelings for this man twined with the already-powerful attraction. She wanted to explore his depths and let the amazing things happening between them explode. Simple desire she understood and appreciated, but this went beyond anything simple, beyond anything she'd experienced before.

"Or we can do both at the same time," she suggested,

her voice dropping huskily as he trailed his wet fingertip down her chin and throat to trace the line of her cleavage.

"There you go again reading my mind," he murmured and captured another grape without looking away, his gaze hot and full of promise. "Let's see if you can guess what I'm thinking now."

Seven

James outlined Bella's full lips with the grape and then ran it down her throat, resting it in the hollow of her collarbone. Slowly, he leaned over and drew the fruit into his mouth, sucking at her fragrant skin as he crushed the grape in his teeth simultaneously.

The combination of Bella and sweet juice sang across his taste buds. She was exquisitely, perfectly made and he wanted her with an unparalleled passion that wiped his mind of everything else.

Flinging her head back to give him better access, she gulped in a breath and exhaled on a low moan that tightened his whole body.

"Instead of reading your mind," she said, her low voice burrowing into his abdomen, spreading heat haphazardly, "why don't you surprise me with a few more strategically placed grapes?"

"You like that?"

Grapes as a seduction method—that was a first. And now he was wishing he'd bought a bushel. Gripping another one, he traced it between her breasts and circled one of her nipples. It peaked beautifully under the filmy sundress.

How had he gotten so supremely lucky as to have such a beautiful, exciting woman within arm's reach? One who didn't require him to rain expensive gifts down on her, but seemed perfectly content with simple trappings and a man paying attention to her.

All the talk of heroics made his skin crawl. She was sorely mistaken if she thought of him as a hero, but the look in her eyes—well, that made him feel ten feet tall, as if he could do anything as long as she believed in him.

The power of it emboldened him.

Urgently, he lunged for her, catching her up in his arms as he laid her back on the blanket. Her lips crashed against his in a hot, wet kiss that went on and on as their tongues explored and dipped and mated. Her body twined with his and finally, she was underneath him, his thigh flush against her core. Her hands went on a mission to discover every part of his back and he reveled in the feminine touch he'd been craving for so long.

Hooking the neckline of her dress, he dragged it from her breast. As her flesh was revealed, he followed the trail with his mouth, nibbling and kissing until his lips closed over her nipple.

She arched against his mouth, pushing herself deeper inside as he reached for a handful of grapes. With little regard for decorum, he lifted his head and crushed the fruit savagely, letting the juice drip onto her peaked nipple. The liquid wetted the tip as she watched with dark eyes; her glistening breast was so erotic, he groaned even as he leaned forward to catch an errant drop on his tongue.

Licking upward until he hit her nipple again, he sucked all the juice off to the sound of her very vocal sighs of pleasure. That nearly undid him.

"I want to see all of you," he murmured and his need was so great, he didn't even wait for her reply. Peeling off that little dress counted as one of the greatest pleasures of his life as inch by inch, he uncovered her incredible skin.

"You're so beautiful," he told her with a catch in his throat.

Something unnamable had overcome him. Something dramatic and huge. But he liked it and before whatever it was fled, he pulled a string of condoms from his pocket and rolled to the side to shed his own clothes so he could feel every gorgeous bit of her against him.

When he was naked, he rolled back, intending to gather up that bundle of heaven back into his arms, but she stopped him with a palm to his chest. "Not yet. I want to see you, too."

Her gaze roved over his body and lingered in unexpected places. His thighs. His pectorals. Her palm spread and flattened over his nipple, as if she wanted to grab hold.

When she couldn't, she purred. "Hard as stone. I like that."

"I like you touching me."

"Allow me to continue." Wicked smile spreading across her face, she ran both hands down the planes of his chest and onto his thighs, right past the area he'd hoped she was headed for. Which of course made him anticipate the return journey.

Her fingernails scraped his leg muscles lightly, and she trailed one hand over his hip to explore his butt, which tightened automatically under the onslaught. *Everything* tightened with unanswered release, including the parts he'd have sworn were already stretched to the point of bursting.

He groaned as heat exploded under her hands. His hips strained toward her, muscles begging to be set free from the iron hold he had on them. "Are you trying to make me barmy?"

"Nope. Just looking for the best places for when it's my turn with the grapes."

"Oh, it's totally your turn," he countered. "This is your dinner, too, and you must be hungry."

"At last." She knelt, grabbed a grape and eyed his splayed body. "Hmm. Where to start? I know."

She stuck the grape in her mouth and rolled it around with her tongue, her hot gaze on his erection. Somehow that was more arousing than if she'd actually tongued *him*. She caught the small globe in her front teeth and bent to run it over his torso, dipping into the valleys and peaks, her hair spreading out like a feathery torture device across his sensitive skin. When she accidentally—or maybe on purpose—dragged her hair over his erection, the light touch lit him up. Fire radiated from the juncture of his thighs outward and just as he was about to cup her head to guide her toward the prize, she leaned up on her haunches.

Plucking the grape from between her lips, she grazed his length with the wet grape, nearly causing him to spill everything in one pulse.

"Enough of that," he growled, manacling her wrist to draw it away from the line of fire. "You've obviously underestimated my appetite. Time for the main course."

She grinned. "I thought you'd never say that."

Fumbling with a condom, he somehow managed to get it secured and then rolled her underneath him. He'd been fantasizing about taking her exactly this way for an eternity. Soft and luscious, she slid right into the curves of his body as she had that day in the sand, except this time, nothing separated their skin and it was every bit as glorious as he'd imagined.

"You—" He nearly swallowed his tongue as she shifted, rolling her hips against his. The tips of her breasts ground into his torso, and it all felt so amazing, he couldn't speak.

And then he didn't have to speak as he gazed down into her blue eyes. Candlelight danced in their depths and he caught a hint of something else that hit him in the gut. As if she'd seen pieces of him that he'd never realized were there and she liked what she'd found. As if she truly saw him as a hero. Maybe she was the only one who could relate. They were both rebels—to the rest of the world—but his pain and difficulties behind the rebellion made total sense to her.

"Bella," he murmured and that was the extent of what he could push through his tight throat.

"Right here." Her low, husky voice became his favorite part of her as it hummed through him. "I was really afraid this would never happen. Make it worth the wait."

It was already so worth it. Worth the lectures from his father, worth the uncomfortable nobleness he'd somehow adopted when around her. Worth sending her away from him on the terrace when all he'd wanted to do was pull that outrageous red dress up to her waist and make her his under the moonlight.

This way was better. Much better. No fear of being caught. No loaded landmines surrounding them, no paparazzi lying in wait to cause a scandal just because they wanted to be together.

He laid his lips on hers and fell into a long sigh of a kiss that grew urgent as she opened her mouth and dove in with her tongue, heightening the pleasure.

And then with a small shift, they joined. Easily, beautifully, as if she'd been specially crafted for James Rowling. It was almost spiritual and he'd never felt such a weight to being with a woman.

He froze for a moment, just letting her essence bleed through him, and then, determined to get her to the same place of mystical pleasure, he focused on her cries, her shifts, her rhythms. He became an instant student of Bella's pleasure until he could anticipate exactly what she wanted him to do next to drive her to release.

And then she stiffened as a volatile climax engulfed her that he felt all the way to his soles. He let go and followed her into oblivion, holding her tight because he couldn't stand to lose contact with her.

As he regained cognizance, he realized she was trying to get closer, too. He settled Bella comfortably in his arms and lay with her to watch the candle flames flicker, throwing shadows of the heavy furniture on the walls of the farmhouse they'd turned into the safest of havens.

This time with Bella…it was the most romantic experience he'd ever had, which sat strangely. For a guy who loved sex and abhorred roots, romance was difficult to come by. Not only had he never had it, he'd never sought it.

Why did something as normal as sex feel so abnormally and hugely different with this woman? He couldn't make sense of it and it bothered him. As the unsettled feeling grew, he kissed Bella's forehead and separated from her.

Bustling around to gather up their abandoned wine glasses and remnants of their dinner, he threw a forced smile over his shoulder. "Ready to finish eating?"

She returned the smile, not seeming to realize that he was trying to mask his sudden confusion. "Depends. Is that code for round two? Because the answer is yes, if so."

Round two. He chugged some wine to give himself a second. Normally, he went for round two like a sailor on shore leave, but the thick, romantic atmosphere and the crushing sensation in his chest when he looked at Bella made him question everything.

What was going on here? This was supposed to be nothing but an opportunity to have fun with Bella, no expectations, no proposals before her brother took the throne.

"No code. Let's eat."

What was his *problem*? A beautiful woman who rocked his world wanted him to make love to her again. Maybe he should just do that, and everything would make sense once they were back to just two people having smashing sex. Will's bet had hashed everything.

"For now," he amended. "Got to keep up our strength."

She grinned and shoved some crackers in her mouth. "All done," she mumbled around the crackers.

Groaning around a laugh, he sat close to her on the blanket and shook off his strange mood. After all, she was Alma's only princess. What role did a disgraced football player have in the middle of all that? Especially when he didn't plan to be living in Alma permanently. In fact, a new contract would get him out from under all of this confusion quite well. He could enjoy a fling with Bella and jet off to another continent. Like always.

Obviously, there was no reason to give any more credence to the heavy weight in his chest.

There was a huge crick in Bella's neck, but she actually welcomed the pain. Because she'd gotten it sleeping in James's arms on a blanket spread over a hardwood floor.

That had been delicious. And wonderful. And a host of other things she could barely articulate. So she didn't, opting to see what the morning brought in this unconventional affair they'd begun.

Once they were dressed and had the curtains thrown open to let sunlight into the musty great room, she turned to James. "I don't know about you, but I'm heavily in favor of finding a café that'll give you a mountain of scrambled eggs, bacon and biscuits in a takeout box. I'm starving."

He flashed a quick grin. "Careful. That kind of comment now has all sorts of meaning attached. You better clarify whether you want me to feed you or strip you."

Laughing, she socked him on the arm. "You're the one who started that with the grapes. And the answer to that is both. Always."

He caught her hand and held it in his. "I'm only teasing. I'll go get breakfast. I wish you could come with me. Is it too much to ask that we go on a real date where I sit with you at an actual table?"

"We'll get there." She kissed him soundly and shoved

him toward the door. "Once I have food in me, we can strategize about the rest of our lives."

Item number one on the agenda: get this farmhouse in livable shape.

The strange look he shot her put a hitch in her stride and she realized immediately how he must have taken her comment. Okay, she hadn't meant it like that, as if she was assuming they'd become a dyed-in-the-wool couple and he needed to get down on one knee.

But what was so bad about making plans beyond breakfast? She'd had some great lovers in the past, but what she'd experienced with James went far beyond the category of casual. Hadn't he felt all the wonderful things she'd felt last night?

She rolled her eyes to make it harder for him to detect the swirl of emotion going on underneath the surface. "You can stop with the deer-in-the-headlights, hon. I just narrowly escaped one marriage. I'm not at all interested in jumping right into another one, no matter how good the prospective groom is at *feeding* me."

Which was absolutely, completely true. Saying it aloud solidified it for them both.

With a wicked smile, he yanked on her hand, pulling her into his embrace. His weird expression melted away as he nuzzled her neck.

Foot-in-mouth averted. Except now she was wondering exactly what his intentions toward her were. A few nights together and then ta-ta?

And when did she get to the point where that wasn't necessarily what *she* wanted? She didn't do all that commitment-and-feelings rigmarole. She liked to have fun and secretly felt sorry for women on husband-hunting missions. Her mother had gotten trapped in that cycle and lived a miserable existence for years and years as a result. *No, thank you.*

Nothing had changed just because of a few emotions

she had no idea what to do with. Her affair with James had begun so unconventionally and under extreme circumstances. If they'd been able to go out on a real date from the beginning, they'd probably have already moved on by now.

Good thing she'd made it clear marriage wasn't on her mind so there was no confusion, though a few other things could be better spelled out.

James sucked on her tender flesh, clearly about to move south, and she wiggled away before her body leaped on the train without her permission.

"That wasn't supposed to be a code word." She giggled at his crestfallen expression but sobered to hold his gaze. "Listen, before you go get breakfast, let's lay this out. Last night was amazing but I'm not done. Are you? Because if this thing between us was one night only, I'll be sad, but I'm a big girl. Tell me."

He was already shaking his head before she'd finished speaking. "No way. I'm nowhere near done."

Her pulse settled. *Good answer.* "So, if you want a repeat of the grapes-on-the-floor routine, I'm all for it. But I'd prefer a real bed from now on. My plan is to put some elbow grease into this place, preferably someone else's, and create a lover's retreat where we can escape whenever we feel like it."

"Are you expecting us to have to hide out that long?" Wary surprise crept into his tone, setting her teeth on edge.

"I don't know. Maybe." What, was it too much trouble to drive out here just to have a few stolen hours together? "Is what I'm suggesting so horrible?"

"No. Not at all. My hesitation was completely on the issue of hiding out. I want to be seen with you in public. I'm not ashamed of our relationship and I don't want you to think I am."

Her heart squished as she absorbed his righteous indignation and sincerity. He wanted their relationship to be aboveboard, just as he'd wanted to clear things with Will before proceeding. And that meant a lot to her. He kept trying to make her think he didn't have a noble bone in his body when everything he did hinged on his own personal sense of honor.

"I didn't think that, but way to score major points." She batted her eyelashes at him saucily. "But that aside, I don't even know if I'm staying in Alma permanently or I'd get my own place. I suspect you're in the same boat."

He'd told her he hoped to get another contract with a professional soccer—sorry, *football*—team, and that the team could be in Barcelona or the UK or Brazil or, or, or… He might end up anywhere in the world. And probably would.

"Yeah. I haven't made a secret out of the fact that I don't plan to stick around," he agreed cautiously.

"I know. So do you really think there's a scenario where either of us would be willing to parade the other across the thresholds of our fathers' houses even if we do clear up the engagement announcement?"

He sighed. "Yeah, you're right. Let's rewind this whole conversation. Smashing idea, Bella. I'd love to help you get this place into shape so I can take an actual shower in the morning."

That was the James she knew and loved. Or rather, the James she…didn't know very well, but liked a whole lot. With a sigh, she let him kiss her again and shoved him out the door for real this time because her stomach was growling and her heart was doing some funny things that she didn't especially like.

Space would be good right now.

The sound of the Lamborghini's engine faded away as she went about taking inventory on the lower floor. Apparently most, if not all, of the original furnishings remained, as evidenced by their arrangement. Bella had been in enough wealthy households to recognize when a place had been artfully decorated and this one definitely had.

The pieces had been placed just so by a feminine hand, or at least she imagined it that way. That's when it hit her that this farmhouse had probably once belonged to an ancestor of hers. Someone of her blood.

A long gone Montoro, forgotten for ages once the coup deposed the royal family. She'd never felt very connected to the monarchy, not even at the palace in Del Sol where some of the original riches of the royal estate were housed. But the quieter treasures of the farmhouse struck her differently.

She picked up a filthy urn resting on a side table. White, or at least it was under the grime. She rubbed at it ineffectually with her palm and managed to get a small bit of the white showing. The eggshell-like surface was pretty.

Maybe it wasn't priceless like the Qing Dynasty porcelain vase sitting in an art niche at the Coral Gables house. But worth something. Maybe it was actually worth more than the million-dollar piece of pottery back in Miami because it had been used by someone.

She'd never thought about worth being tied to something's usefulness. But she liked the idea of having a purpose. She'd had one in Miami—wildlife conservation. What had happened to that passion? It was as if she'd come to Alma and forgotten how great it made her feel to do something worthwhile.

With renewed fervor, she dove into cleaning what she could with the meager supplies at hand, and revised her earlier thoughts. It would be fun to put some elbow grease of her own into this house. Whom else could she trust with her family's property?

When the purr of James's car finally reverberated through the open door, she glanced at her dirty arms and her lip curled. Some princess she looked like. A Cinderella in reverse—she'd gone from the royal palace to being a slave to the dust. A shower sounded like heaven about now.

The look in James's eye when he walked in holding a

bag stenciled with the logo of the only chain restaurant in Alma had her laughing. "There is no way you're thinking what I think you're thinking. I'm filthy."

"Yes, way." He hummed in approval. "I've never seen a sexier woman than you, Bella Montoro. Layer of dirt or not."

There he went again making her insides all melty and that much more raw. She always got the distinct feeling he saw the real her, past all the outside stuff and into her core. The outside, inconsequential stuff was invisible to him. Coupled with the hard twist of pure lust she got pretty much any time she laid eyes on him, she could hardly think around it.

She shook it off. This fierce attraction was nothing more than the product of their secret love affair. Anticipation of the moment they'd finally connect, laced with a hint of the forbidden. It had colored everything and she refused to fall prey to manufactured expectations about what was happening between them.

Get a grip. "Smells like ham and biscuits," she said brightly.

He handed her the bag. "I hope you like them. I had to drive two towns over to find them."

The first bite of biscuit hit her tongue and she moaned. "I would have paid three hundred euros for this."

He laughed. "On the house. You can pay next time."

"Oh?" She arched a brow, relieved they'd settled back into the teasing, fun vibe she'd liked about them from the beginning. "Are you under some mistaken impression that I'm a liberated woman who insists on opening her own doors and paying her own way? 'Cause that is so not happening."

"My mistake," he allowed smoothly with a nod and munched on his own biscuit. "You want a manly bloke to treat you like a delicate hothouse flower. I get it. I'd be chuffed to climb all the ladders around here and wield the power tools in order to create a luxury hideaway, as ordered. You know what that means I get at the end of the day in return, right?"

"A full body massage," she guessed, already planning exactly how such a reward might play out. "And then some inventive foreplay afterward."

That was even more fun to imagine than the massage part of the evening's agenda.

"Oh, no, sweetheart." He leaned in and tipped her chin up to capture her gaze, and the wicked intent written all over his face made her shiver. "It means I get the loo first."

Eight

The farmhouse's great room looked brand-new and James couldn't take all of the credit. It was because the house had good bones and old-world charm—qualities he'd never appreciated in anything before.

Hell, maybe he'd never even *noticed* them before.

Bella finished polishing the last silver candlestick and stuck it back on the mantel of the humongous fireplace, humming a nameless tune that he'd grown a bit fond of over the past day as they'd worked side by side to get their lover's retreat set to rights.

"Did you hear that?" she asked with a cocked head.

"Uh, no." He'd been too busy soaking in the sight of a beautiful woman against the backdrop of the deep maroon walls and dark furniture. "What was it?"

"The sound of success."

She smiled and that heavy feeling in his chest expanded a tad more, which had been happening with alarming frequency all day. Unfortunately, the coping mechanism he'd used last night—grabbing Bella and sinking into her as fast as possible so his mind went blessedly blank—wasn't available to him at this moment because a workman from the municipality was on his way to restore the water connection.

It was a minor miracle the workman had come out on short notice, given the typical local bureaucracy, but once James had mentioned that he was a representative for the Montoros, everything had fallen into place.

He'd have to make himself—and his distinctive green car—scarce. Just as he'd done this morning when the bloke from the electric company had come. But it was fine. The time away had given him an opportunity to talk through strategy with his sports agent, who mentioned a possible opportunity with Liverpool. No guarantees, but some shifting had occurred in the roster and the club needed a strong foot. Brilliant news at an even better time—the sooner James could escape Alma, the better.

"Yep," he said and cleared a catch from his throat. "Only twenty-seven rooms to go."

They'd started on the downstairs, focusing on the kitchen and great room, plus the servant's quarters past the kitchen, where they intended to sleep tonight if the bed they'd ordered arrived on time, as promised. A lot had been accomplished in one day but not nearly enough.

Once they got the master bedroom upstairs cleaned up, James planned a whole silk-sheets-and-rose-petals-type seduction scene. He owed it to Bella since she'd been such a good sport about sleeping in the room designated for the help.

One thing he immensely appreciated about Bella: she joked around a lot about being high maintenance but she was the furthest thing from it. And he knew a difficult, demanding woman when he saw one, like his last semi-permanent girlfriend, Chelsea. She'd cured him of ever wanting to be around a female for more than a one-night stand, a rule which he'd stuck to for nearly two years.

Until Bella.

Since he couldn't lose his mind in her fragrant skin for… he glanced at his watch and groaned…hours, he settled for a way-too-short kiss.

She wiggled away and stuck her tongue out at him. "Yes, we have a lot of work left. But not as much as we would have if you hadn't made all those calls. You're the main reason we've gotten this far."

The hero-worship in her gaze still made him uncomfortable, so he shrugged and polished an already-sparkling crystal bowl with the hem of his shirt so he had an excuse not to look directly at her. "Yeah, that was a brilliant contribution. Hitting some numbers on my phone."

"Stop being such a goof." Hands on her hips, she stepped into his space, refusing to let his attention linger elsewhere. "You're a great person. I'm allowed to think so and don't you dare tell me I can't."

That pulled a smile from him. "Yes, Your Highness."

"Anyway," she drawled with an exaggerated American accent, which only widened his smile, as she'd probably intended. "When I was cleaning the fireplace, I realized I really need to call my father. We can't ignore the press release about my engagement to Will much longer."

Though she kept up her light tone, he could tell some stress had worked its way into her body. Her shoulders were stiff and a shadow clouded her normally clear eyes.

"Maybe we can wait," he suggested, and laced his fingers with hers to rub her knuckles. "Tomorrow's soon enough."

"I kind of want to get it over with." She bit her lip, clearly torn. "But I also really like the idea of procrastinating."

"Why?" he asked, surprising himself. He'd meant to say they should wait. Why do today what you can put off until tomorrow?

He, of all people, understood avoiding conflict, especially when it involved an overbearing father. But the distress evident in the foreign lines around her eyes had to go and he would do whatever it took to solve the problem.

Maybe it wasn't a good thing for him to encourage her to wait. Maybe she needed to get the confrontation over with. But how would he know if he didn't ask?

"My father really wants me to fall in line, like Gabriel did. When Rafe abdicated, it was kind of a big deal." She sighed. "I get that. I really don't want to cause problems because of my own selfishness."

"But you're not," he countered. "How is it a problem that you want to choose the bloke you marry?"

"Because my father says it is." Her mouth flattened into a grim line. "That's why I want to put off dealing with all of this. I'm just not ready for all of the expectations that go along with restoring the monarchy. I mean, I always knew our family had come from a royal line, but that was so long ago. Why is it so important to my father all of a sudden?"

She seemed a little fragile in that moment so he pulled her into his arms, shushing her protests over the state of her cleanliness.

"I wish I could tell you why things are important to fathers," he murmured. "Mine has yet to explain why it's so horrifying to him that I don't want a job at Rowling Energy. Becoming a world-class football player might make some dads proud."

"Not yours?" she whispered, her head deep in his shoulder.

Her arms tightened around him, which was oddly comforting. What had started as an embrace he'd thought she needed swiftly became more precious to him than oxygen.

"Nah. Will's his golden boy."

"Why don't you want to work at Rowling?"

It was the first time anyone had ever asked him that.

Most people assumed he wanted to play football and there was little room for another career at his dad's company. But even now, when he had few choices in continuing his sports career, he'd never consider Rowling an alternative.

His father wasn't the listening type; he just bulldozed through their conversations with the mindset that James would continue to defy him and never bothered to wonder why James showed no interest in the family business.

"It's because he built that company on my mother's grave," he said fiercely. "If she hadn't died, he wouldn't have moved to Alma and tapped in to the offshore drilling that was just starting up. I can't ever forget that."

"Is someone asking you to forget?" she probed quietly. "Maybe there's room to take a longer view of this. If your father hadn't moved to Alma, you wouldn't have discovered that you loved football, right?"

"That doesn't make it okay." The admission reverberated in the still house and she lifted her head to look at him, eyebrows raised in question. "I love football but only because it saved me. It got me out of Alma at an early age and gave me the opportunity to be oceans away. I can't be on the same small island as my father. Not for long."

When had this turned into confession time? He'd never said that out loud before. Bella had somehow pulled it out of him.

"I'm sorry," she said quietly and snuggled back into his arms, exactly where he wanted her.

"I'm sorry you've got the same issues with your father. But there's always gossip in a small town. We're going to be dealing with a scandal over the press release once someone catches on to us shacking up in this love nest. But I support whatever decision you make as far as the timing," he told her sincerely, though he'd be heavily in favor of waiting.

He wasn't royalty though. She had a slew of obligations he knew nothing about; he could hardly envision a worse life than one where you had to think about duty to crown and country.

"I think that's the most romantic thing you've ever said to me." Her voice cracked on the last word.

Puzzled, he tipped her chin up, and a tear tracked down her cheek. "Which part? When I called this jumble of a house a love nest or described our relationship as shacking up?"

She laughed through another couple of tears, thoroughly confounding him. Just when he thought he finally got her, she did something he couldn't fathom.

"Neither. The part where you said you support me, no matter what. It makes me warm, right here." She patted her stomach.

He almost rolled his eyes. That was laying it on a bit thick, wasn't it? "I do support you, but that's what peop— lovers…people in a rela—" God, he couldn't even get his tongue to find the right word to explain the status of what they were doing here.

Maybe because he didn't *know* what they were doing here.

"Yeah," she said happily, though what she was agreeing to, he had no idea. "That's what you do. I get that. You've always done exactly the right thing, from the very beginning. "

He scowled. "I don't do that."

He didn't. He was the guy who buckled when it mattered most. The guy whose team had been counting on him and he'd let them down. The guy who ran from conflict instead of dealing with it. Hadn't she been listening to anything he'd said about why he played football?

His character had been tarnished further with the hooker incident. James Rowling was the last person anyone should count on. Especially when it came to support. Or "being there" for someone emotionally.

"You do." Her clear blue eyes locked with his and she wouldn't let him look away. "You look in the mirror and see the mistakes your father has insisted you've made. I look at you and see an amazing man. You did hard physical labor all day in a house that means nothing to you. Because I asked you to. You're here. That means a lot to me. I need a rock in my life."

She had him all twisted up in her head as the hero of this story. She couldn't be more wrong—he was a rock, all right. A rolling stone headed for the horizon.

It suddenly sounded lonely and unappetizing. "I can't be anyone's rock. I don't know how."

That had come out wrong. He intended to be firm and resolute, but instead sounded far too harsh.

"Oh, sweetie. There's no instruction manual. You're already doing it." She shook her head and feathered a thumb over his jaw in a caress that felt more intimate than the sex they'd had last night. "You're letting someone else cloud your view of yourself. Don't let your father define who you are."

He started to protest and then her words really sank in. Had he subconsciously been doing that—letting his father have that much power over him?

Maybe he'd never realized it because he'd refused to admit the rift between him and his father might be partially his own fault. James had always been too busy running to pay attention. Even now, his thoughts were on Liverpool and the potential opportunity to play in the top league. But more importantly, Liverpool wasn't in Alma—where the woman who had him so wrongly cast in her head as the hero lived. He was thinking about leaving. Maybe he was already halfway out the door.

Which then begged the question—what if he buckled under pressure because he always took off when the going got tough?

The new bed was supremely superior to the floor. Bella and James christened it that night and slept en-

twined until morning. It was the best night of sleep she'd
ever had in her life.

But dawn brought a dose of reality. She hadn't been back
to the Playa del Onda house in almost forty-eight hours.
The quick text message to Gabriel to explain her absence
as a "getaway with a friend" hadn't stopped her father from
calling four times and leaving four terse voice mail messages. She hadn't answered. On purpose.

With the addition of running water and electricity, the
farmhouse took on a warmth she enjoyed. In fact, she'd
rather stay here forever than go back to the beach house.
But she had to deal with her father eventually. If this matter of the engagement announcement was simply a test of
her father's resolve versus her own, she wouldn't care very
much about the scandal of being with James.

But it wasn't just about two Montoros squaring off
against each other. It was a matter of national alliances
and a fledgling monarchy. She didn't have any intention
of marrying Will, but until the Montoros issued a public
retraction of the engagement story, the possibility of another scandal was very real. This one might be far worse
for Gabriel on the heels of the one Rafe had caused. And
hiding away with James hadn't changed that. She had to
take care of it. Soon.

"Good morning," James murmured and reached out to
stroke hair from her face as he lay facing her on the adjacent pillow. "This is my favorite look on you."

"Bedhead?" She smiled despite the somberness of her
thoughts.

"Well loved." He grinned back. "I liked it yesterday
morning, too."

Speaking of which… "How long do you think we can
reasonably hole up here without someone snapping a picture of us together?"

He shrugged one shoulder. "Forever." When she arched
a brow, he grinned. "I can fantasize about that, can't I?

As long as I keep jetting off when people show up, what's the hurry?"

Her conscience pricked at her. James was leaving the timing of forcing the issue to her, but a scandal could be damaging to him as well. It was selfish enough to refuse to marry Will, but she wasn't really hurting him as long as they were up front about it. A scandal that broke before the retraction could very well hurt James and she couldn't stand that.

"I think I need to talk to my father today," she said firmly. "Or tomorrow at the very latest."

James deserved what he'd asked for—the right to take her out in public, to declare to the world that they'd started seeing each other. To take her to a hotel, or dinner or wherever he liked. It wasn't fair to force him to help her clean up this old farmhouse just so she could avoid a confrontation.

Except she wasn't only avoiding the confrontation. She was avoiding admitting to herself that her own desires had trumped her responsibilities. Hurricane Bella had followed her across the Atlantic after all.

"I'll drive you back to Playa Del Onda," he said immediately. "Whenever you're ready."

A different fear gripped her then. What if they got everything straightened out and she and James could be together with no fear of scandal—only for her to discover things between them were so amazing because of the extreme circumstances? The white-hot attraction between them might fizzle if their secret affair wasn't so secret any longer.

That was enough to change her mind.

"I'll probably never be ready. Let's shoot for tomorrow." That was too soon. The thought of losing her allure with James made her want to weep. "Let's get some more work on the house done today. It'll give me time to gear up. Is that okay? Do you have something else you need to be doing?"

"Nothing I would rather be doing, that's for sure. I'm completely open."

"Me, too."

And for some reason, that didn't sit well, as if she was some kind of Eurotrash princess who had nothing better to do than lie around all day getting it on with a hot athlete. That was like a tabloid story in and of itself.

The urn from the great room popped into her head. Usefulness created worth and she wanted to feel that her life had worth.

"You know what I'd like to do?" she said impulsively. "Find out if there's a wildlife conservation organization in Alma."

James, to his credit, didn't register a lick of surprise. "I'll help you find one."

Of course he'd say that, without questioning why. His unwavering support was fast becoming a lifeline. "I was involved in one back in Miami. I like taking care of poor, defenseless creatures. Especially birds. We had wild macaws on the grounds at our house and I always felt like they were there as a sign. I miss them. I miss feeling like I'm doing something to give back, you know?"

"It's a good cause," he agreed. "There are some estuaries on the east side of the main island. Lots of migratory birds and fish live there. Surely there are some organizations devoted to their preservation. If not, you're in the perfect position to start one."

Her breath caught. At last, a use for the title of princess. If her brother was running the show, he could give her backing in parliament to get some state money set aside. Fund-raisers galore could come out of that. "Thanks. I love that idea."

"If we're going to Playa Del Onda tomorrow, you want to swing by the Playa branch of the Ministry of Agriculture and Environment and see if they have any information on wildlife conservation?"

"Definitely. And then I'd like to come back and put together a serious renovation plan for the house. But I'm not suggesting you have to help," she amended in a rush.

Good grief. Everything that came out of her mouth sounded as if she was ordering him around, expecting him to play chauffer and be a general Alma guide. He might have his own life to live. Or he might realize the thrill had worn off.

"I want to help," he insisted. "My assumption is that we're still planning to lie low, even after you clear things up with your father. So that means we need a place to go. I like it here."

She let out the breath caught in her lungs. She shouldn't read into his response. But for some reason, it made her feel a little better that he wasn't already planning to ditch their relationship once it wasn't secret any longer. "I do, too."

She'd started thinking she might like to live in the farmhouse permanently. It wasn't too far from Del Sol, so she could visit Tía Isabella occasionally. If she planned to stay in Alma, she had to live *somewhere*. Why not here? No one else cared about it.

As she lay in the bed James had ordered and smiled at him in the early morning light, it occurred to her that *he* was the only reason she'd even thought about a permanent place to live. As if James and forever were intertwined.

That was enough to propel her from the bed with a quickly tossed-off excuse about taking a shower now that she could.

As the water heated up, she berated herself for dreaming about life beyond the next few days. It was one thing to question whether James would lose interest once they could go public with their affair, but it was another entirely to assign him a permanent place in her life without even consulting him.

What would his place be? Boyfriend? Official lover? She'd be living in the public eye far more in Alma than in

Miami. What if James didn't want that kind of scrutiny? She wouldn't blame him, especially given the past scandals that dogged his steps.

Of course, she didn't know his thoughts one way or another. Maybe he'd be done with their affair in a few days, regardless of the status of their relationship. Maybe the whole concept of being her long-term lover had little appeal.

What was she *thinking*?

What had happened to the girl who used to flit from one guy to the next with ease? Or for that matter, the girl who flitted from party to party? Living out here in the country would make it really difficult to stay in the scene. No jetting off to Monte Carlo or Barcelona for some fun on the Mediterranean when Alma grew too dull. But when she exited the bathroom and saw the beautiful, surprisingly romantic man still in the bed they'd shared last night, sprawled out under the covers like a wicked fantasy, all of that drained from her mind. What party—what other man, for that matter—could compare to *that*?

"Give me a few minutes and we'll get started," he promised. "Let's check out the upstairs today."

God, she was in a lot of trouble. *She* should be the one thinking about cooling things off, not worrying about whether James planned to.

But the thought of ending things with James made her nauseous.

What was she going to do?

Nine

The upstairs master suite had the most amazing four-poster bed Bella had ever seen. When she drew off the drop cloths covering it, she almost gasped at the intricate carvings in the wood. Delicate flowers in full bloom twined up the posts and exploded into bunches at the top corners.

Once she polished the wood to gleaming and whacked the dust from the counterpane and pillows, the bed took on an almost magical quality, as if it had been a gift from the fairy realm to this one.

The rest of the room was a wreck. Mice had gotten into the cushions of the chairs by the huge bay window and Bella could tell by the discoloration of the walls that some type of artwork had originally hung there, but had disappeared at some point over the years.

The floor groaned behind her and she turned to see James bouncing lightly on a spot near the bed. The planks bowed under his weight and then with a *snap*, one cracked in two. Both pieces fell into the newly created hole. It was a testament to James's superior balance and athletic reflexes that the broken plank hadn't thrown him to the floor.

"Oops," he said sheepishly as he leaped clear. "I was not expecting that to happen. Sorry."

She waved it off. "If that's the worst damage we do today, I'll consider that a plus. Why, exactly, were you jumping up and down on it in the first place?"

"When I walked over it, this section felt different, like it wasn't solid underneath. It turns out it wasn't."

Grinning at his perplexed expression, she joined him to peer into the hole. It was a shallow compartment, deliberately built into the floor. "Looks like you found the royal hiding place. Oooh, maybe there are still some priceless jewels in there."

Eagerly, she knelt and pulled the broken board from the hole. "Hand me your phone."

James placed it in her outstretched hand and when she aimed it into the gap, the lighted screen revealed a small box. Leaning forward slightly on her knees, she stuck her hand down into the space and only as her fingers closed over the box did she think about the possibility of spiders. Ick. Since it was too late, she yanked the box out and set it on the floor next to James.

"Anything else?" he asked, his body hot against her back as he peered over her shoulder, lips grazing her ear.

It shouldn't have been such a turn-on, but then, there was nothing about James that *didn't* turn her on. Warmth bloomed in her midsection and as she arched her back to increase the contact with his torso, the feel of him hummed through her.

"Maybe," she murmured. "Why don't you reach around here and see for yourself."

He must have picked up on her meaning. His arms embraced her from behind, drawing her backward into his body, and his fingers fumbled around the edge of the hole without delving more than half an inch into it.

"Nope. Nothing in there." His lips nuzzled her neck as he spoke and she could tell his attention was firmly on her. The hard length grinding into her rear said he'd lost interest in whatever else might be in the decades-old hiding place as well. "But what have we here?"

"I think you better investigate," she said, and guided his hands under her shirt, gasping as his questing fingertips ran over her sensitive breasts.

"You're not fully dressed," he accused her with a naughty laugh. "Ms. Montoro, I am shocked at your lack of undergarments. It's almost as if you expected a bloke's hands to be under your shirt."

"You say that like it's a bad thing." Her core heated as he caressed her, nudging her rear with his hard erection. "And as you're the only man around, you're welcome."

His laugh vibrated along her spine, warming her further. She loved it when he laughed, loved being the reason he was amused. Loved it when he touched her as if he'd discovered something rare and precious and he planned to become intimately familiar with every nook and cranny.

Then he got serious, palming her aching nipples, massaging and working her flesh until she could hardly breathe from wanting him. Would she *ever* get tired of that, of the gasping need and clawing desire? She hoped not.

She whipped off her shirt and tossed it on the bed, granting him full access. Arching against him, she pushed her breasts into his hands and flung her head back against his shoulder. As if reading her mind, he fastened his lips to her earlobe, sucking on it gently as one hand wandered south in a lazy pattern, pouring more fire on top of the flames he'd already ignited as her flesh heated under his fingertips.

Finally, his fingers slid into her shorts and toyed for an eternity with her panties, stroking her through the fabric, teasing her as he kissed her throat. So hot and ready, she could hardly stand waiting until he'd had his fill of exploring.

When she moaned in protest at the delay, he eased her back against his thighs and slipped off the rest of her clothing. Without a word, he picked her up and spun her around, placing her gently on the bed, his dark gaze worshipping her body.

Even that heaped more coals on the fire and she shuddered.

Through hazy vision, she watched as he knelt between her thighs and kissed each one. His tongue traced a straight line across her flesh and then he glanced up at her under his lashes as he licked her core. His tongue was hard and blistering hot and wet.

The flare of white-hot pleasure made her cry out. He dove in, tasting her in a sensuous perusal that drained her mind. *Yes*, she screamed. Or maybe that had only been in her head. Her body thrashed involuntarily as he pleasured her with his mouth, slight five o'clock shadow abrading her thighs as he moved.

Higher and higher she spun, hips bucking closer to the source of this amazing pleasure with each thrust of his tongue. The light scape of his teeth against her sensitive bud set off a rolling, thick orgasm that blasted her apart faster and harder than anything she'd ever felt before.

"Now," she murmured huskily and lay back on the counterpane in invitation. "I want your very fine body on mine."

He complied, clothes hitting the floor in a moment. He stretched out over her, his lean torso brushing her breasts deliciously. She wiggled until they were aligned the way she wanted, reveling in the dark sensation of this man covering her.

Savoring the anticipation, she touched him, letting her hands roam where they pleased. Fingertips gliding over his muscled back—gorgeously bunching as he held himself erect so he wouldn't crush her—she hummed her appreciation and nipped at his lips until he took her mouth in a scorching kiss reminiscent of the one he'd given her at her core, tongue deep inside her.

Wordlessly, she urged him on by rolling her hips, silently begging him to complete her as only he could. A brief pause as he got the condom on and then he slid into her, filling her body as gloriously as he filled her soul.

She gasped and clung with all her muscles.

James.

Absolutely the best thing that had ever happened to her. The sexiest man she'd ever been with, for sure, but also the only one who *saw* her. No pretense. No games. She couldn't tear her gaze from his face and something shifted inside, opening the floodgates of a huge and wonderful and irrevocable surge of emotion.

She let herself feel, let everything flow as he loved her. She couldn't even find the capacity to be shocked. It was dangerous—she knew that—but couldn't help it. Murmuring encouragement, his name, who knew what else, she rode out another climax made all the more intense by the tenderness blooming in her heart for the man who'd changed everything. But the wonderful moment soured as soon as her breathing slowed and the hazy glow wore off. She couldn't tell him she'd discovered all these things inside that had his name written all over them. Could she?

No. Fear over his reaction gripped her and in the end, she kept her big mouth shut. After their affair became public, maybe she could admit he'd done something irrevocable to her. But now, reeling it all back, she lay in his arms, letting him hold her tight as if he never meant to let go.

Later, when they'd finally gained the strength to dress, she noticed the box still on the floor near the broken boards. "We should open that."

She pushed at it with her bare foot and it tumbled over, lid flying open and spilling its contents all over the hardwood planks. Letters. Ten or twenty of them, old and fragile, with spidery pale blue handwriting looping across the yellowed pages.

Picking one up, she squinted at it but in the low light of the still musty bedroom, it was too hard to read. She flipped it over to see more of the same faded writing.

"What are they?" James peered over her shoulder, breath warm and inviting across her neck. "Front *and* back. Looks like someone had a lot to say."

"Oh, no." She shook her head and moved out of his reach with a laugh that came out a lot less amused than she'd intended. "You are banned from coming up behind me from now on."

She was far too raw inside to let him open her up again. Not so soon.

"What?" His wicked grin belied the innocent spread of his hands. "I was curious. I can't help it if breathing the same air as me gets you all hot and bothered."

It was a perfectly legitimate thing to say. They flirted and teased each other all the time. *All* the time, and she normally loved it.

He was just so beautiful standing there against the backdrop of the bed where he'd made her feel amazing and whole, made her feel as if she could do anything as long as he was by her side, holding her hand.

Suddenly, her throat closed and she barely caught a sob that welled up from nowhere. This was supposed to be a fun-filled, magnificently hot getaway from the world. When had everything gotten so complicated?

"I, um… Tía Isabella will want these." Bella held up the letters in one hand with false cheer. "I'm just going to go put them in my bag so I don't forget them."

She turned away from James and left the room as quickly as she could without alerting him to her distress. Apparently she'd succeeded.

And now she was completely messed up because she'd hoped he would follow her and demand to know why she was crying.

They slept in the servant's quarters again because they hadn't gotten nearly enough accomplished upstairs due to the detour Bella had sprung on James.

Not that he minded. She could detour like that all day long.

When he awoke, he missed Bella's warmth instantly. She wasn't in the bed. Sitting up, he sought a glimpse of her through the open bathroom door, but nada.

Shame. He liked waking up with her hair across his chest and her legs tangled with his. Surprisingly. This was officially the longest stretch he'd spent with a woman in… ages. Not since Chelsea. And even then, he hadn't been happy in their relationship, not for a long time. When she'd broken up with him because she'd met someone else, he'd been relieved.

Wondering where Bella had taken off to, James vaulted from the bed and dressed, whistling aimlessly as he stuck his shirt over his head. He felt a twinge in his back at the site of an old football injury. Probably because he'd spent the past few days using a different muscle group than the ones he normally engaged while strength training and keeping his footwork honed. Cleaning decades of grime from a place was hard work. But he liked the result—both in the appearance of the house and the gratitude Bella expressed.

Strolling out into the newly-scrubbed kitchen, he reached for the teapot he'd purchased, along with a slew of other absolute necessities, and saw Bella in his peripheral vision sitting outside on the back stoop. She was staring off into the distance as if something was troubling her.

He had a suspicion he knew what it was. Today they were supposed to drive into Playa Del Onda. Should he pretend he'd forgotten and not bring it up so they didn't have to go? He hated that she'd worked the whole confrontation over the engagement announcement up in her mind into something unpleasant. It really shouldn't be so complicated.

Demand a retraction. Done. Of course, getting her father to agree wouldn't necessarily be easy, but it certainly wouldn't be complicated.

In the end, he opted to join her on the stoop without comment, drawing her into his arms to watch the sun burst from behind the clouds to light up the back acreage. She snuggled into his torso and they sat companionably, soaking up the natural beauty of the wild overgrowth.

A horn blasted from the front of the house, startling them both. "Expecting someone?" he asked and she shook her head. "Stay here. I'll see what it is."

"You can't." Her mouth turned down. "I have to be the one. It's Montoro property."

Enough of this hiding and watching their step and having to do things separately so no one could take a picture of them together. They were catering to the whims of their fathers, whether she realized it or not.

"We'll go together." He rose and held out his hand.

She hesitated for so long, an uneasy prickle skittered across the back of his neck. It was way past time to dispense with all this secrecy nonsense. He wanted to do what he pleased and go wherever he wished without fear of someone creating a scandal. Today was a perfect day to stop the madness, since they already planned to confront her father.

Firmly, he took her hand and pulled her to her feet. "Yes. Together. If someone takes a picture, so be it. We're talking to your father today, so there's no reason to keep up this game of hide and seek. Not any longer."

Heaving a huge breath, she nodded. "Okay."

Together, they walked to the front, where a delivery driver stood on the front drive, waving.

"Tengo un paquete," he said, and touched his cap.

Smashing. One-day delivery, as advertised. James had been worried the gift he'd ordered for Bella wouldn't arrive in time, but obviously the exorbitant rush charge had been worth it.

"Gracias," James responded immediately. *"¿Dónde firmo?"*

Bella's eyebrows quirked. "When did you learn Spanish?"

"In like grade four," he retorted with a laugh. "I grew up in a Spanish-speaking country, remember?"

The driver held out his clipboard and once James signed, the deliveryman went to the back of the truck and pulled free a large parcel. Handing it over, the driver nodded once and climbed back into his truck, starting it up with a roar.

The package squawked over the engine sound.

"What in the world is in there?" Bella asked, clearly intrigued as James carried the box into the house through the front door, careful not to cover the air holes with his arms.

"It's a gift. For you." James pulled the tab to open the top of the box, as the Spanish instructions indicated. The box side fell open to reveal the large metal birdcage holding two green macaws. They squawked in tandem.

Bella gasped. "James! What is this?"

"Well, I must have gotten the wrong birds if it's not abundantly clear," he said wryly. "You said you missed your macaws so I brought some to you. Are they okay?"

He'd paid an additional flat fee to guarantee the birds would arrive alive. They looked pretty chipper for having been shipped from the mainland overnight.

With a loud sniff and a strange, strangled mumble, Bella whirled and fled the room, leaving James with two loud birds and a host of confusing, unanswered questions.

"I guess I muddled things up," he told the birds.

He put the cage on the coffee table and gave them some water as he'd been instructed when he ordered the birds, but his irritation rose as he poured. More water ended up on the floor than in the container.

If he could just punch something, his mood would even out. Probably.

Was he supposed to chase Bella down and apologize for spending money on her? Demand an explanation for why she'd hated the gift so much, a simple thank you was beyond her?

By the time he'd ripped open the package of bird food and poured some in the dish, she hadn't returned and his temper had spiked past the point of reasonableness. So he went in search of her and found her upstairs lying in a tight ball on the bed in the master suite. Sobbing.

Instantly, his ire drained and he crawled into the bed to cuddle her, stroking her hair until she quieted enough to allow his windpipe to unclench. "What's wrong, sweetheart?"

She didn't answer and his gut twisted.

Maybe she'd been looking for the exit and his gift had upset her. Women were funny about expensive presents, thinking a bloke had all kinds of expectations in mind if they accepted the gift.

"There aren't any strings attached to the birds, Bella. If you like them, keep them. If you don't, I'll…" *No returns*, the place had said. "…sort it."

His throat went tight again. If she was done here, the birds were the least of his problems. He wasn't ready to end things, not yet. Eventually, sure. His agent had a phone call scheduled with Liverpool today, but that was only the beginning of a long process that might not net him anything other than dashed hopes.

Had he inadvertently speeded up the timeline of their parting with his gesture?

"I like them," she whispered, her mouth buried in the bedspread.

His heart unstuck from his rib cage and began to beat again. "Then talk to me, hon. I'll uncomplicate it, whatever it is."

Without warning, she flipped to face him and the ravaged look on her face sank hooks into his stomach, yanking it toward his knees.

"Not this. You can't uncomplicate it because *you're* the complication, James."

Circles again, and they didn't do circles. Not normally. She shot straight—or at least she had thus far. Had things changed so much so quickly?

"What did I do that's so horrible?" he demanded.

The little noise of disgust she made deep in her throat dredged up some of his earlier temper, but he bit it back to give her the floor.

"You came in here," she raged, "and tore down all my ideas about how this thing between us was going to go. You understand me, pay attention to me. And worse than all of that, you made me fall for you!"

The starkness in her expression sealed his mouth shut once and for all, and he couldn't have spoken for a million euros.

"And I'm scared!" she continued. "I've never been in love. What am I supposed to do? Feel? I'm running blindfolded through the dark."

Too much. Too fast. Too...everything. He blinked rapidly but it didn't do anything to ease the burning in his eyes. He couldn't...she wasn't... *Deep breath. Hold it together.*

She was afraid. Of *him* and what was happening inside her. That was the most important thing to address first. Cautiously, he reached out and took her hand. He was so completely out of his depth, it was a wonder his brain hadn't shut down.

This was a challenge. Maybe the most important one of his life, and after all his claims of being able to uncomplicate anything, now was a good time to start. No buckling under the pressure allowed. Bella needed to feel as if she could trust him and obviously she didn't.

Heart pounding—because honestly, the freaking out wasn't just on her side—he cleared his throat. "Look me in the eye and tell me that again. But without all the extra stuff."

"Which part?" she whispered, searching his gaze, her eyes huge, their expression uneasy.

"The thing about falling for me." Her nails cut into his hand as they both tightened their grip simultaneously. This was a tipping point, and the next few minutes would decide which way it tipped. "I want to hear it straight from your heart."

His lungs seized and he honestly couldn't have said which way he wanted it to tip. What did he hope to accomplish by making this request of her? But he'd spoken the honest truth—regardless of everything, he wanted to hear it again.

"I'm falling for you," she said simply in the husky voice that automatically came out when she was deeply affected.

Something broke open inside him, washing him with warmth, huge and wonderful and irreversible. And suddenly, it wasn't very complicated at all. "Yeah. I've got something along those lines going on over here as well."

That something had been going on for a while. And he was quite disturbed that Will had realized it first. Bella was special and admitting it wasn't the big deal he'd made it out to be. Because the specialness had always been true, from the first moment her body aligned with his on the beach. It was as if he'd been waiting for that moment his whole life and when it happened, his world clicked into place.

"Really?" Hope sprang into her eyes, deepening the blue. "Like a little bit or a whole lot?"

"With no basis for comparison, I'd say it's something like being flung off a cliff and finding out exactly what maximum velocity is," he said wryly. "And it's about as scary as cliff diving with no parachute, since we're on the subject."

The smile blooming on her face reminded him of the sunrise they'd just watched together outside, before the birds had prompted this second round of confessions.

"Isn't it against the guy code to tell a woman she scares

you?" She inched toward him and smoothed a hand over his upper arm, almost as if she was comforting him—which was supposed to be his role in this scenario.

"All of this is against the guy code." He rolled his eyes and she laughed, as he'd intended. The harmonious fullness in his chest that magically appeared at the sound was an unexpected bonus. "Can you at least fill me in on why I had to pry all of this out of you with a crowbar?"

She scrubbed at her face, peering at him through her fingers. "This is not how it was supposed to go. We were going to have a couple of hot dates and maybe I would end up going back to Miami. Maybe you'd jet off to another country like you always do. No one said anything about losing my heart along the way."

A little awed at the thought of Bella's heart belonging to him, he reached out and flattened his palm against her chest, reveling in the feel of it beating against his hand. "I'll take good care of it."

He realized instantly that it was the wrong thing to say.

"For how long?" She sat up and his hand fell away. He missed the warmth immediately. "Until you get a new football contract and take off? You don't do relationships. *I* don't do relationships. Are you prepared to figure out why the hard way—with each other?"

"Yes," he said instantly. "Stop making this so difficult. *If* I get a contract, you come with me. Simple."

The alternative was unthinkable. Actually, he'd never thought about these kinds of things. Never had a reason to. Women came, women left. But this one—he had an opportunity here to grab on to her tight with both hands and no matter how much it scared him, he wasn't letting go.

Catching her lip between her teeth, she worried it almost raw. "What if we get my father to retract the engagement announcement and everything is wonderful. We can date in the open. And then we find out the only thing we had going for us was the secrecy?"

"What, you're afraid I won't be keen on all of this if we don't have to sneak around?" A laugh slipped from his mouth before he fully registered the serious set of her jaw. It finally dawned on him. "That's what you're afraid of."

She shifted uncomfortably. "It's a real possibility."

"It's a real possibility that you'll figure out the same thing," he shot back and the wracked expression on her face floored him. "You already thought of that."

Ice formed instantly in his stomach. It had never occurred to him while they were confessing unexpected feelings that he hadn't actually removed the complications. The *real* complications might only be beginning. Falling for each other didn't magically make either of them relationship material and the potential to hurt each other was that much greater as a result.

Sometimes, no matter how much you practiced, you still missed the goal. And neither of them actually had much practice. What were the odds of success?

"Why do you think I got so upset?" she countered. "You're giving me everything I've ever wanted, and then you give me things I had no idea I wanted, and my heart does all this crazy stuff when you look at me, and when you kiss me it's like my life finally makes sense, and what if I'm the one who's building up this relationship into something mythical because I really like my men with a side of forbidden?"

"Okay, breathe."

He half laughed and ran a hand through his hair. This rated as the most honest conversation he'd ever had with a woman. And that made it all the more fascinating that he was still here, determined not to buckle. Bella was worth it.

She breathed. And then dropped the second bomb. "What if I want to get married someday? Is that potentially in the cards?"

He let the idea rattle around inside for a long moment,

but it didn't completely unnerve him to consider it. He wasn't saying yes, but wasn't saying no.

"What if it is?" He captured her gaze and held it, refusing to let her look away, where she might miss the sincerity of what he was telling her. "Will that scare you as well?"

His brother had predicted that, too. Silently, he cursed himself and then his omniscient twin. Well, he hadn't proposed yet and no one was saying he would. Grandfather's watch still belonged to James. For now.

"More than I could possibly tell you," she admitted.

But she didn't have to tell him because he had a pretty good idea that the adrenaline racing around in his body closely matched what was going on with her.

"And," she continued swiftly, "I'm not saying that I will want to get married. To you or anyone. But what if I do?"

"You know what?" He tipped her chin up. "I think it's a safe bet that we have more going on here than a forbidden love angle. And I also think that no matter what, we can be honest with each other about what's going on, whether it's marriage or something else. I might be wrong, but I'm willing to take that risk. Are you?"

"Will you hold my hand?" she asked in a small voice. "When you're holding my hand, I feel like the world is a different place, like nothing bad could ever happen."

Yeah, he got that. If they could do this together, it might actually work.

Tenderly, he laced his fingers with hers and held on. "I'll never let go, not even when we hit the water. Jump with me, Bella."

Her smile pierced his heart and he started to believe they might figure this out after all. There were a lot of unknowns, sure, and they still had to sort their families—which wouldn't be as easy as he might be pretending. But it felt as if they were at the beginning of something wonderful.

It wasn't until they'd climbed into the Lamborghini

an hour later that he glanced at his phone and noted two missed calls, followed by a text message…and had the strangest sense of foreboding, as if he'd vastly underestimated the level and complexity of the complications to come.

Ten

James was quiet during the drive back to Playa Del Onda and Bella left him alone with his thoughts.

After all, she'd been the one to change the game, and while he'd admitted his feelings had grown stronger than he'd expected as well, he hadn't argued when the subject of *what ifs* came up. It was a lot to take in. A lot to reconcile.

She still didn't know how she felt about all of this either. She certainly hadn't intended to blurt out something so difficult to take back as "I'm falling for you," but he'd been so sweet, first with the birds and then the way he handled her half-coherent stream of babbling about her fears. If any man was a keeper, it was James Rowling.

So the question was, how hard was it going to be to keep him? Her father was going to freak and there was no getting around the fact that James was still the wrong brother.

No matter. She wasn't ready to let James go, not yet. Whatever happened between her and James, they had a right to pursue it. And she wasn't leaving here without her father's promise to stop interfering.

When they walked into the house—together—Gabriel and her father were waiting for her in the foyer, thanks to a text message she'd sent on the way imploring her brother to play diplomat if the situation called for it.

Judging by the frown on Rafael's face, she'd made a good call.

"What is *he* doing here?" her father demanded, making it perfectly clear that he knew Bella hadn't brought home the correct Rowling despite their similar appearances—and that Rafael's feelings on the matter hadn't changed.

Bella halted but didn't drop James's hand. He squeezed hers tight in a show of solidarity but remained silent, earning a huge number of points. "James is here because I invited him. You've caused us both problems by announcing my engagement to Will Rowling and therefore, we both have a vested interest in resolving the situation."

"The problems caused by the engagement announcement are one hundred percent at your feet, Isabella." Her father crossed his arms over his expensive suit, presumably to ensure he appeared intimidating, but he'd lost any edge he might have had by using that tone of voice with her—and the man she was pretty sure she was in love with.

"Let's not sling accusations," Gabriel interjected and she smiled at him gratefully. "Listen to Bella, Dad. She's a grown woman and this is a friendly conversation between adults."

Rafael deflated. A bit.

Gabriel's "king" lessons had paid off, in Bella's humble opinion. He'd grown a lot in the past few weeks and no one was confused about Serafia's role in that. Her future sister-in-law—also the future queen—was an inspiration and Bella was happy to call Serafia family.

"You have the floor, Isabella." Her father glowered at James but didn't speak to him again, which was fine by her. For now.

"I don't want to marry Will. I told you this already.

Why in the world would you go ahead and issue a press release saying we were engaged? Do you hate the idea of my happiness so much?" Her voice broke against her will.

Why did she still care so much that her father didn't seem to see her as anything other than a bargaining chip?

James stepped forward and addressed Rafael directly. "Sir, you don't know me and I realize I'm not your first choice for your daughter, but please understand that she makes me happy. I want nothing more than to do the same for her. I hope you can respect that."

Well, if there was any question about whether she was in love with him, that speech pretty much shot all doubt to hell. There might even be swooning in her future. She grinned at him, not even caring that she probably looked like a besotted fool.

Her father sighed and rubbed his head but before he could speak, Gabriel held out his hand to James, shaking it vigorously.

"I can respect that." Her brother nodded once at James. "I didn't get a chance to mention it when we first met, but I occasionally watched you play for Real Madrid. Bum deal that they released you. Big mistake on their part, in my opinion."

"Thanks." James smiled and bowed slightly to Gabriel, despite being told the prince didn't like formality. "And good luck to you. Alma is in brilliant hands with you at the helm."

Now that all the small talk was out of the way… "Dad, James and I are going to be a couple. You have to retract the engagement story or we're going to have a scandal on our hands. I don't want that for Gabriel or the Montoro family as a whole."

"All of which would have been avoided if you'd simply gotten with the program," Rafael insisted. "We're all making sacrifices for Gabriel—"

"Hold on a minute." The future king threw up his hands

with a frown. "Don't drag me into this. I never asked Bella to marry Will Rowling and frankly, an arranged marriage is ridiculous in this day and age. I've never understood the reasoning."

"You need the alignment with Rowling Energy," her father sputtered and might have gone on if Gabriel hadn't interrupted again.

"Yes. I do. But Bella is asking us to find another way. What kind of king would I be if I didn't at least try to take her wishes into account?" Gabriel asked rhetorically, his regal voice echoing with sincerity in the grand foyer. "Dad, I think you should consider the retraction, especially if Bella and James's relationship is what they say it is."

Gabriel shot Bella a look that said he'd taken one look at her dopey face and made all kinds of assumptions about the nature of her relationship with James. But then, bringing James with her to the showdown had probably tipped her brother off to that the moment they'd crossed the threshold. "I don't kiss and tell, so you can forget any juicy details, if that's what you're after."

Gabriel mimed putting his fingers in his ears and shook his head with a shudder.

Clearing his throat in his no-nonsense way, Rafael put on his best disappointed-father face. "It's not just the alignment with Rowling Energy that's at stake here, Isabella. You have a tendency to be flighty. Irresponsible. Marriage will be good for you, if you choose someone who settles you. Will is as steady as they come."

The unvoiced and pointed barb directed at James was: *and the man you waltzed in here with is the opposite of steady*. The sting of hearing her father's unvarnished opinion of *her* was totally eclipsed by the negativity directed toward James, who was nothing like what her father assumed.

"That's where you're wrong, Dad. Will might be good at holding a company together, but James is good at holding *me* together. He settles me in a way I've never felt before. I'd rather spend an evening with him washing windows than at a party."

The words were out of her mouth before she consciously planned to say them, but once they took root in her heart, she recognized the truth. She didn't have any desire to be the party girl she'd been in Miami. Her boredom at Will Rowling's party hadn't had anything to do with the difference in party styles across the ocean, but in the subtle changes already happening inside *her*.

"By the way," she threw in. "You haven't asked, but in case you're wondering, your irresponsible daughter has spent the past few days restoring the old farmhouse near Aldeia Dormer that's part of the Montoro holdings. It looks really amazing so far and I couldn't have done it without James's help. I've also spent almost one hundred percent of that time with him, yet I dare you to find one illicit photograph of the two of us."

"What's this about a farmhouse?" Gabriel's eyebrows drew together as he homed in on her.

"I'll fill you in later," she promised. "Can you try to be happy for me, Dad? If you can't do that, I'll settle for that retraction. I do have a strong sense of my royal obligations. I'd just like you to respect the fact that I feel differently about what they are than you do."

"I'll issue the retraction but only to avoid the potential scandal. I cannot condone this relationship. I would prefer that you do not continue seeing him." Her father's sidelong glance at James spoke volumes. There was no doubt he still considered the wrong Rowling a terrible influence.

"I can't do that, Dad. And I'm disappointed that you still can't see the value James brings to my life." Her voice cracked and she cursed herself once again for caring. Regardless, she was getting the retraction she asked for, and she'd take it.

"You're right, I can't. I fully expect that once the thrill

wears off, you'll be back to your former ways, Isabella."
With that vote of no confidence ringing in her ears, her
father motioned to James. "And if you're not, *he* will be.
This is a disaster in the making. Will it do any good for
me to warn you to keep your brother's reign at the fore-
front of your thoughts?"

"I always keep Gabriel in mind," she countered.

"Good, then the three of you can deal with Patrick Rowling." Her father wheeled on Gabriel with a scowl. "Since
you're taking Bella's side in this, I'll let you handle the
delicate matter of ensuring the alliance I painstakingly
put into place won't suffer."

Her father stalked off to go terrorize the staff or something.

"Sorry," Bella said to her brother with a scowl. "I didn't
mean for you to get in the middle of this. At least not that
way. Are you okay with talking to Mr. Rowling?"

Unfortunately, thanks to the hours upon hours of conversation with James at the farmhouse, Bella knew exactly
why Patrick wasn't going to be pleased with the develop-
ments.

"I'll talk to him," James volunteered, and Bella shot
him a small smile.

"That's a good idea." Gabriel's expression reflected the
gravity of the situation. "I'll speak with him as well. But
it's sticky. We have business agreements in place that could
be in jeopardy. You should lie low for a while longer until
matters are a bit more settled."

Great, more hiding. Why was it such a problem that two
people wanted to spend time together? But the mention of
things like business agreements clued her in that there was
more at stake than she might have supposed.

At least her father hadn't forbidden her to see James.
He just said he didn't want her to and made his disappointment in her clear. Fortunately, she had a lot of practice at
living with her father's disappointment. If Gabriel worked

things out with Mr. Rowling, maybe her father would come around. It could happen.

Gabriel and James talked a bit more about the logistics of their impending conversations with Patrick Rowling until James's cell phone rang.

He glanced at it and excused himself to take the call. Based on his expression, it must be shocking news indeed. Gabriel went off to do king stuff as James ended the call.

"What is it?" she whispered, almost afraid to ask. They'd barely confessed their fledgling feelings to each other, their fathers were still potential stumbling blocks in their relationship and she didn't know how many more hits they should be expected to take.

"Liverpool." His tone couldn't have been more stunned. "Management wants to meet with me. Tomorrow."

"Liverpool? Isn't that a city in England?" Then it dawned on her that he meant the football team. "They want to talk to you about a contract? That's great!"

"I have to fly to London." His enthusiasm shone from his face. Then he grew serious. "I don't know what they're going to say. But if it's an offer, it would be hard for me to turn down."

"Why would you turn it down? You can't."

"I would have to live in England for most of the year." His gorgeous eyes sought and held hers as the implications weighed down her shoulders.

This was serious, life-altering stuff, the kind of thing couples with a future considered. While she thought that was where they were headed—thought that was where she *wanted* them to go—it was another matter entirely to have Big Decisions dropped in your lap before you were ready. It was far scarier than accidentally revealing your feelings.

"We'll figure it out," she murmured, as though she knew what she was talking about. "We're jumping together. Just don't let go of my hand, remember?"

Instead of agreeing, or grabbing her hand and shooting

her a tender smile, he scrubbed at his eyes with stiff fingers. "Everything is moving too fast."

Her heart froze.

Everything? As in their relationship, too? He'd volunteered to come with her, to talk to his father and work out the issues between the Montoro family and Rowling Energy—was he having second thoughts now? "One step at a time, James. Go to England and see what they say. Then we can talk."

He nodded and swept her up in a fierce hug. She inhaled his familiar scent, soaked in his essence. That at least felt somewhat normal and it calmed her a bit.

"I'll call you the moment I know something. Guess I'll be gone a couple of days."

Watching him drive away wrenched something loose inside her and the place ached where it used to be attached. She rubbed at her chest and perversely wondered if it would get better or worse if he called with the news that Liverpool wanted to sign him. Because that's when she'd find out once and for all whether removing the temptation of the forbidden caused him to completely lose interest.

James resisted pulling at his starched collar. Barely. If he'd had more notice that Liverpool wanted a meeting, he might have scared up a more comfortable suit. Contract negotiations rarely included the player and the fact that Liverpool specifically asked for James to attend meant… what? He didn't know and it was weighing on him.

The small room got smaller the longer Liverpool's management murmured behind their cupped hands. James could tell from their less-than-impressed faces that his agent's opening pitch hadn't won anyone over.

So maybe the comfort of the suit didn't matter when your entire future was on the line.

Liverpool had expressed definite interest in picking up

James if the price was right, according to his agent, but they wanted to move fast on making a decision.

James was not leaving here without that contract. It wasn't about the money. It was about putting his mistakes behind him and gaining the opportunity to prove his loyalty to a club. He had to. To show Bella he was really the hero material she saw him as. To prove that he was worth all the trouble they'd gone through to be together.

James cleared his throat. "It's obvious you have reservations about me. What are your concerns?"

The three suits on the other side of the table all stared at him with varying degrees of surprise. Why, because he didn't subscribe to the British philosophy of keeping a stiff upper lip?

His sports agent, Spencer Stewart, shot him an annoyed glance and waved off James. "No one has reservations. We're all professionals here. So, give us your best offer and we'll consider it."

"Yes, we're all professionals," James agreed. "But these gentlemen have every right to question my capacity to act professionally. Let's call a spade a spade. I made mistakes. But I'm ready to be serious about my career and I want to play my heart out for a team willing to give me that chance."

All at once, it occurred to him that Alma's reserve team had already offered him that chance. And he'd turned his nose up at it. As if he was too good for what he considered the small time.

That didn't sit well. No club *owed* him a spot on the roster.

Liverpool's manager nodded slowly. "That's fair. As is our original salary offer. The cap is a concern, after all."

James kept his face straight, wishing he could argue. The cap was only a concern for a risky acquisition. They'd gladly pay the fines for going over the cap to gain a player with a less scandalous past. He'd have to take a pay cut if he wanted to play for Liverpool—and work twice as hard to earn it. Simple as that.

And he'd have to move to England.

A few days ago, he would have already been packed in anticipation of relocating as fast as possible. He could avoid his father for good. That conversation with dear old Dad about the agreements between Rowling Energy and the Montoros—the one he'd promised Gabriel he'd have—never had to happen.

Liverpool was the perfect solution to his relationship with Bella—if they had to lie low, what better place to do it than England?

But he couldn't get enthusiastic about it all at once. Bella deserved better than to be required to hide their relationship because of his past. She shouldn't have to move to England if she wanted to be with him, just because he couldn't get another contract.

How had things grown so complicated so fast? The king of uncomplicating things was falling down on the job.

"I need some time to weigh my options," James announced suddenly. Because he'd just realized he not only had options, he also had other people to consider outside of himself. "I appreciate the offer, and it's generous under the circumstances. Mr. Stewart will update you soon on my decision."

Liverpool wasn't the right club for him. Not yet, maybe not ever. Not until he'd proven to everyone—Bella, his father, hell, even himself—that he could stop running away from conflict and deal with the consequences of his actions. He needed to be in Alma to do that. Permanently.

Actually, this wasn't very complicated at all.

James loved football. He'd thought for so long that a professional league contract was his goal, only to find the game had completely changed on him. Bella had changed it. He wanted to be a better man for her. She was the best reason of all to find out whether he could finally stand up under extreme pressure and come out a winner.

James hurried to Heathrow, eager to get back home and tell Bella that her belief in him wasn't misplaced. That he could be the hero she saw him as. He wanted to commit to her, to have a future with her.

As he settled back in his seat and switched off his cell phone in accordance with the flight attendant's instructions, he glanced at his watch. And cursed as he realized what was happening—it looked as if Will was going to be the lucky recipient of Grandfather's watch after all.

When James got off the plane in Del Sol, he powered up his cell phone intending to call Bella immediately. *Surprise. I'm home early.*

But the first text message that popped up was from Will.

Chelsea is here. You better come talk to her. She's camped out in the lobby disrupting business.

What the hell? He swore, dove into his Lamborghini and then drove to Rowling Energy at double the speed limit. The harrowing hairpin turns should have put a smile on his face the way they normally did, but Will's text message had effectively killed any cheer he might have taken from the thrill.

If only he'd called Chelsea back yesterday, when he'd seen the missed calls on his phone, the ensuing fiasco could have been avoided. But Bella had been nervous about confronting her father and he really didn't want to talk to Chelsea in the first place. So he'd ignored her. What could they possibly have to say to each other?

Apparently that had irritated his ex-girlfriend enough for her to go to Rowling Energy and bother his brother. James had dated her for…what, four months? Not long enough for her to remember that James hated Rowling

Energy so much that he rarely set foot in the place. It had taken something as important to him as Bella to get him through the door last week.

His phone beeped. Will had texted him again. Hope you're almost here. Your ex is a piece of work.

Still fuming, James screeched into a parking spot and stomped into the elevator. Why in the hell had she taken it upon herself to disrupt an entire company in order to speak to an ex-lover she'd had no contact with for almost two years? When a bloke didn't ring you back, it meant he wasn't into you.

But when he arrived in the reception area, some of the pieces fell into place. Chelsea, looking less glamorous and far more worn than he recalled, sat on the leather couch bouncing a baby.

A baby.

Obviously she'd been busy since they'd broken up and was clearly hard up for money. What, did she think James was going to fund her for old times' sake? How dare she bring a kid in here as a sympathy ploy? His ire increased exponentially. She *was* a piece of work.

"Chelsea." She glanced up. "Can we take this outside please?"

She nodded, hoisted the baby to her hip and followed him out of the building to a shaded courtyard around the side of the building where employees sometimes ate lunch. It was thankfully deserted.

"You have a lot of nerve barging into my father's company to extort money from me," he said by way of greeting to the woman he'd had only marginal affection for once upon a time.

"That's not why I'm here and besides, you didn't call me back," she reminded him as she settled onto a bench with the baby. "How else was I supposed to find you?"

He bit back a curse. "You're barking up the wrong tree if you think I'm going to give you a dime out of the goodness of my heart because some plonker knocked you up and you're short on cash."

That would explain why she had a bargain basement fashion statement going on. When they'd dated, she spent thousands on clothes and jewelry, usually with his credit card.

"Not someone." Chelsea peered up at him, totally cool. In her element because she'd gotten his attention after all. "You. This is your daughter."

His vision blacked out for a moment as all the blood rushed from his head.

I have a baby daughter. None of those words belonged in the same sentence. Blindly, James felt for the bench so he could sink onto it before the cramp in his stomach knocked him to the grass.

"What are you talking about?" he demanded hoarsely over the street sounds floating through the privacy bushes. "I haven't even seen you in almost two years. That's a baby and they only take nine months to make."

Chelsea smirked and flipped her lanky brown hair behind her back. "She's almost a year old, Daddy. Do the math."

Daddy. His brain couldn't—*could not*—keep up, especially when she insisted on throwing inflammatory monikers onto the woodpile. And now she wanted him to do subtraction on top of it all?

"Why…wha— How…?" Deep breath. His tongue couldn't seem to formulate the right questions. "Paternity test? I want one."

Okay, now he was on top of this situation. Get to the bottom of this pack of lies and toss her out on her no-longer-attractive rear end.

She rolled her eyes. "Fine. I'll arrange one as soon as possible. But there's really no question."

The little girl picked that moment to turn her head, peering directly at James for the first time.

Aqua eyes the exact color of his beamed at him through fringed lashes. Not only the exact color of his, but both Will and their late mother shared the rare shade.

His world tilted and slid quickly off the rails. The paternity test would be superfluous, obviously.

He couldn't tear his gaze away from the baby. His baby. It was real. This was his child, and until five minutes ago he'd had no idea she existed. He'd missed his daughter's birth, along with a ton of other milestones, which he mourned all at once. Chelsea could never rectify that crime.

"Why now, Chelsea? You should have bloody well shown up long before today with this news."

"I thought she was Hugh's." Chelsea shrugged nonchalantly as if they were discussing a pair of pants she'd found in her closet after they'd broken up. "He's the guy I left you for. I must have miscalculated my conception date, but I didn't realize it until recently when her eyes changed color. And I knew I couldn't keep this from you."

There was so much wrong with all of that, he hardly knew where to start. "What happened when her eyes changed color, Chelsea? Did you see dollar signs that Hugh couldn't match?"

"No." She frowned, pulling her full lips into a pout. "I thought it was right that you know about Maisey."

Maisey. His daughter's name was Maisey. And he'd had no say in it. Not that it was a horrible name, but if Chelsea had told him when she got pregnant, he might have been able to participate in the selection process. He'd have liked to name his daughter after his mum. Yet another thing this woman had stolen from him.

"If you thought about me at all, I'm sure it had more to do with things like child support."

He had to get over it and figure this out. Chelsea was his daughter's mother. Period. Like it or not, they were going to have some type of relationship for the next eighteen years, at least. Maybe longer.

Before she could deny her selfishness again, he eyed her. "What did Hugh think about your little error in calculation? Bet he wasn't so thrilled."

Chelsea looked away quickly but not before he saw the flash of guilt in her expression.

"He left you," James concluded grimly. "And you're skint."

She sighed. "Hugh refused to keep taking care of a kid that wasn't his and he might have been slightly ticked to find out that I fudged the details a little about the last time you and I slept together. So yeah, I'm low on money."

God, did the string of dumb decisions this woman had made ever end? This was his daughter's life Chelsea was playing around with, but she seemed to be treating it all like a big game.

The baby made a noise that sounded like a cross between a sob and a sigh and she captivated his attention instantly.

"What was that? Is she okay?" he whispered.

"She's a baby," Chelsea snapped impatiently. "That's what they do. Make noise. And cry. And poop."

This conversation had passed surreal ten minutes ago.

"What do you want from me?" he demanded.

Well, hell. It hardly mattered what she wanted. If this little breathing bundle of hair and pink outfit was his daughter, there was a lot more to consider than what the woman who'd given birth to her hoped to achieve. He had rights. He had options. And he would exercise both.

"I want you to be her father," Chelsea said simply.

"Done. We need to discuss child support and custody arrangements."

Reality blasted him like a freight train whistle. What was his life going to look like from now on? Did he need to reconsider Liverpool so he could be close to Chelsea in England? How would Bella feel about spending weekends with his infant daughter from now on?

He scrubbed at his face. *Bella.* God, this was going to be exactly what her father had predicted—a disaster. She deserved so much more than to be saddled with a boyfriend who had a kid. And what kind of new problems might this cause for her? An illegitimate child surely wasn't going to make her father suddenly approve of James.

"Nothing to discuss." Chelsea shook her head. "I don't want either one. I want you to take her. Forever. I'm signing over all my rights to you."

"You…what?"

Arms crossed mutinously like the immature woman she was, Chelsea scowled. "I'm done being a mum. I hate it. This is your fault, so you take her."

She said it as if they were discussing a stray dog. And she was making his choice easy. He didn't want such a selfish mum raising his daughter anyway. Sickened that he could have ever been intimate with this woman, he nodded grimly. "Seems like the best idea all the way around, then."

Single dad. The voice in his head wouldn't stop screaming that phrase, over and over, and the place in his heart that belonged to Bella ached at this new reality. Just as he'd accepted that he not only *could* do a long-term, roots-into-the-ground relationship, he wanted to. But not like this, with such a huge complication as a surprise baby.

The timing was horrific. Because he'd just realized why this was so difficult, why he couldn't take the Liverpool contract. Why he was so worried about dropping this news on Bella—he was in love with her.

Eleven

By evening, James hadn't called.

Bella tried not to think about it. He was busy with Liverpool. She got that. The one time she'd tried to call him, it went straight to voice mail. Maybe his cell phone had died and he'd forgotten his charger.

If not that, there was a simple explanation for his silence and when he got her message, he'd call. No one would willingly face down her father without having some skin in the game. James had said he'd call and he would. He cared about her. She knew he did.

After a long night of tossing and turning, she had to find something to do to keep busy and the farmhouse still needed work. It kept her mind off the disloyal thoughts that had crept in overnight—that the distance between here and England had given James some perspective and his feelings had cooled after all. Just as she'd feared.

Or he'd decided a princess with a scandal-averse family was too much work for a guy who liked to play the field.

Discovering a bird's nest in the tree close to the back

steps finally pulled her attention from her morose thoughts. She missed her own birds— she'd moved the macaws James had given her to the Playa Del Onda house since she hadn't planned to continue traveling back and forth. These baby birds filled the silence with high-pitched cheeps and she smiled as she watched them from an upstairs window.

It was a much-needed sign. Regardless of what happened with James and the news regarding his contract with Liverpool, she should go forward with conservation work. Birds would always need her and she liked having a purpose.

When she returned to Playa Del Onda, a maid met her in the foyer and announced Bella had a visitor in the salon.

James. Her heart did a twisty dance move in her chest. Of course she'd blown his silence out of proportion and they'd laugh over her silliness. Maybe he'd come straight from the airport and somehow she'd missed his call. As she dashed into the salon, she palmed her phone, already checking for the errant message.

It wasn't James, though, and the man standing by the window almost rendered her speechless. But she found her manners somehow.

"Mr. Rowling," Bella greeted James's father cautiously. "How nice to see you."

They'd met formally once before and she'd greeted him at Will's party, but this was the first time they'd spoken without others in attendance. Did James know he was here? Had he already talked to his father? If Gabriel had spoken to Mr. Rowling, he would have mentioned it to her. She was flying completely blind and nothing good could possibly come of this surprise meeting.

James's father didn't offer his hand but instead bowed as if they'd stumbled into a formal setting without her realizing it. "Princess Isabella. Thank you for seeing me on short notice."

"Of course." Mindful of her father's warning to watch

her step when dealing with matters important to the crown, she inclined her head graciously. "What can I do for you?"

"May we take a seat?" Mr. Rowling indicated the over-stuffed and incredibly uncomfortable couch.

Sure, why not add more formality on top of the already overbearing deference of the elder Rowling? She perched on the cushion and waited for Patrick Rowling to get to the point.

He cleared his throat. "I realize that you and Will have agreed to part ways and that you are seeing my other son. You've made a terrible mistake and I'm here to ensure you understand the full extent of it."

Geez, first her father and now Patrick Rowling? It was as if everyone thought she could be talked out of her feelings if they just tried hard enough. "Will would be a bigger mistake. We aren't interested in each other."

Mr. Rowling held up a conciliatory hand. "I'm not here to talk about Will. Granted, there is sound sense in a match between you and my son, but even I understand that the heart isn't always sensible."

Confused and suspicious, she eyed James's father. "Then why are you here?"

That had come out a little more bluntly than intended, but he didn't seem bothered by her lack of decorum.

Clearing his throat, he leaned forward as if about to impart a secret. "The mistake you're making, the one I'm here to help you avoid, is putting your faith in James. He is not a good choice for any woman, least of all you."

Her temper boiled over but she schooled her features and bit back the nasty phrase she'd been about to say. This man didn't know her and he had a lot of nerve assuming he had insight into what kind of man would be good for her.

But the worse crime was that he didn't know his own son either. That, she could correct.

"James is an amazing man. I'm shocked his own father doesn't recognize that, but since it's clear you don't, despite ample opportunity to come to know your son, I'll tell you. He has a good heart, a generous nature and most of all, he cares about me."

Her voice rang with sincerity. Because she believed what she was saying. He'd call soon and they'd talk about the future. Everything was going to work out.

Mr. Rowling frowned. "I do so hate to disagree. But my son is a notorious womanizer with little regard for anyone's feelings other than his own. Surely you're aware of his indiscretions." He swept her with a pitying once-over. "God help you if you're not."

Foreboding slid down her spine and raised the hair on the back of her neck.

"You mean the photographs in the tabloids?" She crossed her arms, wondering if it would actually protect her against this man's venom. "I'm aware of them."

James had been very upfront about his brush with scandal. Whatever his father thought he was going to accomplish by bringing up the pictures wasn't going to work.

"Oh, no, Princess Isabella." He shook his head with a *tsk*. "I'm talking about James's illegitimate daughter."

Bella's skin iced over. "His...what?" she whispered.

Mr. Rowling watched her closely through narrowed eyes, and she suspected he'd finally come to the meat of the reason he'd casually dropped by.

"James has an infant daughter he fathered with his last girlfriend. Shall I assume from your reaction that he hasn't mentioned any of this to you?"

"No," she admitted quietly as her pulse skipped a whole lot of beats. "I wasn't aware."

And of course there was a reason James hadn't told her. There had to be. Her mind scrambled to come up with one. But without James here to explain, she was only left with huge question marks and no answers.

In all that time at the farmhouse together, he'd never once thought to mention a baby he'd fathered with the girlfriend he'd stopped seeing nearly two years ago? Had she completely misread what he'd confessed to her about his feelings? None of this made any sense. Why would he talk about the implications of moving to England but not tell her he had a daughter?

It was a lie. Mr. Rowling was trying to cause problems. That was the only explanation.

Mr. Rowling eyed her and she didn't miss the crafty glint in his gaze. Neither of his sons took after this schemer in any way and it was a testament to James that he'd ended up with such an upstanding character.

"It's true," he said, somehow correctly interpreting the set of her jaw. "James will confirm it and then you might ask why he's kept it from you. It's a consideration for a woman when choosing whom she has a relationship with, don't you think?"

Yes, a huge consideration. That's what he'd meant by James not being a good choice for her. Because he wasn't trustworthy.

She shook her head against the rebellious thoughts. This was a campaign to poison her against James, plain and simple, but why, she couldn't fathom. "He has his reasons for not telling me. Whatever they are, I can forgive him."

Because that's what people in a relationship did. Not that she had any practice—she'd never had one, never dreamed she'd have one that tested her in quite this way. But James was worth figuring it out.

"You realize, of course, that his daughter is illegitimate." Mr. Rowling countered smoothly. "You're still in line for the throne should something happen to Gabriel. Alma doesn't cater to that sort of impropriety in its monarchy, and citizens have no patience for royal scandals. Frankly, neither do I."

It was a veiled threat, one she understood all too well after the discussion with Gabriel and her father about business between the crown and Rowling Energy. And blast it, he wasn't overstating the point about her position or potential to be queen one day. A princess couldn't drag an illegitimate child through the world's headlines.

Her head started to pound as her father's warning played over and over on an endless loop in her mind. Gabriel wouldn't be on her side with this one, not after what happened with Rafe and Emily and their unexpected pregnancy. Not after she'd already forced her brother to renegotiate agreements with Rowling, which would be very difficult to wade through indeed if Mr. Rowling's threat was to be believed.

If she continued to be with James, the entire future of Gabriel's reign—and indeed perhaps her own—might be in jeopardy.

"Let me ask you another question, Princess Isabella."

The way he said that made her spine crawl but she didn't correct him. Only her friends called her Bella and this man was not in that group. A shame since she'd hoped he would become her father-in-law someday. That dream had rapidly evaporated under his onslaught.

She nodded, too miserable to figure out how to make her voice work.

"What if she's not the only illegitimate child out there?"

God, he was right. The reality of it unleashed a wave of nausea through her stomach. James had made no secret of his playboy past. Since she'd never sat around in virginal white gowns either, it hadn't troubled her. Until now.

She very much feared she might throw up.

"If you weren't aware of the baby, you also probably aren't aware that her mother is here in Playa Del Onda visiting James." Mr. Rowling leaned forward, apparently oblivious to the hot poker he'd just shoved through Bella's chest. "I know you'd like to think that you're special. James has a particular talent with women. But the fact of the matter is that he still has very deep feelings for the mother of his child. Their relationship is far from over."

"That's not true," Bella gasped out. It couldn't be. She wasn't that naïve. "Anyway, James is in England."

The pitying look Mr. Rowling gave her nearly stopped her heart. "He's been back in Alma since yesterday."

"I trust James implicitly," she shot back and cursed the wobble in her voice. She did. But he'd come home from England and *hadn't called* and his silence was deafening. "Why are you telling me all of this?"

Mr. Rowling pursed his lips. "I'm simply making sure you are aware of what you are getting yourself into by refusing to see the truth about James. I have your best interests at heart."

She doubted that very much. But it didn't negate the accusations he'd brought against James. Her throat burned as she dragged breath into her lungs.

No. This was propaganda, plain and simple. She shook her head again as if she could make it all go away with the denial. "I need to talk to James."

"Of course," he agreed far too quickly. "I've said my piece. But before I go, please note that Will is still open to honoring the original marriage agreement."

With that parting comment, Mr. Rowling followed the butler out of the salon, leaving Bella hollowed out. She crawled onto her bed to lie in a tight ball, but nothing could ease the sick waves still sloshing through her abdomen.

Lies. All of it was lies. James could—and would—straighten all of this out and then they'd deal with the issue of his illegitimate child. Somehow.

Except he still didn't answer her call. Twice.

This silence…it was killing her. If he was done with her, she deserved to hear it from him, face-to-face. Not from his father.

She had to know, once and for all. If he wouldn't answer the phone, she'd go to his house.

The Montoro town car had long been on the list of instantly admitted vehicles at the Rowling Mansion gates, so the driver didn't have to announce Bella's presence. As Mr.

Rowling had said, James's green Lamborghini sat parked in the circular drive of the Rowling mansion.

Bella climbed out of the car, her gaze fastened to the Lamborghini, her heart sinking like a stone. James was home. And hadn't called. Nor would he answer his phone. The truth of Mr. Rowling's revelations burned at the back of her eyes but she refused to let the tears fall.

James would explain.

A woman's laugh floated to her on the breeze and Bella automatically turned toward the gazebo down the slope from the main drive. It was partially obscured by foliage but James was easy to make out. Even if she couldn't plainly see the watch on James's arm, Will didn't live here, and neither would he be at his father's house in the middle of the work day when he had a company to run.

The dark haired woman sitting in the gazebo with James faced away from Bella, but she'd bet every last euro in the royal treasury it was his former girlfriend. It didn't mean anything. They were probably talking about the daughter they shared. Patrick Rowling wasn't going to ruin her relationship with James.

Bella had come for answers and now she'd get them.

Feeling like a voyeur but unable to stop herself, she moved closer to catch what they were saying but the murmurs were inaudible. And then James threaded his fingers through the woman's hair and pulled her into a scorching kiss.

And it was a *kiss*, nothing friendly about it.

The back of Bella's neck heated as she watched the man she loved kiss another woman.

James was kissing another woman.

Brazenly. Passionately. Openly. As if he didn't care one bit whether anyone saw him.

His watch glinted in the late afternoon sun as he pulled the dark-haired woman closer, and the flash blinded Bella. Or maybe her vision had blurred because of the tears.

How long had she been playing the fool in this scenario—and was she truly the last to find out? Was everyone giggling behind their hands at her naïvety? Mr. Rowling had certainly known. This was going on in his house and as many times as she'd accused him of not knowing his son… *she* was the one who didn't know James.

It all swirled through her chest, crushing down with so much weight she thought her heart would cease to beat under the pressure.

Whirling, she fled back to the car, only holding back the flood of anguish long enough to tell the driver to take her home.

But when she finally barricaded herself in her room, it didn't feel like home at all. The only place she'd ever experienced the good, honest emotions of what a home should feel like was at the farmhouse. But it had all been a complete lie.

Still blinded by tears, she packed as much as she could into the bag she'd lived out of during those brief, precious days with James as they cleaned up the Montoro legacy. Alma could make do without her because she couldn't stay here.

Everything is moving too fast, he'd said. He'd meant *she* was, with her expectations and ill-timed confessions. The whole time, he'd had a woman and a baby on the side. Or was *Bella* the side dish in this scenario?

Horrified that she'd almost single-handedly brought down the monarchy with her own gullibility, she flung clothes into bags faster. New York. She'd go to New York where there were no bad memories. Her friends in Miami would only grill her about James because she'd stupidly kept them up to the minute as things unfolded with her new romance.

And her brother Rafe would see through her instantly. She couldn't stand to be around people who knew her well.

Within an hour, she'd convinced Gabriel to concoct

some story explaining her absence and numbly settled into the car as it drove her to the private airstrip where the Montoro jet waited to take her to New York. It was the perfect place to forget her troubles among the casual acquaintances she planned to look up when she got there.

The shorter her time in Alma grew, the more hollowed out she felt.

When her phone beeped, she nearly hurled it out the window. *James.* Finally, he'd remembered that she existed. She didn't care what he had to say, couldn't even bear to see his name on the screen. But a perverse need to cut her losses, once and for all, had her opening up the text so she could respond with something scathing and final.

I'm home. Came by, but Gabriel said you left. When will you be back? We need to talk.

She just bet he'd come by—to tell her he was in love with his daughter's mother. Or worse, to lie to her some more.

Bella didn't think twice before typing in her reply.

Not coming back. Have a nice life with your family.

Now she could shake Alma's dust off her feet and start over somewhere James and his new family weren't. New York was perfect, a nonstop party, and she intended to live it up. After all, she'd narrowly escaped making a huge mistake and now she had no responsibilities to anyone other than herself. Exactly the way she liked it.

But Bella cried every minute of the flight over the Atlantic. Apparently, she'd lost the ability to lie to herself about losing the man she loved.

Twelve

The Manhattan skyline glowed brightly, cheering Bella slightly. Of course, since leaving Alma, the definition of cheer had become: *doesn't make me dissolve into a puddle of tears.*

She stared out over the city that never slept, wishing there was one person out there she could connect with, who understood her and saw past the surface. None of her friends had so much as realized anything was wrong. They'd been partying continuously since this time last night. It was a wonder they hadn't dropped from exhaustion yet.

"Hey, Bella!" someone called from behind her in the crowded penthouse. "Come try these Jell-O shots. They're fab."

Bella sighed and ignored whomever it was because the last thing she needed was alcohol. It just made her even more weepy. Besides, they'd go back to their inane conversations about clothes and shoes whether she joined them or not, as they'd been doing for hours. That was the problem with hooking up with casual acquaintances—they didn't have anything in common.

But neither did she want to call her friends in Miami. The problem was that she didn't really fit in with the wealthy, spoiled crowd she used to run around with in Miami either. Maybe she hadn't for a long time and that was why she'd felt so much like a hurricane back home— she'd never had enough of a reason to slow down and stop spinning.

In Alma, she'd found a reason. Or at least she'd thought she had. But apparently her judgment was suspect.

The party grew unbearably louder as someone turned up the extensive surround sound system that had come with the condo when Rafael had purchased it from a music executive. A Kanye West song beat through the speakers and Bella's friends danced in an alcohol-induced frenzy. All she wanted to do was lie on the wooden floor of a farmhouse eating grapes with a British football player who'd likely already forgotten she existed.

Barricading herself in her room—after kicking out an amorous couple who had no sense of boundaries—she flopped onto the bed and pulled the bag she'd carried from the farmhouse into her arms to hold it tight.

The bag was a poor substitute for the man it reminded her of. But it was all she had. When would she stop missing him so much? When would her heart catch a clue that James had not one, but two females in his life who interested him a whole lot more than Bella?

Something crumpled inside the bag. Puzzled, she glanced inside, sure she'd emptied the bag some time ago.

The letters.

She'd totally forgotten about finding the cache of old, handwritten letters under the floorboards of the farmhouse. She'd meant to give them to Tía Isabella and with everything that had happened…well, it was too late now. Maybe she could mail them to her aunt.

When she pulled the letters from the bag, the memories of what had happened right after she'd found the letters flooded her and she almost couldn't keep her grip on the string-bound lot of paper.

James holding her, loving her, filling her to the brim. They'd made love on that gorgeous bed with the carved flowers not moments after discovering the hiding place under the boards.

She couldn't stand it and tossed the letters onto the bedside table, drawing her knees up to her chest, rocking in a tight ball as if that alone would ward off the crushing sense of loss.

The letters teetered and fell to the ground, splitting the ancient knotted string holding them together. Papers fluttered in a semicircle. She groaned and crawled to the floor to pick them up.

Indiscretion. Illegitimate. Love.

The words flashed across her vision as she gathered the pages. She held one of the letters up to read it from the beginning, instantly intrigued to learn more about a story that apparently closely mirrored her own, if those were the major themes.

She read and read, and flipped the letter over to read the back. Then, with dawning horror and apprehension, she read the rest. *No!* It couldn't be. She must have misread.

With shaking fingers, she fumbled for her phone and speed-dialed Gabriel before checking the time. Well, it didn't matter if it was the middle of the night in Alma. Gabriel needed to make sense of this.

"What?" he growled and she heard Serafia murmur in the background. "This better be good."

"Rafael Montoro II wasn't the child of the king," she blurted out. "Grandfather. Our father's father. He wasn't the king's son. The letters. The queen's lover died in the war. And this means he was illegitimate. They were in love, but—"

"Bella. Stop. Breathe. What are you talking about? What letters?" Gabriel asked calmly.

Yes. Breathing sounded like a good plan. Maybe none of this would pan out as a problem. Maybe she'd read too much into the letters. Maybe they were fake and could be fully debunked. She gulped sweet oxygen into her lungs but her brain was still on Perma-Spin.

"I found some old letters. At the farmhouse. They say that our grandfather, Rafael the Second, wasn't really the king's son by blood. Wait." She pulled her phone from her ear, took snapshots of the most incriminating letter and sent the pictures to Gabriel. "Okay, read the letter and tell me I misunderstood. But I couldn't have. It says they kept the queen's affair a secret because the war had just started and the country was in turmoil."

Gabriel went quiet as he waited for the message to come through and then she heard him talking to Serafia as he switched over to speakerphone to examine the photo.

"These letters are worth authenticating," he concluded. "I'm not sure what it means but if this is true, we'll have to sort out the succession. I might not be the next in line."

"Why do you sound so thrilled?" Bella asked suspiciously. That was not the reaction she'd been expecting. "This is kind of a big deal."

"Because now there's a possibility that after the wedding, I might be able to focus on getting my wife pregnant instead of worrying about how to hold my head so the crown doesn't fall off."

Serafia laughed and she and Gabriel apparently forgot about Bella because their conversation was clearly not meant for outsiders.

"Hey, you guys, what do we do now?" she called loudly before things progressed much further. Geez, didn't they ever give the lovey-dovey stuff a rest? "We need to know if this is for real, preferably before the coronation. But who would be the legitimate heir if it's not you?"

God, what a mess. Thankfully, she wasn't in Alma, potentially about to be swept into a much larger scandal than any she'd ever created on her own.

"Juan Carlos," Serafia confirmed. "Of course. If Rafael's line is not legitimate, the throne would fall to his sister, Isabella. I don't think she'd hesitate to pass it to her grandson. It's perfect, don't you think? Juan Carlos has long been one of the biggest advocates of the restoration of the monarchy. He'll be a great king."

Gabriel muttered his agreement. "Bella, send me the letters overnight, but make copies of everything before you do. Can you send them tonight?"

"Sure." It wasn't as if she had anything else to do.

And that was how an Alman princess with a broken heart ended up at an all-night Kinkos on Fifth Avenue, while her so-called friends drank her vodka and ruined her furniture.

When she got home, she kicked them all out so she could be alone with her misery.

JFK Airport had it in for James. This was the ninth time he'd flown into the airport and the ninth time his luggage had been lost.

"You know what, forget it," he told the clerk he'd been working with for the past hour to locate his bags. "I'll call customer service later."

After two delays at Heathrow, all James wanted to do was crawl into a hole and sleep, but he'd spent close to thirty-six hours already trying to get to Bella. He wasn't flaking out now.

The car service ride to the address Gabriel had given him took another forty-five minutes and he almost got out and walked to Bella's building four times. He worried his lip with his teeth until he reached the building and then had to deal with the doorman, who of course wasn't expecting anyone named James Rowling.

"Please," he begged the doorman. "Buzz Ms. Montoro and tell her I'm here."

It was a desperate gamble, and she might very well say, *James who?* But he had to see her so he could fix things. He might be too late. His father might have ruined everything, but he had to take this shot to prove to Bella that she could trust him. That he'd absolutely planned to tell her about Maisey but everything had happened too fast.

"No need. Here I am."

Bella's voice washed over him and he spun around instantly. And there she was, wearing one of those little dresses that killed him every time, and he wanted to rush to her to sweep her up in his arms.

But he didn't. Because he didn't understand why she'd left Alma without at least letting him explain what was happening with Maisey or why his life had spiraled out of control so quickly that he'd managed to lose her or why just looking at her made everything seem better without her saying a word.

"Hi," he said, and then his throat closed.

He'd practiced what he'd say for a day and a half, only to buckle when it mattered most. Figured.

"Hi," she repeated, and glanced at the doorman, who was watching them avidly. "Thanks, Carl. It's okay."

She motioned James over to the side of the lobby, presumably so she could talk to him with a measure of privacy. "What are you doing here?"

"I wanted to talk to you." *Obviously.*

Off kilter, he ran a hand over his rumpled hair. Now that he was here, flying to New York without even calling first seemed like a stupid plan.

But when his father had smugly told him that he'd taken the liberty of informing Bella about Maisey, James had kind of lost it. And he'd never really regained his senses, especially not after his father made it clear that Bella wasn't interested in a bloke with an illegitimate child. As though it was all sorted and James should just bow out.

That wasn't happening. Because if Bella was indeed no longer interested in him because of Maisey, he wanted to hear it from Bella.

"So talk." She crossed her arms and he got another clue that things between them had progressed so far past the point of reasonable, there might be no saving their relationship. He was on such unfamiliar, unsteady ground, it might as well be quicksand.

The damage was far more widespread than he'd hoped. "Why did you leave before I could explain about Maisey?"

"Maisey? Is that your girlfriend's name?" Her eyes widened and she huffed out a little noise of disgust. "Surely you didn't expect me to sit around and wait for you to give me the boot."

"Maisey is my daughter," he countered quietly. "Chelsea is her mother. I'm sorry I didn't get a chance to tell you about this myself. I'm very unhappy with my father for interfering."

"Well, that couldn't have happened if you'd just told me from the beginning." He could tell by her narrowed gaze that she'd already tried and convicted him. "Why couldn't you be honest with me?"

"I was going to tell you. But you left first." With no clue as to where she was going. Was that her way of saying a lover with a kid was *no bueno*? Sweat dripped between his shoulder blades as he scrambled for the right thing to say. "Why didn't you wait for me to call like we discussed?"

"Wait for you to—are you mad at *me*? You're the one who should be on your knees begging my forgiveness. And you know what else? I don't have to explain myself to you!"

She stormed to the elevator and he followed her, only just squeezing through the doors before they closed.

Obviously *that* hadn't been the right thing to say. And she was far more furious than he'd have ever dreamed.

Yeah, he'd messed up by giving his father an opportunity to get between them, but hadn't he just flown thousands of miles to fix it? Shouldn't he at least get two minutes to make his case?

Or was it too late and was he just wasting his time?

"Actually," he countered as anxiety seized his lungs. "An explanation would be smashing. Because I don't understand why you don't want to hear what I have to say. I thought we were a couple who dealt with things together."

And now he was shouting back at her. Good thing the elevator was empty.

He'd thought they were headed for something permanent. He had little experience with that sort of thing, but he didn't think jetting off to another continent without so much as a conversation about the potential complexities was how you did it.

He'd *wanted* to talk to her about Maisey. To share his fears and ask her opinion. To feel less alone with this huge life-altering role change that had been dropped on him. Even the simple logistics of flying to New York hadn't been so simple, not the way it used to be. It had required him to sweet-talk Catalina, one of the Rowling maids, into babysitting Maisey—totally not her job, but Cat was the only person James trusted implicitly since they'd grown up together. As soon as he got back, finding a nanny for his daughter was priority number one.

She wheeled on him, staring down her nose at him, which was an impressive feat since he was a head taller. "A couple? Really? Do you tell Chelsea the same thing? I saw you two together. You must have had a good laugh at my expense."

"You saw me and *Chelsea* together? When?"

"The day I left Alma. Don't shake your head at me. I *saw* you. You were very cozy in that gazebo."

Gazebo? He'd never set foot in any gazebo.

"That would be a little difficult when Chelsea and I

were in my lawyer's office signing paperwork to give me sole custody of Maisey." They'd obtained the results of the fastest paternity test available and then James had spent a good deal more cash greasing the works so he could be rid of Chelsea as soon as possible. "And then she immediately left to go back to England."

He'd been relieved to have it done. The meeting with his lawyers had taken far longer than he'd expected but he had to deal with that for his daughter's sake before he could untangle himself to go talk to Bella. Unfortunately, those few hours had given his father the perfect window of opportunity to drive a wedge between James and Bella.

"She…what?" For the first time since he'd entered the elevator, Bella's furious expression wavered.

"Yeah. I came to tell you everything but you'd apparently just left. Gabriel gave me some lame explanation, so I texted you, remember?"

The elevator dinged and the doors opened but Bella didn't move, her expression shell-shocked. Gently, he guided her out of the elevator and she led him to the door of one of the apartments down the hall.

Once they were alone in the condo, James raised his brows in silent question.

"I remember your text message. Clearly," Bella allowed. "If Chelsea left, who were you kissing in the gazebo?"

"Kissing? You thought I was kissing someone?" His temper rose again. "Thanks for the lack of trust, Bella. That's why you took off? Because you thought I was two-timing you?"

Suddenly furious he'd spent almost two days in pursuit of a woman who thought so little of him, he clasped his aching head and tried to calm down.

"What was I supposed to think, James?" she whispered and even in his fit of temper he heard the hurt and pain behind it. "Your father told me you still had feelings for Chelsea. I thought he was lying, so I went to the Rowling mansion to talk to you. Only to see you kissing a dark-haired woman. I wouldn't have believed it except for your watch."

She glanced at his bare arm and her face froze as he held it up. "You mean the watch I gave to Will?"

"Oh, my God."

In a flash, she fell to the ground in a heap and he dashed to her, hauling her into his arms before he thought better of it.

"Are you okay?" he asked as he helped her stand, his heart hammering. "Did you faint?"

"No. My knees just gave out." She peered up, her gaze swimming with tears as she clutched his shoulders, not quite in his embrace but not quite distancing herself either. "It was Will. The whole time."

He nodded grimly. Such was the reality of having a brother who looked like you. People often mistook them for each other, but not with such devastating consequences. "Welcome to the world of twins."

Now he understood her animosity. No wonder he'd felt as if he was on the wrong side of a raging bull. His father's interference had caused even more damage than James had known.

And who the hell had *Will* been kissing in the gazebo?

"Why didn't you tell me you gave him your watch? You always wore it. I know how much it means to you and I just…well, I never would have thought you'd…" Her eyes shut for a beat. "I know, I left before you could tell me. I'm sorry. I shouldn't have jumped to conclusions."

"Yeah, on that note. Why did you?"

His temper hadn't fully fled but it had been so long since he'd been this close to her, he couldn't quite make himself let her go. So he sated himself on the scent of her and let that soothe his riled nerves.

"You said everything was moving too fast," she reminded him. "It's not that I didn't trust you. You've always been honest with me, but… Chelsea's your child's mother. You didn't call and your father said you were home from England. Your car was in the drive and he dropped the news about a baby and tells me you have feelings for your old girlfriend. Maybe you thought it was the right thing to try again with her."

That was so far off the mark…and yet he could see the logic from her perspective. It was maddening, impossible, ridiculous. "Not for me. I love *you*."

"You do?" The awe in her face nearly undid him. Until she whacked his shoulder with her fist. "Then why didn't you call me when you got back from England?"

"Blimey, Bella. I'd just had the news about the baby dropped on me, too."

She recoiled. "Wait. You mean you *just* found out you had a daughter?" Her eyelids flew shut for a moment. "I thought…"

"What, you mean you thought I knew from the very beginning?" He swore. Everything made so much more sense. Scowling, he guided her to the couch. "We need to get better at communication, obviously. Then my father wouldn't have been able to cause all of these problems."

She nodded, chagrin running rampant across her expression. "I'm sorry. I told you I wasn't any good at relationships."

"We're supposed to be figuring it out together. Remember?" Without taking his gaze from hers, he held out his hand. "I promised not to let go. I plan to stick to that."

She clasped his hand solemnly, no hesitation. "Are you really in love with me?"

"Completely." Tenderly, he smoothed a stray hair from her cheek. "I'm sorry, too, sweetheart. I was trying to get everything settled in my barmy life before I settled things with you. I jumbled it all up."

This was entirely his fault. If he'd told her every minute what she meant to him, she might have very well marched up to Will and demanded to know what he was doing. And realized it wasn't James. None of this would have happened.

He'd been missing this goal since day one, yet kept kicking the ball exactly the same way. No wonder she'd assumed he didn't want her anymore.

"So are things settled?" She searched his gaze and a line appeared between her eyes. "What did you mean about Chelsea signing over custody? What happened?"

And then reality—his new reality—crashed over him. They'd only dealt with the past. The future was still a big, scary unknown.

James shook his head. "She dumped the diaper bag in my lap and told me she was too young to be tied down with a baby she hadn't asked for. Being a mum is apparently too hard and it's interfering with her parties."

"Oh, James." Her quiet gasp of sympathy tugged at something in his chest.

"I'm quite gobsmacked." This was the conversation he'd intended to have when he went to her house in Playa Del Onda. Only to find that she'd taken off for New York. "I have a daughter I never knew existed and now she's mine. I'm a single father."

And he'd have to relinquish his title as the king of un-complicating things. There was no way to spin the situation differently. No matter how much he loved Bella, she had to decide if he was worth all the extra stuff that came along with the deal.

Now the question was…would she?

James was a single father.

When she'd seen James across the lobby, she'd assumed he'd come to grovel and planned to send him packing. But then the extent of his father's lies and manipulation had come out, changing everything. The instant James had held up his bare wrist, she'd known. He wasn't the man his father made him out to be. The explanation she'd sought, the forgiveness she knew she could offer—it had all been right there, if only she'd stayed in Alma.

Part of the fault in all of this lay with her. She shouldn't have been so quick to judge, so quick to believe the worst in him. So quick to whirl off and leave broken pieces of her relationship with James in her wake.

And still James had said he loved her. Those sweet words…she'd wanted to fall into his arms and say them back a hundred times. If only it were that simple.

But it wasn't.

"That's…a lot to take in," Bella allowed with a small smile. Her mind reeled in a hundred directions and none of them created the type of cohesion she sought. "How old is she?"

"Around ten months. I wish I knew what that meant in terms of development. When will she start walking, for example? It's something I *should* know, as a father. But I don't." He shut his eyes for a beat. "I'm learning as I go."

Her heart dipped. This must be so hard. How did you learn to be a father with no warning? James would have to get there fast and probably felt ill-equipped and completely unready. "You'll be a great father."

He'd stepped up. Just as she would have expected. James always did the right thing.

"I'd like you to meet her. If you want to."

"I do," she said eagerly and then the full reality of what was happening hit her.

Dear God, was *she* ready to be the mate of a single father? She barely felt like an adult herself half the time. When she'd confronted her father to demand her right to see James, she'd taken huge steps to become the settled, responsible person she wanted to be.

But she wouldn't exactly call herself mother material, not yet. Maybe in the future she could be, after she'd spent time alone with James and they'd both figured out how to be in a relationship. But they didn't have the luxury of that time. She couldn't decide in a few months that it was too much responsibility and whirl away, leaving a broken family in her wake. Like her own mother had.

She loved James. After everything, that was still true.

But was love enough when their relationship had so many complications, so many things going against it? Adding a child into the mix—an illegitimate one at that, which would reflect poorly on the royal family—only made it worse.

And in the spirit of figuring it out together, they had to talk about it.

"Your daughter is a…" She'd almost said a *problem*. "A blessing. But I'm a princess in a country very unforgiving of indiscretions. I'm still in line for the throne. You realize there's a potential for our relationship to…go over very badly, right?"

The tabloids would have a field day, eviscerating the royal family in the press. She was supposed to be forging alliances and solidifying the new monarchy in the country of her heritage. Not constantly dodging scandals.

"Yeah." He sighed as she gripped his hand tighter. "I know. We don't make any sense together and you should toss me to the curb this minute. I'm a lot of trouble."

Her heart fluttered in panic at the thought. But that's what they were talking about. Either they'd make a go of it or they'd part ways.

"Seems like you warned me how much trouble you were once upon a time."

Continually. He'd told her he was bad news from the start. She hadn't believed him then and she still didn't. James Rowling had character that couldn't be faked. His father couldn't see it, but Bella did. He was every inch her hero and the rest of the world would see that, too. She'd *help* them see it. And that decided it.

She smiled as she cupped James's face. The face of her

future. "Turns out I like my man with a side of trouble. We have a lot of obstacles to leap. We always have. But I think you're worth it, James Rowling. Jump with me."

"Are you sure?" he asked cautiously even as he pressed his jaw more firmly into her hand. "You don't worry about losing out on your fun lifestyle and how Maisey will tie you down?"

Once, that might have been her sole consideration. No longer.

"The party scene is empty and unfulfilling." As she said the words, they felt right. She'd been growing up all along, becoming a woman she could be proud of, one ready for new challenges. "Maybe someone who hadn't had a chance to sow her wild oats might feel differently. But I don't regret moving on to a new phase of life. Just don't let go of my hand, okay?"

"Never." He grinned back. "You're right, by the way. My grandfather's watch is very special to me. Will bet me that I would ask you to marry me before Gabriel's coronation and the watch was the prize. I fought like hell to keep it, but in the end, it was only fair to hand it over."

"But you haven't asked me to marry you." Because she'd run off and almost ruined everything.

"No, I haven't. Allow me to rectify that." He dropped to one knee and captured her hand. "Isabella Montoro, I love you. I don't deserve a minute of your time, let alone forever, but I'm so lost without you. I have sole custody of my daughter and it's selfish to ask you to be an instant mother. Despite all of that, I'm asking you to marry me anyway. Let me treat you like a princess the rest of your life."

Just when she'd thought he couldn't possibly get any more romantic, he said something like that. How could she say no? "Before I decide, I have a very important question to ask."

"Anything," he said solemnly.

"Do I have to move to England?"

His laugh warmed her. "No. I turned down Liverpool. My heart is in Alma. With you."

"Oh." And then her ability to speak completely fled as she internalized what she'd almost missed out on—an amazing man who'd quietly been making her his top priority all along. "Then yes," she whispered. "The answer is always yes."

He yanked on her hand, spilling her into his lap, and kissed her breathless, over and over until she finally pushed on his chest.

"I love you, too," she proclaimed. "Even though you made a stupid bet with your brother that lost you a watch and almost lost you a fiancée. What if I'd said no? Would you still ha—?"

He kissed her. It was a very effective way to end an argument and she hoped he planned to use it a whole lot in the future.

Epilogue

Bella still loved Miami. Thanks to the double Montoro wedding that had concluded a mere hour ago, she'd gotten an opportunity to come back, see her friends and spend some alone time with James. Which was much needed now that they were settling into life with a baby.

James's arm slipped around her waist as he handed her a glass of champagne. Still a little misty from the ceremony where her brothers had married their brides, she smiled at the man she loved.

Bella sighed a little over the romantic kiss her brother Rafe shared with his new wife, Emily, as they stole a few moments together in a secluded corner. Of course, they probably didn't intend for anyone to see them, but Bella had been keeping her eye on her new sister-in-law. She'd been a little unsteady due to her pregnancy.

Serafia Montoro, Bella's other new sister-in-law, toasted Gabriel and laughed at something her new husband said. They were going to be just as happy together as Rafe and Emily, no question.

The reception was in full swing. Five hundred of the world's most influential people packed the party. The governor of Florida chatted with Bella's father, Rafael III, near the bar and many other of Montoro Enterprises' key partners were in attendance.

"You ready to do this with me soon?" James murmured in her ear.

She shivered, as she always did when he touched her. Looked at her. Breathed in her general direction. Oh, she had it bad and it was delicious.

But who could blame her when she'd fallen in love with the only man in the world who got her? The only man who settled the hurricane in her heart. She'd returned to Alma to meet his daughter, who was the most precious thing in the world. And she looked just like her father, which was a plus in Bella's book. She'd instantly bonded with the little sweetheart.

Then James had helped Bella launch a fledgling organization dubbed the Alma Wildlife Conservation Society. A graphic with twin macaws served as the logo and no one had to know she'd secretly named them Will and James.

It was a healthy reminder that things weren't always what they seemed. As long as she always communicated with James, no one could tear them apart. It was their personal relationship credo and they practiced it often.

Bella smiled at James. "I'm afraid I'm out of siblings so our wedding ceremony will have to star only us. And Maisey."

James cocked his head. "You'd want her to participate? Babies and weddings don't necessarily mix."

"Of course," Bella insisted fiercely. "She's my daughter, too."

Maisey had surprised everyone by uttering her first word last week—*bird*. Her proud father couldn't stop smiling and Bella had decided then and there to have another baby as soon as possible. *After* she and James got married.

The Montoros didn't need any new scandals.

Not long after she'd returned to Alma, Gabriel had appointed a royal committee to authenticate the letters Bella had found at the farmhouse. After careful and thorough examination and corroborating evidence culled from the official archives, the letters proved valid.

The late Rafael Montoro II wasn't the legitimate royal heir, which meant no one in his line was either. His grandson, Gabriel, and granddaughter, Bella, weren't eligible for the throne. The legitimate line for the throne shifted to Isabella Salazar nee Montoro, Rafael's sister, who was unfortunately too ill to take on her new role. Therefore, her grandson, Juan Carlos II, long the only Montoro with the right heart to lead his country, became the sole legitimate heir.

Despite Bella's willingness to brave the tabloids with James, to weather the storm over the unfortunate circumstances of his daughter's birth, in the end, no one paid much attention to Bella and James as the world's focus shifted to Juan Carlos.

Bella wasn't the only Montoro to express relief. Gabriel looked forward to spending time with his new wife instead of balancing his personal life with his public reign. Their cousin would take the throne of Alma, leaving the three Montoro siblings to their happily-ever-afters.

* * * * *

MILLS & BOON®

Desire™

PASSIONATE AND DRAMATIC LOVE STORIES

A sneak peek at next month's titles…

In stores from 21st August 2015:

- **Claimed** – Tracy Wolff
  and **Maid for a Magnate** – Jules Bennett

- **The Baby Contract** – Barbara Dunlop
  and **His Son, Her Secret** – Sarah M. Anderson

- **Bidding on Her Boss** – Rachel Bailey
  and **Only on His Terms** – Elizabeth Bevarly

Available at WHSmith, Tesco, Asda, Eason, Amazon and Apple

Just can't wait?
Buy our books online a month before they hit the shops!
visit www.millsandboon.co.uk

These books are also available in eBook format!